A HUNDRED
WORDS FOR HATE

A REMY CHANDLER NOVEL

THOMAS E. SNIEGOSKI

A ROC BOOK

ROC
Published by New American Library, a division of
Penguin Group (USA) Inc., 375 Hudson Street,
New York, New York 10014, USA
Penguin Group (Canada), 90 Eglinton Avenue East, Suite 700, Toronto,
Ontario M4P 2Y3, Canada (a division of Pearson Penguin Canada Inc.)
Penguin Books Ltd., 80 Strand, London WC2R 0RL, England
Penguin Ireland, 25 St. Stephen's Green, Dublin 2,
Ireland (a division of Penguin Books Ltd.)
Penguin Group (Australia), 250 Camberwell Road, Camberwell, Victoria 3124,
Australia (a division of Pearson Australia Group Pty. Ltd.)
Penguin Books India Pvt. Ltd., 11 Community Centre, Panchsheel Park,
New Delhi—110 017, India
Penguin Group (NZ), 67 Apollo Drive, Rosedale, Auckland 0632,
New Zealand (a division of Pearson New Zealand Ltd.)
Penguin Books (South Africa) (Pty.) Ltd., 24 Sturdee Avenue,
Rosebank, Johannesburg 2196, South Africa

Penguin Books Ltd., Registered Offices:
80 Strand, London WC2R 0RL, England

Published by Roc, an imprint of New American Library, a division of Penguin
Group (USA) Inc. Previously published in a Roc trade paperback edition.

First Roc Mass Market Printing, February 2012
10 9 8 7 6 5 4 3 2 1

For Mulder

*A hundred words . . . far too few to describe how much it
hurts that you're gone. Until we see each other again, you
will always be in my thoughts, and in my heart.*

ACKNOWLEDGMENTS

With love to my wife, LeeAnne, and to our newest addition, Kirby, for not sending *me* back to New Jersey.

Thanks are also due to my pal Christopher Golden, Ginjer Buchanan, Liesa Abrams, James Mignogna, Dave "Do These Slacks Make Me Look Fat?" Kraus, Pam Daley, Mom and Dad Sniegoski, Mom and Dad Fogg, Pete Donaldson, Kenn Gold, Thomas "Blessed" Hope and the lovely Rachael, Timothy Cole, and the Evolution Revolution down at Cole's Comics in Lynn.

Tom

PROLOGUE

The Jungles of Paraguay: 1929

The first of humanity lay as if dead in the cool semidarkness of the underground chamber and dreamed of another time—of the Garden, of what he had lost to the poison of original sin. It had been so very long ago, but the memories lingered, as sharp as a viper's tooth and three times as venomous.

Adam had lived every moment of his multitudinous years with endless regret. The apologies to He who had created him—who had breathed life into what had once been dirt—were far too numerous to count, yet always fresh upon his lips.

Even when he dreamed, he begged for forgiveness. In the land of sleep he was free of the ravages of time, and he scraped and bowed before the glory of his Creator, praying for blessed forgiveness and eternal rest beneath the grounds of Eden.

And of late, he had entertained the idea that it might just happen.

For he'd been dreaming of the Garden like never before.

She was returning.

Soon.

Jon shielded his eyes, squinting as he gazed up through the jungle canopy at the noontime sun. He was late; a game of marbles with one of the younger boys—in which he'd won a cat's-eye, an aggie, an oxblood, and three new clearies—had delayed him. The teenager hoped he wouldn't be met with a lecture as he ran, sandaled feet slapping rhythmically along the worn jungle path.

He knew they all had a responsibility in tending to the needs of the patriarch. To the novice's eye, the withered form appeared as though dead; even Jon's grandfather could not remember a time when he had moved. But to the Sons of Adam, this ancient man was so very much more.

He was the first father, and their sole purpose for existence.

Jon and his people were the direct descendants of the first children of the world. They were charged with caring for the father of them all, and praying for the day when they could return to Paradise.

Although he would never dare voice it, Jon doubted that would ever happen. The patriarch had already lived for thousands of years, existing in a state of living death. Why would a God who allowed this to happen to the first of His creations show mercy after all this time? Most in the order believed He would.

But Jon was skeptical.

He stopped before the entrance to an ancient, vine-covered Incan temple. He expected to find Nathan waiting for him, an annoyed look upon his face.

This wasn't the first time Jon had been late.

But Nathan wasn't there; neither was Josiah, nor any other member of the order. Jon was suddenly filled with an odd sense of foreboding that made the guilt he was already feeling expand into full-blown panic.

What if something had happened to Adam? What if the first father had needed something and he, Jon, hadn't been there?

His mind raced as he climbed the decaying stone steps and made his way down the cool, torchlit passage toward the patriarch's resting chamber in the belly of the temple.

As Jon grew closer, he noticed an eerie, pulsing orange glow emanating from within the normally semidark room.

He reached into the pocket of his robes, feeling the leather pouch that held the spoils of his latest victory, and took strength from them. Then he quickened his pace.

Jon's imagination flared. Perhaps some of the oil used to keep the passage torches lit had spilled—*ignited*—and his brethren were attempting to extinguish the flames before any harm could come to . . .

But there was no fire burning within Adam's chamber.

As Jon passed through the stone archway, he saw the cause of the unearthly glow, and struggled to believe his eyes.

How is this possible? he asked himself in disbelief. But wasn't the entire order based upon things that the rational world would find unbelievable? Why, then, would this sight be any more implausible?

Josiah and Nathan were kneeling just inside the chamber, held in rapt fascination by the sight of the angel (for what else could it be?) that stood before the patriarch's sleeping alcove.

The being seemed to be comprised of light, and the huge wings upon its back radiated a warm, pulsing glow. It was at least seven feet tall, its powerful body covered in layers of flowing robes that appeared to be cut from the fabric of the night sky, and decorated with the stuff of stars.

And when it turned to look at him, Jon felt the strength leave his legs, and they began to tremble with uncontrollable fear.

The angel's face was fierce, its eyes like bottomless caverns of pitch, its pale features sharp and angled as if chiseled from stone—its flowing hair and beard seemingly composed of fire.

Jon wanted to run, but it was as if a large pair of invisible hands had clamped down upon his shoulders, forcing him to kneel beside his friends.

And then came its voice, sounding like every instrument in the world's largest symphony playing the same beauteous note at once.

"The Gardener's life draws to a close," the strange being proclaimed.

In the confines of the stone chamber it was the loudest sound Jon had ever heard, and he winced in agony as he covered his ears.

"From across the void I have heard his plea," the angel continued.

Josiah and Nathan fell upon their sides, writhing under the assault of the messenger's booming voice.

"Eden draws near. . . ."

Its voice was like knives relentlessly stabbing into Jon's brain and he opened his mouth in a scream of agony that he could not hear.

"And I have come to bring him home."

CHAPTER ONE

Fernita Green could not remember what she had lost, and that was why Remy Chandler was there.

He stood in the kitchen of the old woman's home, surrounded by the accumulations of her very long life. Plastic bags filled with other plastic bags and scraps of what he could describe only as trash, but kept by Fernita because it just might—one day—be important. Stacks of newspapers like ancient rock formations grew up from the rubbish-strewn floor, some leaning dangerously, but somehow defying the laws of physics.

The counter near the sink was covered with empty bottles and flattened cereal boxes. Tin cans and glass jars had been rinsed clean and stacked amid the debris.

Remy found the teakettle behind a stack of plastic Meals On Wheels containers. They had been washed out as well.

The inside of the sink was relatively clear, and he placed the empty kettle beneath the faucet. He turned on the water, gazing over a row of knickknacks and through the grimy window at the lushly overgrown backyard while the kettle filled.

A little more than three weeks ago, Fernita had started calling his office. She had wanted him to help her find something, but she couldn't remember what it was. Remy had tried to dissuade her, encouraging her to call a family member instead. But she had continued to call him—

sometimes leaving as many as four messages a day—until he had finally agreed to pay her a visit.

That had been two weeks ago, and he'd been visiting regularly since.

"How do you want your tea this time?" he called out from the kitchen as he turned off the faucet and took the kettle to the stove. He had to push aside a stack of fine-china plates that he didn't remember seeing there last time.

"With some milk, baby," he heard Fernita call out from the living room.

Sometimes she liked her tea dark . . . *"like the color of my skin,"* she would say with a chuckle, letting the bag steep in her cup for a good long time. Other times she'd take it with milk, like today.

Remy moved the plates to a tiny dinette set in the corner under a pair of windows. He had to push aside Easter baskets filled with green plastic grass to make way for them.

He returned to the stove only to find Fernita's cat, Miles, sitting in the center amid the four burners. The black cat with the white bib of fur stared at him with intense green eyes.

"Hello, Miles," Remy said as he placed the kettle on one of the electric burners and turned it on. "Careful, now; this is going to get hot."

"Hungry," the cat said in its feline tongue.

Remy looked over at the two dishes on the floor beside the refrigerator. One was filled with water, and the other had some Friskies in it. "There's food in your bowl," he told the cat, turning around to search out two clean cups.

"No," the cat growled. *"Hungry."*

Remy opened the cabinet to the left of the sink, catching a stack of recipes torn from the pages of magazines before they could drift to the floor. There were plenty of cups inside as well—enough to offer tea to the whole city of Brockton.

"And I said there's food in your bowl." Remy pointed to the dish on the cluttered floor.

The cat jumped down from the stove, his paws crinkling

some stray plastic bags that lay there as he padded over to his dishes.

"See?" Remy said as he opened the box of tea bags that was left on the counter. He would have much preferred coffee, but finding the coffeemaker in the chaos that was Fernita's kitchen was far too daunting a task. Tea would have to suffice.

"*No*," the cat said again, pawing at the nuggets in his dish.

"Stop playing with your food," Remy scolded, but Miles didn't listen.

One by one he removed the pieces of food from his dish and left them on the floor. "*No, hungry.*"

"Did anybody ever tell you you're a pain in the ass?" Remy said as the teakettle began to whistle.

Miles answered no.

One can of tuna and two cups of tea later, Remy was sitting in an overstuffed wing-back chair across from the old black woman as she went through box after box of *stuff.*

"I just don't know where it all came from," Fernita said, picking up one piece of wrinkled paper, dropping it back down into the box, only to pick up another. "I think I might've been saving these for the tax man."

The pieces of paper appeared to be old, very old, and Remy doubted the IRS would have any interest in them now. "Why don't you just throw them away?" he suggested. He placed his cup on a coaster beside his chair and reached for a plastic trash bag that he'd brought from the kitchen. "Just throw them right in here and you won't have to worry about it anymore."

Remy watched as the old woman seemed to consider this. "I guess I could," she said slowly, and he almost believed he was getting through to her. "But what if I should need them?"

"Do you really think you will?" he asked, his tone urging her on.

Fernita's wrinkled hand reached into the box again and picked up some of the papers that she'd already looked through. "I'd better hang on to them," she said with a pretty, yellowed smile. "It would be just my luck to have the tax man bang on my door, and me not have my papers in order." She put the box atop three others also filled with things she might need someday.

In the old days, she would have been called a pack rat, but now, in this more politically correct age, when everyone's quirks were diagnosed with a fancy name and a weekly series on the Discovery Channel, she was definitely a hoarder.

And perfectly fine with it.

"And what if what I'm looking for . . ." Her voice trailed off as she gazed around the cramped confines of the sitting room. It was stuffed with old furniture and boxes of God knew what.

"What if what I'm looking for is inside one of these boxes?" she finished.

"I suppose." Remy sighed, drinking more tea and wishing it were coffee.

"All right, then," she said with finality. "I'd better not be putting anything in that trash bag." She leaned back in her chair and took a sip from her cup, looking at him through the thick lenses of her glasses. They made her dark, watery eyes look huge as they fixed upon him. And then she began to laugh.

Remy couldn't help but do the same.

When he'd asked her why she had called him, Fernita told him that an old friend named Pearly Gates had once told her that if she ever had a problem to give the detective a call. She'd produced an old business card from the pocket of the flowered apron she was wearing. It had been a long time since Remy had used that particular card—at least thirty years.

He had no idea who Pearly Gates was, but the name amused him.

Fernita was suddenly very quiet, staring off into space as if seeing something beyond the room.

"Are you okay?" he asked her.

She seemed startled by the sound of his voice and

looked at him inquisitively. For a moment Remy was certain she had no idea who he was.

A smile then appeared, and he knew she had returned from wherever she had temporarily been.

"Remy Chandler," she said happily. "It's so nice that you visit me."

He smiled, reaching out to take her hand. "I like that you let me."

And it was true. Remy had actually started to look forward to his visits with Fernita, who had lost something very important, but couldn't quite remember what it was. He had to wonder if maybe it was her dwindling faculties she was missing, and was desperate to have back.

But there was something about this wonderful old woman, something he couldn't quite put his finger on.

The grandfather clock, nearly hidden by stacks of old magazines, tolled the hour, and Remy counted twelve. He had planned to stay only until lunchtime. He had things to finish at the office, and he was going out tonight.

His stomach did a little bit of a flip, and he felt the nature of the Seraphim coiled in slumber at his core stir.

"I need to get going," he said to Fernita, almost too quickly.

He reached out and patted her hand affectionately, then stood and retrieved his heavy leather jacket from the banister near the front door.

"Where are you off to now?" Fernita asked from her chair.

"I've got to get back to the office and help more people," he told her. He was tempted to tell her what he was doing tonight, knowing that she would get a kick out of it, but he really didn't feel like talking about it at the moment.

"You're a good man, Remy Chandler," she said.

"Thanks for noticing." Remy slipped into his jacket as Miles sauntered toward them from the kitchen.

"And there's my other handsome boy," Fernita said, making a noise for the cat to come to her. Remy had to give Miles credit—he didn't ignore her, jumping into her lap and settling down to be petted.

"When will you visit again?" Fernita asked Remy, her eyes wide through the thick lenses of her glasses. "You know I'm never gonna find that thing without your help."

"I'll try to stop by toward the end of the week; how does that sound?"

"That would be wonderful!" She stopped petting Miles and held him firmly. "Now, you be sure to close that door quick," she ordered Remy. "My little friend here is dying to get outside, but I'm afraid the world is just a little too tough for Miles."

"*Out*," Miles meowed, trying to jump from Fernita's lap.

Remy hurried out the door.

"You take care," he called to her, closing the door gently behind him before the cat could escape into the cold, cruel world.

The Seraphim was confused.

The angelic nature could sense his master's distress, and waited for the inevitable release.

And waited . . . and waited some more . . .

He longed to be free; to spread his golden wings . . . to wield the fires of Heaven once more.

To reduce his enemies to smoldering ash.

But the loosing did not come.

So the Seraphim waited, and waited some more.

Forever patient.

Remy breathed in sharply through his nose, and exhaled through his mouth. He was standing in front of the mirror in his bedroom, gazing at his reflection and feeling the pressure.

He would rather have been doing just about anything other than what he was about to do this night. Briefly he wondered what the Black Choir was up to, and how hard it would be to attract their attention.

The Seraphim churning inside him would surely appreciate that.

He was wearing a tie, and wasn't sure if he liked the look.

"What do you think?" he asked, shifting his gaze slightly

to look at the reflection of the black Labrador retriever sitting sphinxlike on the bed behind him. "Tie or no tie?"

"*Tie!*" Marlowe barked.

"What do you know?" Remy asked.

"*Know lot,*" Marlowe responded indignantly.

"You think?" Remy reached up to tighten the knot on the blue-and-red silk tie. "Worn a lot of ties, have you?"

Marlowe remained silent, watching his master.

Remy laughed as he turned from the mirror to face the dog on the bed.

"Honestly, do I look all right?"

The dog just stared, droplets of drool leaking from his loosely hanging jowls and staining the bedspread.

"Your silence speaks volumes." Remy moved to the bed to ruffle the black dog's velvety soft ears and kiss the top of his hard, blocky head. "I've got to get going," he said, feeling a lead ball form heavily in the pit of his stomach.

He turned to leave the bedroom, and heard the familiar thud as the dog leapt to the floor to follow.

"*Out?*" Marlowe asked, looking up from Remy's side.

"I am, but you're not," Remy told the animal as they started down the stairs.

He'd been dreading this night since he'd planned it a little more than a week ago. Every day since he'd tortured himself with the question of why he had done it, swearing he would cancel.

But he never did, and now it was too late.

"*Why?*" Marlowe asked, having already forgotten what they'd discussed earlier in the day.

"Because I have to go someplace where they don't allow dogs," Remy explained, going to the hallway closet for his heavy jacket. "I know it's hard to believe that there are actually places in this city that won't welcome your smiling face, but it's true."

The dog plopped heavily onto the living room carpet just inside the doorway.

"*Work?*" he asked, tilting his triangular head quizzically.

"I wish it was," Remy answered with a sigh, slipping into the leather coat. "But no."

He'd debated for weeks and then made the call in a moment of weakness. He'd finished watching Streisand and Redford in *The Way We Were*, and blamed the film for lowering his resistance.

Remy went to the kitchen, took a Red Delicious apple from the bowl on the counter, and cut it into pieces.

"This should hold you until I get back," he told the black dog, as he returned to the living room and dropped the pile of chopped apple on the rug in front of him. "I shouldn't be too late."

The dog didn't seem to notice him anymore, scarfing down the apple as if he hadn't been fed in days.

Remy said good-bye again, and left the house.

The Seraphim nature stirred within as it sensed his anxiety.

If only the current situation could be resolved by unleashing the heavenly might of his angelic essence, it would be one of the few times he wouldn't regret the loss of control.

But this wasn't the time for an angel's rage, for beating wings and flaming swords.

It was freezing outside—typical January weather for Boston, but Remy paid the harsh temperatures no mind. He had other things to think about as he walked to his car and drove the few blocks to Boylston Street.

Everybody had told him he was doing the right thing . . . well, *everybody* meaning Steven Mulvehill, homicide cop and Remy's closest human friend.

Madeline had been Remy's anchor in this human world, and so much more, but it was nearly a year since her death now, and he'd had no one in his life since. Mulvehill argued that this was causing his friend to disconnect from the humanity Remy had worked so hard to create.

Remy's true nature surged with the thought. He was, after all, a creature of Heaven . . . a warrior angel . . . a Seraphim . . . but Remiel—as he had once been called—had grown tired of the fighting, and the war, and the death, and he had left the Kingdom of God, heading to the world of man to find an easier life.

A happier life.

A human life.

And after a few thousand years, give or take, Remiel had found just that as he made the Earth his home. He'd chosen the name Remy Chandler, and started his work as a private investigator, and suddenly it had all fallen into place.

That was when a beautiful woman had applied for a job as his office secretary, and suddenly he wasn't pretending to be human anymore.

He *was* human.

The love of her—of Madeline—had transformed him into so much more than what he had been.

He wished more than anything that their love could have gone on forever, but the Lord God had seen fit to make His most favored creations mortal; a very sad flaw in the Creator's design, Remy believed.

So Madeline was gone now, taken by cancer and age, and he was left alone to grieve for his beautiful wife, and his slowly faltering humanity.

It had been so much easier being a thing of Heaven, serving the Almighty with nary a question. And the business of being human? That was truly a chore, but despite the confusion and pain, it was something Remy was desperate to hold on to.

That was what brought him out here on this cold January night. It was all about his need to connect again. To find that special thing . . . that special someone to tie him to the world of man, and keep his eyes from straying to the heavens.

The power inside him would return to its master in an instant, but Remiel . . . Remy had seen far too much as a soldier of God and preferred the grimy city streets of Earth to the golden spires of Heaven.

Remy handed off his keys to the valet in front of Mistral and headed toward the restaurant. As he reached for the brass handle on the door, he felt as if the world were dropping away from beneath his feet, and he tried to recall whether he had felt this anxious when stepping through the passage to the Hell prison of Tartarus.

He didn't think so.

He took a deep breath and stepped into the lobby, un-zipping his leather jacket as he scanned the dining room.

"Hi, may I help you?" asked an attractive woman with long blond hair and a radiant smile.

Remy returned the smile. "I have a reservation for Chandler," he said, not seeing his date.

The woman studied the open book on the podium. "Yes, sir, seven fifteen, for two," she said, looking up at him. "The other member of your party hasn't checked in yet. If you'd like to wait in the bar, and I'll call you as soon as . . ."

Remy felt a blast of January air as the door opened be-hind him, and he turned to face it.

Linda Somerset stood in the entryway.

Her cheeks were a rosy pink, and there seemed to be a touch of panic in her gaze as she looked past him to the restaurant beyond. She pulled the floppy woolen hat from her head and combed her shoulder-length, chestnut brown hair with her fingers.

Remy couldn't help but smile as her gaze turned to him and recognition dawned on her pretty face.

Linda laughed, reaching out to grab hold of his arm. It was a nice sound, and she had quite a grip.

"I didn't even notice you," she said, her eyes never leav-ing his. "I was afraid I was late."

"No worries," Remy said. "I just got here myself."

The manic look he'd seen when the woman had first en-tered started to recede, and he found himself suddenly feel-ing more comfortable as well.

What's that all about? he wondered, staring at Linda. Mere seconds ago he was ready to jump out of his skin, now . . .

She was the first to break their gaze, reaching into her coat pocket for a wrinkled Kleenex. "I'm sorry," she said, laughing again as she brought the tissue to her nose. "My nose runs like crazy when it's cold. I don't want to embar-rass myself any more than I have to."

She looked self-conscious, turning away from him as she wiped beneath her nose and quickly put the Kleenex away.

"There, perfect," she said with an exaggerated eye roll.

"Perfect," Remy agreed. "Shall we head in?"

Linda nodded.

"May I take your coats?" the hostess asked as she stepped from behind the podium.

Remy helped Linda off with hers, then took his own off and gave both to the woman. They waited as the hostess hung them in a closet behind the podium, then returned, picking up two leather-bound menus.

"This way," she said, holding the menus to her chest.

Remy gestured for Linda to go first, and followed close behind.

This is it, he thought.

Once more into the breach.

Hell

The floor of the underworld bucked and heaved like a succubus coming down from a weekend of gorging at the all-you-can-eat soul buffet.

Didn't even have the common courtesy to wait until I died, the Guardian angel once of the angelic host Virtues thought as his injured form was thrown about the shifting landscape.

Fraciel—now called Francis—held on to his fleeing consciousness, staving off inevitable death, in order to bear witness to what was happening in the realm of Hell.

Lying upon his back, the ground beneath him moving like the Magic Fingers beds at the no-tell motel out on Route 114, he lifted his head to see the ice prison of Tartarus—that most horrible of places, created by God to imprison those who had taken up arms with the Morningstar—crumble and fall, disintegrating before his very eyes.

There's something you don't see every day, he thought in a pain-filled haze, watching as gigantic hunks of glacial ice cascaded toward the surface of Hell, only to stop midway and float inexplicably weightless through the debris and ash-choked air. Pieces of Tartarus, like an asteroid field above the quake-ravaged surface, gradually dissolved into a thick cloud of swirling matter.

Hell was coming apart at the seams, and Francis had a front-row seat.

After centuries of servitude, he had been given the job as Guardian of one of the many gates—*passages*—from the world of man to the Hell realm and the prison of Tartarus. It had been his way of making amends with the Almighty for temporarily siding with the Morningstar. And he had served his God well, helping those fallen angels released from their time in the icy prison to prepare for the remainder of the penance they would do on Earth.

He'd also shown some initiative, and managed to maintain a lucrative business as a professional assassin. Very selective in those he killed, Francis had eliminated only the worst of the bad. It had been the one saving grace in his exile upon the planet of man—that and his friendship with the Seraphim Remiel.

Known now as Remy Chandler.

The remains of Tartarus swirled in the air, a maelstrom of ice, dust, dirt, and rock.

And the storm was growing.

Francis lay upon the trembling ground watching in awe. He knew that was where Remy had been going when last he saw him, and wondered if the Seraphim had anything to do with the cataclysm that threatened the Hell realm.

Of course he did.

The ground beneath his back grew incredibly hot, but Francis didn't have the strength to move. He was thankful Hell decided to do this for him.

There was an explosion of foul-smelling gas, the force of the blast propelling him up into the air, only to land on his belly at the edge of an expanding pool of lava.

Francis barely managed to hold on to consciousness, the sucking darkness of oblivion pulling him slowly closer. He tried to pull himself away from the burning fluid, but managed only to turn onto his back, where he could once again look up into the rubble-filled sky.

Pieces of Hell and Tartarus had mingled together, a

growing, swirling vortex of all the misery, hate, and sorrow that defined this horrible place created by a supposedly loving God.

It wouldn't be long until Francis too joined the maelstrom, sucked up with everything else into the yawning maw of the voracious funnel cloud.

What did you do, Remy? Francis wondered as he felt the first, burning touch of liquid rock on his battered flesh. *What did you find inside the prison that could have led to . . . this?*

And as if some higher power had heard his question and, knowing that he would soon no longer be among the living, took pity upon him, showing him the answer.

The vortex spun above him, opening wider and wider. And inside its mouth, floating in the dust-, dirt-, and ash-choked air, untouched by the madness of what was happening around him, floated a figure.

The figure . . . he was like the sun, repelling the darkness with a golden light that emanated from his perfect form.

Francis remembered this being, and how he had once stood alongside the Almighty.

The answer to his question hovered in the center of the storm.

The Morningstar had risen.

And Francis knew that nothing would ever be the fucking same again.

CHAPTER TWO

"So, what's your story, Remy Chandler?"

Linda Somerset's voice echoed inside Remy's head as he drove past the Museum of Science on his way to Somerville, where he'd promised to meet Steven Mulvehill for a nightcap.

The date had gone well—nothing spectacular, but good. There were no fireworks or wedding plans or joint checking accounts in the foreseeable future, but the night had been okay. There'd been lots of small talk, conversation establishing a comfort zone for the two of them. Normally, Remy would have been bored to tears, but from Linda, it was like opening the window on a gorgeous spring day after a particularly harrowing winter.

And it *had* been a harrowing winter.

"So, what's your story, Remy Chandler?"

He heard her ask the question again. She had just finished talking about everything from her fear of spiders and her love for Japanese monster movies to her failed marriage and how it had taken her a very long time to get her head straight again.

She had paused, brought her second merlot to her lips, and asked him over the rim of her glass:

"So, what's your story, Remy Chandler?"

And strangely enough, he had told her. Not everything, of course, just the things that wouldn't make her run screaming into the night. No, there'd be plenty of time for that business on the second date.

The second date.

The thought troubled him. It wasn't that he didn't want another; he'd had a pretty good time with Linda, but he just couldn't shake the guilt.

He felt as if he were cheating: cheating on the memory of Madeline.

Remy parked his car at a meter across from the Bowman. The usual barflies were hanging out in front of the neighborhood tavern, smoking their cigarettes, even though the windchill had to be well below zero. The cigarette smoke mixed with the exhalation from their lungs formed thick clouds of white that billowed in the air before them.

Remy passed through the cloud bank and pulled open the heavy wooden door to a blast of warm air that stank of stale beer and age. He looked around and found Mulvehill hunched over the bar, contemplating the secrets of the universe in a Scotch on the rocks.

"Should you be drinking that now?" Remy asked as he joined his friend, removing his heavy leather jacket and placing it over the top of a high-backed stool. "Isn't it a school night?"

"I won't tell if you don't," the homicide detective said, gesturing for the bartender. "What do you want?"

"I'll have whatever he has," Remy told the proprietor as he took a seat beside Mulvehill.

"So?" Mulvehill asked, taking a careful sip of his drink, barely disturbing the ice.

"So what?" Remy replied, knowing full well what his friend was getting at.

"Didn't you have plans tonight?" Mulvehill said with a smirk.

The bartender returned with another Scotch on the rocks and placed it on a napkin in front of Remy. "Thanks." Remy nodded as he picked up the drink and took a long sip of the golden liquid.

"Maybe," he said to Mulvehill as he smacked his lips and set the glass back on the napkin.

Mulvehill laughed. "Asshole," he said with a shake of his head.

"Coming from you, that means a lot."

"I know assholes," Mulvehill said, pointing to himself as he stifled a laugh. "And you're exceptional."

Remy lifted his drink in a toast to his friend. "Why, thank you, sir," he said. "I have at last achieved greatness."

Mulvehill picked up his own drink in response and they both drank, silently savoring the alcohol and the friendship they shared.

"So, did she show?" the detective asked, finally breaking the silence.

"She actually did," Remy answered, staring straight ahead at the elaborate assortment of liquor bottles behind the bar. "Imagine that."

"Imagine." Mulvehill nodded. "How'd it go?"

"Well, I'm here now, aren't I?" Remy turned his gaze to his friend with a smile.

Mulvehill cringed in mock horror. "Ouch," he said, screwing up his face in an expression of pain. "Sorry, dude."

Remy laughed. "No, it was fine," he said. "Nice, actually."

"Nice?" Mulvehill asked. "What, did you go out with my mother?"

"No, that would have been *hot*." Remy wiggled his eyebrows for effect.

"Now you're just getting gross," Mulvehill said with a disgusted look.

Remy took another sip of Scotch. "Really, we did have a nice time."

Mulvehill watched him carefully. "Really? A nice time? The sky didn't open up and rain toads or anything?"

Remy shook his head. "Nope, it was a nice time." He could still feel the guilt inside, squirming around, keeping company with the essence of the Seraphim, and he hoped his friend wouldn't notice.

"Then why does your face look like that?" Mulvehill asked, turning on his bar stool to study Remy.

"Like what?" Remy asked, feigning innocence. He leaned over the bar to get a better look at himself in the mirror behind the liquor bottles. "I'm telling you, there's nothing wrong. I went on a date, we had a nice time, and that's it. Nothing more."

"You're so full of shit you stink," Mulvehill growled. "I'm going to need another one of these just to talk with you." He gestured for the bartender.

"I might as well too," Remy said, lifting his glass toward the bartender.

"So if you had such a nice time, why do you look like you ate a bad piece of fish?" Mulvehill pressed.

"Bad piece of fish?" Remy echoed. "I look that bad?"

Mulvehill nodded. "Something isn't sitting right with you."

The bartender brought them two fresh drinks, and was off to the other end of the bar in a flash.

"It's stupid," Remy said. He drained what remained of his first drink and set it down before picking up the second.

"Figured as much," Mulvehill said. "Why don't you share the stupidity so I can get a good laugh."

"It's because I had a good time," Remy mumbled, embarrassed as he heard himself speak the words.

"You look like you're smelling low tide at Revere Beach because you had a good time? What's wrong with this picture?" And then Mulvehill's expression changed. "This is about Madeline, isn't it?"

Remy said nothing.

"Jesus, Remy," the homicide cop said. "Can't you cut yourself the tiniest bit of slack?"

Remy knew that Steven was right, but it didn't change how he felt. "I know it's crazy," he admitted, "but I can't shake the feeling that . . ." He stopped, staring at the ice in the bottom of his glass.

"That you're cheating on her," Mulvehill finished the sentence for him, his voice low and rough.

Remy nodded once. "Yeah, something like that."

"You know that's not true, right?"

"Yeah." Remy nodded again.

"This isn't helping you at all, is it?" Mulvehill said.

Remy started to laugh. "Not at all."

Steven laughed too, picking up his drink and taking a large swig. "You're your own worst enemy, Remy Chandler," the homicide cop said.

"Ain't it the truth," Remy had to agree.

They were quiet again, the sounds of the bar swirling around them as they sat and drank. There was a tickling at the base of Remy's brain, and suddenly he could hear a voice—a prayer—ever so softly from someone in the bar. The person was praying for his mother, who was dying. He was praying that her life would end soon.

That there would be an end to her suffering.

"So where'd you leave it?" Steven asked, the distraction an answer to Remy's own silent prayers.

"We're supposed to have lunch tomorrow."

"So you're going to see her again?"

"Yeah," Remy said.

"Good. You shouldn't be alone."

"You're alone," Remy countered, turning to look at Steven.

"But, you see, that's the difference between us," the cop explained. "I'm better off alone because I'm a miserable bastard, but you . . . Let's just say you need a good woman to keep you in check, and we'll leave it at that."

Steven was right.

Since the death of his wife, Remy was finding it more and more difficult to control the angelic nature that writhed and churned inside him—desperate to be released, desperate to do what he was created for.

The Seraphim was a soldier—a warrior of God—and he existed to burn away anything that was a blight in the eyes of God. A power such as that had to be controlled.

Steven knew that, and knew that it was the love of Madeline that had kept the destructive, divine power in check for all these years, a love that had kept Remy anchored to the mask of humanity he'd created for himself as he lived upon the world of God's man.

An anchor that was now missing.

"What makes you think Linda will be able to fill that role?" Remy asked him.

Steven shrugged. "I don't, but at least you're out there trying . . . acting like all the other poor schmucks looking for love."

"Except you," Remy said.

"I eat love for breakfast and it gives me the wind something awful," Mulvehill said with a snarl as he finished what was left of his drink. "I need a cigarette and my bed, in that order."

He fished his wallet out from the back pocket of his pants as he slid from the stool. "I got this," he said, pulling out some wrinkled bills and placing them on the bar. He gestured to the barkeep and took his coat from the back of his chair.

"Wow, even after I pissed you off you're still picking up the tab," Remy said, slipping into his own leather jacket.

"What can I say," Mulvehill said, pulling a crumpled pack of cigarettes from an inside coat pocket. "I'm generous to a fault."

Remy followed his friend outside into the freezing cold. The smokers who had been there when he'd first arrived were long gone.

"Shit, it's cold," Mulvehill said as he yanked the collar of his coat up around his ears. A cigarette protruded from his lips, and he brought a lighter up to ignite its tip.

"It's January in New England; what do you expect?" Remy commented.

"Thank you, Al fucking Roker," Mulvehill said dryly, making Remy laugh. "Where'd you park?"

Remy pointed to his Toyota across the street. "There she be," he said. "Where are you?"

"I walked; figured it'd be one of those exasperating nights where I needed many drinks to keep from strangling you."

"And was it?" Remy asked.

"You were one Scotch away from being throttled," his friend said, cigarette bobbing between his lips.

"Guess it's my lucky night," Remy said. "Want a ride?"

Mulvehill shook his head. "Naw, gonna walk off the buzz." He started to back up down the street.

"Talk to you later, then," Remy said, walking into the center of the street. There wasn't a trace of traffic as he strolled to his car.

"Hey, Chandler," Steven called out as Remy stuck his key in the door of his car.

"Yeah," he answered.

"Can't imagine she wouldn't want you to be happy," his friend said.

"You're probably right," Remy answered, letting the words slowly penetrate, knowing full well whom Steven was talking about. Pulling open the car door, he waved good night before climbing inside.

Can't imagine.

Odd jobs—that was all he could remember doing for . . .

It seemed like forever.

They called him Bob, but he had no idea where the moniker had come from. He couldn't remember his real name.

He couldn't remember much of anything.

Bob was waiting in front of the Home Depot with ten others, waiting for work. They would do just about any form of manual labor for a day's pay—gardening, painting, yard cleanup . . . odd jobs.

Odd jobs.

Bob stood by himself, away from the others, as he usually did, eyeing the entrance to the parking lot.

The smell was upon him first, a wave of hot, fetid aromas—the stink of a primordial jungle, lush with thick, overgrowing life. Bob closed his eyes, suddenly feeling as though he'd moved through time and space to another location.

A place that he could almost see inside his mind. A place where he had been before.

This wasn't the first time he'd experienced this, but it was stronger of late, the smells more specific, the imagery more precise, and he kept hoping that one day soon, he would remember more.

More than the odd jobs.

"Hey, you comin'?" a voice asked, interrupting his thoughts.

Bob opened his eyes to see a thin Hispanic man standing in front of him. The others were already climbing into the back of a silver pickup truck.

"Yes," Bob answered quickly, the lingering scent of the forest fading from his nostrils as he joined the other day laborers.

After a short drive, they ended up in a well-to-do neighborhood, clearing an overgrown lot to make way for the renovation of an existing property. Bob knew little more than that, and really didn't care.

He couldn't forget the latest assault to his senses. It was right there, teasing him, telling him something he needed to know, but didn't understand.

Almost as if the memory were in some foreign tongue.

Bob stood in the lot, a scythe in his hand, cutting a swath through a thick wall of overgrown weeds. He concentrated on the rhythmic, back-and-forth movement of the blade, trying to forget the smells, the sensations, but elusive echoes remained, just beyond his reach.

The morning sun climbed high in the sky, and his shirt was soaked with the perspiration of hard work. Heart hammering in his chest, Bob let the scythe drop and removed his shirt, exposing his well-muscled flesh to the sun's rays.

The high-pitched sound of a child's laugh caught his attention and he gazed back toward the well-kept yard beyond the lot. The man who owned the property—Bob didn't remember if he had even told them his name—was spraying a gleefully shrieking little boy with a garden hose.

Bob's eyes were riveted to the scene, locked on the image of the happy child racing around the yard, trying to avoid his father's attempts to soak him. It was all so ... *familiar*.

And suddenly, the laughing child was replaced by the image of a man and a woman ... naked, perfect in their form. They too ran through a gently falling rain.

A rain that fell upon a garden.

The Garden.

Bob let out a scream of agony and fell to the dusty ground he'd just cleared. For years—*centuries*—he had waited for a time when his visions would reveal their secrets, but now he wanted them to stop.

His fellow workers crowded around him.

"Is he okay?" the home owner called out. "Should I call nine-one-one?"

The silence in Bob's mind was nearly deafening now, and he felt that the world had stopped for him—waiting to see what was to come.

Waiting for him to remember.

The man still had the hose in his hand, a steady stream of water arcing through the air to drench the grass.

The child stood watching, wet and shivering.

Why does he shiver? Bob wondered. *Does he sense what I do? Does he know it's coming?*

Something was returning after so very long away.

It was almost here . . . but what was it? The images pounded furiously in Bob's skull, and he screamed as the visions exploded in front of him.

If only the others could see, they would be screaming as well.

He saw the Garden, in all its wondrous glory, and in its center was the Tree . . . the Tree pregnant with fruit.

Forbidden fruit.

Bob was standing before the Tree, gazing at the pendulous growths that hung from its verdant branches, and somehow he knew that a piece of fruit was missing.

The sword of fire that he clutched in his armored hand blazed all the brighter . . . hotter . . . fiercer. And he was incredibly sad, for he knew that they must be punished.

They. Must. Be. Punished.

A hand . . . a human hand dropped down upon Bob's bare shoulder, rousing him from his vision.

But now he knew.

He gazed into the frightened eyes of his fellow workers.

"Call nine-one-one," the Hispanic man who had brought them here called out to the man with the hose.

"No," Bob said, reaching out to grab hold of the man's wrist. He could already feel his body changing. His skin was on fire . . . the flesh starting to bubble, pop, and steam.

The Hispanic man started to scream, but only briefly as his body ignited as if doused with gasoline.

And then they were all screaming . . . screaming as Bob's flesh melted away, dripping like candle wax to the parched earth that he knelt upon. There was metal beneath the faux flesh, metal forged in the furnaces of Heaven, and it glistened unctuously in the noonday sun.

Bob rose to his feet, twice as tall. Powerful muscles on his back tensed painfully, then relaxed as a double set of mighty wings unfurled, shaking off flecks of fire that hungrily consumed the dry grass around him.

The fires of Heaven raged, the cries of his fellow workers abruptly silenced as they were returned to the dust from whence they came.

Remy and Madeline were sitting side by side in two white wicker chairs on the front porch of their cottage in Maine.

This had always been their favorite time, when the day eventually succumbed to the night. Usually they'd had their supper, and then retired with a cup of coffee, or a cocktail, to the peace of the porch and the surrender of daylight.

The nocturnal bugs were tuning up, preparing a woodland symphony just for them. At least, that was what they had liked to think: a concert of clicks, buzzes, and hums for their listening pleasure only.

"Hey," Madeline said, reaching across to give Remy's hand a loving squeeze.

"Hey back," Remy said, smiling at her. It was always good to see her, even though it broke his heart every time.

"Good day?" she asked, as they gazed into the darkness beyond the porch. It sounded as if every insect in the woods had something to say . . . something to sing about.

Remy was silent, not quite sure how to answer.

"What?" Madeline asked, turning to him with the smile that transformed his insides to liquid.

"Interesting day ... and night," he said, not looking at her.

"Is that a touch of guilt I hear in your voice?"

Remy shrugged noncommittally, even though he knew she had the answer.

"You realize that's a waste of perfectly good guilt," Madeline stated, continuing to rub the side of his hand with her thumb.

"Perfectly good guilt?" he repeated with a grin, finally turning to face her with a look of feigned innocence.

"Mmmmm-hmm," she replied with a quick nod. "All that energy could be put to good use elsewhere, like returning your phone calls, or giving to that kid outside the Market Basket collecting for Pop Warner."

"I didn't have any change that day," Remy protested.

"And taking Marlowe to the Common," Madeline continued, ignoring his outburst. "Poor baby hasn't been to the Common in days."

"It hasn't been days," Remy attempted, before realizing that she was right.

"See, perfectly good guilt going to waste over me."

"Nothing ever went to waste over you," he said, missing her more at that moment than he had in some time, knowing that this wasn't real, but realizing it was better than nothing.

"Ah, flattery." She squeezed his hand. "So, what was it like?" Madeline asked. "Being out on a date after all this time?"

"Different," Remy said. "Nerve-racking." He started to laugh.

"What's there to be nervous about? You always gave good date."

"Gave good date?" Remy repeated with a chuckle.

"It's true," Madeline said. "You were the best I ever dated. I always had the nicest times with you."

"You brought out the best in me." Remy leaned forward and kissed her hand.

"See?" Madeline said. "Even now you're giving good date."

"This is a date?" Remy asked.

"What would you call it?" asked the woman he had loved for more than forty years. "You've created this place in your head so we can spend some time together, and here we are, enjoying each other's company. I'd call it a date."

"Well, I'm not sure what kind of date I was the other night," Remy said, reflecting on his dinner with Linda.

"Why, did you make her run screaming from the restaurant?"

"No."

"She didn't eat with her hands, did she?"

"No, she knew how to use a knife and fork."

"Phew." Madeline rolled her eyes. "For a minute there I thought maybe—"

"She wasn't you," Remy interrupted quickly, his heart filled with emotion for the woman who had made him what he was.

Who had made him human.

"Excuse me?" she asked.

"I don't think I was very good company because I kept thinking that I'd rather be with you."

"You're so sweet," Madeline said. She reached over and placed her warm hand against his cheek. "And I'm flattered, really, but I'm also dead, Remy. The only way we can see each other is like this. Just you and me . . . and your very active imagination."

They were both silent for a moment, listening to the insect song.

"You didn't bring me up, did you?" Madeline asked finally.

"No," Remy said. "I didn't think it would be appropriate."

"Thank God for that," she said with a gentle laugh.

"Hey, I'm not as hopeless as you think I am," Remy defended himself.

Madeline leaned over and put her head on his shoulder. "You're not hopeless at all," she told him. "Just a little bit stubborn sometimes."

"Ya think?" Remy asked, putting his arm around her.

They sat like that for quite some time, Remy not wanting to speak—not wanting to ruin the moment. It felt like it had when everything was perfect.

When everything was just right.

"Did you have a little bit of fun?" she asked him.

"Maybe a little," he answered, immediately feeling that twinge of guilt.

"How much?" Madeline asked, sitting up and turning to face him. She held up her thumb and forefinger about an inch apart. "This much?"

Remy shrugged. "Maybe a little less. She had a runny nose."

Madeline wrinkled hers. "Really?"

Remy nodded. "Yeah, it was cold, though, so I guess I should cut her some slack."

"I guess," Madeline agreed. "Do you think you'll see her again?"

Remy didn't want to answer that question.

"Remy," Madeline said, trying to get his attention.

He looked at her then, wishing with all his heart that this could be real.

"I asked you a question," she said, her beautiful gaze urging him to answer.

"Yes," he finally replied, and as the words left his mouth, the sounds of the forest were suddenly—eerily—quiet. "Yes, we're having lunch tomorrow."

Madeline smiled then, a smile that he'd seen thousands of times, a smile that had never failed to warm him to his core, a smile that personified the love she'd felt for him, reflected back as the love he had for her.

"Good," she said. "I like her."

"She isn't you."

"And you wouldn't want her to be," Madeline said, slowly shaking her head. "What we had belongs to us."

"And only us," Remy added.

"Exactly." She leaned forward in her chair, her lips suddenly so close to his.

"No more wasted guilt," she whispered, as their lips touched.

*   *   *

Remy opened his eyes to the reality of his world.

The Maine cottage was gone, as was his wife. Instead he
sat at his desk, where he had been finishing some billing
when he'd closed his eyes and let his consciousness wander.
An angel needed no sleep, but often he would enter a kind
of fugue state to rest his weary mind and spend time with
his wife.

Marlowe lay flat on his side on the rug beneath the desk,
legs outstretched as if he'd been shot, his dark eyes watching Remy.

The clock at the bottom of the computer screen said
that it was after three a.m., and the street outside his Beacon Hill brownstone was quiet. Maybe it was time to allevi-
ate some more of his burdened conscience.

"Hey," Remy said to his dog.

Marlowe sat up at full attention, head tilted, waiting for
Remy to ask the question.

And he did. "Want to go to the Common for a walk?"

No more magickal words had ever been spoken.

The Labrador immediately sprang to his feet and began
to anxiously pace.

"Guess that's a yes." Remy stood and stretched, then
headed for the stairs, a very excited Marlowe at his heels.

As Remy was getting ready to take Marlowe on a nighttime walk, Fernita Green was dreaming.

She had fallen asleep in her living room chair, as she was
wont to do these days, surrounded by the clutter of her life,
Miles the cat curled tightly in her lap, also deeply asleep.

Sharing the dream of his mistress.

Fernita walked through the jungle, tall grasses and thick
underbrush moving aside to allow her to pass.

Leading her.

Miles purred and chirped, enjoying the freedom of this
place that could only be the world found on the other side
of the window.

The big outside.

Something deep inside told Fernita that she knew this

vast, primordial place, and this calmed her as she walked the path that appeared beneath her bare feet.

Where are my shoes? she wondered briefly, for there were far more important things to worry about. Although she could not remember what they were.

Only that she was the answer.

The jungle path abruptly stopped, a curtain of thorny vines blocking her way. Fernita stood before the obstruction, waiting for the vegetation to show her the way around, but the green did not react, softly rustling in the warm, gentle breeze that caressed this wild place.

The wild was awakened in Miles the cat, his large eyes scanning the grass and trees for signs of birds, or bugs, or squirrels—signs of prey.

But, disappointingly, there were none right then. There were only the plants here in the big outside.

The jungle closed in around her. Fernita watched with a growing sense of unease as the path she'd walked slowly filled in behind her, reclaimed by the abundant overgrowth. A twinge of panic struck, but she managed to keep it under control as she turned her attention to the wall of thick, spotted vines dangling before her.

She did not know why, but she was suddenly overcome with the desire to touch them. Before she could even question this nearly overpowering compulsion she reached out, then quickly withdrew her hand with a hiss as a thorn pierced the underside of two of her fingers and her palm. For a moment she stared at the dark blood pooling in her hand, then returned her attention to the thick vine before her.

At first she believed it to be a trick of her eyes. There was blood on the vines where she had touched them . . . where she had been stuck, but the blood seemed to be fading away, gradually absorbed into the body of the vines.

How odd.

And as the last of her blood was taken in, the vines began to sway and shake, slowly pulling up and away like the thick velvet curtains of the old movie palaces, to reveal not the white of a screen, but a dark, winding path beyond.

Fernita crouched at the opening, Miles cowering beside her, neither sure they wanted to go any farther, even though every fiber of Fernita's being screamed that she should.

The high grass had again receded, forming a snaking passage through the abundant jungle to a clearing. And in the clearing was a tree; perhaps one of the largest trees Fernita had ever seen. She could just about make out the vast network of thick branches that grew out from its massive trunk, tapering upward into the velvet black sky.

How odd the stars appeared, almost as if they were too close.

Fernita's eyes were just returning to the path . . . to the glorious tree, when something stepped out of the shadows to block her view.

It was huge, its body covered in golden armor that reflected the brightness of the burning sword it clutched in one of its massive, gauntleted hands.

Frozen in fear, she could only look up into its face, which was equal parts eagle, lion, and man.

What are you? she wanted to ask it, but the answer was upon her, floating up from the darkness from where it had been hidden.

Cherubim.

"You do not belong," the creature shrieked, roared, and bellowed in one discordant voice that made her bones shake.

And Miles hissed, his body pressed flat to the grassy ground, fur standing on end as if electrified.

It pinned her there with its multiple sets of eyes, its large form casting a cold shadow across her naked form.

It was the first moment that she recognized she was unclothed, and it would have caused her much confusion if she hadn't been in the presence of a looming weapon of Heaven.

The Cherubim lumbered ever closer; four sets of strangely beautiful wings unfurled from its armored back. Though terrified, she could not help but marvel at its fearsome beauty, staring up into its three faces as it lifted its sword of fire.

"You do not belong," it announced again, prepared to strike.

And Fernita watched, unable to move as the fiery weapon descended, her mouth opening, not in a scream as she believed would pour forth from the depths of her very soul, but another sound that proved she was the answer.

That she did *belong.*

Fernita awakened from the dream, the answer to a question that had plagued her for so very long dancing upon the tip of her tongue.

For a moment it was there, but as the recollection of the jungle drifted away like the morning mist, it too was gone. And in a matter of seconds, she had forgotten that she had even dreamed at all.

Miles had moved from her lap to an open portion of windowsill, staring intensely out at the cold, predawn world, a strange trilling sound, as if he were excited by the sight of a bird or a squirrel, coming from his furry throat.

"What do you see out there, crazy cat?" she asked sleepily, as she reached out and stroked his back with old fingers, crooked with age.

Miles continued to stare, repeating the strange sound over and over again, answering the question that the old woman asked of him.

"*It's coming,*" the cat told her, even though she did not understand.

"*The big outside is coming.*"

CHAPTER THREE

"**W**atch out for the rats," Remy called out to Marlowe as he stuffed the dog's leash in his back pocket and sat on a bench in Boston Common.

"*Rats?*" Marlowe questioned, stopping beside an old oak tree. He looked around, his nose twitching in the cold early-morning air.

"I didn't say there were any waiting to attack you; just be careful. You don't want to get bitten and have to go to the vet for shots."

"*No shots,*" Marlowe growled, nose to the frozen ground. "*No rats . . . no bite . . . no shots,*" the Labrador grumbled, a checklist to make this visit next to perfect.

Remy chuckled. It was still relatively dark in the Common, and he and Marlowe seemed the only living things willing to brave the more than chilly early morning. Still, he wanted to keep an eye on the dog; sometimes Marlowe's enthusiasm got away from him.

"And don't eat any garbage!" Remy called out as an afterthought, one more thing for the checklist. The dog didn't respond, but Remy was sure he'd heard.

Remy settled in on a bench, crossing his legs and resting his arm atop the back, looking as though he were relaxing on a mild summer's night. It was so cold that even the homeless who often frequented the Common appeared to have sought more protective shelter elsewhere.

Good for them, Remy thought. This was the kind of weather that could kill if you weren't careful.

Looking around at his surroundings, Remy realized that it had been some time since he and Marlowe had been here, long enough for the city to put in some new, freshly painted trash barrels to replace the old rusted and dented ones. He considered pointing them out to his dog, who was pawing at a patch of frozen grass, but decided it would be better not to offer an opportunity for food. Marlowe's appetite was voracious, occasionally getting the better of him, and Remy preferred not to deal with the consequences.

A spot of rich green amid the skeletal branches of a nearby tree caught Remy's attention, and he found himself staring. It was odd to find such vibrant leaves in the dead of winter—and even odder to find so many.

And then he noticed that the explosion of plant life seemed to be all around him, in the trees, in the bushes, and even in thick patches of grass that seemed to have erupted up through the old snow and ice.

A sudden barrage of barks distracted him from the oddity of nature, and Remy quickly stood to find his dog.

The sun was just about ready to rise, and he could see Marlowe had something pinned against one of the new trash barrels. He was darting from side to side, barking and growling.

"Marlowe, no," Remy commanded, knowing exactly what he'd find as he headed for the ruckus.

The rat was huge, fat, and it glared at the dog, its beady eyes glistening red in the first light of morning, bristling, brown-furred back pressed against the barrel.

"*Rat*," the dog barked angrily. "*Rat take bread.*"

"What bread?" Remy asked as he approached, careful not to slip on the packed snow as he left the relative safety of the paved walkway.

"*My bread*," Marlowe barked again, lunging at the now hissing rat.

"You don't have any bread," Remy reminded the frenzied animal. And then he saw it. The overweight rodent had taken possession of the end of a submarine sandwich roll . . . a roll to which a certain Labrador retriever, even though he'd been warned not to eat any garbage, had taken a particular shine.

"No," Remy ordered, reaching over to grab his dog's collar. "It's not your bread. . . . It's garbage, and what did I tell you about garbage?"

"*Not garbage.*" Marlowe's eyes were riveted to the roll. "*Bread.*"

"If you found it on the ground, it's garbage." He tugged on the collar as Marlowe tried to pull away.

Remy looked at the rat and spoke in its primitive tongue. "We're sorry," he said. "Take your prize and go."

The rat glared at him, its damp nose twitching in the air, testing for danger. It did not trust him.

Remy pulled Marlowe away.

"*No!*" the dog protested with a pathetic yelp.

"No?" Remy repeated. "How about *yes*?"

The rat's bulk loomed over the piece of roll as it eyed them cautiously. "*Mine,*" it squeaked. "*Hate dog. Hate man,*" it added with a dismissive hiss, as it snatched up the bread and scampered off.

"And furthermore, what did I tell you about rats?" Remy asked the dog, releasing the hold on his collar.

"*Filthy,*" Marlowe said, already sniffing at the ground and ready to move on.

"Yeah, filthy," Remy said. He glanced at his watch and saw that it was nearing five thirty. "Want to go home and get some breakfast?"

That caught the dog's attention.

"*Eat?*" Marlowe asked.

"Would I lie to you?" Remy questioned, smiling, the love that he felt for this simple animal nearly overwhelming.

"*No lie,*" the Labrador said, excitement in his doggy voice. "*Eat. Eat now.*"

"Well, c'mon, then." Remy gestured for Marlowe to follow him.

As he turned, he caught sight of three figures on the path up ahead of him, and took Marlowe's leash from his pocket. "Come here." He reached down to clip the leash to the dog's collar. "Just in case you get any ideas about bothering these early risers."

"*No bother*," Marlowe said, but his tail was already wagging furiously. Marlowe loved people, but could never understand that some people didn't love dogs, especially big ones that seemed overly excited.

"Behave yourself," Remy told him, pulling up on the leash as they grew closer to the three figures.

He saw that they were eyeing him and he made it a point to pull Marlowe even closer.

"Good morning," Remy said to the first of the men, a short, dark-haired, dark-skinned fellow, probably in his mid-twenties, bundled up in a heavy woolen cap and puffy jacket. The other two men were similarly dressed.

The three stopped and watched Remy as he passed, Marlowe struggling, desperate to say hello.

"Don't worry about him," Remy explained with a smile. "He just gets excited around people. Doesn't have an aggressive bone in his body."

He tugged at the dog's leash, continuing toward the exit when he heard one of them speak.

"Remy Chandler?"

He stopped and turned.

"Yes?"

"You are Remy Chandler . . . the private investigator?" the shortest of the three men said.

"I am," Remy answered. "And you are?"

"My name is Jon," the man said, pulling off one of his gloves as he stepped toward Remy, offering his hand. "We've been looking for you."

Remy shook the man's hand as the other two nodded. The handshake was warm and firm.

"Really," he said. The man had an odd speech pattern, as if he was quite hard of hearing.

Marlowe pulled forward on the leash, barking for some attention.

"Knock it off," Remy said, giving the leash a tug.

"That's all right," the man said, squatting down to vigorously pet the dog behind the ears. "He seems like a good dog."

"*Very good*," Marlowe grumbled, finally getting the attention he so desperately craved.

"He tries," Remy said, giving Marlowe's butt a swat. "So, you say you've been looking for me?" There was a strange vibe coming off the men, but one he couldn't quite read. The only thing that he could tell—could feel—was that they weren't dangerous, and meant him no harm.

"We have," Jon said, his breath coming in roiling clouds of white as he slid his hand back into his glove. "We were told you were here, but we didn't know where exactly. It's so cold we were about to give up."

The others smiled as they nodded again, obviously pleased they had managed to stick it out.

"That's funny," Remy said. "I don't remember telling anybody that I'd be here."

"You didn't have to," Jon said. "We listen to our surroundings, and in turn, they tell us what we need to know."

Okay, not dangerous, but very likely crazy.

"So your surroundings said I'd be at the Common, walking my dog?"

Jon bent at the waist in a stiff bow. "They did indeed. I believe it was an elm. . . ."

"Maple," one of the others corrected.

"Ah, yes, thank you. A maple tree on Pinckney Street told us that you had passed with your friend here."

Remy smiled carefully. "A tree told you I went to the Common?"

"It mentioned you had passed, as did the others you walked by on your way here."

"More than one tree talked to you?" Remy asked incredulously.

"All plant life upon this planet talks to us," Jon said with a beatific smile. "You probably think we're mad," he added.

Remy laughed. "Well, since you brought it up."

"We are the Sons of Adam," Jon said, pointing to his comrades, and then to himself.

It took a moment for their identities to sink in.

"Sons of Adam," Remy repeated slowly as the meaning

of the words began to permeate his thick skull. "*The* Adam?"

"Exactly," Jon said. "And he's sent us here to find you."

Marlowe, tired of all the talking, flopped down onto the cold path, lifted his leg, and began to lick at his lower regions.

A real class act.

Remy was silent, anticipating what was coming next.

"The first father has need of your special skills," Jon continued. "Adam needs you to find something for him. He asks that you find the key . . .

". . . the key to the Gates of Eden."

Hell

Francis really didn't know what to expect when he died, but it wasn't this.

Every inch of his body ached. Even thinking hurt, and although he tried to throw himself into a pool of sweet, sweet oblivion, it just wasn't meant to be.

He'd always said thinking could be bad for you, but this was the first time he had actual physical proof.

Tiny hand-grenade blasts were going off inside his skull, all over the surface of his brain, and they forced him to scream like a little girl.

A tough little girl with a penchant for medieval weaponry, and a dry wit.

Francis cautiously opened his eyes. His brain was on fire, as was his skin. Even his eyelids felt as if they'd been ripped from his skull, and put back with random staples.

He rolled over on what appeared to be the floor of a cave, the sounds of Hell still reshaping themselves in the distance. As his eyes adjusted to the gloom of his surroundings, he forced himself to look around.

A flash of memory—like a hot poker being shoved into his ear—jumped into his thoughts, but was quickly gone in a flesh-rending screech of spiked tires.

Gone, but what he had seen was not forgotten.

He remembered lying on the ground, ready to die . . . ready to be swallowed up by one of the many molten pools opening up on the blighted surface of Hell. And just as he was about to give in to the fury being unleashed, he saw the figure of a man.

A hooded figure wearing tattered robes, and holding a staff that appeared to be made from polished bone.

But then the ground vomited up a cloud of noxious gas and bubbling lava, and he saw the man no more, succumbing to the flirtations of sweet unconsciousness, as what he believed to be the final curtain came down.

The show wasn't over, though; in fact, it had just been an intermission, and now the main feature had begun.

Francis lifted himself into a sitting position, the pain of this action making him wish for a quick, numbing death, just to make it all stop. Propped against the wall, he quickly examined himself. He was naked; the nasty wounds he'd received in recent battle and the tantrum thrown by the hellish environment had been dressed.

He lifted an arm that felt as though it weighed a ton, and examined the covered wounds. Thick wads of drying Hell-ash had been placed upon his injuries. Hell-ash had natural healing attributes, but if the proper kind wasn't used—the deeper layers found beneath new accumulations—it could also be extremely toxic.

Whoever had taken care of him knew what they were doing.

He checked himself out; his filthy, naked form was covered with the healing ash. His body had endured a lot of punishment, and Francis realized that he should have been dead.

He took a deep breath and continued to peer through the gloom at his surroundings. He wasn't too far from the entrance to the cave, and he found that if he leaned slightly to the side he could just about make out what was going on outside . . . and it didn't look good.

From what he could see, it looked as though he had been taken to one of the caves that dotted the high hills just beyond the valley that had held Tartarus.

The sky outside the cave was dark and still filled with screeching winds and swirling debris. He guessed that Big Daddy Morningstar was still doing his thing: taking Hell apart piece by piece. What he was going to do once that was finished was the ten-million-dollar question.

Something moved in the darkness behind him, and Francis turned toward the sound. Maybe his mysterious benefactor was about to make an appearance.

"Hello?" he called out, his voice sounding incredibly small as it bounced off the walls of the cave. "Thanks for patching me up. Don't often see folks do such good work with Hell-ash . . ."

Something growled in the shadows, and Francis realized that he might have been a little premature with his thanks.

A Hellion padded toward him from the back of the cave, head low and growling. The Hell beast looked just as nasty as Francis remembered after having gone a few rounds with the filthy fuckers when Tartarus first started to come apart at the seams: thick bodies seemingly devoid of flesh, showing off powerful red musculature. Beady eyes glared at him from its skull-like head.

He tried to move, summoning all the strength that he could muster, but didn't accomplish anything other than sliding over on his side and rolling onto his belly. Lifting his head, he saw that the beast had paused, watching him.

Viscous drool that hissed and spattered like hot grease as it landed upon the floor of the cave dripped from its mouth in a continuous stream as it finally determined that Francis was no threat, and started toward him again.

Francis tensed as the monster drew closer, emitting a strange, high-pitched keening sound incongruous to its great size.

"C'mon, then—what are you waiting for?" the former Guardian angel growled as he watched the beast's red, exposed muscles suddenly tense before launching its ferocious mass at his prone and helpless form.

"I hope you fucking choke."

Fernita couldn't find her telephone.

She stood in what little open space there was in her living room, closed her eyes, and tried to remember.

The problems with her memory were getting worse, and

had been for quite a few years. The old woman did what she could to accommodate the changes. She didn't go out much anymore, preferring to remain in her home, in a safe environment, where the routines she'd established for herself could be maintained.

Outside, those routines didn't exist, and things had a tendency to become very confusing. There was something about a trip to the grocery store. She couldn't recall the exact details, but she knew it had been bad, and that was why she had become more or less housebound.

But she didn't mind, most of the time. Here in the safety of her home, surrounded by her things, she felt as though she had some control.

That life wasn't slipping away between her fingers like grains of sand.

Most of the time, but now was one of those times when the familiarity of routine began to crumble, and she was finding it very hard to hold it all together.

"Where are you?" she whispered, eyes still closed, rocking ever so slightly from side to side.

She tried to remember the last time she had used the phone, and decided it was when she had spoken with that nice man Remy Chandler.

Wasn't it a coincidence that he was exactly who she needed to talk to now?

To tell him that she'd found a clue.

Fernita opened her eyes for a moment, glancing toward the area of the room where the clue had been uncovered. It gave her an uneasy feeling in her stomach to see it there, very much like the feeling she got those few times she had to leave her house.

Her mind started to wander again as she attempted to recall how it was that she'd found the clue, but she was able to pull herself back to the matter at hand.

For a moment, what exactly she had been desperate to find suddenly eluded her, but then she remembered— grabbing hold of the memory with both hands and holding fast—the phone. She needed to find the phone so she could call Remy.

Miles meowed from his perch upon the windowsill, rubbing the side of his neck against the corner of some boxes stacked beside the window.

"Help your mama out here, cat," she said. "Where did I put that phone?"

The cat looked at her intensely, making a little chirping sound, as if to answer her. He then jumped down into her seat, flipping onto his back as if to show off the black fur of his belly.

"That's not helping me. Shoulda had a dog," Fernita said with mock disgust. "I could just say, 'Fetch me the phone,' and he'da found it for me already."

Miles rolled onto his side, letting his head hang over the cushion. One of his paws dangled off the chair and he started to swat at the handle of a grocery bag that she'd brought into the room for some reason or another.

It had something to do with apples, she inexplicably remembered.

Fernita was drawn toward the bag, the chair, and her cat.

She leaned forward, peering inside the open bag to see that it was filled with the peelings and core of an apple she'd had for a snack. When, she could not recall, but it couldn't have been that long ago.

It was probably a good idea that she put the bag, and its peelings, in the trash before it started to stink up the place, she told herself as she reached for the handles.

Miles swatted at her outstretched hand, nicking the top of one of her dark knuckles with the hook of his claw.

"Ouch!" Fernita squawked, pulling back her hand, one of her fingers catching the handle of the plastic bag.

The loud rustling of the shopping bag startled Miles, and he bounded from the chair, his panic to flee setting off a kind of chain reaction that began with the boxes he'd been rubbing his scent on earlier.

The boxes tipped toward the seat, spilling magazines and coverless paperback books onto her chair and the floor beneath.

"Guess I was right," Fernita muttered as she dove forward to stem the avalanche. "Should've got a dog when I had the chance."

And then it came to her: a memory seemingly sunk to the bottom of the lake that was her recollection.

She was eating an apple right before she'd called Remy Chandler.

The bag of apple droppings still hanging from her wrist, Fernita stepped back from her chair to take in the big picture and found what she was looking for.

She had placed the old rotary phone on the floor while she had cut her apple, and it must've been pushed out of sight by her comings and goings.

"Found it," she said happily, holding on to the arm of her chair as she bent down to retrieve the phone. She brought it up from the floor, careful not to get the cord caught on anything else that could tip or topple.

She dropped the bag from her wrist and placed the phone on a stack of *Better Homes and Gardens* by her chair.

Strangely enough, she never had a problem remembering where she kept the private eye's phone number, and removed the old business card from inside her apron along with some old tissues. Letting the Kleenex fall to the floor, she studied the number on the card and slowly began to dial.

As she waited for her call to be answered, her eyes drifted to the other side of the room, where something odd had been uncovered after her dreams that night.

She had no idea where it had come from—multiple vertical lines of peculiar writing, obviously some foreign language, written in black on the lower half of her walls. Long hidden by her things, it seemed to shift in and out of focus.

She heard Remy's voice, and immediately prepared to speak, before realizing it was just his answering machine. Fernita waited for it to finish, waiting for her chance to let the nice man know she had something for him.

Though she wasn't sure exactly what it was, she knew it was a clue to what she had lost.

CHAPTER FOUR

Remy gazed out the window of the private jet at the thin, wispy clouds floating past, and experienced the sudden pangs of longing. His shoulder blades had started to ache where his wings would be if he allowed them to unfurl.

To beat the air in glorious flight.

He squirmed, tightening his seat belt before turning his eyes to the clouds again. Suppressing the urge to fly, he found his mind start to wander, thinking not of the unusual client who had sent a private plane for him, but of breakfast that morning and with whom he'd had it—Linda Somerset.

They were supposed to have had lunch, but the urgency of the Sons' request had convinced Remy to make the trip to see Adam as soon as possible. The Sons had said that they would call him with the information about the flight sometime later that morning, which had given him an idea. He would call Linda and see if she could do breakfast instead.

It was unusual, in retrospect, Remy thought, continuing to stare out the window. Here was his opportunity to step back from the discomfort he was feeling about the whole dating thing, but he hadn't. He didn't cancel, and had immediately thought of a backup plan.

It was clear that he really wasn't in his right mind at the moment. Thoughts of Adam, the first father, and a missing key to the Garden—and what this all meant—were using up valuable space inside his skull. That had to be the answer; why else was his thinking so scattered?

Linda had answered the phone sleepily. He didn't even think to check the time that he was calling. It was only a little bit before seven a.m., and he'd woken her up.

Just another example of his brain not functioning at top form. *What's wrong with me?* he wondered. That had been bad enough, but it didn't stop there.

After he apologized profusely, she had accepted his offer, telling him that she needed to be in the city early for some school stuff anyway, and that she would love to have breakfast.

Remy saw in his reflection on the circular plastic windowpane that he was smiling, and didn't quite know how to feel about that.

They had met at a small deli near Coolidge Corner, and it was then that he'd realized the next thing that had completely escaped him: Not really knowing how long he was going to be with Adam, he needed somebody to take care of Marlowe for him. Nothing big, mind you, just walking, feeding, playing, and stuff.

Remy had apologized for being rude, telling her that he needed to make an important phone call. He called Ashley and spoke with her mother, and was reminded—*again*—that Ash was heading to Killington for some skiing with friends.

As he hung up, Linda must have seen the look on his face, and she asked what the problem was. He explained that the person who normally looked after Marlowe when he was away was not around.

Remy remembered the look on Linda's face as if she were still there, sitting in front of him. And then he remembered her words.

"I'd love to watch Marlowe for you."

Remy had actually hesitated, not knowing exactly how he was feeling about Linda's offer, but she seemed genuinely eager to do it, and something just felt really right about the situation, so he'd agreed.

Not that he wasn't a little anxious.

He might've been nervous, but Marlowe was ecstatic, excited as all get-out about going to the pretty female's house. As he'd handed over Marlowe's leash to her, the Labrador had told him that Linda smelled good.

Remy hadn't responded to the dog's statement, but he had to agree.

She told Remy not to worry, that the two of them were going to have an excellent time. And Remy knew that they would, and honestly had felt a little bit jealous of his four-legged best friend.

The Sons of Adam had sent a car for him, which had brought him to T. F. Green Airport in Rhode Island, where he'd boarded a private jet, and here he was.

He glanced at his watch to see that they'd already been in the air a little over two hours. It wouldn't be much longer.

And as if on cue, he felt the plane begin its descent. He leaned his forehead against the cool plastic of the window.

Adam, and his Sons, were living in a secluded place that Jon had lovingly referred to as the Garden. He hadn't given Remy much more than that, which was why Remy searched the gradually approaching land below.

He was somewhere over the Arizona desert, the brownish red landscape below starkly beautiful in the rays of the afternoon sun.

And then he saw it.

It was totally out of place in the harsh desert surroundings, a white bubble ... a dome, looking as though it had erupted up from the dry brown earth ... a kind of boil on the flesh of the bleak desert skin.

As the plane banked to the left in its descent, he saw how large it actually was, the white dome even having its own runway. The private jet came in for a landing, smoothly touching down and rolling to an eventual stop.

The pilot emerged from the cabin with a gracious smile, opening the door and extending the steps. Remy unbuckled his seat belt and stood.

"Thank you," he said, and the pilot touched the rim of his cap as Remy exited the plane. There was something in the man's eyes that told him he too was a Son of Adam, something that said he had lived upon this world far longer than normal men.

The desert heat was stifling as Remy walked down the steps to the runway. There was a van waiting for him, and he saw Jon, no longer dressed in his heavy New England–winter clothing, but now wearing chinos and a white short-sleeved shirt.

Jon had the look in his eyes, as did the others who had accompanied him to Boston earlier this morning.

Remy had known about the Sons for many, many years: direct descendants of the first man, they exhibited longevity uncommon to most humans, almost as if they had a special purpose. Most had sworn an oath to care for their seemingly eternal ancestor, forming a kind of secret community around him.

The Sons believed that their most holy ancestor had been wrongly accused by God, and waited for the day when the Almighty would see the error of His ways, and allow His first creation to return to Paradise.

As Jon approached, hand outstretched, Remy had to wonder if the rift with the Daughters of Eve had ever been mended. That was a bit of a mess that had gone on for centuries, and might still be going on, for all he knew.

"Mr. Chandler," Jon said as they shook hands. "Thank you again for coming."

"No problem," Remy said, following the man to the waiting van. "Pretty impressive," he added, eyeing the dome in the distance as he prepared to get into the air-conditioned vehicle.

"Wait till you see it from the inside," Jon said as he turned the van around on the runway and onto a road that would bring them to the fenced area surrounding the half bubble bulging up from the desert.

"I can't wait," Remy said as they drove closer. "Is this where the Sons are living now?"

"Some of us," Jon said as he rolled down the window as they approached a high gate. He removed a key card from his shirt pocket and slid it into the face of a metal security box atop a post, and the gates began to slide apart to grant them access.

"Over the years some of us have decided to go out into the world, occasionally returning when necessary, but a large majority of us remain together, looking after Adam's needs."

Jon brought the van alongside the great dome and got out. Remy followed, standing alongside the man as they approached what Remy imagined was an entrance.

There was a keypad on this door as well, and Jon again used his card to grant them access.

"After you," he said, gesturing for Remy to step inside as the door slowly slid open with a hydraulic hiss. Doing as told, Remy immediately noticed the temperature difference from outside.

"The electric bill must be enormous," Remy said jokingly.

"We supply all our own power here," Jon said, heading down a corridor. "If you weren't aware, this is a biosphere, a self-sustaining environment all beneath this dome."

"Nice," Remy said.

"We do research here in energy, agricultural genetic engineering, and alternative medicine, as well as some excursions into the fringe sciences," Jon explained.

"I always wondered what you guys did for fun," Remy commented slyly. Jon didn't appear to be all that up on sly.

"We hold a number of very profitable patents that allow us to live the life of seclusion our order requires," he said as they passed through another door into a circular atrium. The room was white, blindingly so, and very cold and antiseptic—not at all what Remy would have expected of an order that had existed for so many thousands of years.

There were multiple doors surrounding them, and Jon gestured to one in particular. "You'll be going in there," he said, the door sliding open on its own as they approached.

Passing through the door, Remy could see nothing but green, the air so thick with humidity that for a moment it was almost difficult to breathe.

"It's beautiful," he said, looking around at the equivalent of a tropical rain forest in the middle of a desert. The rich colors were stimulating to the eye, brightly colored birds flitting around above them, their joyous cries reminding the Seraphim of a familiar place from so very long ago.

"It's our temporary piece of Paradise," Jon said, looking around the jungle. "And hopefully, someday soon ... with your help ... we'll be able to have the real thing."

"Maybe," Remy answered him, uncomfortable with how to respond. As far as he understood, the first of humanity had been banished from Eden for their sins against God, and the Garden of Eden was cut loose from reality to prevent it from becoming a beachhead during the war with Lucifer and his followers, but then again, maybe there was something he didn't know.

Remy hoped that this meeting with Adam would help clear up some things.

"The one you need to speak with is down there," Jon said, pointing down the length of the path that disappeared into the thick jungle foliage.

"You're not part of this meeting?" Remy asked.

Jon shook his head. "This is not the place for someone like me. I'll see you after."

He turned away, leaving Remy alone in the man-made jungle, alone in this attempt to re-create the Garden of Eden on Earth.

Remy followed the path into the shadows, pushing aside the leathery leaves that blocked his way. Something squawked loudly as he stepped out into a clearing, and he looked up to see a large parrot perched upon a thick branch, peering down at him with one beady eye, its head cocked at a bizarre angle.

"No fear," he told the parrot, reassuring the colorful jungle resident that he meant it no harm. The bird seemed to accept his word, going back to breaking open with its powerful beak the nut that it held in its taloned foot.

In the distance, beside an artificial stream, he saw the box. It appeared to be made mostly from clear plastic, and reminded him of a high-tech coffin. There was a housing for machinery that hummed softly that was attached to the back of the box, which was standing in an upright, vertical position. Remy could see that there was something—*someone*—inside the box as he came up alongside it.

Peering inside, he saw the almost mummified body of a man, his thin, leathery dark skin pulled tight across his skull and body—as if his skeleton had been dipped in a brownish paint and that was all that covered his bones. His eyes were barely open, see-through, tinted goggles that appeared to provide moisture for the ancient orbs in his withered face.

Stepping closer to the front of the box, he could see that the man's bare arms and legs were adorned with tubes that disappeared beneath the thin flesh like burrowing worms, a series of monitors on the front of the coffinlike box providing readouts on his health.

The box was helping to keep him alive.

"Hello, Adam," Remy said sadly, placing the palm of his hand against the front of the plastic case.

If this could be called living.

Flashes of memory appeared before his mind's eye as the nature of the Seraphim at the center of his being was stirred by the memory of the one within the box.

He saw the actual Garden and all the wonders within her, including the magnificent specimens that would eventually become the prototypes for the human race.

But he also saw Eden in turmoil, the destructive aftereffects of original sin, and God's displeasure with His most prized creations.

"It's been quite a long time."

Remy sensed the presence almost at once; the air was suddenly charged with an ancient power.

He turned, the Seraphim inside ready to emerge.

Standing before him was a being of immeasurable might, although he too was wearing the guise of humanity—a tall older man in a finely tailored suit, with closely cropped white hair and beard—but Remy could see through his disguise.

See him for what he was—and what he had once been in the scheme of things.

"Malachi," he said in the language of the Heavenly hosts.

"Remiel," the angel responded, his voice reminiscent of the celestial choir. "Thank you for coming."

The Garden of Eden: During the Great War in Heaven

The Seraphim Remiel soared above the Garden of Eden, sword in hand and ready for battle.

They had said that the legions of Lucifer would come here, to this beautiful place created for the Lord God's most spectacular creations, but which was now empty of them.

The humans had been banished . . . punished for the sin of disobedience—a sin that Lucifer Morningstar had predicted.

Remiel landed amid the thick greenery, the stench of God's anger still tainting the air. It was peaceful here, the clamor of battle, the sounds of brother killing brother not yet reaching its emerald expanse.

Yet.

The Son of the Morning had said that God had given them too much, that the humans would take His gifts for granted and disobey Him in their arrogance.

And in an attempt to prove that his words were true, Lucifer tested them, tempting the first of the humans with the fruit of the Tree.

The Tree of Knowledge; the Tree that was forbidden them.

And Lucifer was proven right; they did betray the trust of their most beatific Creator, but it did not stop the Lord God from continuing to love His newest creations—though He was immensely disappointed.

Which led to their punishment.

For their sin, the humans had been driven from Eden.

Remiel trudged through the forest, his sword of fire cutting a swath through the overgrowth toward his destination. With the humans gone, Eden had grown wild and overgrown—those chosen to be the gardeners no longer there to tend it.

But this punishment wasn't enough for the Son of the Morning, who wanted these two insolent whelps wiped from existence—for the Almighty to recognize that He had already conceived His most magnificent of creations.

The angels were all that He needed; the angels would love only Him, and never disobey.

But how quickly was that proven false?

Despite their flaws, God did not forsake His human creations. Instead, He chose to love and guide them, picking them over all others.

This enraged the Morningstar, and many others of the Heavenly hosts, and war was declared against Heaven. They decided that they no longer needed Him, that they no longer loved Him, and chose to disobey Him in any way that they could.

Rumor had it that Lucifer and his followers planned to take Eden as theirs, to use it as a stepping-stone—a beachhead—to eventually taking Heaven itself.

This, Remiel would not allow to happen.

Others had been given the chore to cut the Garden loose, to cast it adrift, severing its connection to God's Kingdom, but here it remained.

This concerned the Seraphim, which was why he was at the ready, cautious that the Morningstar's legions had already arrived.

If this were the case, it would be up to him; he would need to be the one who prevented Eden from falling into Lucifer's hands. It was a job he was ready to perform.

A chore that he was ready to die for, if need be.

Having been here before, Remiel had a sense of where he was despite the thick overgrowth. Hanging vines sizzled and popped, dropping to the grassy floor of Eden as the burning blade cut through them, exposing to him the clearing, and what was growing huge and bountiful there.

The Tree of Knowledge.

The sight, more magnificent than the last time he'd viewed it, was marred by a scene of violence and death. The angel soldiers who had been sent to perform their task had been slain, their bodies broken and bleeding—their blood seeping into the rich earth to feed the great Tree.

Only one of the soldiers remained alive.

He was of the Heavenly host, Cherubim, and he knelt amid the carnage, his head of many faces staring with unwavering intensity.

Remiel knew him as Zophiel, a sentry of the Tree.

"Brother," the Seraphim called to him, but the kneeling angel did not seem to hear. Remiel moved carefully closer, his warrior's senses on full alert.

"Caution," said a voice nearby.

Remiel leapt into the air, his burning sword at the ready, only to pull back as he dropped to the ground.

Malachi emerged from behind the great Tree, his vestments of shimmering light spattered with the blood of angels.

Malachi had been one of the originals that sprang from God. First there had been Lucifer, the Light Bringer—and then there had been Malachi, he who would bring life.

"Forgiveness," Remiel said, averting his gaze temporarily from the great elder angel. Slowly his gaze returned to the dead, and the powerful Cherubim that knelt among them.

"What has happened here?"

Malachi emerged further, his body radiating the power given him by the Almighty.

"It was as if Zophiel had been touched by madness," the angel explained. "He had been here, guarding the Tree, when the soldiers arrived, and when told to step aside, he seemed to snap . . . and this is what occurred."

Remy rose to his feet, stricken by the words of the Life Bringer.

"How is this possible?" Remiel asked, still staring at the angel kneeling among the dead.

"Perhaps a flaw in his design," Malachi suggested, having assisted the Lord God in the execution of the Cherubim's creation. Malachi had assisted in the design of them all; this was what he had been created for—an extension of God's artful hand.

As Malachi spoke, the Cherubim Zophiel looked up, madness burning in the three sets of eyes.

"No!" the powerful angelic force bellowed, rising up to his full and impressive height. His armored form was shaking—trembling—as if fighting off some invisible force.

"Quickly, Remiel," Malachi ordered. "Before more damage is done."

Remiel knew what he had to do; it was the same thing that had been needed from him since the war began, what seemed like an eternity ago.

Zophiel continued to vibrate as he swayed upon powerful armored legs, eyes suddenly falling upon a mighty sword protruding from the back of one of the angels he had slain.

"Don't do it, brother," Remiel warned, his own sword at the ready.

Zophiel hesitated, and for a moment Remiel saw in the Cherubim's look a Heavenly being in the throes of torment.

But as quickly as the expression had come, it was gone, leaving only a maniacal force of violence behind.

With a bellow that combined the enraged cries of eagle, lion, and man, Zophiel grabbed hold of the mighty sword's hilt and yanked it free. The sword pulled from the ground, but the body of the fallen angel still hung upon the large ebony blade. The Cherubim roared again, spreading his multiple sets of wings, raising his corpse-adorned sword to strike.

Remiel leapt into the path of the descending blade, blocking the sword's burning arc with his own sword of fire. The fire from his weapon jumped to the corpse hanging limply from his attacker's sword, voraciously consuming the dead Heavenly flesh and armor till nothing remained.

"The time for mercy is at an end, Remiel," he heard Malachi say from behind. "Put the poor beast out of his misery before more bad comes of this."

Using his sword, Remiel shoved his attacker back, spreading his own wings to put the Cherubim on the offensive.

"Nothing good can come of this, Zophiel," Remiel

roared, swinging his weapon in cracking arcs of fire. "Yield. . . . Set down your sword and surrender."

The madness had taken the Cherubim's voice, rendering the former sentry for the Garden nearly animal in his responses. He brought his black weapon down with a piercing cry as Remiel soared up into the air to avoid its bite. The sword cleaved the earth, the grass and flowers growing wild there withering before catching fire.

Remiel descended, his own weapon poised to deliver a killing blow. The Seraphim drew back the sword, aiming the blade for the base of the Cherubim's neck, where his armor ended. Thrusting forward with the sword, Remiel's aim was true, but Zophiel, in his maddened state, was faster. The sword blade slipped past its target, allowing the Cherubim to reach up and grab hold of Remiel's chest plate and snatch him from the air.

Wings flapping wildly to get away, Remiel was thrown backward, slammed into the Tree of Knowledge's trunk with enough force to shake the Tree so violently that fruit upon its branches began to rain to the ground.

Things were momentarily black, but the Seraphim struggled back from the abyss, surging awake to find the sword he had dropped.

Remiel lunged for his weapon, his slim fingers gathering around the hilt just as Zophiel's armored foot dropped down to pin the blade to the ground. Remiel looked up into the faces of the Cherubim to see him standing there, the black blade raised above his head.

But it did not fall.

Remiel could see the struggle going on behind the Cherubim's eyes—the inner conflict threatening to rip the angel sentry asunder with its fury.

"Put down your weapon," Remiel told the tormented angel, sensing that there might be a solution that did not involve one of their deaths.

Zophiel stumbled back, his huge sword dropping to his side as his free hand grabbed at his head. The Cherubim was struggling, unable to do battle on two fronts.

"Strike while you can, Remiel!" Malachi commanded.

The Seraphim reacted, picking up his sword and springing from the ground prepared to deal a killing blow to his foe, but Remiel pulled back on the savagery, watching the Cherubim in the midst of some great inner struggle.

Malachi was suddenly beside him, wrenching the sword from Remiel's hand.

"Slay him now, while we have the chance," the elder angel bellowed, as he turned to face their beleaguered foe.

And just as Malachi was about to strike, the air was filled with a trumpet's blare.

"Lucifer," Remiel said, gazing up into the heavens.

Malachi and Zophiel were listening as well as the wail of the battle horn was replaced with the sound of flapping wings . . . hundreds and hundreds of flapping wings.

Sensing that his moment was fleeting, Malachi swung out with the sword, hoping to catch the Cherubim unawares. But Zophiel was at the ready, parrying the blade and lashing out with his other hand, swatting Malachi aside like some bothersome bug.

"No!" Remiel yelled, recapturing his sword to finish what he should have done before, his moment of compassion perhaps leading to their undoing.

The Cherubim did not press the attack, instead stepping back and away. He looked to the sky as the pounding of angels' wings filled the air, before looking back to Remiel.

And without another word, the angel sentry spread his own wings, leaping into the air, and then was gone in a crackling discharge of energy as he tore through the veil that separated this reality from others.

"After him," Malachi hissed, crawling to his feet, but this time Remiel did not heed his command.

"No," the Seraphim said, quickly walking from the clearing.

"No, brother?" Malachi asked incredulously.

Remiel turned to face the powerful angel. "Eden cannot be allowed to fall into their hands," he said as he pointed toward the sky. "The Cherubim is the least of our problems now."

Malachi did not respond, but the sneer upon his radiant features told Remiel that the old angel was not used to having his words go unheeded, but there was no time for delicate feelings. There was a war on, and his Lord God was depending on what he would do next.

"Quickly, now," Remiel said to him. "Come with me or be trapped here forever."

The elder said nothing more as wings emerged from his back, and with a single, powerful thrust, he launched himself into the heavens and was gone.

Thoughts returned to the mission at hand, he hacked his way through the verdant jungle, hoping that he wasn't too late. Remiel knew where Lucifer and his legions would try to enter the Garden, and he made his way quickly toward the entrance to Paradise. Emerging from the dense wall of green, Remiel saw the twin stone posts from which the gates to the Garden hung.

Still open wide and beckoning.

This would be where they would try to gain entrance.

The sounds of winged flight and the bleating of war horns echoed through the air as Remiel passed through the passage to gaze up into the sky.

Soldiers still in service to the Lord God were in battle with the followers of Lucifer . . . the blood of angels raining down from the air to quench the thirst of the lush Garden below.

Outside the posts, Remiel spread his arms, taking hold of the gates in each hand, ready to slam them shut and sever the tie between Eden and Heaven. He hated the thought of it, Eden being such a beautiful place, but the Morningstar planned to corrupt it, turning it against their Lord and Master.

He could hear the legions of Lucifer in the sky above, their screeching cries growing louder as they readied to drop down upon him—to prevent him from doing what the Almighty desired.

"Remiel!" called a voice that he knew belonged to the Morningstar; it wasn't even necessary to turn.

"Paradise isn't for you, Lucifer," Remiel roared to the

heavens, using all his strength to swing the mighty metal gates closed.

And as they came together, the locking mechanism slipped finally into place with a sound like the cracking of the universe's largest bullwhip, and the floor of Eden, just outside the locked gates, began to tremble and shake.

The ground began to disintegrate beneath his feet, and Remiel took to the air, watching as the Garden of Eden started to become less and less defined, no longer attached to the Heavenly Kingdom—cut away, and slipping from the present reality into another.

Cast adrift in a sea of realities too numerous to count.

Likely never to be seen by Heaven—or any other—again.

"This is a surprise," Remy said, the memory of the last time he'd seen the elder angel fresh in his thoughts.

"I gather you never imagined you would see the likes of me again," Malachi said as he reached up to bend a beautiful flower toward himself so that he could smell it.

"These days I never rule anything out," Remy said, and smiled at the ancient being. "Let's just say I've learned from experience."

"Experience," Malachi said with an accepting nod. "And what experience, may I ask, brought you to this?" the elder asked as he scrutinized Remy's appearance.

"Let's just say the affairs of Heaven no longer agree with me," Remy replied, attempting to be respectful, but having a difficult time keeping the annoyance from his tone. "So I've removed myself from the equation."

"You live as one of them?"

"I do."

"Fascinating," Malachi said. "Do you see what you've inspired?" the elder then asked the unmoving form of Adam.

"Can he hear you?" Remy asked, moving closer.

"Yes, he can," Malachi answered. "But the passage of time is finally catching up to him." The elder turned his gaze from the withered form inside the transparent sarcophagus to Remy.

"So he's dying?" Remy asked, pangs of sudden emotion tightening in his chest.

"They were never meant to live forever," the designer said. "The fact that he's lived this long is quite remarkable."

Remy recalled his fascination with the first humans: how he would perch unseen in a tree within the Garden to watch these fabulous new creations that God had brought into existence. He had always known how special they would be, even though many of his kind did not.

"And this has something to do with needing to find the key to Eden?" Remy asked, remembering what brought him across the country.

"It does," Malachi said. The elder was staring again at the withered form inside the see-through box. "It's all connected, I believe," he said, reaching up to wipe away a smudge from the front of the case.

"Connected to what?"

"It's coming back, Remiel," Malachi said, his dark eyes growing wide with excitement. "The Garden . . . Eden . . . it's coming here . . . drawn to this world. Drawn to him."

Remy couldn't believe his ears. He'd thought the Garden had been destroyed countless millennia ago, when the gates were slammed closed and it snapped away from reality.

"But that's impossible . . . isn't it?" Remy asked. "I thought that once it had been severed from its connection to Heaven that . . ."

"Did you honestly believe you would ever see me again?" Malachi asked.

"Got me," Remy said with a smirk. "Like so many others of our ilk, I thought you had been a casualty of the war."

There was a stone bench beside the stream and Malachi went to sit. Remy followed, listening as the elder explained where he had been.

"The war," he said sadly. "I watched it from a distance with a disbelieving eye, never imagining the horrors that transpired. Here were the beautiful creatures that I helped to create, slaughtering one another with such abandon, jealous of their Lord . . . jealous that He did not love them enough."

Malachi stared off into the man-made jungle, reliving what he had experienced.

"I could no longer stand the sight of it and left," he said, disgust in his tone. "So I headed out there . . . into the universe. What I was searching for, I did not know."

Remy could understand what the elder had felt, for he had experienced it as well, though his personal search had not taken him to the stars, but to the Earth below.

"I found nothing out there to assuage my feelings of sadness, of disgust," Malachi said.

"So you came here," Remy stated.

"I wandered the planet for some time, hiding myself away, observing the Earth as it evolved," Malachi answered. "I found myself drawn to him . . . to Adam. . . . Like a light far off in the distance, I went toward it, searching for purpose."

Malachi stood up from his seat, walking toward the life-support unit, his back to the detective.

"And I found it with him, and those who care for him. I believe it has something to do with his . . . *our* connection to the Garden," the elder said. "Somehow his impending death is calling Eden here . . . to this plane of existence. To make things complete again."

Malachi was silent as he stared within the life-sustaining case at the first of humanity.

"We have a bond, he and I," the elder whispered. "And as the last of his days draw near, I want to grant him his final wish."

"And what would that be?"

"He wants to go home," Malachi said as he slowly turned to face him. "He wishes to be laid to rest beneath the soil of Paradise."

"It was where he was born."

Malachi agreed with a nod. "And where he wishes to finally die."

"And you need a key to get in . . . to open the gates that I closed."

"The key is in two parts," Malachi explained, holding up two slender fingers. "Adam is the first section of the key, with his mate providing the other."

"His mate? You mean Eve?"

"The temptress," Malachi said with a distant smirk. "I had a sense after her creation that she would be trouble, but never imagined how much."

"I hate to be the bearer of bad news, but from my understanding, Eve is dead."

Malachi cocked his head to the left and looked toward the clear coffin as if hearing something. "Yes, we're aware of that, but the key remains in her bloodline. There is always one who carries the knowledge."

"And this is the key that you need me to find."

"Precisely," Malachi said. "With the two halves a whole, all that is needed to turn the lock will be present."

Malachi left the clear coffin again to approach Remy.

"They are both the lock and the key," the elder explained.

"I'm not sure I'm following," Remy said honestly.

"It is their repentance to God, and their forgiveness of each other for the sin committed in the Garden so long ago, that will open Paradise to them again."

The enormity of what was being asked of him gradually crept up into his lap like an affectionate elephant.

"Let me see if I've got this," Remy said. "The Garden of Eden is going to manifest on Earth, and you need me to find the other part of the key . . . a descendant of Eve . . . so that the gates into the Garden can be opened again. And this is all so that you can bury Adam in his place of birth. Am I missing anything?"

"Very good, Remiel," Malachi said, clapping his hands together in silent applause. "I now see why Adam requested that it be you."

"I'm flattered, but I haven't a clue how to begin."

Malachi looked confused.

"You need me to find somebody . . . a specific descendant of the first woman . . . of Eve. That's like asking me to find a needle on the planet of the haystacks."

"Planet of the haystacks?" Malachi repeated, not understanding his amusing way of getting a point across. Remy was sure that Francis would have laughed at that one.

"Forget that," Remy said. "All I'm saying is that it would be nearly impossible for me to locate this woman without some kind of lead . . . a trail that I could follow that might eventually take me to her."

"A trail to take you to the needle on the haystack planet," Malachi said.

"Right," Remy said. "I'm good, but I'm not that good."

Malachi considered the situation.

"We might be able to assist you with this," the elder then said.

"I'm all ears," Remy stated. "Anything to narrow things down a bit would be greatly appreciated."

Malachi turned to Adam again. "If you will excuse us," he told the withered figure inside. He then proceeded past the bench and into the jungle. "Follow me."

Remy hesitated for a moment, his attention on Adam.

"I'll do what I can," he told the first of humanity, and then reached out to lay his hand upon the clear plastic cover. He then left the silent figure to follow Malachi farther into the man-made jungle.

He found the elder angel standing at a metal door, waiting.

Without a word, Malachi opened the door to reveal a set of steps that traveled down into a muted yellow light. Remy followed, one set of steps after another, until they reached a second door.

There was a loud buzz, followed by the opening of an electronic lock, and Jon stepped out to greet them.

"Hello again, Mr. Chandler," he said, holding the door open.

It was warm inside this room as well, probably warmer than the jungle Remy had just left, but it didn't take him long to figure out why.

There was a tree growing in the center of the room.

But not just any tree; it was a young version of the Tree of Knowledge.

"Is that what I think it is?" Remy asked, noticing that the sapling was hooked up to all manner of machines, rooted not in soil, but in some sort of clear fluid.

"It is," Malachi answered. "Grown from a single seed from the fruit of the original. The Sons had it in their possession for countless millennia, never realizing the potential it carried."

The elder had approached the platform, studying the growing tree with a scrutinizing eye.

"Multiple lifetimes have gone by as we tended the sapling, hoping that someday it might provide for us answers to the questions that have haunted the first of humanity, and his offspring."

Remy could see that a single piece of fruit hung from the spindly branch. He remembered the actual Tree, and the overabundant bounty of life that dangled fat and ripe from its branches, and this wasn't even close.

"Seems unhealthy," the detective commented.

"We're lucky that it looks this well," Jon said. "It took close to fifty years to find the proper nutrient solution to feed the tree, and even that is a far second to the soil of Paradise."

Malachi stood close to the tree and reached out, his fingers wrapping around the body of the single piece of fruit. "But our time has finally run its course," the elder ominously said as his grip tightened, and he gave the fruit a sharp tug, separating it from its branch.

Jon audibly gasped as the elder's hand came away from the tree holding the sickly growth, presenting it to him.

"And now we must find the answers."

Jon carefully took the piece of fruit from Malachi's hand and brought it to a table in the corner of the room. He placed it on a metal tray, clicked on an overhead light, and removed a pair of rubber gloves from a box nearby. Like a doctor prepping for surgery, he slipped them on with a snap.

Malachi came to stand beside him as they both watched.

Jon grabbed a scalpel and, holding the body of the fruit in one hand, began to cut away the thick skin.

"And what are we doing here?" Remy asked.

"The tough, leathery skin must first be cut away," the elder explained as they continued to watch Jon work. "To reach the tender fruit beneath . . . as well as the answers hidden there."

Jon had peeled away all the skin, and had separated it to one side of the metal tray. The skin was very thick, reminding Remy of a deflated football. The fruit that remained was small, looking a bit like a peeled grape.

"We're ready," Jon said, looking up from his work, a serious expression upon his face.

"I'm guessing that somebody is going to be eating that," Remy commented.

"You are correct," the elder angel answered. "And, sadly, it will likely be the last thing he ever consumes."

CHAPTER FIVE

The Garden. It was all about the Garden.

The creature that had called himself Bob hung in the cold vacuum of space, watching as the Earth spun languidly below him.

It was all coming back.

Slowly. Very slowly . . . in jagged, razor-sharp pieces that cut into his mind, memories oozing from the wounds like the flow of blood.

Bob saw the images they formed before him, but he could not yet understand.

Random images that held no meaning.

But they shared a common theme.

The Garden.

Bob held tightly to the memory of that sacred place. And as he floated in the void, he could see similar places on the world below, jungles vibrant with color and life of every conceivable size and shape, but nothing like the Garden.

Something of dire importance had brought him to this place, something that could endanger the Garden.

And Heaven beyond.

Bob suddenly saw the earth of Paradise churning and bubbling like water as something writhed beneath it, and then, just as quickly, it was gone, replaced by the image of another: one like himself.

A servant of Heaven, a blade made from the light of the divine in his hand.

"*This is for the good of us all,*" the brother of Heaven said as he stepped forward, his knife flashing seductively just before . . .

Bob's mind was afire; he screamed noiselessly in the black expanse of space—the pain as real as if it were happening at the moment.

But it was all just a memory.

Eventually the pain subsided, and he found himself still floating in the void above the Earth. His multiple sets of eyes were fixated on the blue planet, and he knew that the reason he still existed was to be found beneath him.

The angel—yes, he knew what he was now—believed it to be only a matter of time before all was revealed to him.

He had to have patience.

And the perseverance to see the mission—*whatever it may be*—through to the end.

The angel Bob floated in the darkness of space, watching the Earth below him.

Waiting for a sign.

Hell

The Hellion pounced with a gurgling growl.

Francis felt its razor-sharp claws flex on the flesh of his back as he struggled beneath the Hell beast's weight. Saliva like acid rained down upon his skin, and he knew it was only a matter of minutes before his spine was torn out when he felt the warm breath of the Hellion on the nape of his neck.

"Do it," Francis hissed, too weak to do anything but await oblivion as he ended his life as Hellion Chow.

He felt the beast tense, its claws digging deeply into his back as it let loose a sound that reminded Francis of the screech of breaks on a rain-slicked highway.

It was the sound of doom, and this time he was on the receiving end.

He lay there, waiting for the feel of powerful jaws closing around his neck, and the savage shake that would sever his spine.

But it didn't come.

"No!" a mysterious voice suddenly commanded. "Off!"

And after a moment's hesitation, Francis felt the weight of the monster leave his aching back. The Hellion wasn't happy in the least; he could hear it growling somewhere to the left of him.

Francis mustered his strength and, maneuvering onto his side, managed to pull himself around to face the back of the cave.

And his mysterious savior.

He prepared to say thanks, but the words became lodged in his throat as he beheld the raggedy figure standing in the opening to the farthest reaches of the cave, the snarling Hellion by its side. His robes were dirty, tattered, and torn, his long, grimy white hair pulled back into a crude ponytail, and his full beard was equally filthy. But Francis could feel the energy—*the divinity*—radiating from him; there was no mistaking that this was an angel of incredible power.

Francis studied the angel's face, searching for something that would spark a moment of familiarity, finding nothing.

"Did you really think I dragged your carcass across the shifting Hellscape and up a mountain face into this cave, and then dressed your wounds, only to feed you to my beast?" the mysterious angel asked, a twinkle of madness in his black, bottomless eyes.

"Thank—," Francis began, his voice nothing more than a dry croak.

"No," the angel interrupted, continuing his rant. "I've been waiting too long for you to arrive, to just let you die." He shuffled toward Francis, the Hell beast loping obediently by his side.

For the first time he could remember, Francis was speechless. "I don't—" He started to cough, the dust and dirt from the transforming hellish landscape outside choking his voice. "I don't know what you're talking about," he finally managed.

The angel reached down and grabbed his throat in a powerful grip, lifting Francis from the floor of the cave.

"Of course you don't," the angel said, holding him aloft

with one hand, while the other searched for something in the folds of his filthy vestments.

Francis squirmed in the angel's grasp, finding it ever harder to breathe as his feet danced in the air just above the ground.

"If you did, you wouldn't be trying to thank me," the angel continued, as he pulled out a delicate knife of light and plunged its glowing tip straight through Francis's forehead.

The former Guardian angel beheld a curtain of darkness, the last of the angel's words cryptically echoing through the halls of oblivion before the silence.

"You'd be cursing me with your last breath."

Miles carefully approached the exposed wall, sniffing at the strange, archaic writing.

"Get away from that!" Fernita cried out.

The animal froze, looking at her with wide, fear-filled eyes, before scurrying off to hide.

Fernita wrung her hands nervously as she stared at this newest piece of writing, wondering what it meant and how it got there as her eyes slowly traced the odd shapes.

A strange buzzing started in her brain, as if bees were trapped inside her skull, and it seemed to grow louder the more she looked at the foreign words written in black upon her walls.

How much more is there? she wondered, gazing around at the furniture and boxes that still hid most of her walls.

She was afraid to look, afraid of what she might find.

Her eyes traveled back to the exposed wall, and the humming inside her head continued to build.

Is this what I've forgotten? she asked herself.

The buzz became a mechanical whine, and the image of a spinning saw blade cutting through a length of tree, guided by hands encased in thick leather gloves, took shape in her mind. At first she had no idea what the imagery meant, but suddenly she remembered, the recollection floating free, like a child's balloon released into a blue summer sky.

Her father had worked at the mill ... where she herself had lived until ...

The whining of the saw blade was replaced by the discordant thrum of a poorly tuned guitar and the sound of a piano.

Fernita smiled, her tired old eyes filling with hot tears at the memories—for that was what these images were, *memories*.

But her happiness quickly turned to terror as the pleasant visions were savagely replaced by one of fire. The old woman let out a scream, throwing her hands over her face and falling backward into piles of yarn that spilled from a wicker sewing basket.

The images burned her brain, living fire consuming the piano that only moments before brought tears to her eyes with the song it played.

The sounds of screams drifted hauntingly through the air, screams that drew the living fire like moths to a flame.

Burning. Killing.

Fernita knew not to cry out herself; someone had told her to be quiet as she was dragged through the burning room, someone special, but she couldn't remember who it was.

Bodies littered the floor, bodies claimed by the living fire as it searched the room ... searching for ...

The head of a lion formed from the flames roared and came at her. Fernita could feel the intensity of its breath as it surged. And then it was gone, wisps of smoke drifting past her mind's eye.

The old woman managed to sit up, her breath coming in short, gulping gasps as she pushed herself backward toward the doorway. She propped herself against its wooden frame, watching the writing on her wall, feeling its mysterious pull on her fragile mind, and anger filled her. She didn't want it there anymore ... didn't want it unlocking secret memories.

And before she even realized what she was doing, Fernita was on her hands and knees, crawling across the cluttered living room floor.

"Go away, damn you!" she cried out, licking her fingers and rubbing at the black markings. She rubbed and licked, and rubbed, and rubbed and licked some more, her lips and chin smeared black as she tried to erase the alien scrawl that had brought such fear into her life.

But the more she rubbed, the louder the buzzing whine inside her skull became, as if somebody—something—was angered by her actions.

How dare you wipe away the words.... Don't you know what this means? Don't you realize what this will do?

And as the words started to disappear, it was as if a door had been opened, and more memories began to flow.

A deluge of the forgotten.

CHAPTER SIX

A door opened on the far side of the laboratory and Remy watched as a young man, who might have been one of the two who had accompanied Jon to Boston, entered. He was wearing only a T-shirt and baggy shorts now.

Malachi stood silently, watching with an unwavering eye.

"So he's going to eat the fruit?" Remy asked, as the young man sat in a leather chair that had been brought from a closet and placed in the center of the room.

"Yes," Jon answered. He too was watching the man, but his expression told Remy that he was clearly upset. "Nathan . . . excuse me, the volunteer will ingest a piece of the fruit, and we'll record the results." Jon cleared his throat and coughed nervously. "Hopefully his sacrifice will not be in vain."

"The effects of the fruit are that powerful?" Remy asked.

Jon nodded. "We started our research with some of the older seeds, but the results were pretty horrible. It created a psychic link too powerful for a human being . . . even a Son of Adam, to withstand."

Technicians began to fasten the young man's wrists and ankles to the chair with thick leather straps.

"Is that really necessary?" Remy asked.

Malachi answered this question. "Even though the effects are diluted by ingesting the meat of the fruit as opposed to the seeds, the result can still be quite . . . violent," the elder angel explained.

Remy stared at the volunteer, now looking small and defenseless beneath the humming fluorescent lights. "Are you sure this is the only way to get what we need?"

Jon looked to Malachi, but this time the angel remained silent, the human visage that he wore grim.

"It is the only way," Jon confirmed softly. "We believe he'll be linking with the actual Tree of Knowledge, in effect with the Garden itself, and in doing so, he'll know what the Garden knows, and be able to tell us where the other half of the key is located."

"Let us begin," Malachi said, waving Jon on with his hand.

Remy watched the man's features tighten as he steeled himself; then Jon picked up the tray of fruit and walked over to the volunteer restrained in the chair. The two looked at each other for a moment.

"Are you ready?" Jon asked, setting the tray down on a small table beside the chair.

"I am," the man who Jon said was named Nathan replied.

Jon nodded, accepting his friend's words, and stood, staring . . . waiting.

"You're going to have to help me," Nathan said finally, looking down to his bound hands and feet.

Jon laughed nervously as he reached for a pair of tongs. He used the tongs to pick up a slice of fruit and brought it toward Nathan's mouth.

"You're sure about this?" he asked again.

"Just get on with it," Malachi growled impatiently.

Nathan closed his eyes and opened his mouth slightly.

Carefully Jon placed the fruit on his friend's tongue and stepped back, his shoulders slumped. He tossed the tongs on the table and gestured for the techs. "Take this away," he ordered.

Nathan's expression had been almost trancelike as he began to slowly chew the piece of fruit in his mouth.

But that suddenly changed.

In the blink of an eye, it went from dreamy to nightmarish, his body going rigid, straining against his bonds.

Jon moved toward his friend, placing a comforting hand upon his shoulder. "Relax," he said. "Let it come."

Nathan looked at Jon, eyes pleading, the veins in his neck bulging and pulsing rapidly with the beat of his heart. "I didn't know. . . ." He gasped, white foam spilling from the corners of his mouth. "I wouldn't have—" His words were cut off as his body was racked with bone-breaking convulsions.

Remy was tempted to go to the man, to find some way of helping him. And as if reading his mind, Malachi's hand dropped upon his shoulder.

"It is necessary," the elder stated, eyes riveted to the horrific scene unfolding before them.

Nathan's head thrashed from side to side so unnaturally fast that the movement was actually blurred. He screamed as if his soul were being torn from his body.

"Isn't there something we can do?" Remy asked, not wanting to watch, but unable to look away.

"Nothing," Malachi answered in an emotionless drone. "The fruit must take hold. Only the Sons of Adam can do this. . . . They are from a special human strain, and only they can withstand the punishment of making the connection. Any other human would have been dead in seconds."

Nathan's head finally stopped moving, but his face was scarlet red and the blood vessels in his eyes had burst.

Jon was staring at Nathan; a single tear began to run down his cheek, and he quickly wiped it away. Remy could only guess how horrible it was for him to watch what was happening to his friend, knowing that he couldn't help.

A loud crack, like ice beginning to thaw on a frozen pond, startled Remy from his thoughts. At first he couldn't find the source of the sound; it was repeated again and again, and each time the body of the man in the chair shook with a violent spasm. Blood began streaming down Nathan's face, running into his screaming mouth, and then hanks of hair and bits of flesh-covered bone began to fall away as his skull opened.

The sight was so horrific that Remy didn't even notice that the volunteer had stopped screaming.

An electrical hum filled the air of the lab and grew in intensity as Nathan's brain swelled, oddly resembling a cake rising in a pan that was too small. Crackling bolts of electrical energy were released from the pulsing gray matter, slicing across the room, into the sapling version of the Tree of Knowledge. More tendrils of energy erupted from the tree, crisscrossing about the room, making contact with everything . . . and everybody.

Remy gasped as the energy touched him; it struck like a scorpion's stinger, entering through his chest and exiting just as quickly through the toe of his left shoe, rousing the Seraphim inside him.

The power touched Malachi as well, the elder standing perfectly stiff as the strange energy moved through his body.

It seemed to be affecting the Sons of Adam even more, as one by one they dropped to their knees.

"What's happening?" Remy asked.

"They are all connected now," Malachi explained.

"Us too?" Remy asked, feeling nothing but the eagerness of the Seraphim to be free.

Malachi shook his head. "No, we are not of the Garden."

Nathan's head looked like the Fourth of July on the Esplanade, jagged bolts of energy shooting from the pulsing gray surface illuminating the air above it.

"It is closer than you think," the man suddenly proclaimed, his voice sounding as though it were coming from an old stereo system. "Bouncing from reality to reality, it comes to us. . . ."

Malachi strode past Remy. "The key," the elder angel demanded from Nathan. "Where can we find the other half of the key?"

"The key," the man repeated. "One half is with us, close by, and the other . . ."

Jon let out a low moan, his head swinging loosely upon his neck.

Remy noticed that two of the techs were on their feet

now, stumbling across the room to their workstations, pulling out their chairs and sitting down as if drunk. One of the pair, a heavyset man with a haircut like Moe Howard's, pulled a drawing tablet from the things on his desk and began to draw. The other was leafing quickly through a book of maps.

"The Garden yearns for its children," Nathan announced. "For too long they have been apart. . . . Too long have they known loneliness."

The Sons were crying, and Remy almost wished he could experience what was happening in their heads, for he remembered the Garden too, and envied them.

"We shall be together again," the man's voice boomed. "Forgiveness bestowed as you pass through my open gates."

Then the man's eyes began to flutter crazily, and the corners of his mouth twisted downward in what appeared to be a pain-racked frown. Remy glanced around the room and saw that all of the Sons were wearing the same bizarre expression.

"Come quickly, my children, for there is danger present."

Malachi stepped closer to the ranting Nathan.

"A secret enemy grows within my bosom," he said, writhing against his bonds. "A danger that threatens not only Eden . . . but the world of man . . ." His voice grew louder and the electrical discharge from his exposed brain became more intense.

"And Heaven itself!"

A searing flash accompanied those words, disintegrating Nathan's chair. His body was lifted into the air on tendrils of blue energy, and the acrid smell of burning ozone filled the air.

"Let me show you this evil," he proclaimed.

The Sons were listening, their faces twisted in expressions of pain as they waited for Eden to show them their enemy.

Malachi stepped into the pulsing blue light, the crackling rays of mental lightning raining down upon him as he reached up to drag the figure down to the ground.

"What are you do . . . ?" Remy began as the elder pinned the thrashing figure to the ground with one hand and reached for Nathan's obscenely swollen brain with the other. Malachi wrapped his clawlike fingers around the pulsing gray brain matter and squeezed.

The Sons began screaming, grabbing for their heads, and a searing flash of blue forced Remy to cover his eyes as Nathan's brain popped in Malachi's constricting grip.

Remy lowered his arm and, as his vision cleared, he saw that the Sons were scattered about the floor, writhing and moaning in pain. He quickly looked to Malachi, who stood above the newly dead volunteer, wiping his gore-covered hand on a handkerchief.

"What did you do that for?" Remy demanded, stunned by the sudden violent act.

Malachi dropped the filthy cloth, letting it flutter down to cover the volunteer's ravaged face. "I know of the secret enemy," the angel said. "It is a clear and present danger to us all . . . a danger that lurks around every corner, watching . . . waiting for us to expose ourselves."

Remy didn't understand, his look urging the elder angel to continue.

"There are those who would refuse Adam his birthright," Malachi offered.

Jon rose on shaky legs and stumbled across the room, nearly falling as he knelt by his friend's side.

"Why did you kill him?" Remy asked of Malachi, watching as Jon took his friend's blood-spattered hand in his own.

"There was no choice," the elder angel replied. "The connection was growing and he would have felt it."

"Who? Who would have felt it?"

"He who would see Adam die here . . . never to be embraced in the bosom of Eden."

The Sons of Adam were coming around now, rising shakily to their feet, the experience having left its mark.

"You know him from your last encounter in Eden," Malachi explained. He was looking at his hand, still wet and glistening from the brain of the volunteer. "The Cherubim sentry," he said.

"Zophiel."

Remy wondered why nothing could ever be easy.

According to Malachi, Zophiel had eventually ended up on Earth as well, and now that Eden was returning to this plane of existence, he too was hunting for the keys. The elder angel had mentioned violent incidents at other Sons of Adam locations around the globe as proof that this danger was real.

Remy glanced to the left at Jon, who was driving him back to the airstrip. He didn't look so good.

"You all right?" he asked.

Jon didn't answer, lost in thought and staring straight ahead at the desert road.

Remy reached across and touched his shoulder.

Jon started, looked at him, and then back to the road. "I'm sorry. Is there something wrong?"

"No." Remy shook his head. "Just wanted to be sure you're okay."

Jon gave him an odd look, then reached up, pulling a tiny hearing aid from his ear and stuffing it into the breast pocket of his shirt. Remy hadn't even noticed it was there.

"Sorry about that," he said. "The batteries must be dead. You're going to have to speak a little bit louder."

"Have you always had a hearing problem?" Remy asked, raising his voice.

The man shook his head. "I lost it in my early teens," he said, staring out through the windshield. The plane came into view through the shifting dust blowing across the desert. "Actually it was when Malachi first arrived."

He smiled, but Remy could see little amusement there.

"The whole voice-of-the-divine thing," Jon explained. "He was rather loud with his proclamations and damaged my eardrums."

They reached the plane; Jon shut off the van's engine and turned toward Remy.

"I want to thank you for coming," he said, extending his hand.

Remy shook it. "My pleasure. I hope I can help."

"Those should make certain you can," Jon said, pointing to the papers resting in Remy's lap.

When the volunteer's mind had connected with them, showing the Sons all that Eden had to share, two had written down what they had seen, providing Remy with a detailed map and specific information on where the second half of the key could be found and who it was the detective had to find.

"The pilot has already been instructed to bring you to an airport in Thornwell. From there you can rent a car and head to the designated location," Jon said as they got out of the van.

He met Remy in front of the vehicle and reached out to shake the detective's hand.

"Good luck," Jon said. "Hopefully we'll be seeing each other again soon."

"Take care," Remy said, clutching the important papers beneath his arm as he proceeded toward the foldout stairs that would take him up into the jet.

The pilot was standing there waiting, saluting Remy as he passed through the rounded doorway inside. The stairway was retracted, and the door closed and secured as Remy took the same seat he'd sat in on his way out. Buckling himself in, he removed his phone from his jacket pocket to check for messages.

This was a new phone, finally replacing the archaic one that he'd had for the past ten years, and he had to think about the steps to play back voice mails.

A message from Fernita was the first he heard. It wasn't uncommon these days for him to get calls from the older woman, but this one sounded a bit off. Remy didn't like the hint of panic he heard in her voice. If he'd been heading home, he would have taken a drive over just to be sure she was okay. He considered calling her back, but then thought better of it, deciding that maybe it would be best to just wait to see her until this case was over and done, but the tone of the old woman's voice disturbed him.

An idea began to take shape. An insidious concept, but one that the more he thought about it, the better it became.

The new phone had texting capability—his old one probably had too, but it wasn't something Remy had ever thought to use. He tried to recall what he'd read in the owner's manual as he set about sending his very first official text message.

Madeline would have been so proud of him. His wife had always been the first to embrace technology. He probably wouldn't have even owned a cell phone if it weren't for her.

Slowly his fingers played over the tiny keyboard, spelling out the message he would then send to Steven Mulvehill. Remy finished the message, then read it over and could barely contain his smile. He had told his friend about the wonderful old woman recently, and Steven had seemed genuinely amused, wanting to meet her. Well, here was his chance. In the message he asked if Steven would mind stopping by and checking things out, just to be sure that she was all right. As a special incentive, Remy promised the homicide cop a steak dinner at the Capital Grille and a bottle of twenty-five-year-old Macallan single-malt if he did this special favor for him.

There was very little Mulvehill wouldn't do for a steak and a good bottle of Scotch.

The plane's engine began to whine, the private jet starting to taxi down the runway, preparing to take him on to the next leg of his journey. He hit Send, watching the message disappear into the ether, and smiled as he returned the phone to his coat pocket.

Remy was certain he'd be hearing some serious shit from Mulvehill on this one, but what were friends for if they couldn't be taken advantage of?

Nathan had been Jon's closest friend.

They had grown up together in the various Sons of

Adam communities, mortal enemies at first, but gradually becoming as thick as thieves.

And so much more.

Jon ran his key card through the security gate and entered the biodome, placing the card back inside his pocket. Nathan had always wanted to help; he was just like that. If it would advance the cause in any way, he would be the one to try to march it through. When they'd first begun to discuss human testing in regard to the fruit of the tree, he was the first to put his name on the list.

Nathan had described it as wanting to do something, to not sit around waiting for things to happen, but to actually contribute to things moving forward.

I hope wherever you are, you're happy, Jon thought angrily. There were plenty of others in the Sons who would have volunteered, others Jon wasn't so close to. It made him feel awful, but he secretly wished that one of them had been the one to taste the fruit, and not Nathan.

Another door slid open before him with a hiss of hydraulics, and he was hit with a blast of unusually frigid air. The air-conditioning must have been on the fritz again.

As he moved down the silent corridor, his mind continued to wander. A chill not caused by the air-conditioning ran down his neck as he recalled the moment Nathan's thoughts—imbued with the power of Eden—touched his mind. Jon had never experienced anything like it, and hoped never to again.

He had been dwarfed by the immensity of it, a feeling so big that it threatened to swallow him up where he would disappear forever. Was that what returning to the Garden would be like? he wondered. Becoming part of something so big that one would lose any chance of individuality? If that was the case, he would much rather stay where he had been born.

From birth he'd been taught about the Sons of Adam's holy mission, and had applied himself to the rules and regulations of the order's cause, but deep down he had never expected their beliefs would come true.

Although he'd kept those thoughts to himself.

And now they were that much closer to its actually becoming a reality. The Garden of Eden was coming here . . . to Earth. It was a concept that he was having a difficult time wrapping his brain around.

Jon's mind raced as he passed through a doorway into the cafeteria. A cup of coffee was what he needed, before the sad task at hand.

It was strangely quiet, even for this time of day. He paused, looking around, and saw no one. Not even the cafeteria staff.

"Huh," he muttered to himself, moving on through the empty hall, the reason he had come there forgotten.

Distracted from his coffee needs, he exited into another corridor, continuing on to his destination with a heavy heart.

He'd promised Nathan that he would take care of his remains. Neither of them had been sure what would be left after the exercise, but Jon had promised to dispose of them with dignity and respect.

It was when he'd seen Nathan's body, after Malachi had . . .

Go ahead, he thought. *It's true. How else could it possibly be described?*

After Malachi had killed him.

It was as he looked down at his friend's ruined form that he knew where he would take Nathan's remains.

His friend wouldn't be around now to return to the Garden, but he could at least find peace in the beauty of the biodome's garden. That was where Jon would take him and lay him to rest. It was the least he could do for his friend.

Nathan's body had been taken to one of the dome's freezer units, where many of their medical supplies requiring refrigeration were stored. He was certain that Nathan wouldn't have minded taking a short break there until Jon could get back to him.

The medical wing was empty as well.

"What is going on here today?" Jon said aloud as he entered the empty wing and went to the cold-room door. Taking a few deep breaths, he grabbed the door handle, pulled it open.

The stretcher with Nathan's body resting atop it was waiting for him. At least that was where it was supposed to be, he thought as he grabbed the chilly ends of the metal stretcher and pulled it from the refrigerated room.

Another wave of sadness spilled over him as he maneuvered the stretcher down the hall and toward the exit. The Sons of Adam lived a very long time, some stretching into the hundreds of years, and it was quite disappointing—no, worse than that, tragic—that his friend wouldn't be around to share those years with him.

But Nathan was all about the sacrifice, especially since Malachi's arrival to the order.

Before the angel came, the Sons had just existed, living their day-to-day lives, caring for the father, and waiting for a sign that the sins of the first man and woman would be forgiven.

Many believed that Malachi was that very sign, an agent of Heaven brought to them to help make their reasons for existing a reality. Jon believed that the angel had come to them with a purpose, but wasn't quite sure if said purpose was to benefit the Sons' cause, or something more personal. These were his own intimate thoughts, thoughts that hadn't been uttered to a soul.

Except for Nathan.

Hands on the corner of the cold metal of the stretcher, Jon stopped to gaze down at the sheet-covered form lying there before him. He'd been able to hold himself together, but he felt the grief inside him build to an incalculable level, and there was no amount of strength that could hold it back.

In the currently empty corridor he began to cry. As the tears came, memories washed over him, the two friends throughout the many years their kind were allowed to live. For a brief moment he wished that he were like all the other human beings out there, no longer special—no longer of the special line—for he would likely be close to death now, and wouldn't have to know this pain much longer.

He was tempted to pull away the sheet, to look upon his friend's broken remains, but didn't care to soil his memory of him. He remembered how he had looked in the lab . . . how he had looked before Malachi had . . .

Killed him.

Jon ran the back of his hand over his face, wiping away the tears and snot, wiping away the residuals of his sadness. Steeling himself, he continued to wheel the stretcher down the empty corridor on the way to what would be Nathan's final place of rest.

Reaching the entrance to the botanical garden, Jon walked around the stretcher to open the door. Always the efficient one, he was already reviewing the supplies that he would need in order to prepare Nathan's grave. He knew that there were shovels inside, so that would pretty much take care of it: a shovel, and perhaps a nice rock to mark where he lay. Jon reached inside his pocket and removed something that he had brought from his room. It was a leather pouch filled with his collection of marbles that he had accumulated over the years. Nathan had always admired them, and Jon thought that he would bury them with him—a piece of himself to accompany his friend. Jon was about to lose it again, so he sucked it up, preoccupying himself with the thought of where he'd need to dig, and how long it would take him to finish.

The door started to slide open as he walked around the stretcher, but he noticed that the door had opened only three-quarters of the way. *Great*, he thought, *something else for maintenance to look at.*

He returned to the door to check whether something was obstructing the track.

The first body was just inside the door, a splayed arm jammed against it preventing the door from sliding completely back.

Jon didn't know what to think entering the botanical garden, about to ask the man—his name was Rudolf, and Jon had never really liked him all that much—what the matter was as he knelt down beside him, but Jon knew that he was dead before the words could even leave his mouth.

Instantly slipping into emergency mode, Jon stood and headed for a phone just inside the room to the right of the doorway.

This was when he noticed the other bodies all along the path leading into the garden. They appeared broken ... bloody.

Were those bite marks? he wondered with escalating horror.

He then knew why the other areas of the dome had been so quiet—the residents were all here. Not realizing it, he had begun to walk the path, stepping over the bodies of the people he had known all his life. All dead, all wearing expressions that could best be described as shock ...

No ... the look was surprise.

Reaching the clearing, he noticed that the tropical forest was completely quiet; even without his hearing aid, he could hear that the bugs' and birds' voices were silenced. Maybe they knew to be silent ... or maybe they were dead too.

The most bodies were in the clearing, stacked like a huge pile of dirty laundry ... dirty, bloody laundry. Jon froze, searching the green of the man-made jungle, sensing that he wasn't alone.

"Show yourself."

The words left his mouth before he could consider them, and they brought with them a response that he really didn't care to experience.

There was laughter from the jungle, low and rumbling, more like a growl. He could feel it low in his stomach, as well as hear it. Jon couldn't tell exactly where it was coming from; it seemed to come from all sides ... from everywhere.

And then there came the fire.

It was like a living thing, leaping out from the concealment of the trees and bushes ... tongues of flame consuming everything in their path as they made their way toward him.

Jon spun around, running across the body-strewn path on his way to the exit. He imagined the bodies, his friends, reaching up to grab at his legs and feet, not wanting him to get away, not wanting him to survive. He could feel the fire growing in intensity behind him, nipping hungrily at his heels.

He could see the door up ahead, the stretcher holding the body of his friend just outside it. That was his goal, he decided, feeling a tongue of fire lick at the salty wetness of sweat on the back of his neck. He wanted to reach his friend.

If he was to die, he wanted it to be with him.

Jon made it to the exit, passing through the doorway with one final push, jumping onto the stretcher, feeling the body of his friend beneath him as Hell opened its awful mouth to consume them all.

CHAPTER SEVEN

The airplane shuddered.

Remy casually glanced out his window expecting to see the beginnings of a storm, but saw only cottony white clouds, so inviting that he was tempted to lay his weary head upon them.

The jet shook again, harder this time, and now he could hear the alarms going off in the cockpit up front. His hand was reaching to unbuckle his seat belt when the plane trembled yet again, so violently that the overhead storage bins flapped open.

"Is everything all right?" Remy called out, holding on to his seat as he made his way up the short aisle toward the cockpit.

The alarms continued on the other side of the door as he rapped on it with his knuckle.

"Is everything . . ."

There was an explosion of air that could only have been the roar of decompression, followed by the shriek of the jet's fuselage as it tried to maintain its integrity.

The plane began to fall.

Remy was about to kick open the cockpit door when part of the wall to his right was ripped away with the whine of twisting metal, and the screech of the wind as it rushed in to fill the void.

Remy attempted to hold on to something—anything—as his body was wrenched toward the yawning hole.

And through that hole he caught a glimpse—a glimpse of something large and terrible, something that had done this on purpose. Something that had willfully attacked the plane.

Then a rush of air tore at Remy's clothing as he lost his grip and was sucked into the void. Spinning through the clouds, he caught sight of the plane—one engine and part of a wing gone, the other engine engulfed by orange flame and leaking black, oily smoke. The cockpit was gone, shorn away, along with the pilot.

Over the deafening roar of free fall, he could just about make out a sound, and craned his neck to face the Cherubim Zophiel, large and powerful, and as filled with rage as the last time Remy had seen him.

The Cherubim flew past with the speed of a jet fighter, then banked around to match the speed of Remy's descent, a trinity of faces—eagle, lion, and man—studying his form as he plummeted to Earth. Malachi had warned of this—of the hatred Eden's sentry had for the Sons of Adam and their mission.

The ground loomed closer, and Remy knew what he had to do, although it enraged him. He would have to call upon his other side—the side of Heaven.

The Seraphim.

Let's get this over with, Remy thought. He dug deep within his psyche to where his other half waited. He was there, as he always was, sitting impatiently behind the mental barriers Remy had erected. He reached for the divine spirit, calling him forth, and the Seraphim surged forward, ferociously wild and eager to be free.

The Cherubim flew toward Remy, all three of his mouths shrieking a cry of doom. The renegade angel was almost on Remy, reaching out to snatch him from the air, but just as his metal claws were to close about him, the Seraphim manifested in a flash of Heavenly fire.

Zophiel wailed, rearing back from the hungry flame as Remy spread his wings, slowing his descent to face his adversary.

"Let's end this the way we should have a very long time ago," the Seraphim cried over the howling winds.

The Cherubim roared his response, moving with the speed of a lightning strike, slashing out with multihued wings as sharp and deadly as the finest blades forged in the fires of Heaven.

Remy glided back, but he wasn't fast enough and the tip of one of Zophiel's wings cut a bloody line across the middle of his chest. The Seraphim was angry now. If he hadn't been sequestered away, and had been allowed to roam free, nothing could have caused him harm.

Coming around again, the Cherubim came at him with murder in his eyes. *Let it come*, the Seraphim thought, wings holding him aloft, watching as the sentry flew closer, and closer still.

Just as he and Zophiel were about to collide—a runaway freight train about to hit a Volkswagen Beetle—Remy flew up and turned, landing on the back of his attacker.

The Cherubim screamed, his wings flapping wildly as he attempted to dislodge the bothersome insect that had attached itself, but the Seraphim held tight, angling his body to avoid the knifelike feathers of the Cherubim's wings.

Remy reached out and grabbed hold of the Cherubim's long black hair. He channeled his inner fire, igniting the sentry's hair like a fuse, the divine power burning down its oily black length until it engulfed all three visages. The Cherubim screamed wildly as he thrashed and spun his armored body around before plunging earthward in an attempt to extinguish the flames.

Spreading his wings, Remy released his grip, attempting to avoid a collision with the quickly approaching desert floor, but Zophiel had decided otherwise. The Cherubim grabbed the Seraphim's ankle with a gauntleted hand, dragging his prey down with him.

Remy struggled, but it was useless; the Cherubim's grip was too powerful, and the pair struck the ground at full velocity—a mushroom cloud of sand and rock blossoming from the desert floor.

The Seraphim crawled up from the crater, burning with rage and the desire to see his enemy vanquished, but the

Cherubim was nowhere to be found. The angel fluttered his golden wings, shedding a thick layer of dust and some slivers of rock that clung to them. He was about to take to the air again, when the humanity that had been momentarily forgotten attempted to reassert its control.

The Seraphim did not care for this, fighting the attempts to again force him down to the darkness. But the humanity was still stronger, wrestling with the warlike nature of the angel, pulling it down and forcing it to heel.

Remy was again in control. It took a moment for his head to clear, a warrior's rage still burning in his every muscle.

He did not put his angelic form away entirely, still needing the ability to fly. There was a part of him that would have loved to chase after his attacker, but also a part that thought of the biodome, and the safety of the Sons of Adam. What if Zophiel had come for him after first attacking the dome?

The Seraphim had no care for the Sons or their cause. All that concerned him was to see his enemy destroyed, and he argued to be free again against Remy's mental restraints.

But Remy was stronger, and he kept the warrior nature at bay. Fearing for the lives of the biodome's residents, he unfurled his wings and took flight, soaring just above the desert surface, on his way back from where he had come.

Unnoticed, the tiny lizard emerged from beneath the sand, watching as the Seraphim took flight. It waited there patiently, watching with large, dark eyes filled with intelligence, until the angel was just a dwindling speck on the horizon.

Waiting until it felt confident that it could abandon the reptilian form it currently wore for something far more efficient.

To proceed with the plans that it had set in motion.

Remy hoped that he was wrong, that Zophiel had come after him, not bothering with the innocents inside the dome, but something told him otherwise . . . *something* and the roiling black clouds that his superior eyesight saw reaching up into the sky way off in the distance.

To get there all the faster, Remy allowed his wings to enfold his body, his mind thinking about where he needed to be at that very moment—where he had been—and when his wings opened again, he had reached that very destination, dropping down to the earth in front of the chain-link gates leading up to what remained of the biodome.

Remy flew up and over the security fence into the actual compound. He could not pull his eyes from the sight before him. Where the dome had once stood, growing out from the desert floor, now there were only the shattered, broken, and burning remains of the home to the Sons of Adam.

Remy stepped around the charred, twisted pieces of metal that littered the ground on his way toward the jagged, broken hole in the side of one of the walls that still managed to be standing. He peered inside, the stink of burning flesh and chemicals assailing his heightened senses. Remy recoiled from the stench, stepping back to again assess the damage. There had been a powerful explosion from within, he imagined. He imagined the beastly form of Zophiel releasing his Heavenly might within the facility, the unleashed power of Heaven tearing the biodome asunder.

Scanning the ruin for survivors, Remy could find only the burned and broken bodies of the dead. The Sons of Adam had the gift of longevity on their side, but it was nothing against the power of Heaven released.

He was about to leave this place of death, to continue with the mission he'd accepted, when he heard what sounded like a cough. Remy stood perfectly still, expanding his senses just to be sure. Was it possible? Could somebody have actually survived, or was he just hearing the final death sounds of the installation?

Standing at the edge, he looked down into the smoldering crater, the first level having collapsed and given way to levels beneath. Again he heard a sound, soft, but distinct, and flew down into the remains, searching for signs of life.

Remy guessed that he'd reached what had once been the man-made garden, the broken shapes of colorful birds strewn upon the charred floor.

"Hello?" Remy called out, eyes scanning the rubble for any sign of movement.

It sounded like a gasp for breath, but nonetheless it was a sound of somebody or something still alive in the remains of the biodome, now rendered a tomb. Something shifted beneath a felled section of the garden wall, and Remy flew above the broken concrete, searching for the source of the sound. There was scraping beneath the rubble, and the angel touched down beside it. He grabbed a huge piece of concrete, and in a display of supernatural strength hauled it up and tossed it aside.

Beneath he found a body. The remains were badly damaged. There was no way that the sound could have come from him, but Remy again heard something: this time a muffled cry.

Rolling the corpse over to one side, he found what looked to be a metal stretcher. Something stirred beneath the stainless steel, and Remy lifted it up to reveal the shape and the still-living body of a man covered in thick dust, dirt, and blood.

Reaching down, Remy carefully took hold of the man's arm and pulled him from the rubble. Despite the destruction around him, the survivor appeared to be unscathed other than some minor burns, cuts, and bruises.

"Are you all right?" Remy asked, kneeling beside him.

The man turned a dirty face toward him. "You're going to need to speak up, Mr. Chandler," he said.

Remy was startled, even more surprised when he realized that the survivor was the man called Jon.

"What happened here?" Remy asked, remembering how it had once looked, but now seeing only devastation.

Jon crawled across the rubble to the body that had lain atop him. He knelt beside it, taking one of its burned hands in his. "I was going to bury him," he said. "In the garden . . . when I found them all dead."

Remy realized that the corpse belonged to the volunteer, and his belief that Jon and he had been more than friends was affirmed by the intensity of the man's emotion.

"All dead?" Remy asked.

"Something got into the dome and killed everybody. I only survived the initial attack because I was dropping you off at the plane. I came back to bury Nathan. . . ."

Jon stared at the broken and bloody corpse again, stroking its hand. "That was his name. . . . His name was Nathan."

"Stay with me, Jon," Remy said. "What did you find when you returned?"

"The place was unusually quiet. . . . It was when I entered the garden that I found the bodies."

"Did you see who did it . . . ? Was it Zophiel? The Cherubim?"

Jon shook his head. "I don't know. . . . All I heard was a laugh, and then there was this horrible fire and—"

"What happened to Malachi and Adam? Did you see either of them?"

Jon thought for a moment before answering. "No . . . no, I didn't see them."

"Then they might have survived," Remy said. "Escaped before they could be hurt."

"Yes," Jon said as he started to rise, nearly falling over as the rubble shifted beneath his feet. "I believe Adam still lives," he said. "I think I'd have felt it if he died."

"Then there's still a chance of getting this done," Remy said. "Of finding the key."

"Do you still have the map and drawings?" Jon asked. He was still gazing down at Nathan's body.

"I was attacked, as well. Zophiel brought the plane down," Remy said. "The map and drawings were lost."

Jon looked to him with a nod. "I see," he said, and then walked closer to Nathan's remains. "I'd like to bury him before we go," he said.

Remy stared, not entirely understanding what was being said.

"We?" he questioned.

Jon nodded. "I'm the only one still alive who saw what he did," Jon said, pointing at Nathan's corpse. "You're going to need me to get us where we're going to find the second half of the key and open the Gates of Eden."

Remy now understood completely.

"But before we go anywhere, I need to bury my friend," Jon said, going to the body. "Will you help me?" he asked of him, as Remy nodded.

It was the least he could do for the man.

Zophiel ... I am Zophiel.

The Cherubim floated above the Earth in the cold vacuum of space and continued to remember. Splintered pieces of memory came at him from every side and he snatched at them, eager to put the imagery together ... eager to know what had happened to him.

Eager to know what had yet to be done.

Invisible feelers trailed from his drifting form, leading from his armored body down to the planet below.

Zophiel knew the answers were there, and he would find them. All he needed was patience.

The feelers drifted across the surface of the Earth, telling him much about the place to which the Almighty had taken such a shine. It was a special world filled with a myriad of life, and bountiful resources, and so much more, but the answers still eluded him.

The Cherubim felt his anger begin to spike, and he resisted the temptation to descend upon the planet, laying waste to its vast cities until the answers to the mysteries in question revealed themselves to him. It was an option that he was seriously considering when he felt the first twinge.

Like a spider in its web, Zophiel felt the thrum of an ancient power through the tendrils of webbing that trailed from space to the planet below. It had not been there before, but now it was.

Just a hint of something that had once been hidden.

A taste.

The Cherubim drifted in the cold of space, ready to act upon the next sign. And it came again: another faint tremble in the ether, vibrating up through the invisible line from the earth below.

Zophiel squinted his many eyes, following the connection from space, down through the atmosphere and clouds. It was there that he would find what he was searching for.

Spreading his massive wings, the Cherubim dropped from the stars in search of answers.

Heaven help any who dared stand in his way.

Steven Mulvehill pulled up in front of Fernita Green's house a little after six, and again considered what he was doing.

Taking one last puff from the cigarette in his mouth, the homicide cop shoved the smoldering remains into the open ashtray, which resembled a kind of cigarette cemetery, the butts sticking up like tombstones.

Leaning over in the driver's seat, he looked out the passenger window at the house across from him.

He'd received his friend's message after a particularly grueling day on a Charlestown double homicide with no witnesses, or at least that was what they were saying. The folks of that particular Boston neighborhood had their own ideas on justice and how to handle things. He'd seriously considered ignoring Remy's text, but realized that his alternative—at least three hours of paperwork—wasn't any more attractive.

Remy had talked about this Fernita Green and what a hot shit she was a few times, and Steven had even said that he would get a kick out of meeting her, but the real reason he didn't say no was because of who was asking the favor.

How could somebody say no to an angel of Heaven?

It sounded fucking stupid even as he thought it, but there was some semblance of truth even with the stupidity.

To most, Remy Chandler was just a guy, a relatively good-looking middle-aged private investigator. Nothing more than that.

But Steven knew otherwise.

He knew some of the details: that Remy had left Heaven after some war, fed up with all the bullshit that was going down as a result of the conflict, and ended up here. He'd been hanging around Earth for a really long time, eventually becoming a private eye, falling in love with an amazing woman, and losing her to cancer.

Mulvehill was sure there was more, all kinds of details

connected to what Remy actually was, and the reality of the
kind of world in which Steven was living where a warrior
angel every so often had to deal with a situation like the
impending Apocalypse, or that the Devil was taking control of Hell again.

Yeah, weird shit happened, but it was the kind of shit
that Mulvehill would rather not know about. Just being
privy to the knowledge that Remy wasn't really human was
more than he cared to know, a peek into a reality that, because of his friendship with Remy, he now knew existed,
and wished that he didn't.

The pair had a rule when they were together. The weird
shit was kept to a minimum. Steven believed that this rule
was a good thing, helping to keep Remy grounded in his
attempt to be as human as the next guy, and it also prevented Steven from knowing things that he shouldn't.

Things that weren't meant for someone like him to
know.

So he had driven all the way from Boston to Brockton in
rush-hour traffic, no mean feat, out of respect for what
Remy was, and the things he had done in service to humanity, but mostly he did it because Remy was his closest friend.

And, of course, he'd been promised dinner at the Capital Grille, and a twenty-five-year-old bottle of Macallan.

Score one for the homicide cop!

Steven left the warmth of his car and walked up to the
house. It was a nice place, a Dutch Colonial, but it was starting to look a little run-down.

Remy had mentioned that he thought Fernita might be
showing the first stages of Alzheimer's. He could understand why Remy had asked him to check up on the woman.
Steven wasn't entirely sure of the connection between the
old woman and the private eye, vaguely recalling something being said about her hiring him to find something
that she had lost, but that was all Steven could remember.

He walked up the wooden steps onto the porch and
wondered if Fernita knew that he was coming. He had
called Remy about an hour ago to ask that very question,
but the call hadn't gone through.

Standing in front of the door, he hoped that Remy had mentioned him in passing to the old gal, so that he was at least vaguely familiar to her. Raising a knuckle, he rapped on the glass panel. Steven waited a little longer, pulling the collar of his winter coat up tighter around his neck, before knocking again. There was still no response, so he leaned into the door, listening, and heard movement from inside.

"Fernita?" he called out, knocking again a little louder. "Hi, I'm Steven Mulvehill ... Remy Chandler's friend? He asked me to stop by."

The sounds inside grew louder, more frantic.

"Fernita?" he called again. "Is everything all right?"

Steven was reaching for the doorknob when the door came suddenly open, and Steven stood face-to-face with an older black woman who could only have been Fernita Green.

"Hi," he said again. "I'm Steven...."

And then he noticed the look on her face, and the wild glint in her eyes behind her thick glasses—never mind the fact that she was wearing green rubber gloves.

"I don't have time for this bullshit," she said furiously. "Everything's coming together and here I am at the door talking with the likes of you. Get offa my porch or I'll call the police," she snarled, ready to slam the door in his face.

Mulvehill was startled. This wasn't the nice old woman Remy had talked about; this lady was crazy with a capital C.

"I *am* the police, Fernita," Mulvehill told her, placing a hand on the door to keep her from closing it. "And Remy Chandler ... You remember Remy, right? He asked me to stop by ... to make sure you were ..."

She abruptly turned her back, leaving the door open as she disappeared inside the house muttering to herself.

Steven had no idea what to do. He stood there for a moment, then took a deep breath and followed her in, carefully shutting the door behind him. "Fernita?" he called out. "Hey, Fernita ..."

He immediately noticed the stacks of magazines and newspapers just inside the door. Remy had hinted that she was a bit of a hoarder, and from what he could see he had to agree.

"Hello?" he called again, moving tentatively down the hallway, turning slightly to the side to avoid knocking over any piles.

"Remy was worried, and asked me to ..." Mulvehill came to the archway into the living room and found his voice immediately stolen away.

The amount of stuff ... Boxes and bags and stacks and piles were everywhere, making it look as though she were packing her things to move, but he knew that wasn't the case.

He couldn't see Fernita, but he could hear her.

Mulvehill gingerly stepped into the room, careful not to disturb anything as he searched. He found her in a far corner, on her hands and knees, a bucket of dirty, soapy water beside her. She was using a brush and scrubbing at a section of wall in front of her.

"What are you doing?" he asked, his eyes going to the strange writing in black that she was working hard to erase. Mulvehill stared at the writing, his eyes tracing over the unknown alphabet, certain that he had never seen anything quite like it before, and he felt the hair at the back of his head begin to stand up, and he realized that this wasn't just a case of him being asked to check in on a potentially sick old woman.

No, this was more than that.

This was one of those other cases ... the cases that he preferred that Remy not talk about.

It was one of those weird-as-shit cases.

"I'm gonna fuckin' kill him," Mulvehill muttered beneath his breath, watching as the old woman continued to furiously scrub at the bizarre writing on the wall.

Desperate to make it go away.

CHAPTER EIGHT

Arkansas, 1932

Fraciel drove the blade of the Enochian dagger through the angel's heart, closing his eyes as he listened to the final cries of the once-Heavenly creature.

The angel tried to escape him, spreading its powerful wings and flapping wildly in a futile attempt to take flight, but Fraciel held him tight as he twisted the blade, stealing away the angel's last bit of strength.

"Nothing personal," he said softly as he lowered the body of the angel to the wet ground of the alley—a soft Southern rain falling upon them.

The angel, who had taken the human name of Luke, looked up at him with wide dying eyes.

"F . . . Fra . . . Francis," he said in a strangled voice as dark blood oozed up from somewhere inside him and ran from the corners of his gaping mouth. "Why?"

Fraciel—*Francis*—did not respond. Instead, he removed a handkerchief from the inside pocket of his suit coat and cleaned the angel's black blood from his blade. But the question echoed inside his troubled mind.

Why? It was something he'd asked himself a lot recently.

Why? Because God said so. That was why.

Francis was a killer for the Allfather, ending the lives of those who ran afoul of Heaven, penance for his own terrible sin.

He watched as Luke died on the filthy ground, his last breath trailing off in a whistle as the light of life left his eyes.

He had found this particular angel in the tent of a traveling church revival on the outskirts of Oak Bluff, Arkansas, preaching to those who believed that the Lord God was actually watching them.

Francis had been amused; as far as he knew, the only ones being watched were those humans who posed some sort of threat to Heaven and angels who had escaped to Earth after the Great War to avoid punishment. But the country was in the grip of a depression, and people were desperate.

Desperate for God to notice them.

Francis had attended the revival meetings, participating in the fervent praise to God, waiting for the opportunity to carry out his mission. Finally, at the end of a particularly zealous meeting, he had approached Luke, and although he was able to mask his true identity, even to other angels, Luke must have sensed a kindred spirit.

For some reason, Francis had allowed friendship to blossom, breaking his own cardinal rule. Though it was painful to admit, he had enjoyed having a friend, and hated to see it end in such a way.

But there was no choice.

Francis could sense his Masters' impatience, and knew it was time to finish the job. He and Luke had been passing out flyers announcing a special meeting dedicated to asking for God's forgiveness, and were on their way back to the revival tents when Francis saw his opportunity, suggesting they take a shortcut through the alley.

Luke had been so happy, brimming with excitement at the chance to preach God's mercy to such a large gathering. Francis could practically feel the energy radiating off of him.

God's mercy indeed.

Briefly, Francis wished it didn't have to end this way, but he had no choice. He too awaited forgiveness, and if that was ever to happen, he had to kill this angel, and any other deemed an enemy of God.

It was the price he had to pay.

The act itself had been quick, as merciful as Francis was able, but it didn't stop the questions.

What had Luke done to deserve this?

Francis returned the dirty handkerchief and blade to his inside coat pocket and waited; it usually didn't take *them* very long to respond after one of the divine had met his fate.

The Thrones appeared in a blinding flash, followed by a sound like all the keys on the world's largest pipe organ being played at once. The Thrones resembled balls of fire . . . six balls of fire covered with eyes, spinning in the air before him.

"It's done," Francis said, glancing at the corpse at his feet.

The angelic beings remained silent, rolling in the air, sparks of divine fire spewing from their awesome forms to sizzle in the puddles that had formed on the alley floor.

Francis wanted nothing more than to get as far away from them, and what he had done, as possible. *A couple of stiff drinks are in order*, he thought. Even during Prohibition there was always a way to get good and drunk if one really wanted to; and after the night he'd had, Francis wanted to.

"What took you so long?" the Thrones asked as one, their powerful voices ringing inside his head like the bells of Notre Dame.

Francis was quiet, not sure how to answer. He didn't want to tell them that he had actually grown fond of Luke, and had enjoyed having a friend. He could just imagine how that would have gone over.

"I was waiting for the right time," he finally said, refusing to look into their many eyes. "It took longer than I expected."

"Is that all?" the balls of roiling fire asked suspiciously.

"That's all," he answered, keeping his anger in check.

The Thrones watched him for what seemed like forever, then finally glided through the air to hover above the body of the angel. Tendrils of white flame trailed down from their revolving bodies, wrapping around the dead angel and drawing him up into their fire.

Francis had seen them do this so many times, and still didn't know exactly what they were doing with the bodies. Maybe they were storing them for transport back to the City of Light, or maybe they were burning them—not a trace of anything to show that the angels had ever existed.

Or maybe they were just being eaten.

Whatever the case, *they* weren't offering any explanations, and Francis wasn't about to ask.

"Am I done here?" he questioned, eager for the taste of gin in his mouth.

"You will be done when we tell you," the Thrones admonished as the last of the angel Luke was drawn up into their burning bodies.

Not a trace of anything to show that he had ever existed.

Francis felt his ire rise, but knew better than to let it show. He reached up, removed the fedora from his head, and slicked back his dark, thinning hair before putting the hat back on. He would wait; he had all the patience in the world.

Especially if that patience would someday lead him to redemption.

"This is done," the Thrones said, and Francis turned to leave, until the words, "But there is another," stopped him dead in his tracks.

Once again, he faced his Masters.

"Another? So soon? Usually there's some time between them."

"This time there is not."

"Obviously."

"Do you grow tired, servant?" the Thrones asked him. "Should we relieve you from your duties? Perhaps you'd prefer to serve out the remainder of your penance in a cell deep within Tartarus?"

Just the mention of the hellish prison, where angels were made to relive their sins over and over again, was enough to set him straight. Francis couldn't think of a worse torture.

Worse even than dealing with the Thrones.

"Sorry, I meant no disrespect," Francis said, averting his eyes. "I'm just surprised that—"

"Surprised that the Lord God has many enemies?" the Thrones interrupted, their color becoming darker—*fiercer*—with anger. "The Almighty cannot . . . will not rest until *all* who oppose His glory are a threat no more."

Francis didn't respond, knowing he was better off keeping his mouth shut.

"There is another," the Thrones repeated.

"Where?" Francis sighed, the taint of death still lingering around him like a bad smell.

One of the fiery orbs was suddenly in his face, a thick tendril of burning matter emerging from its body to touch the center of his skull. It was excruciating at first, and he was certain that they enjoyed his pain immensely, a little payback for disrespecting them.

It was done before he could scream, the tentacle of flame disappearing back into the spinning ball, as it returned to hover with its brethren.

Francis's head was now filled with images: images of where he would go, and whom he would kill in the name of the Lord.

"Go," the Thrones ordered, as they disappeared with another searing flash and a sound that could have been mistaken for thunder; the puddles that had been beneath them bubbled and steamed.

Francis cleared his throat and spit into one of the boiling puddles. Then he lifted a hand and began to utter an incantation that would take him to his next assignment. It was a little bit of magick bestowed upon him by the Thrones, since he had lost his wings after siding with Lucifer during the Great War.

He moved his hand in the air before him, opening a tear in the fabric of time and space, a passage to where he'd find the next to die. The only consolation was that he'd be going to a speakeasy.

And he could finally get his drink.

*   *   *

Located on the edge of Beauchamp, Louisiana, the Pelican Club didn't even have a sign.

For all intents and purposes, it was an abandoned general store, but that was only for folks who weren't in the know.

The Thrones were in the know, and knew where the latest offender of Heaven could be found, and now Francis knew as well.

Strolling up the quiet, rain-swept street, he took note of the building, and the large black man sitting on the front porch, a mean-looking dog of many breeds seemingly asleep at his feet. But Francis knew otherwise. That dog would be up with fangs bared as soon as it sensed even the slightest inkling of a threat.

He observed mostly folks of color strolling up to the building.

He stood in the shadows and willed his flesh a darker shade, then fell in behind a group of four men as they drew near the club. One at a time they climbed the steps, greeting the big man with a nod and a "good evening," then sticking out their hands for the monstrous beast to sniff. The brave ones went as far as to pat the animal on top of its large head.

It was his turn.

"Nice dog," Francis said to the big man.

He grunted. "Huh. See if he thinks you're nice."

Francis held out a brown hand. The beast ignored the offered appendage, choosing instead to look up into the fallen angel's eyes. A communication passed between them, a sharing of information about each other. Francis learned that the dog was a good dog, a faithful dog, but if he felt like it, he could do some serious damage. And the dog learned that Francis was a good person, a faithful person, but that he too could do some serious damage if he wanted.

In seconds they came to an understanding, and the dog extended his snout and licked Francis's hand with a thick pink tongue.

"Thattaboy," Francis said, scratching behind his ears.

The dog rolled over onto his back, allowing Francis to rub his dark, fleshy belly.

He glanced up at the large man, noting the surprise on his face.

"Guess I am nice," Francis said with a grin.

"Huh," the man said as he hooked a thumb, gesturing for Francis to head inside.

It was dark in the Pelican Club, the room lit by a few bare bulbs on a wire that stretched across the wooden ceiling. It was more crowded than Francis expected, as folks were standing around in small groups and others sipped refreshments from jelly jars at tables positioned in pockets of shadow throughout the room. There was a makeshift bar—three two-by-fours laid across two cracker barrels—and it called to him.

Francis asked the barkeep if he had any gin, and the man just laughed, pouring him a jelly jar of something from a brown jug that he pulled up from the floor.

"This'll do," Francis said as he paid for his drink. He returned the man's smile and brought the glass to his lips, taking a sip. The moonshine burned as it went down, and he let it. He liked the warm feel of the illegal whiskey. If he'd wanted to, he could have shut it all down, canceling out the effects of the alcohol with just a thought.

But where was the fun in that?

Francis leaned on the bar and scanned the room, looking for his target. He saw no one who matched the image the Thrones had placed in his brain, but if they said the target would be here, it would be. All Francis had to do was relax, have himself a drink or two, and wait.

He found an old stool against a wall and sat. It was a strange place for the Thrones to have sent him; there wasn't a renegade angel or supernatural being to be found, just some poor folks looking to let off a little steam.

Francis finished his drink and slid off his stool to get another.

"Hit me again," he told the barkeep, handing him the empty jelly jar.

"Still want that gin?" the man asked, pouring more of the whiskey from the jug into the glass.

"What's gin?" Francis asked.

The barkeep got a big kick out of that, laughing up a storm.

Francis stayed by the bar this time, deciding that he'd like to share the company of the man tending the bar. He looked like a good egg, and good eggs were hard to come by these days.

"Never seen you in here before," the barkeep commented as he poured a drink for a little old lady who looked as though she could be on her way to church services.

"That's because I've never been here before," Francis answered.

The barkeep nodded, and then held out his hand. "Name's Melvin," he said.

Francis stared at the hand for a moment before taking it firmly in his.

"Francis," he said as the two shook.

"So, what do you think of the Pelican?" Melvin asked, taking some more jelly jars from a wooden crate and placing them on top of the bar.

"Nice," Francis said as he took a short sip of the white lightning. "I imagine it helps people forget their problems for a while."

"It certainly does that," Melvin said. "And it puts some money in my pocket."

Francis looked at the barkeep over the rim of his glass. "Is this place yours?"

"It is," Melvin said. "I pay the man who used to own the general store here a slight fee for the use of his premises, but I maintain the place, keep the jugs full, and bring in the entertainment."

"Entertainment?" Francis laughed. "You've got entertainment here?"

"I sure do," Melvin said. "Don't tell me you never heard of the Swamp Angel?" he asked incredulously.

Francis shook his head.

"Then you're about to now," Melvin said. "She's comin' on as soon as the band is ready." The barkeep gestured with his chin to an area where a sheet had been strung like a curtain. Francis could see some men and their instruments taking their places on a makeshift stage.

The crowd gradually started to notice as well, clapping as the men sat down on old chairs and stools and began to tune up their musical instruments. There was a very thin fiddle player, a guy who easily could have tipped the scales at three hundred pounds with an old bowler hat on top of his big head and a beat-up guitar in his lap, and a third man at an old piano.

Instruments tuned, the musicians gave one another a look that said they were ready and the place became eerily quiet.

Then from behind the curtain she stepped, a striking woman wearing a simple white dress that smacked of being handmade. She wore no jewelry or makeup. Her skin was like mahogany, and Francis wasn't sure whether he'd ever seen in the flesh a creature quite so beautiful. She stood on the small stage, looking out over the silent audience, and he was reminded of a scared little animal caught in the head-lights of an oncoming truck.

For a moment, he thought she might take off, jumping from the stage and heading out the door in sheer terror, but he watched as she took a couple of deep breaths and looked at the smiles of the three men who were ready to accompany her. Slowly she nodded.

The men began to play, and she began to sing.

Francis had heard the celestial choirs of Heaven, but they couldn't hold a candle to what he was hearing now. He stood statue still, whiskey in hand, with no urge to drink it. All he wanted to do was listen as the woman—the Swamp Angel—sang from the very depths of her soul and, in turn, touched every single soul in the room.

It was a shame he was going to have to kill her.

Francis left the memory of Louisiana and the sweet, sweet sound of the Swamp Angel's voice, and returned to Hell.

Louisiana? he questioned as he slowly emerged from the mire of unconsciousness. *I've never been to fucking Louisiana . . . especially not during the Depression.*

But he had. He just hadn't remembered until the crazy angel that had saved him stuck a knife into his brain.

The former Guardian opened his eyes with a pathetic yelp, recalling the feeling of the glowing blade as it violated his skull.

He was on his back facing the ceiling of the cave, stalagmites—or were they stalactites? He never could remember—hanging down. He tried to move, but couldn't.

Again he heard the rumbling sounds of Hell changing somewhere off in the distance, and he knew he was still a guest in the Magick Kingdom.

Francis tried to move again, and this time realized that his wrists and ankles were bound by thick leather restraints.

"What the fuck?" he said aloud, his voice sounding weird as it bounced around the confines of the cave.

Fighting a wave of dizziness, he lifted his head for a better view of his surroundings. His stomach flipped, threatening to make him yak up his insides, but he really hadn't eaten anything since . . . When was the last time he had eaten? How long had he been in Hell? Time moved differently here; it could have been days, or maybe even months.

What I wouldn't give for a Hot Pocket about now.

Through bleary eyes he saw the angel. His back was to him, and he appeared to be working, standing in front of a slab of black rock that seemed to have grown up out of the floor. And there was somebody else . . . someone who looked to be in even worse shape than Francis lying atop the slab. The Hellion was curled in a tight ball of nastiness at the angel's feet.

"Hey," Francis squeaked, his throat tight and dry.

"You're awake," the angel commented, continuing to work.

The Hell beast lifted its obscene head and hissed.

"Let me just finish here and I'll be right with you," said the angel.

Then he dropped something wet and red. It plopped to

the floor of the cave with a spatter, and the Hellion reacted immediately, snatching it up into its awful mouth, chewing eagerly.

"Glad you won't be needing that anymore," the angel said with a chuckle to the being laid out before him.

Then he turned to face Francis. The front of the angel's robes, already filthy with the dirt and soot of Hell, were now spattered with blood. He held his glowing blade in a relaxed hand, and Francis again recalled the agony as it had entered his head.

Though the muscles in his neck were screaming, the former Guardian angel could not—would not—lower his head. He could see the other figure lying upon the slab now. It had once been an angel. Francis guessed he was likely one of the few who had managed to escape the tortures of Tartarus, reverting to barbarism on the plains of Hell. Now his stomach had been opened, the skin peeled back.

Something that could have been a mountain crumbling roared somewhere outside the cave, and the angel tilted his shaggy head slightly, listening to the sound.

"The changes are coming closer," he said. "I wonder what it will be like when *he's* finished?"

"What the fuck are you doing?" Francis demanded. A while ago he had expected to be dead, but now? He had a front-row seat on the crazy bus and it didn't show any sign of slowing down soon.

"It's all about change, really," the angel said. The glowing scalpel disappeared somewhere inside his robes. "Take this poor beast, for example." He gestured toward the angel on the slab.

"You wouldn't believe the changes his body has undergone, living the way he did . . . changes that I never foresaw, and I was partially responsible for his design."

Responsible for his design? Who is this madman? The thought coursed through Francis's fevered brain as he fought to keep his head up.

"His internal workings have evolved to survive the rigors of Hell," the angel continued.

Francis had no idea what this lunatic was talking about,

but as long as it kept him from using the light-saber scalpel to open him up, he could keep right on talking.

"To survive what is coming, we must all evolve. I learned that quite a long time ago, but I've only recently come to truly understand it."

The angel approached Francis, and he squirmed on the slab, but to no avail. He wasn't going anywhere.

"But I knew that things were finally about to come around when I found you out there. It was a surprise, but not really."

The angel reached out with a bloody hand to stroke Francis's bald head.

"I knew you would be coming; I just didn't know when."

The scalpel was in the angel's hand again, and all Francis could do was stare in horror at the figure looming above him.

"I was always proud of the Guardian's design," he said.

"Who the fuck are you?" Francis growled.

"You don't remember me . . . yet," the angel said with a smile that would have given Charles Manson the creeps. "But you will."

He leaned toward Francis, one blood-encrusted hand holding the former Guardian angel's head steady as the scalpel once more slipped effortlessly into his skull.

Like a hot knife cutting through butter.

CHAPTER NINE

Remy helped Jon bury Nathan as the sun started to set over the Arizona desert.

They were silent as they shoveled dirt over the poor man's battered corpse with tools they had found after foraging through the wreckage of the biodome.

"Tell me about him," Remy said, desperate to ease the uncomfortable silence.

"Nothing much to tell, really," Jon said. He had begun to place large rocks atop the fresh earth in an attempt to keep the desert predators away. "He was a good man . . . a kind man, and I loved him."

Jon looked at Remy with a sad smile as the tears began to flow down his dirty cheeks.

"There, I said it." He looked skyward. "I said it, and the heavens didn't open up, and fire didn't rain down from the sky."

"Did you think it would?" Remy asked him.

Jon shrugged. "Relationships like ours were frowned upon in the Sons," he said. "So we kidded ourselves by ignoring our true feelings . . . lying to everyone around us, as well as ourselves."

The man looked back to the fresh grave, then bent down to retrieve more rocks.

"How pathetic is it that only after he is dead can I say it out loud." Jon shook his head in disgust. "You should have left me to die under the rubble."

"He knew that you loved him," Remy said.

Jon laughed bitterly. "Yeah, I'm sure he did."

"I can sense these things better than most, but one would have to be in a coma to not see and feel the connection you two had."

Jon knelt beside the grave. He stayed like that for a little while.

"Thank you for that," he said finally.

"It's the truth."

"Well, thank you anyway."

"You're welcome," Remy said.

Jon stared at the grave again. "It's kind of funny," he said. "I can still feel him around me."

"Not such a bad thing, is it?"

"No, not at all. It's really kind of nice."

"We should probably think about going," Remy suggested.

"Yeah," Jon said.

"From what I remember of the map, we're going to Louisiana, right?" Remy asked.

"Louisiana it is," Jon agreed. "But we'll have to be careful. It has to be done just right, or it could be disastrous." He seemed to almost physically shake off his emotions, and was suddenly very professional. "The first thing we need to do is find some batteries for my hearing aid, and then get ourselves cleaned up. I doubt the Daughters of Eve would talk to us if we look as though we've just fought a war."

"Do you think they will talk to us?" Remy was curious, given the feud between the two groups.

"Sure," Jon said. "Right before they find out who we are, and try to kill us."

Fernita Green reached into her bucket of filthy water and removed a rag.

"Here," she said to Mulvehill, handing him the dripping cloth. "Start scrubbing. Anyplace you see this writing."

For some reason he took it, soapy water dripping from his hand to patter on the threadbare carpet.

"Listen, Fernita," Mulvehill started. "Why don't we talk about this . . . ?"

"There's no time to talk," the old woman snapped as she frantically rubbed at a blackened smudge on the wall. "I have to get it all off."

Mulvehill wasn't familiar with the scrawl, but it looked old, and he got an odd, itchy feeling at the backs of his eyes when he looked at it for too long.

"All the things I forgot," Fernita said as she scrubbed. "The more I wipe away, the more I remember. . . . It was horrible . . . just horrible."

The old woman was sobbing as she dunked her brush into the bucket beside her and brought it out again to scrub at the wall.

Cautiously Mulvehill knelt beside her, feeling the spilled water from the bucket soak into the knees of his slacks as he gently put his arm around her. "It's all right," he tried to console her. "Everything is going to work itself out. Why don't we take a break, talk a little, and see what—"

"They were burnin'," the old woman said, staring at him with eyes red from crying. "All those folks inside, they all got burned up because of me."

Mulvehill felt horrible. Fernita Green was in genuine pain; he could practically see it eating away at her.

"He was trying to kill me," she said between sobs, and then with a desperate moan she attacked the wall again, rubbing with all her might to make the markings disappear.

"Who, Fernita?" Mulvehill asked. "Who was trying to kill you?"

The old woman slumped forward, sliding down the wall until her face and hands were touching the ground. She was exhausted, barely able to hold herself up anymore.

"The angel," she said into the floor, and he thought for sure that he must have misheard her words.

"Who?" he asked again, squeezing her tighter.

"The angel," she said again, raising her head. "The angel wanted to kill me."

"Shit," Mulvehill said, fingers of icy dread tickling the

length of his spine. "This just keeps getting better and better."

Jon and Remy were at a motel on the outskirts of the Sonoran Desert, cleaning up before beginning their search for the Daughters of Eve.

The van from the biodome had been singed a bit in the explosion, but it had proven to still be road-worthy. They'd made a quick stop at the closest megastore, picking up some fresh clothes, a map, and Jon's hearing-aid batteries.

Remy had just run himself through the shower, and he came out of the bathroom to find Jon sitting on the corner of one of the beds, staring at the room's green carpet with laser-beam intensity.

"You all right?" Remy asked, drying his dark hair with a towel.

It took a moment or so, and he was about to ask the question again when Jon pulled his eyes away from the rug.

"I'm good," he said, but Remy wasn't sure he believed him. The man was pale, sick-looking, and he hoped that it was just the reality of their situation catching up with him.

"Are you done in there?" Jon asked, rousing himself.

"It's all yours." Remy stepped aside as Jon grabbed a plastic bag containing his purchases and disappeared into the bathroom, closing the door behind him; seconds later the water in the shower was running.

Remy had bought a new pair of jeans and a powder blue dress shirt. He tore the price tags off and dressed, glancing toward the bathroom, wishing he were alone on this leg of the journey. Something told him that things were only going to get worse, and Jon had already been through enough.

From another bag on the floor, Remy took out the maps he'd bought and unfolded them on the bed, planning the quickest route to Louisiana and hoping the van would last long enough to get them there.

Steam swirled around the bathroom as Jon held on to the edges of the sink, staring at his fogging reflection in the mirror.

But it wasn't himself he was looking at; it wasn't a person at all. Jon was seeing a place . . . a place not seen by man or woman for a very long time.

Eden was coming.

He was both in awe of and terrified by the immensity of the place, the wildness of its smell. It was closer now than it had ever been, and soon it would be here.

If only Nathan could have lived to see it.

But it was his sacrifice that had allowed Jon to connect to the special place in a way that his people never had before.

It was as if he were actually there, walking amid the lush, tropical green, feeling the moisture of the humidity upon his naked skin.

The pain was sudden, like stepping on shards of glass with bare feet.

Jon recoiled, his entire body shivering with the intensity of the agony. His gaze fell on the ground at his feet and he realized that where he was standing was inexplicably dead. The Garden around him was lush and thriving, but this area now appeared leached of life.

And then he heard the sounds. They were coming from the dead zone, somewhere very close.

Something was stirring.

Something beneath the earth.

And as it stirred, Jon felt himself growing sicker . . . weaker . . . as if his very life force were being sucked away.

Remy had just finished leaving Linda Somerset a message, explaining that he'd be gone longer than he thought, but would make it up to her when he got back.

First Mulvehill's bottle of twenty-five-year-old Scotch and steak dinner, now Linda, and he was sure Marlowe would have something to say when he returned.

Jon emerged from the bathroom, interrupting Remy's thoughts. He was completely naked, and looked even paler, if that was possible.

"We have to find the key right away," he said, swaying on his bare feet.

"I agree," Remy said carefully. "I've already gone over the maps and I think—"

"No." Jon shook his head. "We have to get there fast...."

"Yes, I know, and I'm pretty sure I've mapped out the fastest route—"

"Faster," Jon interrupted, panting, as if he'd overexerted himself in the shower. "It has to be faster. We have to be there now."

Remy rushed to the man's side as he began to fall, grabbing hold of his arm to steady him. "What's happened, Jon?"

"Something's happening in the Garden," he said, gasping. "Since Nathan did his thing I'm more connected.... I had a vision.... Something's killing it."

"Did your vision show you what's killing it?" Remy asked. "Is it Zophiel or ..."

"I don't know what it is," Jon said with a shake of his head.

"So not only do we have to get the second half of the key and get Adam home; now we have to save the Garden as well."

"Looks like it," Jon agreed. He pulled out the chair to the desk and sat, elbows resting on his bare knees. "We need to get to Louisiana as fast as possible, and the quickest way is you."

Remy didn't like the sound of that. "Me?"

Jon looked up, face pallid and sweating. "You're an angel; I saw those wings when you rescued me from the wreckage of the dome."

"You want me to fly us there?"

"Don't play stupid, Remy," Jon said. "You know you do more than fly."

"And you received your doctorate in angelology from what school?"

"From the school of answering to one for more than seventy years," Jon retorted.

It was easy to forget how old Jon actually was, and how long he'd been in the company of Malachi.

"I don't know where we're going," Remy said. "I have to have some sort of connection."

"I do," Jon said. "After Nathan ate the fruit and connected us to the Garden, it was like I was there."

Remy shook his head. "But it didn't happen to me."

"It's in my blood now. The scent of the place is in my blood."

Jon had received a gash on the side of his head in the biodome explosion, and although it had stopped bleeding some time ago, it appeared to be seeping a bit since his shower. He reached up, touched the wound, and held his bloodstained hand out to Remy.

"You can follow a scent. Track this. . . . It should bring us there, or at least pretty close."

Louisiana: 1932

Francis had become a regular at the Pelican Club.

Leo, the big man on the porch, greeted him nightly with an accepting nod, and Cleo, his dog, with an excited wag of the tail.

He was okay as far as they were concerned.

If only they knew the truth.

Melvin greeted him the same way from behind his two-by-four bar every night—with a big smile and a jelly jar full of moonshine.

Francis liked being a regular, liked the fact that folks smiled at him as he entered, assuming he was one of them.

If only they knew the truth.

The Thrones had sent him here on a mission of murder, and as he sat on the rickety wooden stool, sipping moonshine whiskey from a jelly jar, he waited for his target.

He had been waiting for days.

It wasn't that his target hadn't made an appearance; in fact, she had been there every night. He liked to tell himself that he was waiting for the opportune moment.

But he knew otherwise.

It was always the same. He arrived at the Pelican intent on carrying out his assignment, but then she'd open her mouth to sing, and it was like nothing mattered anymore.

Tonight the Swamp Angel was singing once again, but there was a difference; tonight she was looking at him. It was bad enough that her voice had such an effect on him, but now, as her eyes touched his, it was a whole new ball of wax.

"I think somebody's noticed you," Melvin said as he used a rag to dry the inside of a recently washed jelly jar.

"What are you talking about?" Francis asked, not able to tear his gaze away from the Angel.

"I think you know what I'm talking about," Melvin said. "You'd have to be dead not to notice."

The situation was going from bad to worse, and this target wasn't even a real angel; she was human. Francis picked up his drink and retreated to one of the darker corners. He had to think.

The Swamp Angel finished her first set, climbed down off the stage, and grabbed a drink from the bar. She and Melvin talked for a moment, both glancing toward Francis.

Quickly the former Guardian angel willed himself invisible, appearing to humans as only another shadow in the darkness of the corner.

The woman took her drink and headed toward him. And certain that he couldn't be seen, Francis watched her, nearly mesmerized by her beauty. She was wearing a frilly white blouse and a blue skirt that came down past her knees. The clothes looked as though they might have had some years on them, but it didn't matter. She wore them well.

She stopped before him and took a dainty sip from her whiskey. "Do you like my singing?" she asked.

Francis looked over his shoulder but there was no one else there.

"Are you not answerin' my question because you don't, or are you just being rude?" she asked.

She can see me.

The Swamp Angel smiled, and held out a delicate hand. "Well, I'm not rude," she said. "I'm Eliza. Eliza Swan."

Not good. Not good at all.

*   *   *

The smell of Eden was most certainly in Jon's blood.

He had quickly dressed, then given Remy a facecloth he had used to wipe the blood from the laceration on his head.

His blood reeked of magick, and Remy could follow magick.

With the scent of Eden filling his nostrils, Remy reluctantly called upon the Seraphim. He felt the transformation begin, as his clothing shifted from cloth to armor, and wings of gold unfurled from his back. His angelic nature eagerly attempted to fully assert itself, but he forced it back, allowing only a small part of the divine power to come forth.

Remy leaned in close to Jon, capturing a whiff of fresh blood from his still-weeping wound.

An explosion of imagery filled his mind. He knew where they were going.

"Are you ready for this?" Remy asked.

Jon nodded, although his expression wasn't as certain.

Remy took hold of Jon's shoulders and closed his wings around both of them. In his mind, he saw the place where they were headed and tightened the embrace of his wings as he felt reality begin to shift.

The strong bleachy smell of the motel room was replaced with the thick aroma of honeysuckle and the heavy, damp smells of a swamp.

They had arrived.

Remy opened his wings, and Jon spilled out onto the ground, where he immediately began to vomit.

"Sorry about that," Remy said as he took full control back, pushing away the fearsome visage of one of God's soldiers. "I've heard it can be a little rough."

"S'okay." Jon wiped his mouth and climbed unsteadily to his feet.

"So, where are we?" Remy asked, looking about the heavily wooded area.

"It's called Eden Parish," Jon said, beginning to make his way through the forest.

"Of course it is," Remy said, following.

Jon pushed through the thick underbrush to emerge in what looked like a small junkyard. Old, rusted-out cars were parked here and there, and a school bus without any wheels listed to one side, and appeared to be sinking into the soft earth.

"Is this right?" Remy asked, the place not where he imagined one of the descendants of Eve to be found.

"I think it is." Jon continued to walk across the yard, past corroded car engines and shopping carts overflowing with pieces of scrap metal. There was a dilapidated trailer ahead, and Remy could see a small child sitting on some wooden steps that led up to a screen door.

The child was filthy, and was playing with a black-and-white kitten in her lap.

"Hello," Jon said, smiling at the child.

She looked at him and scowled before placing the kitten in the crook of her arm and heading toward the door.

"It's all right," Remy said, stepping forward.

The little girl had the screen door open halfway, but let it close, her eyes never leaving Remy's.

"I know what you are," she said almost dreamily.

"She can see me," Remy said to Jon. "Really see me."

"She probably can," Jon answered. "Just like I can see you."

"You can see me?" Remy asked him, surprised by the admission.

"Certainly," he said. "The original bloodlines are very attuned to all things divine. That's how I found you in the park that night; I could see your glow."

"I glow?"

The little girl clutched her kitten closer. "I know what he is, and I know what you are as well," she said, scowling at Jon.

"What am I, darling?" Jon asked, gently.

"You're one of the bad men," she said.

"He's not bad," Remy began to explain. "He's a nice man who—"

"No, to her I am bad," Jon interrupted. "Remember, she's a child of the original bloodline ... of Eve's original bloodline. . . . Our two lines have been at each other's throats for millennia, one blaming the other for what transpired in the Garden. She can tell what I am, and hates me. It's practically genetic."

The little girl stared at Jon, and Remy could feel her anger.

"You know the old saying about how Eskimos have a hundred different words for snow?" Jon asked Remy.

Remy nodded, having heard something like it before.

"Well, they say that the Daughters of Eve have a hundred words for hate . . . all directed at the Sons of Adam."

A large woman, her gray hair pulled back in a tight ponytail, appeared at the screen door. "Lydia, get your ass in here." She opened the creaking door just enough for the child to scoot inside. "What the hell do you want?" she asked, turning her angry gaze on Jon and Remy.

The woman's not-so-pleasant disposition went from bad to worse as she continued to stare at Jon.

"I was hoping you could help us," he said as politely as he could.

"You've got a lot of balls coming here," the woman snarled. "We've killed people like you for less than trespassing around these parts."

"Please," Jon said. "We don't want any trouble. We just . . ."

A shotgun muzzle slid out from behind the screen door, aimed at Jon's chest.

"We don't like your kind in this parish," she warned. "So if you don't want to end up at the bottom of the swamp I suggest you take your sorry asses and get . . ."

Remy stepped in front of Jon.

"We don't mean to cause you any problem, ma'am," he said. At first he thought he might get shot, but gradually her expression began to soften, and she lowered her weapon.

"What the hell is one'a you doing with the likes of him?" she asked, disgusted by the idea of anyone—never mind an angel—being seen with a Son of Adam.

Jon bravely stepped out from behind Remy.

"Haven't you felt it?" he asked her.

"Felt what?" she barked, the shotgun starting to rise again.

"You know what I mean," Jon said. "We've all been feeling it . . . all of us who are of the blood."

"I don't know what you're—"

"I see it in my dreams," Jon interrupted. "A place so beautiful that I wake up with my face soaked with tears. It was supposed to be our home . . . where the first of us were to live with our families, and our family's families . . . forever."

Remy could see the woman's eyes grow glassy with emotion. "But then there was the sin," she mumbled.

Jon moved closer to the steps. "But what if there's a chance that sin could be forgiven?" he proposed eagerly. "That all the hate we have for one another . . . all the guilt, could be made to go away?"

Tears were running down the woman's leathery face as she stared at him from the doorway of the mobile home. "Why haven't I shot you yet?" she asked, wiping away the tears with her free hand.

"Because you can sense that what I'm saying is true," Jon replied. "That there's a chance *they* can finally be forgiven."

"What do you want from me?" she asked.

"There's a house on stilts," Jon said, gazing past the mobile home. "Out there in the swamp. I need to speak to the woman who lives there."

The woman's expression turned to one of surprise.

"What do you need her for? She's crazy."

"Aren't we all?" Jon said with a soft smile, and the woman smiled as well, the urge to kill him no longer a priority.

CHAPTER TEN

Fernita's poor old eyes blurred as she tried to focus on the latest row of foreign scribbles that adorned the wall of her living room, behind the sofa.

Remy's friend was with her, trying to get her to stop, but he just didn't understand. Wiping the markings away . . . it was like washing a window covered in thick dirt, and finally being able to see what was on the other side.

Some of the memories were horrible, yes, that was true, but others . . .

Others were special beyond words.

Louisiana: 1932

She didn't know why the man with thinning black hair caught her eye the way he had, but there was just something about him.

Eliza had seen him out there in the audience every night for the last week, listening as she sang. Maybe it was the way he watched her, as if he could feel what she did as she sang her favorite songs.

The songs made her feel whole. Complete.

And it had been a very long time since she had felt complete.

No one knew how long she'd been hanging around this sad old world. She knew that she didn't look to be any older than her mid-twenties, but looks were deceiving.

She was much, much older than that.

Her grandmother once told her it had something to do with their bloodline, that they were one of the first, and it made them age slower.

All Eliza knew was that she had experienced a lot of things in her life—war, slavery, freedom, of a sort—but nothing made her happier than singing her songs.

Her family hadn't approved of her singing in clubs. They kept telling her that her voice was a gift from the Lord, and she should use it only on special occasions. But Eliza couldn't understand that. Why would the Almighty have given her this gift if she wasn't allowed to share it with everybody?

That was the question that made her leave her family, setting out for Louisiana in the middle of the night. That was why she was here, sharing her songs with everyone. But tonight, for some reason, she didn't really didn't care about everyone. Tonight she wanted to share her songs with only this man.

What is it about him?

She'd seen him talking to Melvin, but her boss didn't seem to know who the stranger was. Just some guy coming to hear her sing, he'd guessed.

Still, she wanted to know, and decided she'd get what she needed from the horse itself.

He seemed surprised that she was even talking to him, and now as she stood before him, hand out, waiting for him to reply, she wasn't sure if he was just rude or touched.

"I'm Pearly Gates," he said finally, taking her hand in his.

The moment was special beyond words.

The moment that Eliza Swan fell in love.

Zophiel flew just above the sea of clouds, a shark swimming the ocean waters following the scent of blood.

One moment it was strong, taunting him with its proximity, and the next it was gone, driving him to the brink of madness.

But he did not stop searching; this was what he had come to this world to find.

What he had sworn to destroy.

It was there again, wafting in the atmosphere. He took the scent into his being. This time it was strong, and growing stronger.

His powerful wings, sheathed in the armor of God, beat the air with increasing fury, his speed intensifying as he followed the trail. The smell of it had become even more intense, his preternatural senses aroused to the brink of overload.

Zophiel was so close.

But he mustn't become careless, for he had been this close before....

The memory bubbled up from the morass of his subconscious, reminding him of his folly.

Zophiel had no recollection of how long he had been in the world of God's man, or why, until he'd sensed the power.

It called, teasing him with its poisonous taint. He did not know why he hated it so, only that he had to destroy it.

Circling the land from above, the Cherubim found the source of his rage, and descended upon it with the combined shriek of his three faces.

He landed in a crouch before the fragile wooden structure, the scent of his prey driving him forward. A sentry and its faithful four-legged beast attempted to bar his way, the human firing a noisy weapon that spit fire and flecks of metal, but to little avail.

The Cherubim briefly admired the bravery of the human and his animal before turning the fires of Heaven upon their fragile forms, wiping away any evidence that they'd ever existed.

The power continued to cry out from within the structure, and the Cherubim threw himself upon the closed wooden doors, taking them and most of the front wall down as he made his entrance.

Screams of terror erupted from the human bugs inside, their frenzied attempts to escape a distraction from his purpose. The fire leapt from his fingertips, igniting the room and its scurrying inhabitants as it searched for the source of his outrage.

The Cherubim's three faces sniffed the air, the smell of forbidden power prevalent over the choking aromas of wood smoke and burning flesh.

"There," Zophiel proclaimed.

His quarry stood, staring wide-eyed at his awesome visage. She was a woman, a human woman with a power so dangerous that it threatened Heaven itself.

And nothing would stop him from destroying her.

But something had stopped him.

Zophiel hovered over the world as the memories flooding his brain became a trickle, and then trailed off to nothing.

Something had prevented him from carrying out his duty, but the memory of what it was eluded him. The Cherubim was frustrated, and that quickly turned to anger. He turned his attention toward the Earth below, knowing that the answers he sought would be found there, amongst the hairless monkeys that had captured the love of the Heavenly Father. Strangely enough, this thought calmed him, the knowledge that he would soon have answers to temporarily sate his fury. The Cherubim returned to the hunt, finding the elusive scent again, and flying toward it.

This time he would not be stopped.

The woman had agreed to take them.

Remy sat across from Jon in the boat, the woman at the back, steering with the craft's outboard motor. Behind them, the little girl stood on the wooden dock watching them leave, kitten still clutched in her arms.

"I don't know how she'll feel about this," the woman said as she piloted the craft through the thick, brackish waters, between twisted, primordial-looking trees hanging thick with moss.

"We'll just explain ourselves like we did with you," Jon said, slapping at the bugs that were trying to feast upon his blood.

"Huh," the woman responded, taking them deeper and deeper into the swamp.

Remy let his senses wander. There was something here, something ancient and powerful. He could feel it emanating from the trees, from the animals that hid as they approached, from the water.

"It's beautiful," he said as the boat moved deeper into the swamp's embrace.

"It is," the woman replied. "But that beauty'll kill you if you're not careful."

"I'm sure it would." Remy watched an alligator, at least eight feet long, slither from a mud-covered bank into the still, oily water, where it disappeared.

"How much longer?" Jon asked, still slapping at bugs that seemed intent on eating him alive. The bugs didn't bother Remy—he had lowered his body temperature so as not to be all that enticing.

"Not long," the woman said.

The swamp grew thicker—denser—almost completely blocking out the rays of the hot sun as if night had suddenly fallen.

"There," the woman said, pointing through the thick mist rising from the water at something in the distance ahead.

At first Jon and Remy couldn't see anything, but then they saw . . . something.

It was a single, tiny ball of orange, and then there was another, resembling a set of fiery eyes peering out through the darkness, but that illusion was dispelled by the appearance of another, and another after that. Multiple orbs of light hung in the mist, like stars in the sky, before Jon and Remy could figure out what they were seeing.

Before the thick, smoky mist pulled apart like a delicate spiderweb, and they saw the stilt house, looking like some large, prehistoric beast standing in the midst of the swamp on tree trunk–sized legs. Burning lanterns hung from the structure.

"It's almost as if she knows we're coming," Jon said, his eyes never leaving the house.

"Oh, she knows," the woman said.

Remy's sense of an ancient power was even stronger here. The hair on his arms and the back of his neck stood on end as they drew closer.

A wooden ladder hung from the elevated platform, and the woman piloted the boat as close as she could before cutting off the engine.

"This is as far as I go," she said.

Jon stood, grabbing for the ladder. "Maybe you should join us," he said. "Help explain that we don't mean her any harm."

"She doesn't need to hear anything from me," the woman said. "She'll make up her own mind about you."

Remy stood carefully so as not to tip the boat, and joined Jon at the ladder.

"Thank you for this," he said.

"It's all right," she answered. "Whatever happens from here on is out of my hands."

"Thank you for not shooting me," Jon said, starting to climb the ladder.

The woman laughed. "You might be wishing I did after you've dealt with Izzy."

Remy followed Jon up onto the platform, the two of them watching as the woman piloted her motorboat back into the embrace of the thick swamp mist. Not only did it swallow her up, but it swallowed the sound of the outboard as well, leaving them alone in an eerie silence.

"I suggest we get this over with," Jon said, reaching up to adjust his hearing aid as he turned and walked toward the front door of the house. "The sooner we do this, the sooner we can reconnect with Adam and Malachi and . . ."

A woman stood in the open doorway.

Jon noticed her with a start, jumping back and bumping into Remy.

She was older at first glance, but exactly how old was tricky. She looked forty, but could have very easily been sixty, considering her pedigree. She had smoky skin and piercing, light-colored eyes. She was wearing a loose-fitting cotton top and a flowing peasant skirt in multiple colors. She was exotically attractive, but what really stood out was her hair, long and frizzy with streaks of white—like lightning bolts shooting from her scalp and running through the length of her wavy curls.

"Well, hello," Jon said, recovering quickly. "I'm Jon, and this is Remy, and we've come to—"

"I know why you've come," she said. Remy didn't like her tone and immediately went on full alert. "I've been waiting for a long time."

Her eyes gave the first sign that they were in trouble. In less than a second, they changed from a light shade that could have been the palest green to something dark and murky, like the swamp waters surrounding them.

The many bracelets adorning her wrists jangled noisily in the stillness as her hands shot out to either side of her, supernatural energy leaking from the tips of her fingers. Remy could feel the power start to surge, permeating the air as it intensified. It was all happening too fast.

The magick was loose, charging the very air around them with an aura of danger. Remy pushed Jon aside, moving to the forefront in an attempt to quell their growing predicament, but it was too late for that, and she told him so.

"You're too late, angel," she said, with a smile that showed off pearly white teeth and bands of magickal energy squirming across their ivory surface. "I've prepared for the likes of you two."

The winds began to howl, and the still waters seethed. The trees seemed to be moving—snaking closer to converge on the stilt house. The wood beneath their feet began to vibrate, and Remy was forced, yet again, to call upon the power of the Seraphim. But again he wasn't fast enough.

Something surged up, something sculpted from the mud and water and wildlife of the swamp.

The monster was in human form, mouth like a swirling vortex opened to roar its might, but it was like nothing Remy had ever seen before. It towered above the platform, then flowed down in a tsunami of thick, foul-smelling mud, to snatch them from their perch.

Dragging them down into the murky depths.

*   *   *

Louisiana: 1932

Francis was totally smitten by Eliza Swan.

He had never felt anything like this before. Certainly he'd had his dalliances with human women over the numerous centuries he'd been on Earth cleaning up God's messes, but none had ever managed to touch him so precisely . . . so deeply.

It was like magick.

He was at the Pelican Club again, listening to Eliza sing, and this time he knew that she sang to him.

Her voice made him feel more alive than he had in forever. It made him forget the dark days of war, when he slew his brothers in the name of a cause that he eventually came to realize was insane. She made him truly feel.

As if he were loved by God again.

But no matter how loved he was feeling, it didn't change the fact that he'd been given an assignment, and the Thrones weren't all that crazy about insubordination.

Eliza Swan was supposed to die, and he was the one who had to see to it she did. The Thrones wanted Eliza's blood for whatever reason, and they would not be denied.

She was singing one of his personal favorites, a beautiful, melancholy tune called "Searching for Paradise," and he let her sweet, sweet voice wash over him.

This one is something special, he thought, wondering why the Thrones would want her dead. Maybe it was the spell she seemed to have over anyone who heard her voice.

She finished her song to wild applause, and flashed Francis an amazing smile from the stage, leaving no doubt she'd sung that song for him.

There had to be a solution to this problem that didn't involve killing her. Part of him argued to just do the job and move on—that nothing, and no one, was more important than being able to pass through the gates of Heaven again and bask in the glory of the Almighty.

He imagined that was the same part of his nature that had been beguiled by the words of the Morningstar. He shouldn't have listened then, and he wasn't going to now.

He picked up his drink, and it was about halfway to his mouth when he felt it, a strange tingling in his spine. He'd heard humans make reference to the sensation as someone walking over their grave, and he couldn't have said it better himself. Although it was just the feeling he got when others of his kind were around.

Francis scanned the room. He wasn't sure what he was expecting, doubting he'd see the flaming, eye-covered orbs of the Thrones floating around the Pelican, but then again, he hadn't followed through on his orders, and the Thrones were impatient sons of bitches.

But it wasn't the Thrones. It was an angel, tall and dressed to the nines in a dark suit and tie. The angel's human guise was a striking one, with hair and beard of glacial white. He looked like some sort of aristocrat who had decided to see how the simple folk lived.

He was headed directly for Francis, other patrons instinctively moving aside, allowing him to pass.

Francis casually set his jar of moonshine down, letting his arm brush against his coat pocket. The Enochian dagger was still there, resting . . . waiting . . . eager for another taste of angel blood.

But he would wait, see what the creature of the divine wanted first. Who knew, maybe he just stopped by for a drink, saw Francis, and was coming over to say hi.

And maybe pigs had suddenly learned to fly.

Eliza was wailing beautifully upon the stage, this time accompanied only by the fat man—Big James—on his guitar.

Francis watched her, but was totally aware of the angel now standing before him. "Can I help you with something?" he asked, his eyes never leaving the woman onstage.

"No, I don't think that will be necessary," the angel said, his voice oozing authority.

Francis glanced quickly at the angel and was surprised to see that he too was staring at Eliza.

"I believe we've both found what we're looking for," the angel said.

"Maybe you should start by telling me who you are and what you want," Francis said, feeling what could only have been sharp pangs of jealousy.

The angel slowly turned his gaze to meet Francis's.

"I am Malachi," he said in a way that made Francis think it should have meant something to him.

"Am I supposed to know you?" he asked, retrieving his whiskey from where he'd placed it on the floor beside his stool. "Because I'm sorry to say I have no idea who you are ... other than you're obviously from that grand ball-room upstairs."

"Grand ballroom?" Malachi questioned, before it eventually dawned on him. "I see, you make light of the King-dom." He nodded ever so slowly to show he understood, but Francis doubted that he really did. "You're trying to be like them—the humans. I could never understand the need for this sense of humor. It was a trait I would have deemed worthless in the initial design, but the Allfather saw things differently."

Malachi's words were like a jab with a sharp stick. This talk of design and the Allfather piqued the former Guard-ian angel's curiosity to the extreme.

"Now do you know who I am?" Malachi asked.

Francis knew of a powerful angel, one of the first to be created. It was he and the Morningstar who had stood by the Lord God's side as He created the Heavens and the Earth below.

And yes, he had been called Malachi, but why would an angel of such power be here?

"You're *that* Malachi?" Francis asked, hoping that he was mistaken.

"I am," the angel said.

"But why are you *here*?"

"I am here for the same reason you are," Malachi said, staring at the stage where Eliza and her band were decid-ing what song they would do next.

Francis's hand drifted down toward his pocket. "You're here to kill her."

"No." Malachi looked at him. "To save her."

Francis's head was spinning, and he was about to ask the angel to step outside so they could talk freely when there came a horrible commotion—the sound of smashing glass and splintering wood, followed by the screams of the Pelican Club patrons.

Francis jumped from his stool, removing the deadly blade from his pocket. The screams intensified as the air became rank with the smell of burning flesh and something else.

Something divine.

The smell of angel.

The cries of the fearful and the dying replaced Eliza's songs. Francis watched in growing horror as the club's patrons, engulfed in fire, ran to escape, too terrified to realize that they were already dead as the hungry flames burned them to nothing.

A Cherubim emerged from the smoke with a discordant roar. It had been a very long time since Francis had last seen one of the more beastly of the Heavenly hosts. The Cherubim were the Lord's guard dogs, and he briefly considered the fate of Leo and Cleo on the front porch of the establishment.

What is something like that doing here? Francis wanted to know.

He watched as Melvin stood bravely before the forbidding angel, grabbing hold of a chair and swinging it wildly at its multiple faces in an attempt to drive it back.

It was the face of the lion that decided the club owner's fate, its ravenous jaws opening to ridiculous proportions, snatching the man up, and biting him in half.

Francis had seen enough.

He was moving toward the Cherubim, knife poised and ready. But something grabbed hold of his arm with a steely grip.

Francis spun around and looked into the face of the angel Malachi.

"You won't do much damage with the likes of that," the elder angel said, making reference to Francis's Enochian blade.

The Cherubim lifted its trifaced head, and its multiple eyes locked upon the angels. He spread his wings, fanning the smoke-filled air eagerly before he started to charge.

"He's looking for her," Malachi said, taking his eyes briefly from the monstrosity coming at them to look at Eliza frozen upon the stage.

"Eliza!" Francis cried out, noticing for the first time that she was still inside.

But the Cherubim had noticed her too, changing his course and barreling across the club floor, tossing tables and chairs aside as if they were nothing.

"Get her to safety," Malachi ordered. "You have to protect her for me."

Then Francis saw that the angel held his own weapon in hand, a blade, long and narrow, that seemed to have appeared from nowhere, and looked as though it might have been made from a piece of the sun.

And for a brief moment, Francis actually believed that the two of them had a chance against the rampaging Cherubim.

Right before Malachi plunged the burning dagger into Francis's eye.

Hell

Francis screamed at the top of his lungs, struggling against the restraints that held him upon the stone table.

Malachi withdrew his blade, the smell of burning angel flesh trailing behind it like a tail.

"There," the angel lord said, placing a cold, dirty hand against Francis's hot, sweating brow.

"What did you do to me?" Francis asked, his voice nothing more than a strained whisper.

"I made you forget," Malachi replied with a knowing smile. Hell rumbled outside the caves, sending shock waves through the mountains. Dust and dirt rained down from the ceiling upon them. "But I left you with enough to do what needed to be done."

Malachi turned and picked up a bucket nearby.

"She had to be protected," he said, pulling a ladle of water from the bucket and bringing it to Francis's lips. "And I could think of no one better to do that than a member of the Guardian host."

Francis did not want the water; he wanted answers, but as the ladle touched his lips he slurped greedily until Malachi took it away.

"I don't fucking understand," Francis said as the angel tossed the ladle back into the bucket.

"And you shouldn't," Malachi said. "But it will all become clear as we progress."

The scalpel was in his hand again, and Francis began to thrash in anticipation of what he knew was to follow.

"Let us continue," Malachi said with cold efficiency.

And Francis steeled himself against the incredible agony, eager to know what this was all about.

Desperate to remember.

CHAPTER ELEVEN

The swamp is trying to kill us, Remy thought as he was dragged deeper and deeper beneath the thick, muddy water.

But Remy was having none of that, thank you.

He called upon the Seraphim, but the essence of Heaven that resided inside him did not respond.

Swamp grass reached up from the silt-covered floor, wrapping around his ankles and drawing him down to the bottom of the swamp. Remy struggled in its grip as supernaturally invigorated currents swirled about his face, trying to force him to breathe.

Just take a deep breath, he imagined the swamp water saying in a thick Louisiana accent. *Suck it in deep, boy, and all your troubles will be over.*

He commanded the Seraphim to manifest, but somehow it denied him. He could feel it deep in the darkest part of his being, watching as his human nature struggled with its newest plight.

So weak and fragile, he heard it growl. *But still you cling to it.*

This is not the time, Remy said, oxygen deprivation starting to take its toll.

I have nothing but time, the Seraphim replied. *Time to lie here buried deep within the darkness of your being, waiting to be called upon when needed . . . imprisoned and hated when not.*

The grass was drawing him down, catfish and snapping turtles stirred by his presence, hearing the siren call of the swamp to attack.

Perhaps it would be better to die, the Seraphim continued. *To allow the fragile guise of humanity that you wear to choke upon the black water, to suffer no more.*

His lungs were about to burst, explosions of color blossoming in the darkness. There was nothing Remy could do other than call the Seraphim's bluff.

He opened his mouth, foul water pouring in to fill the cavity, and for a moment, he knew what it might be like to drown.

For a moment.

The Seraphim flew up from the darkness, filling his every fiber with the power of its being, chasing away the opportunity for death. Remy's body burned with the fires of Heaven, the heat from his armored flesh causing the water that surrounded him to boil with such intensity that nothing could live near him.

So glad you decided not to die, Remy chided, wrestling with his angelic nature so that it could not assume total control. Beneath the churning waters, he spread his powerful wings and sprang from the bottom of the swamp in a roiling cloud of silt, dead fish, and turtles.

The world had turned to muffled chaos.

Jon thrashed, trying desperately to keep his head above water as the swamp tried to pull him under. He could feel things around him, beneath the stinking water, things that bit at his clothes, trying to get to the flesh beneath, things that wrapped about his ankles, trying to yank him below.

"Please!" he screamed, moving his head away as a wave rushed at him, trying to enter his mouth to silence his voice and steal his life. "We don't mean you any harm."

He could see Izzy still standing on the platform in front of her house, hands glowing with supernatural power that flowed from her fingertips down into the water.

"My daddy said you'd be coming someday," she cried over the groans of the swamp bending to her will. "You'd be coming here to try to find out about my mama, and nothing good would come of it."

Something in the water tugged hard upon his ankle, and Jon screamed once before being pulled beneath the surface. His hearing aid buzzed and whined as it was submerged. Frantically Jon reached for his foot, feeling the slimy blades of grass wrapped around his shoe. Before his lungs could explode, he tore the shoe from his foot and struggled back to the surface.

Jon broke the surface, gasping for air, and found himself gazing up into the face of the woman using the swamp as her weapon.

"Just . . . just let me talk to you." He gasped, struggling to keep his head above the thrashing water.

"You're not dead yet?" Izzy asked, her voice filled with annoyance. Then she raised her hand, sending a writhing blast of magickal power out into a wooded section of the animated swamp. "I can fix that."

The waves grew, breaking over Jon's head, their weight trying to push him down again. He fought the watery onslaught, arms flailing, desperate to grab on to something, anything that could keep him afloat.

Through stinging, bleary eyes he saw something floating in the water not too far from his reach, but as he reached out to take hold of what he thought was a thick branch, he caught sight of two yellow eyes.

Alligators, his brain screeched in full panic. *I'm about to be eaten by alligators.*

Jon spun in the water, and began to swim as hard as he could away from the approaching predators, but Izzy wasn't going for it.

"Where are you going?" she called out from the deck. "Don't you want to meet some of my babies?" She started to laugh, directing even more of her magick into the water surrounding her stilt house.

Jon imagined he could hear the sound of the gator swimming closer, its hissing breath as it anticipated its next meal, its jaws creaking like an old hinge as it opened its mouth wide for the first bite.

A wave of black water dappled with dead fish and God knew what else rushed at him, throwing him backward into the path of the advancing alligator.

"You shouldn't have come," Jon heard Izzy say over the whine of his water-damaged hearing piece.

At least I'll be with Nathan soon, he thought as he slowly turned, looking into the cold stare of reptilian death.

But then the alligator came to an abrupt stop as the water around them became suddenly hot.

It began to froth, and glow an eerie yellow as something rapidly rose to the surface.

The angel erupted from the swamp in an explosion of blazing light and clouds of steam, his mighty wings flapping powerfully, holding his majestic form above the frothing waters.

Remy scanned his surroundings with the eyes of a warrior, searching out the nearest threat.

He saw Jon bobbing in the water below, an alligator too close. Remy angled his body down toward the water, and reached down to snatch Jon from the water.

A bolt of magickal force struck the metal of his chest plate and he cried out, almost dropping Jon back into the swamp. He quickly recovered, shrugging off the pain and flying toward the stilt house, where he released Jon and turned to face Izzy.

"Get away from my house," she cried, more and more magickal energy leaking from her body. The sky had begun to rumble; the trees swayed with winds that had begun to pick up. "I'll bring something worse than Katrina down on your heads," she spat.

Remy looked at her intensely, furling his powerful wings. "I don't want to fight you," he said.

"I tried to tell her," Jon said between gasps, but Remy held up a hand, silencing him.

"Look at me," Remy ordered Izzy. "Really look at me.... I know you can feel my intentions. I don't want to hurt you."

The magick continued to swirl around her. "I swore I would stop you," she said through gritted teeth.

"Stop us from what?" Remy asked. "All we want to do is talk to you."

Izzy held out her hands palms up, showing him the magickal power that swirled there.

"If you're lying, I'll make you eat this," she said with a sneer.

"Deal." Remy pulled back on his angelic essence with little difficulty, and returned to his very wet but human form.

Jon was looking down at his bare foot.

"I lost my shoe," he said.

"Maybe one of the gators has it," Remy said. "Want to go ask?"

This got a laugh from the woman, who was staring at Remy with a tilt of her head.

"There's something about you," she told him.

"I've heard that," Remy joked.

"No," she said seriously. "There's something familiar about you . . . something that I trust."

"And that's a good thing," Remy said.

"Yeah," she agreed with a nod, pulling open the screen door and gesturing for them to follow her inside.

"If it wasn't, the two of you would be dead right now."

Steven Mulvehill tried to reach Remy again, and again he got nothing.

"Son of a bitch," he hissed beneath his breath, sliding the phone back inside his jacket pocket.

"He did this," Fernita said, waving a rubber-gloved finger at the writing upon the wall. "He did this to protect me."

This whole situation was going from bad to worse. He thought it was crazy enough that angels were trying to kill her; now she was telling him that somebody wrote on her walls to keep her safe. God bless Remy and his weird shit.

"Who did, Fernita?" Mulvehill asked with a sigh.

"Pearly," she screamed. "My husband . . . Pearly Gates."

Her expression changed from one of anger to one of complete surprise, as she slowly raised a shaking hand to her gaping mouth.

"What is it?" Mulvehill asked. "Are you all right?"

"My husband," she repeated. "He was my husband. . . . I forgot that too."

She began to rock from side to side and Mulvehill moved to put a comforting arm around her shoulder.

"It's all right," he said, his compassionate side making a surprise appearance. "I think you're probably just a little confused right now," he told her. "Why would your husband want to make you forget him?"

Mulvehill would have loved to forget his marriage and the subsequent divorce, but that was another story entirely.

"He didn't do it to be mean," she said, sniffling. "He did it to protect me. He did it to hide me away from it."

"From the angel that was trying to kill you?"

"Yes," she said. "If I couldn't remember who I was, then it couldn't find me." She tentatively looked back to the wall she'd been cleaning. "I'm afraid," she said.

"You don't need to be afraid," Mulvehill told her. "I'm here with you."

"I'm afraid of what else I might've forgotten."

At first Steven thought it was a plane he heard flying overhead, low and rumbling.

And getting louder.

Closer.

And then the air itself seemed suddenly charged. He felt as though bugs were crawling on the back of his neck, and he quickly reached up to make sure that wasn't true. There were no bugs on his neck, but the hair was standing on end.

Every instinct he'd developed in his twenty years as a homicide cop was screaming.

Screaming for him to get the hell out of there.

The sound from outside was louder, and there was no mistaking that steady, rhythmic beating of the air.

Wings.

"Fernita, we need to get out of here," he urged, gazing up at the patterns on the water-stained ceiling.

"I can't go," Fernita said, spinning around to return to her work. "I need to see what else I've forgotten. . . . I need to remember."

Mulvehill's senses were shrieking.

"No, we're leaving." He grabbed her arm and pulled her along as he headed toward the door.

She struggled for a moment, but then noticed the sound also.

"Oh, no," she said, her voice a fear-filled whisper. "Is it him?"

"Let's hope it's not," Mulvehill said, hauling her through the rubbish-strewn living room and down the the hallway. At the end, he quickly turned the knob, opening the front door.

"Miles," she said.

"Who?" Mulvehill asked, and then he saw the large cat crouched in the doorway to the kitchen. Its eyes were huge as it looked all around. Then it suddenly bolted, disappearing with a snap of its bushy black tail.

"He'll be fine," Mulvehill told the old woman, pulling her out the door.

Roiling black clouds filled the sky above them as they hurried down the sidewalk to Mulvehill's car.

"It's cold out here," Fernita complained. "I should probably have a coat."

"I've got heat in the car," Mulvehill told her.

She started to argue, but a sound behind them interrupted her, and they both turned to look back at the house.

Something large fell from the sky, punching an enormous hole through the roof and into the attic.

They could hear the racket of destruction, and Mulvehill knew they didn't have much time before whatever had just made its grand entrance realized they were no longer in the house. He pulled open the door on the passenger side of his car and practically threw Fernita into the seat, slamming the door shut.

He raced around to the driver's side, chancing a final look at the house before getting into the car. A piece of furniture—a love seat, or it could have been a couch—flew through the front window to land broken and burning upon the lawn.

Steven Mulvehill got inside his car, turned over the engine, and put it in drive.

Cursing the name of Remy Chandler as he screeched away from the curb.

Malachi had never cared for humanity.

There was just something about them that he despised; maybe it was their basic design. He saw flaws in just about every aspect—soft flesh, easily broken bones, internal workings that would eventually wear down and cease to function.

And the soul.

A spark of the Almighty present in each and every one of them.

Malachi had balked at the concept, but was overruled by a much higher authority.

God wished it, and so it was. He believed they would be His greatest creation, that this tiniest piece of His essence would enable them to do great things in His name.

Malachi remembered how Lucifer had laughed, telling the Lord God that these creatures ... these newest creations of His ... would only bring Him sorrow.

And the Almighty had said if that was what they wished to do, so be it. He would give them the ability to make decisions on their own; they would be the masters of their own existence.

Free will, a magnificent gift that Lucifer was certain would be squandered by these hairless monkeys that had so captured the Allfather's eyes.

Malachi had been there when the first had been placed in the Garden created for them. The elder had felt his disdain grow as he watched the creature move through the lush jungle, asserting its mastery over the lesser life that already lived there.

And then there were two, male and female, with the ability to create more of their own kind, to propagate a species in their garden habitat.

Oh, how the Lord God had loved them, but Lucifer's warnings had left their mark. The idea that these creatures would bring Him great sadness must have worried the Creator. And so to prove a point, He fashioned a test.

In the Garden the Almighty had grown a Tree; and in this Tree He had infused His knowledge, and He forbade His creations from feeding from this Tree, telling them that no other fruit would be forbidden them—except for the bounty of this Tree.

This Tree of Knowledge.

Malachi was amused; having observed the humans and their innate curiosity, he knew it was only a matter of time before they disobeyed their Creator. But they did not partake of the Tree's fruit, choosing instead to avoid the tree that God had forbidden them to feast upon.

The elder angel wasn't sure when the obsession had taken root, but he soon found himself thinking of the Tree, and the fruit that hung swollen and ripe from its branches. He could feel the power radiating from the Tree, and he could have sworn that it called out to him, tempting him with its ripened promise of forbidden knowledge.

Malachi knew that it was not only the humans who were forbidden to partake, but his kind as well.

But try as he might, he could not forget the Tree's promise, and became consumed with the idea of partaking of the fruit.

Lucifer fit the plan that Malachi eventually formulated. Of course, he told the Son of the Morning about the Almighty's test for His newest creations. Lucifer's jealousy of God's new humans made him desperate to have his prediction come true, and so, armed with Malachi's tale of the Tree of Knowledge, the Morningstar walked the Garden in search of the humans. Clothed in his finest armor of Heaven-forged scale mail, the Morningstar found the pair—this Adam and Eve—and enticed them with a promise of godhood.

He drew them to the Tree, telling them that they could sit at the right hand of God—all they needed to do was ignore His command.

The humans were afraid of their God, and what might happen if they were to disobey Him, but the silver-tongued Lucifer reassured them that He would be unable to do anything, for they would be like Him.

They would be His equals.

Malachi remembered the joy he felt as he watched the female approach the Tree, reaching up with trembling hands to grab hold of one of the fruits, swollen with knowledge of God.

Will she do it? he wondered. Had Lucifer managed to convince them to disobey their most Holy Father?

He had.

The fruit came away in her hands, and she stared at it with great longing before bringing it to her mouth. Adam was soon beside her, fear in his gaze, but her confidence won him over, so desperate was their desire to be like Him whom they loved so very much.

So Adam joined his mate, and both partook of the forbidden fruit.

The Lord God Almighty was not pleased.

The Garden of Eden was besieged by a terrible storm reflecting God's anger with His rebellious creations.

The humans ran away in fear, chased by the fury of God's wrath, dropping what remained of the special fruit.

And in all the excitement, while no one was watching, Malachi retrieved that piece of fruit from the storm-swept ground, holding what he believed to be his destiny in his hands.

As the humans were tempted, so was he. The elder angel brought the future to his mouth, and tasted it.

And he saw.

Hell

"I saw as He saw," Malachi said aloud, twisting the blade of his scalpel ever so carefully within Francis's brain.

The former Guardian cried out, straining against the straps that held him to the stone table.

"I gazed into a future of chaos, and the inevitable end of all things."

Malachi stepped back, his surgical tool in hand.

"How could I allow something like that to occur, I ask you?" he said, seeming to confide in his captive. "The fall of the humans and their banishment from Eden was just the beginning . . . the catalyst for the nightmare to follow."

Malachi stopped for a moment and listened to the sounds of a world changing outside the caves.

"It wasn't long after that we were at war," the elder continued. "The humans' failure proved that Lucifer was right—that humanity was not the answer—but the Allfather did not listen, still faithful to what He perceived to be His greatest creations."

Malachi looked down at the suffering Guardian's glazed and unfocused eyes. He wasn't sure how much more the fallen angel could withstand, but he had to find it.

He had to find what had been so expertly hidden away for just this precise time.

"The war, as horrible as it was, provided me with the perfect cover," Malachi said. "The perfect distraction to set my own plans for the future—*for my destiny*—in motion."

He leaned in close again, tenderly stroking the Guardian's sweat-soaked brow.

"I just want you to know how important you are to the coming future, and how much I appreciate all that you've done, and what you are about to sacrifice."

"I...I don't have a...a fucking clue...what...you're...talking about," Francis managed.

"Which is how it was supposed to be," Malachi said, pressing his hand more firmly against Francis's brow, holding his head steady on the stone table. "It was all part of the plan."

Malachi placed the blade in the corner of Francis's left eye and slowly pushed it into his brain.

"You've been holding something for me," the elder said, twisting the blade and making Francis shriek.

"Now all I have to do is find it."

Remy and Jon sat by the wood-burning stove so that their clothes might dry.

"How do you like your coffee?" Izzy asked from the tiny kitchenette.

"Black is good," Remy said.

"Do you have any cream?" Jon asked, trembling from the dampness.

"Got no cream," Izzy snarled, handing Remy his cup.

"Then black is good," Jon said.

"It sure is," Izzy muttered as she returned to the stove for Jon's cup and her own.

She handed Jon his coffee and sat down in a lounge chair across from them. "I hate to break it to you, but you two almost got yourselves killed for nothing."

"How so?" Remy asked after taking a sip of the scalding hot brew. It was good, or maybe it wasn't; maybe it was just because he hadn't had a cup of coffee in a while.

"You're looking for my mama, and I don't have a clue as to where she is."

"You couldn't have just told us that?" Remy asked. "Maybe skip the whole siccing-the-swamp-on-us business?"

Izzy laughed. "Now, what would have been the fun in that?"

"We spoke the truth, you know," Jon said. "We don't mean you or your mother any harm. We've come on a mission of forgiveness."

"For who?" Izzy asked, scrunching up her face.

"Eden is coming," Jon said. "You must have sensed it."

"I've been having a lot of dreams," Izzy admitted, holding her coffee mug in one hand as she rubbed her eyes. "I figured something was up, which is why I was ready for you." She blinked several times as she brought the mug to her mouth. "You still haven't told me who's being forgiven."

"The first father," Jon said.

She looked a little confused.

"Adam," he said. "Adam is dying and wants to be buried in Eden."

"*Adam* Adam?" she asked incredulously. "Are you serious? He's still kickin'?"

"Yes," Jon responded. "He's . . . still kicking, but we need your mother . . . the other half of the key to gain entrance to Eden once it returns."

"Too bad Eve can't have that same luxury," Izzy said angrily as she set her mug down on a tray table beside her chair.

"It is too bad," Jon said. "But there's nothing we can do now to change what happened in the past. It was a long time ago, and my brethren believed—misguidedly—that the way to forgiveness was to punish the sinner."

"It takes two to tango. You idiots burned her alive," Izzy spat angrily.

Remy had heard that during the early 1600s the Sons of Adam had found Mother Eve and, in an attempt to make things right with the Almighty, had sacrificed her on a burning pyre. The relationship between the Daughters and the Sons had been toxic ever since.

"An act that I did not believe in," Jon assured her.

"Aren't you something wonderful." Izzy gave him a look that could seriously maim, if not kill. "I couldn't help you find my mother . . . this other half of the key you're lookin' for, if I wanted to. My father feared for her safety and hid her someplace that I don't even know."

"Your father," Remy said as he sipped his cooling coffee. "He wasn't human, was he?"

Izzy looked at him with anger in her eyes. "Who are you to call my daddy—"

"He was like me, wasn't he?"

Remy had felt the touch of the divine in the way that she'd manipulated the elements. He had no doubt that she was the product of the mating of angel and human. Although he was surprised that she hadn't been driven completely insane by the angelic side of her nature, as was the case most of the time.

"Let's just say he was something special," Izzy said. "Just like my mama." She became very quiet, gazing into her coffee mug, and Remy could hear the sound of thunder in the distance as her mood affected the elements.

"What do you want from me?" she finally asked. "I can't tell you where she is, or even if she's still alive . . . though I think I'd know if she was dead, but that's beside the point. I don't know where my daddy hid her; he disappeared not long after that. He didn't want to draw attention to me or the Daughters."

"Attention from whom?" Remy asked her.

Izzy stared past them as she remembered. "The angels," she said. "I saw them once ... after Ma had already been hid. Daddy was talking to them."

Remy was confused. He'd thought the threat came from the Cherubim, but her words suggested otherwise, that new players had just entered the field.

"There was more than one?" he asked.

"Yeah," she said, her eyes glazing over as she remembered. "They were like miniature suns, fireballs covered in eyes, lighting up the darkness of the swamp."

Remy physically reacted. The Thrones. What the hell did they have to do with this?

"They weren't happy with my daddy at all," she mused with a smile. "Wasn't long after that he disappeared ... but not before telling me to watch out for folks looking for my mother ... and to show them that it wasn't healthy for them to be doing so."

Remy's mind was buzzing as he tried to keep up.

"What was your father's name?"

"Pearly," she said with a huge smile. "Pearly Gates."

A gaping pit opened in Remy's stomach.

"Pearly Gates?" he repeated, just to be sure he had heard correctly, although he knew he had.

Izzy nodded. "I don't remember him as good as I'd like, but what I do know is that he was something special." She paused, lost in a memory. "I remember him being kinda sad," she said after a moment. "Like he had done something bad, and he was trying to make up for it. But he was good to me and my mama, and he made me promise to be strong when Mama, and then he, had to go away."

Tears had started to leak from her eyes, trailing down her high cheekbones, and Izzy quickly wiped them away.

"And I have been strong," she said. "Strong for a very long time."

Jon set his half-drunk mug of coffee down at his feet.

"Is that it, then?" he asked, obviously exasperated. "The vision I was given goes no further. If she's not here ..."

"Don't give up just yet," Remy said, cautiously optimistic. Things were suddenly ... strangely, falling into place.

"Your mother and father," he said to Izzy. "You wouldn't happen to have any photos of them, would you?"

Izzy stared at him, her demeanor very still. It was almost as if she didn't want to share what little she had of her parents with them.

"I don't have much," she said. "It's practically nothing."

"That's fine," Remy said. "I would just like to see them . . . if that's all right."

He could feel Jon staring at him, anxious to know what he was up to.

Izzy hesitated.

"Please?" Remy flashed her a smile that he'd been told once or twice was quite charming, although that had come from his wife, and she'd had a tendency to lie to make him feel better, or to get what she wanted.

But it worked this time too. Izzy got up from her chair, leaving the cramped living room space and disappearing through a doorway into what Remy figured was her bedroom.

"What's this about?" Jon asked. "How could her pictures help us in—"

"Trust me," Remy told him, as the woman returned carrying a wrinkled paper bag.

"I've been meaning to get a book," she said, plopping down into her seat and opening the bag. "Y'know, one of those books you put pictures in?"

"A photo album?" Remy suggested.

"Yeah, yeah, a photo album . . . I need one of those."

She removed a stack of old photos and began to shuffle through them. "Most of these are just friends who helped raise me after my folks were gone."

And then her face lit up with a smile as she stopped at one photo in particular. "Here it is," she said. "I guess she was quite the singer when she was young."

Hesitantly, she handed the picture over to Remy.

Remy recognized the woman at once—much younger, of course, but there was no mistaking Fernita Green.

"This is your mother?" he asked.

"Yes."

"Your mother is Fernita Green," he said.

Izzy's face scrunched up. "No." She took the picture back. "My mother's name is Eliza Swan."

Remy's heart began to race. His mind immediately went to his many visits with the old woman he knew as Fernita Green, her missing memories, how she was looking for something very important that she'd lost.

Now Remy knew what that something was. And he also knew that he might just have put a very good friend in a lot of danger.

Jon was staring at him, trying to read the expression on his face.

"What is it?" he started to ask, but was interrupted by Izzy, who was handing another photograph to Remy.

"This is the only one I have of my dad," she said. "I don't know what it was for, or who even took it, but one of the Daughters gave it to me to remember him by."

The picture was old and grainy. It looked as though it might have been taken inside some sort of club. All the patrons were black, and Remy recognized a young Fernita Green—Eliza Swan—singing on a stage.

"Daddy's the one in the front row staring at Mama as if there wasn't another living person on the planet," Izzy said proudly.

The photo was black-and-white, and the man whom Izzy pointed out as her father was a tad blurry, but he looked pretty much the same as the last time Remy had seen him, other than having a little bit more hair—and being black.

Remy knew Pearly Gates by another name.

He knew him as Francis, and suddenly things became a whole lot more interesting.

And dangerous.

"We have to leave," Remy said, standing quickly. "We have to get back to Massachusetts right away."

CHAPTER TWELVE

Hell

The memories actually helped to lessen the pain.

Francis let his mind go, allowing the buried recollections to float to the surface as they attempted to squeeze themselves between what he did remember, changing the past to something altogether new.

Brockton, Massachusetts: 1953

Eliza was crying.

She understood why it had to be this way, but it didn't make it any easier to accept.

"How much will it take from me?" she asked softly.

Pearly knelt at the base of the wall, drawing strange symbols with a black paint that he'd made from crushing hard-shelled beans grown inside a dead man's skull, and mixing the powder with a bit of blood from each of them.

"Most," he said, working on the symbols from memory. They had to be laid out just right, or they wouldn't work.

"You?" she asked, her voice trembling. "Izzy?"

The mention of their child just about broke him. He had never imagined he could feel such pain.

"I'll mostly be gone," he said, feeling as if the blade of his Enochian dagger had been thrust through his heart. This whole situation was killing him, but he kept telling

himself over and over again that it was for her own good—it
would keep her alive.

If he didn't . . . if they stayed together . . . she was as good
as dead.

"You'll remember me as somebody you knew . . . but
little more than an acquaintance."

The forces of Heaven wanted Eliza Swan dead, and
Pearly was going to do everything in his power to see that
they didn't get their way. The magick originally used to
hide her from the Thrones would work on beings of that
power level for only so long, which was why Malachi had
suggested something more . . . permanent.

Eliza began to sob, and Pearly had to fight the urge to go
to her, to take her into his arms and tell her that everything
would be all right.

Because then he'd be lying.

Everything wasn't going to be all right.

When he finished this spell, her memory would be incomplete; huge gaps of her past would be missing; characteristics that defined her as who she was as a person, gone.

In effect, she would be somebody else.

The elder had told him to take her away, to hide her
from the eyes of those who would do her harm. He still
wasn't sure why Malachi was so keen to protect her, other
than the fact that he had said she was special . . . and important for the future. It made Pearly a little uncomfortable,
but he would do anything to protect Eliza.

Massachusetts was as good a place as any. The former
Guardian angel had always had a fondness for New England. And he had met somebody very special here once,
one of his own—an angel of Heaven—and his being here,
in the same state as Eliza, made Pearly feel that much safer
about leaving her.

He stopped his work momentarily, wiping his hands
upon a rag before reaching into his back pocket for his wallet. He removed a business card—the Seraphim's business
card. He lived among the humans, as a human. This angel—
this Remy Chandler—helped them as a private investigator. A detective.

"Take this," he told Eliza, handing her the business card.

"Who is it?" she asked, her voice still shaking with emotion as she read the card.

"If there ever comes a time that you need help," he assured her, "this man will help you. That's what he does ... he helps people."

Her lips mouthed the name.

"I don't understand," she said as the tears flowed from her eyes.

"You will if it's necessary," he said. "He's a good man...."

"Like you?" Eliza said, reaching out to touch his face, but he stepped away to avoid her tender touch.

"Not like me at all," Pearly said, the faces of the angels and the men that he'd killed in service to the Thrones flashing before his mind's eye.

He returned to his work, finishing the last of the sigils before climbing slowly to his feet.

Eliza had become strangely quiet. Pearly turned toward her and found her simply standing, staring off into space, not noticing him, the angelic magick already going to work on her.

He hated this more than anything he'd ever experienced in his very long existence, but Malachi had said that it was necessary to protect her. And Pearly would do anything in his power to keep her safe.

Even if it meant losing her forever.

He watched her as she stood there, her eyes glazed as they traced the symbols drawn upon the wall. And as her eyes finished their review, the marks gradually faded away, blending with the paint of the wall.

She wouldn't even know they were there, keeping her hidden from those who wished to do her harm.

Pearly stood beside her, resisting the urge to reach out to her, resisting the urge to take her into his arms and hold her for one last time. She would be safe here in the life he had created for her. The house was paid for, and there was money in a special bank account, the residuals of his being on the Earth for so many years, and having such a knack for killing. Somebody always wanted someone dead, and he was more than happy to oblige—for a price—when not kowtowing to the Thrones.

He wanted to tell her that he loved her, and that he was sorry. . . .

But she didn't even know he was there.

Eliza blinked her beautiful brown eyes, and then went about her business, humming a tune, strangely off-key, as she assumed the functions of her new life. Even her talent for song had been taken away.

Pearly stopped at the door for one final look. She was in the kitchen, putting some glasses away in the cabinet.

"You take care of yourself, Fernita Green," he called out, using her new name.

Then he opened the door and stepped out into the New England cold. He liked this part of the world, the change in seasons. He hoped that Eliza . . . Fernita . . . would like it too.

Francis took one final look at the house in the quiet Brockton neighborhood as he stood upon the walk.

He had never imagined that he could feel such pain, and not even have a sword plunged through his chest.

Malachi had been very specific that they meet after he had hidden Eliza away. The abandoned church in Italy's San Genesio seemed just as good a place as any.

Francis pushed open the door and stepped into the run-down structure to see the elder sitting in one of the pews, gazing up to where a crucifix had once hung. There was a stain against the yellow wall over the altar in the shape of the cross.

"Is it done?" Malachi asked, not even turning around.

"Yeah," Francis replied, the weight of the word nearly exhausting.

"And nobody knows her location but you?" The elder angel turned his head ever so slightly.

"That's right," Francis said. "Only me."

Malachi left the pew and came to stand before him.

"Then everything is as it should be," he said.

Malachi then reached into the inside pocket of the suit jacket he wore and removed a scalpel. The light from the blade was momentarily blinding, and Francis reflexively stepped back.

"What's that for?" he asked.

"The final step," Malachi answered.

Francis didn't quite understand.

"It's to take that very important memory away," the elder explained.

"You're going to cut out my memory?"

"Not exactly," Malachi said. "I'm going to take it and move it to someplace else in your mind. Someplace where it will be waiting when we need it."

Francis considered that.

"Will I still remember her?"

Slowly, Malachi shook his head.

"All your memories of her will be put away," the elder explained. "That way no one will ever know where to find her . . . until it's necessary."

"And when will that be?"

Malachi turned back to the altar, gazing at the cross-shaped stain upon the wall.

"When it is time," he said. "When all the pieces have fallen into place."

Francis was suddenly afraid. He wanted to know exactly what all of this meant. He wanted to know exactly what role he and Eliza played in Malachi's vision of the future.

The questions were just about to flow when Malachi turned back to him, scalpel of light still in his hand.

And before the words could leave Francis's lips, the blade shot toward him.

Cutting away the brightest light he had ever known, and leaving behind only the darkness.

Hell

Malachi dug deeply within the angel's brain, allowing the flow of memories to bleed out, flowing into and up through the scalpel and into the elder's own mind.

"There you are," the angel said with a joyous grin, digging deeper beneath the gelatinous folds to find—at last—what he had been seeking.

"Just a little bit deeper," he said to Francis, who twitched about on the verge of death beneath the elder's ministrations.

"And I should have it all."

"You have me," the angel said, opening his palms to show that he was unarmed.

Francis blinked wildly, momentarily unsure of what had just occurred. He had completed a side job in Italy when he had sensed the nearly overpowering presence of one of his own.

An angel of incredible power somewhere close by.

He had found the angel in the church: Malachi, he believed he was called, an important angel of the highest order that had betrayed the Lord of Lords during the Great War.

Malachi had sided with the Morningstar, but fled to Earth after the rebellion was squelched. If Francis's memory served him correctly, the Thrones wanted this one very, very badly.

Francis had a gun in his hand, and it was pointed at his quarry.

He wasn't sure whether the Thrones wanted this one dead or alive, but he was more than willing to use the Colt .45 loaded with special bullets made from lead mined from the resources of Hell, bullets that could end an angel of Heaven despite its divinity.

"Are you going to kill me?" the angel asked.

Francis was tempted, but at the same time could feel little malice for the betrayer, for he too had fallen under Lucifer's spell.

Although Francis had realized the error of his ways.

"All depends on how hard you want to make this, or how merciful I'm feeling at the moment."

The angel just stared.

"I could end it now for you," Francis said. "One shot to the head would take it all away."

"Yes," Malachi said. "Yes, it would."

"They'll put you in Tartarus," Francis told him. He had seen the prison, and had often been threatened with a cell there by the Thrones. He wasn't certain which would be worse: death or time spent in the Hell prison.

"They will," Malachi said, seemingly resigned to the idea.

"And that's all right with you?"

"It's how it is supposed to be," the renegade angel said.

And suddenly there was a sound like the loudest thunder, and the air behind them began to tremble and bend as a passage was opened from the other side. The Thrones were again upon the world of God's man.

Four of the flaming, eye-covered orbs floated from the opening out into the church, lining up in a row behind Francis.

"Thought you might be interested," he said, pistol still pointed at the angel called Malachi.

"We are," the Thrones answered as one.

Malachi stood with his hands crossed before him, eyes upon the Thrones.

"Didn't know if you wanted this one dead or—"

"No," the Thrones hissed. "This one must be made to suffer," they said as one.

The four floated around Francis and encircled the renegade.

"What have you been doing?" they asked the elder angel directly, their voices eager. "Share with us, and your penance will be less . . . harsh."

"It's as if you believe I've been up to no good," Malachi said, and chuckled.

"Tell us," the flaming orbs covered in bulging eyes demanded.

"There's nothing to tell."

Tentacles of fire shot out from the bodies of the Thrones, enwrapping the elder angel in their fiery grasp.

The angel was burning, but he did not scream.

"What do you think he did?" Francis asked, disturbed by the sight of Malachi's flesh bubbling—melting—as the

Thrones' fiery appendages continued to entwine and caress.

The Thrones ignored the question, converging on the elder as his body began to tremble from the agony he was experiencing.

But still he did not cry out.

Francis had seen a lot of terrible things in his long life, and this had to be right up there with the worst. The Thrones must have had a serious mad-on for this guy for them to be paying this much attention to him.

Malachi had dropped to his knees, head drooping to his chest. His hair was on fire now, his blackened scalp starting to show the seared bone of his skull.

Francis still pointed his weapon, feeling his trigger finger begin to itch. He was tempted to fire, to put one shot in the angel's head to end his torment. Nobody deserved this.

"Keep it up and there won't be anything left for Tartarus," he called out.

The Thrones' multiple sets of eyes darted quickly to him, bulging at his insolence. He half expected to feel those tentacles wrapping around him at any second.

"The fallen Guardian is correct," the Thrones said, withdrawing their hold on Malachi as he crouched there, smoldering from their touch.

The air behind them began to vibrate and blur as a passage for their departure was summoned. Francis could see the forbidding shape of the icy prison fortress, Tartarus, behind them, stepping back as the acute smell of brimstone and despair wafted out from the opening.

The Thrones again took hold of the charred and still-smoking angel, dragging him toward the passage and a fate more horrible than an eternity of death.

Malachi's head bobbed as he was pulled through the pulsing rip in the fabric of time and space, slowly lifting his chin to look at him just as he passed over the threshold from the realm of Earth, into Hell.

"It's how it is supposed to be," Malachi said through cracked and blistered lips, seemingly accepting his fate.

Then the doorway began to waver, the passage to Hell's prison closing up behind them.

Hell

Malachi admired the glint of his blade.

The information he had been seeking for so very long, extracted from the brain of the fallen Guardian, dangled wetly from its tip.

"Hello, lovely," he purred.

How long had he waited for this moment? The elder truly couldn't say. The time spent confined within an icy cell in Tartarus had seemed like an eternity. But he'd had his transgressions to keep him company, and his plans for the future of the universe, while he patiently waited for the inevitable to occur.

The fruit of the Tree had shown him a possible future; he just needed to have the patience to wait for it to happen.

"Eliza," Francis hissed from the stone table below him.

Malachi glanced down at the former Guardian, whose gaze was locked upon the drop of hidden knowledge hanging from the edge of the scalpel.

"Oh, yes," the elder agreed. "It's all about the lovely Eliza ... without whom I would never be able to enter the Garden."

Francis struggled to speak. "Hidden ..."

"Yes ... yes, she was, but now she is found," Malachi said happily. "I would thank you for keeping this for me, but I seriously doubt you'd accept my gratitude."

He watched as Francis's mouth moved fitfully as it attempted to shape more words.

"What is it?" Malachi asked. "Are you going to prove me wrong?"

"K-kill you," Francis managed, eyes blazing with a repressed rage.

"You would try, wouldn't you," Malachi told him. "The only hope for the future and you would see it dead." He shook his head in disgust. "It's how we have come to this," Malachi proclaimed. He motioned toward the passage from the cave. The howls and rumbles of Hell were all the louder.

"The Morningstar is free, and here we are at the precipice of war once more . . . all of creation hanging in the balance. It's time for a level head to prevail."

Malachi held the scalpel up to his face and studied the thread of knowledge, careful not to let it fall. His servant in the world beyond needed it. With a quick jab, he plunged the razor-sharp instrument, and the retrieved information resting on the tip, through the flesh of his forehead and on into his skull.

Malachi gasped aloud as he felt the scalpel blade—and the prized knowledge—enter his mind in a heated rush that was not too far from pleasurable.

"There," the elder said, yanking the surgical tool from his head with nary a drop of blood. "He should have everything he needs."

He returned his attention to Francis.

"And we are that much closer to success."

The former Guardian glared up at him weakly, hate shooting from his eyes. Malachi hadn't expect him to understand. Francis was part of the old ways, averse to change, even though it was all for the better.

Malachi leaned closer, the dim light of the cave reflecting off the scalpel in his hand. He could see Francis tense, but instead of cutting his flesh, Malachi cut through the leather straps that bound the fallen angel.

Malachi stepped back, watching as Francis slowly—painfully—sat up.

"I—I don't understand," Francis squeaked, his voice dry.

"Of course you don't," Malachi told him. "You're really not supposed to."

Francis carefully slid his bare legs over the side of the stone platform, letting his feet dangle.

"What now?" he asked, far too weak to do much of anything else.

"Now, that's the proper attitude," Malachi said with a nod and a grin. "There is actually one more thing you must do for me."

*   *   *

Mulvehill wasn't at all familiar with the back roads of Brockton, but that didn't prevent him from driving like a bat out of hell.

He thought about asking the old woman where they were, but doubted that she was in any mental state to tell him.

Christ, I'm barely in the mental state to drive.

The road was empty, and that was good. He hated to think his speed would hurt anyone. He risked a quick glance at Fernita, buckled into the passenger seat next to him. She appeared to be in a kind of catatonia, staring ahead through the windshield, mouth slightly agape. He considered asking her whether everything was all right, but figured he already knew the answer to that.

The image of something huge dropping from the sky and crashing through the old lady's roof flashed before his eyes again, and he got that awful tickling sensation in his crotch that told him if he wasn't such a big boy, he would have been pissing himself.

It was nice to see that he at least had control of that.

There was a turn up ahead and Steven took it—big mistake. It turned out to be a private drive, leading to what appeared to be an unfinished housing development.

"Ah, shit," he grumbled, bringing the car to a complete stop, and then throwing it in reverse. He thought about giving Remy a call again, but decided that he didn't want his blood pressure getting any higher. When—*if*—Mulvehill ever saw him again, Remy would be buying the homicide cop twenty-five-year-old Scotch every week for years, taking him out to Morton's for breakfast, lunch, and dinner, and then to the nearest Kappy's for more Scotch just for good measure.

That would fix him.

Mulvehill backed out of the dead end and slammed the car into drive, hitting the gas just as the sky—or at least a piece of it—fell into the road in front of them.

It landed with an explosion of asphalt and dirt, but it didn't slow him down. It couldn't. Mulvehill knew deep in his gut that he had to keep going forward, to get them out of there before ...

His thinking stopped. It had no experience with things like this, so it had nowhere else to go. All he knew was that they had to escape or something very bad was going to happen to them.

"Hold on," he told Fernita, trying to sound calm, as if this were something he did all the time, but he was sure it came out high and squeaky, like some fucking cartoon character.

The air was filled with thick, choking dust, but Mulvehill swerved to the left and drove right through it—only to come to an abrupt stop. Both he and Fernita pitched forward before their seat belts snapped them back. Mulvehill's foot was still on the gas, and he could hear the engine screaming—feel the tires spinning, but they weren't going anywhere.

Eyes darting up to the rearview mirror, he tried to see through the dust behind them. Something—something huge—had the bumper in its grip and it wasn't going to let them go.

Mulvehill put the car in reverse and gunned the engine, sending the car rocketing backward to hit something horribly solid. He snapped the gear to drive and stomped on the gas pedal. This time the car shot forward, but the damage to the back end made it difficult to control and they fishtailed off the road and careened down an embankment.

Fernita screamed as branches whipped at the windshield and boulders tore at the underside of the car, their out-of-control descent coming to an abrupt and violent stop when they hit the base of an old oak tree. The front of the car crumpled like an accordion.

Now Remy owes me a fucking car, Mulvehill thought just before his forehead bounced off the soft center of the steering wheel, making the horn toot briefly and his brain vibrate painfully inside his skull.

He thought he might like to grab a little nap, but frantic hands were shaking him.

"Hey," Fernita called. Mulvehill was going to tell her to

leave him alone, but the sound of sheer panic in her voice roused him more fully, and he remembered their situation.

"I've got it," he said groggily, having no real idea what that meant, but he was already on the move, undoing his seat belt and pushing open the driver's-side door. The ground was at an incline, and he dropped to his knees, sliding a bit toward the front of his car before regaining his footing. Steam hissed from the obliterated radiator, and he again cursed the name of Remy Chandler as he hauled himself up and around the back of the car to get Fernita. Pulling open the door, he leaned inside to help her undo the seat belt.

"Leave me here," she said quietly, and he stopped, staring through the thick lenses of her glasses into her deep brown eyes filled with panic.

"What are you talking about?"

"It doesn't want you," she said. "Leave me and get yourself away from here."

"Like hell I will," he said, and practically pulled her from the seat. "Be careful here," he told her. "The ground isn't level and . . ."

A roar from the direction of the road interrupted him. It was like the blast of an eighteen-wheeler's air horn, only with more of an I-want-to-kill-and-eat-you kind of vibe to it.

Mulvehill had never heard of an angel who did anything like that, but he also knew there was quite a lot he didn't know about angels and the like.

That he didn't *want* to know.

Fernita looked at him hopelessly, and he felt a shiver go through her thin frame.

"C'mon," he said, helping her down into the wooded area. He had no idea where they were going, but figured the farther away from this particular spot they were, the better off they'd be.

The old woman was doing far better than he would have expected. Mulvehill held her arm as they traversed the uneven terrain. He didn't hear the horrible roaring again, and wondered if perhaps whatever it was that was chasing them had given up and gone after easier prey.

An old woman and an out-of-shape homicide cop—how much fucking easier could it be?

And suddenly their pursuer passed over them in a powerful rush of freezing air, leaving torn branches and withered leaves from the winter trees in its wake. It was moving so fast that Mulvehill couldn't even see it, but he could hear it, the sound of its powerful, flapping wings as they ravaged the air.

Fernita slowed, cowering against him as she searched the open air above them.

"Keep moving," Mulvehill ordered, pulling her along.

The angel dropped heavily into the woods, landing in a disturbance of fallen leaves.

Fernita gasped as they looked upon it, and Mulvehill found that he had stopped breathing, a terrible tightness forming in his chest reminding him that he'd be dead all the sooner if he didn't take oxygen into his lungs.

Would that have been the better way to go?

It was like no angel that he had ever imagined, more monstrous than heavenly.

It crouched on all fours, but he could tell that it was huge. Its powerful body was covered in filthy armor that hinted at something once beautiful to behold. Mulvehill could just about make out intricate etchings beneath the layers of grime on the tarnished, golden metal plates that covered its large body.

But it was the face—*faces*—that made that terrible feeling in his lower regions return, and he had to make a conscious effort not to embarrass himself. The angel had one large head, but three faces—an eagle, a human, and the face of a lion, all side by side, forming one nightmarish appearance.

And they were all looking at him and Fernita with murder in their gazes.

The monster angel tensed, and Mulvehill could see that it was about ready to pounce. He reacted instinctively, reaching beneath his arm to draw his gun, chamber a round, and fire four times into the many faces.

"Go!" he cried to Fernita, not sure how far the old

woman could get on her own, but wanting at least to give her a chance.

The angel reared back, one of its armor-covered hands wiping at its faces. The bullets must have at least annoyed it.

It wasn't much, but it was something.

He glanced quickly over his shoulder to see how far Fernita had gotten, and was surprised and happy to see that her old legs had taken her into a more densely wooded area.

About to take off himself, he turned back to find the angel directly in front of him. He hadn't even heard it move, and there it was, as big as life, looming over him and smelling like an overheated truck engine. Mulvehill raised his weapon, aiming for the human eyes.

But the angel had had enough of that, thank you very much.

It bellowed, a deafening sound, before reaching down with one of its clawed, metal-covered hands to rip away the gun and toss it above the treetops.

Mulvehill cried out as two of his fingers snapped like twigs.

If somebody had described this scenario to him, he would have imagined himself curled in the fetal position on the ground, but instead he felt more angry than anything else.

Angry that two of his fingers had been broken . . . angry that his favorite gun had been tossed away into the woods . . . angry that he was probably going to die at the hands of something that he had been taught as a child was a thing of beauty and a loving servant to God.

And more specifically, he was angry at Remy Chandler for kicking open the doorway and exposing him to a world that he shouldn't even know existed.

The anger boiled up inside him, and he reacted, hauling off and punching the monstrous thing of Heaven in the faces as hard as he could with his unbroken hand.

The angel recoiled, its many eyes at first expressing surprise, but then the lion pulled back the flesh of its maw, showing off fearsome teeth, and Mulvehill was sure he was about to be eaten.

When there was a voice.

"Hello, Zophiel, what do you have there?"

The monster angel spun around, its multiple sets of wings unfurling in a defensive posture.

As the heavenly creature moved, Mulvehill could see who had spoken. It was an older guy, maybe someone who had seen his wrecked car from the road and come down to help.

Mulvehill almost screamed for the man to run away, but something about his appearance stopped him. Something told Mulvehill that this probably wasn't just a normal man. That he was something else entirely . . . something of this strange new world that Mulvehill had been unceremoniously thrown into.

"You've been on the hunt for too long, Cherubim," the man with the white hair and beard said, a sly smile spreading across his face. "Wasting your time menacing a helpless human—is that not below you?"

"Malachi," the Cherubim said in an unearthly growl as it tensed and sprang, even more furious now than when Mulvehill had shot it in its faces.

"You are the cause of this," the monster angel roared, landing upon the stranger and driving him back to the frozen ground.

Mulvehill clutched his injured hand to his chest and stumbled back, away from the impending carnage.

The stranger appeared helpless beneath the bulk of the armored attacker, but then the homicide cop heard the oddest of things—laughter.

As the angel lay upon the man, armored claws reaching down to tear and rend its prey, the stranger was laughing.

The sound of merriment only proved to enrage the angelic beast all the more. Its body glowed with an unearthly light, and liquid fire began to drip from the tips of its hooked fingers and its three open mouths.

"And you have been a thorn in my Master's side long enough," the stranger announced, his expensive suit already starting to smolder and burn, but it seemed to have zero effect upon the person inside it.

Mulvehill was catching snippets of their heated debate. It was obvious that these two knew each other, and weren't the best of buds.

"Your fetid touch has brought me to the brink of madness," the Cherubim wailed, struggling to hold the stranger down. "For millennia I have fought the aftereffects of your influence, and only now am I able to see what must be done for Heaven to be saved."

The stranger was laughing all the harder now, even as his body began to change.

"Do you think my Master would sully his touch upon a worthless creation such as yourself?" asked the old man, who wasn't an old man anymore. "You're nothing more than a stupid beast . . . a guard dog that outlived its usefulness a very long time ago. . . ."

The stranger had become another creature, and Mulvehill hadn't a clue whether this was another kind of angel . . . or something more demonic.

Its skin was a dingy white, and covered with strange markings, like some of the tribal tats that he'd seen on many of the scumbags he'd arrested over the years.

"What madness is this?" the Cherubim hissed. "You are not the traitorous elder."

"I am what should have been," the pale, tattooed thing said, its body almost like liquid as it flowed around the now struggling Cherubim. "And what will be very, very soon."

"You are an abomination!" Zophiel bellowed, panic clearly in its voice. "The Lord God would never allow you to exist, Shaitan!"

The pale-skinned thing had wrapped multiple limbs around its foe, powerful, knifelike fingers attempting to make their way between the seams of the angel's armor. Zophiel's movments were frenzied, its four wings flapping wildly as it attempted to flee the battleground, but its equally monstrous attacker would not allow it, the liquid flesh of the shape-changing foe slithering onto the Cherubim's wings, preventing flight.

"Then we shall need to do something about the Lord God," the new aggressor spoke. "But first things first."

The pale-skinned thing spread across Zophiel's body, constricting the Cherubim's four mighty wings and wrapping around its throat.

Mulvehill knew that he should be getting the hell out of there, but he couldn't take his eyes from the epic struggle before him. He had no idea whom to root for, sensing that either of these creatures would be the death of him—and Fernita.

It didn't look good for the Cherubim. The shape-shifting thing had almost completely enveloped the angel's armored form. At that point Mulvehill decided that he should probably move along, and had just started to turn when the Cherubim let loose a deafening cry, equal parts scream and thunderous roar. The angel's fury echoed through the winter woods, the tormented sound shaking free the dead leaves that still clung to the trees.

Zophiel tore away the liquid flesh of its attacker, the Cherubim's armored form now glowing white-hot with the heat of its divine body.

The pale, tattooed thing writhed upon the frozen ground, steam rising from its smoldering body, but within only seconds it appeared fine, returning to its more human shape to taunt its Cherubim foe.

"You have met your better, sentry," the shape-changer said. "Accept your fate now, for your kind, and all the hosts of Heaven, will soon bow before my brothers and sisters. The Almighty will be made to see the error of His ways, and a great change will be brought upon the Shining Kingdom and all the worlds that bask in the light of its glory."

Mulvehill started to back away as muscular tentacles shot out from the tatooed beast's body toward the angel, whose form still glowed like white-hot metal.

"What now?" he said, running in the direction he'd last seen Fernita go, a battle of monsters still raging behind him.

Dreading what new insanity would be waiting ahead.

CHAPTER THIRTEEN

The dead man moved.

Fernita had been making her way through the woods, trying not to slip and fall, when she came across the body.

It was wrapped in an old red blanket, propped up against the base of a birch tree. She wanted to run past it, knowing she had to get as far away as she could from the monsters behind her, but she could not.

It was as if it were calling out, beckoning for her to come closer.

For a moment, Fernita hesitated, trying to force herself to go on, but her mind was filled with the images of a wondrous place of green, a jungle unlike anything she had ever seen.

The old woman stepped closer to the body.

And suddenly the memories came flooding back.

She remembered the place she saw when she opened her mouth and bared her soul in song. She remembered who she really was.

Pearly had tried to hide that too, but now Fernita Green was just another fading memory. She was Eliza Swan, and always had been.

Eliza could feel a song bubbling in her heart as she climbed over the mounds of frozen leaves and broken branches toward the body, a song starting to move from her heart—her soul—up through her chest and into her throat.

How long had it been since she had sung?

It started as a hum as the words came to her.

A song of Paradise, a song of the place she saw so vividly inside her head.

She stumbled then, her slippered foot catching on half-buried roots, and sprawled on all fours in front of the corpse. She reached out to steady herself, brushing against the dried, almost mummified flesh of the body's foot.

And the images that filled Eliza's head were explosive.

They came at her all at once, a sensory rush of pictures and emotions, and in the course of a moment she lived a lifetime, born into the Garden from the rib of a man....

This man before her.

She saw and felt it all: the temptation, the sin, the loss of innocence.

She could taste it in her mouth ... the taste of the fruit.

The taste of their fall from grace.

The sin had become part of them, following them from the Garden, growing in the hearts and souls of their bloodline. Never to be forgotten.

Never to be forgiven.

Until ... now.

Eliza recoiled, pulling her numbed hand away from the body. She had no idea what had just happened, but she understood what was on the horizon.

Eden was returning for him ... this corpse....

This man.

Eliza understood whose body it was that lay before her.

"Adam," she said, staring at the withered remains wrapped in the red blanket.

The corpse tilted its head ever so slightly toward the sound of her voice; its eyes slowly opened to look upon her.

And she began to scream.

He had worn the guise of his master for so long that Taranushi had actually started to believe that he was the elder angel Malachi.

But as he took his true form, he was reminded of the truth, and his purpose.

Taranushi was the first of the Shaitan: the beings of

darkness and fire that would soon replace the angels of Heaven.

He looked down upon his foe, tightening his grip upon him. The Cherubim was tired, the fight nearly drained from him.

The Shaitan momentarily took his dark eyes from the angel, and gazed off in the direction of the scream he had heard moments before. It was the one out there whom he wanted: she was the reason he was upon this Earth ... waiting.

Waiting for the Garden to arrive.

Taranushi turned his black-orb eyes back to the Cherubim. Still the angel pathetically struggled.

"Why can't you just die?" the Shaitan asked, aggravated now.

Heavenly fire leapt weakly from Zophiel's hands but it had no effect on the shape-shifter.

Again Taranushi looked off into the woods. If he did not act, she might elude him again. He knew that he should go.

In a display of savagery, Taranushi shaped his malleable form into something distinctly terrible, with claws and teeth so fierce that not even God's armor would protect. The Shaitan ravaged his foe, biting and clawing, ripping and tearing away pieces of the Cherubim's armor and the divine flesh beneath.

The blood of the angel was like the strongest of acids, but Taranushi used the pain as his fuel, maiming the heavenly sentry to the point where it struggled no more.

The Shaitan looked down into the faces of its foe, seeing in the many eyes expressions of failure. The Cherubim knew that his end was here, that he had been brought to the edge of death by his better.

His eyes begged for release, but the Shaitan did not know the meaning of mercy. Instead, he left the angel to die slowly as his life force poured from his torn flesh.

Once again the Shaitan assumed the dignified form of Malachi.

An appearance far less frightening to the human whom he sought.

The human who would grant him access to the Garden and bring about the birth of his people.

And the fall of Heaven.

Zophiel knew that he was dying, but it did not stop him from attempting to rise. The pain was great, but it did not compare to the agony he felt at the core of his being at the failure that had come to define him.

As he struggled to stand, his mind wandered back to the time when he'd discovered the threat to them all.

The threat to Heaven and to his Lord God.

If there was but one thing for which he could thank the monster that had mauled him, it was this moment . . . this clarity of thought. Impending death had cleared the fog from his damaged mind, and he saw what had brought him to the brink of madness.

He had been in the Garden of Eden after the fall of the humans, guarding the sacred place as the war with the Morningstar raged in Heaven. There had been rumors that Lucifer would try to take the Garden as his own, and Zophiel remembered his bravado. As long as he was sentry, nothing would dare threaten that holy place.

He had sensed a disturbance not far from the Tree of Knowledge, and upon investigating, had discovered several strange, fetal creatures writhing in the dirt at the base of the Tree. Zophiel was familiar with all the beasts in the Garden, but he had never seen the likes of these. They were pale, hairless, their bodies adorned with black sigils of power . . . sigils that caused the fire of his sword blade to ignite ominously as his six eyes passed over their odd shapes.

What are these . . . things? the Cherubim wondered, instincts attuned to danger already beginning to thrum.

And then an angel stepped into the clearing from the dense forest, holding one of the mewling life-forms lovingly in his arms. He was the elder Malachi, the one to whom God had given the gift of creation.

"What is this?" Zophiel remembered asking.

And the elder angel had explained that they were his

attempts to create a better servant for the Almighty—a better angel—that he had been secretly working on his Shaitan, as he called them, for quite some time.

Zophiel recalled his own reaction to the word *secretly*, and when prodded, Malachi explained that the Lord knew nothing of his experiment . . . that it would not be wise for Him to know about the creatures that would one day replace His Heavenly hosts.

The Cherubim was about to demand that Malachi explain himself, or be brought before the Thrones, when the elder did the unthinkable.

Malachi suddenly dropped the infant life-form to the ground and lunged at the sentry, dagger of light in hand.

Zophiel had no chance to react.

He remembered the pain as the blade slid through the middle of his faces, and how everything, in a matter of seconds, had turned to madness. The thoughts would not come; there were only pain and confusion. The need to retaliate, to strike back at the one who harmed him, who had threatened the Creator and all that He had built, was all a-jumble.

The dagger had brought about the insanity, and Zophiel was nothing more than a wild beast trying to remember the purpose of its rage.

But now he remembered.

Now, in time to die, he remembered.

Zophiel painfully spread his wings, blood leaking from his ravaged body to pool upon the frozen ground. He had to get away; he had to do something to stop Malachi.

The Cherubim leapt skyward, flying above the clouds.

Not sure how much longer he, or the Kingdom of Heaven, had left.

The screams had drifted off, but Mulvehill still surged ahead.

He listened as he wove between the trees, listening for the sound of pursuit, but so far there was nothing.

Maybe they killed each other, he thought, just as he found the old woman, kneeling in front of a birch tree. *Wouldn't that be something*.

"Fernita," he called, then caught sight of something wrapped in a red blanket leaning against the tree.

A body.

She turned at the sound of his voice, and he could see that her face was damp with tears, but there was something in her expression.

Something in her eyes.

Clarity. That was the only way to explain it.

"This is Adam," she said. "And he needs our help."

Mulvehill stepped forward and knelt beside Fernita. He was shocked by the condition of the body leaning against the tree. It reminded him of a mummy that he'd seen at the Museum of Science a few years back, only this mummy was somehow alive.

"I don't know how much time we have," he said, his eyes drawn to the dark, sunken orbs in the body's—in Adam's—skull. Mulvehill felt as though he were falling into them, suddenly feeling a sense of calm despite the current situation.

"You help him," Fernita said, holding on to Mulvehill's arm as she awkwardly climbed to her feet. "I'll be fine."

Mulvehill gently placed one arm behind Adam's back and the other under his knees, and carefully lifted him from the ground. His injured hand throbbed painfully with each rapid-fire beat of his heart, but he didn't have a choice. They had to move, and move now.

It was a little disconcerting, the corpselike figure in his arms seeming to weigh close to nothing. Skin and bones, that was all he was.

"If we head this way, I think we'll be close to the highway," Fernita said, leading them away.

There was that look again, Mulvehill observed as he followed with Adam. There was that clarity.

"Where do you think you're going?" a voice boomed from somewhere behind them.

Mulvehill spun around to see the white-haired, older gentleman, but he knew better. He was about to tell Fernita to run faster, when the bearded man was suddenly right in front of him, his movement a blur.

"I believe you have something that belongs to me, monkey," the thing wearing the mask of humanity said with a knowing smile. It knew that Mulvehill was aware of its deception. "Give him to me," he demanded, holding out his arms.

"Why don't you go fuck yourself?" Mulvehill said, knowing that probably wasn't the smartest thing to say.

The figure before him stared blankly before seeming to explode. First there was a bearded guy in a suit, and then there wasn't—the man's shape flowing up and out, expanding and contracting as it became something else.

A thick tentacle of pale, tattoo-adorned flesh lashed out, slapping Mulvehill with such speed and ferocity that he found himself airborne before striking a nearby tree and dropping to the frozen earth in a heap of agony.

The taste of blood filled his mouth. And through bleary eyes he saw that the creature was holding the blanket-wrapped Adam in an arm that coiled about the ancient figure like the body of a large snake.

"Respect," the creature said, fixing Mulvehill with its inhuman gaze. "Humanity will know its betters soon enough."

"Steven," a frightened voice called out.

Mulvehill turned his head slightly and saw Fernita moving toward him through the trees. His heart sank.

"There she is," the creature said happily, a grin, absent of any real joy, spreading across its gaunt, skull-like features.

Fernita knelt before Mulvehill, placing a cold hand against his cheek.

"I told you that you should've left me," she scolded.

"I could be saying the same thing to you," Mulvehill replied, trying to shake off his pain but only making everything hurt all the more.

Fernita turned to face the strange beast that held the body of Adam in one tentacled arm.

"You're here for me . . . aren't you?" she asked.

"Oh, yes," it said, a tremble of what could only be excitement passing across the creature's body and making it vibrate. "I've been trying to find you for a very long time."

And with those words, another boneless limb lashed

out, wrapping around the elderly woman's waist and drawing her to it.

Mulvehill reached for Fernita as she was yanked away, but the movment made him dizzy and he fell over on his side, too weak to right himself.

Face pressed to the cold winter ground, he watched as the tattooed beast admired its two prizes.

"Master, I have them both at last," it said almost gleefully. "Now I have the key."

The very air around the creature began to stir, to swirl, picking up leaves, snow, and twigs, as if they were in the eye of a cyclone.

Through blurring vision, the homicide cop watched as one moment they were there, and the next they were gone.

One moment he was conscious, and the next . . .

The air above Fernita Green's cluttered living room floor began to shimmer and quake.

Something from somewhere else moving from there to here.

Remy and Jon had been at the stilt house in the middle of the Louisiana swamp, and now they were in the old woman's home in Brockton.

"Oh, God, that's awful," Jon said, stumbling out from beneath Remy's wings.

Remy didn't waste any time, ignoring the Son of Adam, who was doing everything he could not to retch upon the carpet. Remy was about to call out for Fernita, for Steven, but his eyes were instantly drawn to something that filled him with fear.

The walls were covered in powerful sigils: the kind used in angel magick. Remy could feel the power leaking from the markings that remained, but he noticed the bucket of filthy water, the scrub brush floating within it, and the sections of old wall smeared black where the sigils had been wiped away.

Remy's eyes darted over the writing as he tried to discern their meaning . . . their purpose.

"What is it?" Jon asked, some color returning to his pale features.

Remy's mouth moved as he translated what he could. It had been ages since he'd seen an angelic spell this complex, but he pretty much got the gist of it.

"This writing ... It's there to make you forget," he said, ice flowing in his veins as he recalled the numerous discussions he'd had with the poor old woman, blaming her condition on age and ailment.

"Like that you're actually somebody named Eliza Swan?" Jon asked.

"Something like that," Remy said, eyes darting about the room. He lunged toward a chair overflowing with loose clothing, books, and magazines, grabbing the piece of furniture and sliding it across the room to see what lay hidden behind it.

It was as bad as expected.

"Remy!" Jon called out.

He hadn't realized that the man had left the room, and went to find him. At the end of the hall, Remy found Jon in the kitchen. It looked as though a demolition team had come by and turned the room on its ass.

"What happened here?" Jon asked, looking up at the enormous hole in the kitchen ceiling to the second floor, and then up through another jagged hole into the attic. One of his hands tugged at his damaged ear nervously as he gazed up through the ragged openings.

"Whatever it was came through the roof," Remy said. He allowed his angelic senses to expand, sniffing the air for the scent of anything familiar, and he found it.

Cherubim.

"Fernita?" he called. "Steven?"

He tensed his legs and flapped his powerful wings once, flying up to the second floor.

"Hello?"

The stink of the angel sentry was strong up there as well, and he began to feel afraid. If Zophiel had found Fernita and Steven here ...

He pushed the troubling thoughts aside, not wanting to

think about the outcome. Expanding his senses farther, Remy listened beyond the sounds of the house to the neighborhood outside, and beyond that.

The sound of sirens.

He flew up through the gaping hole in the ceiling of the second-floor hallway, through the attic, and then outside, his powerful wings keeping him aloft as he scanned the area with vision sharper than a bird of prey's. In the distance he saw a plume of smoke and immediately flew toward it, a tightening in his gut warning him of what he might find.

From the air he looked down at multiple fire engines as they doused a car that had gone off the road into the woods and hit a tree.

A very familiar car.

"Son of a bitch," Remy hissed, dropping out of the sky toward an ambulance parked a way up the back road. He willed himself unseen, touching down beside the open doors as a paramedic hopped out, calling to his partner, who was speaking with one of the firemen.

Remy withdrew his wings and angelic essence, assuming his human guise as he looked into the back of the emergency response vehicle to see a battered Steven Mulvehill strapped to a stretcher.

Silently he hopped in.

"Hey," he said, feeling almost giddy that he'd found his friend alive.

Mulvehill's neck was immobilized by a white plastic brace, and for a moment Remy thought he might have been unconscious.

He reached out, taking his friend's hand in his.

And Mulvehill's swollen eyes shot open, bulging wide as they looked upon Remy.

"It's only me," Remy said, smiling warmly at his friend.

"I know it's you," Mulvehill answered, alarm in his tone.

Remy checked Steven out. He was banged up pretty badly, but nothing looked to be too serious.

"What happened?" he asked, the guilt already beginning to grow.

"What happened," Mulvehill repeated. "What the fuck

happened?" Steven's voice was growing louder, more intense. "You fucking happened is what happened. . . . You, Remy fucking Chandler."

The words were like physical blows, but Remy could understand his friend's anger.

"I'm sorry," he said truthfully. "I had no idea. . . . I didn't know." He didn't know what else to say; no amount of Scotch or steak dinners would make things right at the moment.

"Leave me alone," Mulvehill said, closing his eyes.

"Where's Eliza?" Remy asked.

Mulvehill looked at him strangely.

"Fernita," Remy corrected himself. "Where's Fernita?"

"She's gone," the homicide cop said. "Taken by some fucking monstrosity . . . a Shaitan or something; I don't fucking know." He moaned and closed his eyes again.

Hearing the word was like taking hold of a live wire. There had to be some kind of mistake.

"Shaitan?" Remy repeated. "Where did you hear that?"

"It's what the angel with the three faces called it," Mulvehill said, opening his eyes and scowling. "Now, will you please get the fuck out of here and leave me alone?"

"Steven . . . ," Remy began again, desperate for his friend to know how badly he felt. How sorry he was.

"Just get away from me," Steven said, the fight going out of him as he finally succumbed to whatever drugs he had been given. "Please go away."

Remy wanted to say more, but it wasn't the time. Steven needed a chance to heal, time to wrap his brain around what he had experienced and survived.

Willing himself unseen, Remy jumped from the back of the ambulance as the two EMTs approached, one getting in the back with Steven while the other closed the doors and climbed into the driver's seat.

Remy stood watching with a heavy heart as the ambulance was driven away, lights flashing and siren wailing.

For better or worse, his friend would never be the same again.

And for that, Remy was truly sorry.

* * *

Jon approached a portion of wall once hidden by stacks of boxes, his eyes focused on a block of sigils now exposed to the room.

It's there to make you forget, Remy had said. He ran a finger over the strange shape, wondering whether it could have an influence over him, or if the spell was specific to this Eliza Swan.

There was part of him that would have liked to forget what he'd been through over the last twenty-four hours.

The image of Nathan strapped to the chair in the biodome, his body under the influence of the fruit from the tree, came to mind. He would have liked to forget that, to forget the screams of pain from the man he loved.

His vision started to blur, his eyes were so fixed upon the black shapes, but nothing changed. The horrible memories of the last day remained, still painful and raw, at the forefront of his thoughts. The magick had been only for Eliza.

But why? What did she have to forget that was so bad?

He guessed that it would all come to light once—and if—the woman was found, and the three of them were reunited with Malachi and Adam when the Garden returned.

A chill of excitement passed through him at the thought of Eden. How long had his people dreamed of that wonderful place denied to them? The Sons of Adam always had plans for the Garden; it had been the core of their mission since the order's inception. They believed that once Adam was forgiven, Eden would return for him, and those who had cared for the first father's needs would be allowed to live in Paradise forever.

He had never really believed that any of it was possible, but here it was on the verge of being true.

Jon made out the familiar sound of flapping wings from the kitchen, and knew that Remy had returned.

"Any luck?" he asked, tugging at his ear as he rounded the corner and came face-to-face with a living nightmare.

He let out an unmanly scream, stumbling backward into the hall.

Zophiel slowly approached, and Jon realized the Cherubim was injured.

Steady drips of angelic blood leaked from horrible wounds and from beneath sections of its filthy, and damaged, armor. The three faces that made up its fearsome visage appeared slack, unfocused, experiencing the effects of its injuries.

"You're hurt," Jon said, stating the obvious.

The creature of Heaven stopped, tilting its large head to one side, as if noticing him for the first time.

The face of the lion twitched, its nostrils flaring as it sniffed the air.

"There is danger in the Garden, Adam-son," the Cherubim said, the voice coming from all three of its mouths, and loud enough that he could hear perfectly well. It lurched toward him, crashing to its armored knees as the blood continued to weep from its wounds. "Danger to us all."

The Cherubim knelt there, its massive head bobbing as it struggled to remain conscious.

Jon surveyed the damage to the being. Huge pieces of its armored body had been ravaged, torn. . . . *Are those bite marks?* he wondered, seeing large areas of pale, bleeding flesh.

"What did this to you?" he asked in awe.

"The emerging danger," Zophiel answered. "The first of the Shaitan to be born . . ." The Cherubim shook its head from side to side. "But not the last if Malachi returns to the Garden."

The great angelic beast lurched, rising to one knee.

"The Garden must remain closed," the Cherubim said. It reached toward its side, and pulled an enormous flaming sword seemingly from out of thin air. "If you must be slain to make this a reality"—the monstrous angel had risen to its full height, raising the burning blade to strike at him— "then so be it."

Jon tensed, watching as the giant swayed on shaky legs, preparing to strike him dead. The sword descended in a hissing arc, cutting into and through the wood floor as he managed to evade the blazing strike.

He darted toward the angel, hoping to get around it and into the kitchen, where he could escape through the back door.

The angel roared, lashing out with its armored wings and tearing huge chunks of plaster from the wall as it spun to follow. Jon dropped to the floor, crawling on all fours as fast as he was able as the Cherubim pursued him.

"Do not make this harder than it has to be, Adam-son," Zophiel said, two huge strides of his powerful legs allowing him to catch up to the fleeing man in an instant.

Jon flipped onto his back just in time to see the Cherubim again raise his sword. He continued to backpedal, sliding across the debris-covered floor until his back hit up against the lower kitchen cabinets.

"It is for the good of us all," Zophiel roared as the blade started its descent.

The burning sword hissed as it fell, reminding Jon of some huge snake darting forward to strike. He reached for the cord of a microwave that had been knocked to the floor during all the damage, and was about to lift it up, he hoped to block the blade's fall, when another winged figure dropped down from the hole in the ceiling in front of the attacking Zophiel.

Remy.

Jon was about to call out, but saw that the angel needed no such urging, reacting instinctively, as his warrior breed was wont to do. Remy lunged, grabbing hold of Zophiel's wrists, preventing the giant blade from finishing its arc.

Remy lashed out with his foot, kicking Zophiel in the center of its chest plate with enough force to send it rocketing back into the hall.

"You might want to get out of here," Remy said, turning briefly before charging after the Cherubim.

Jon saw the kitchen back door—and his way out—and almost went for it, but couldn't leave his friend. Unwavering loyalty had always been one of his more endearing characteristics.

He hoped that it didn't get him killed.

CHAPTER FOURTEEN

Zophiel had landed upon his back in the hallway, thrashing upon the ground like some giant turtle on its shell, attempting to right itself. Remy didn't want to give the Cherubim the chance, flying the brief distance from the kitchen to the hallway to land upon his foe, slamming him back to the floor.

"This ends here, Zophiel," Remy cried, the Seraphim inside howling with glee as the warrior's instincts and skills were allowed to flow. He reached out, grabbing hold of a wooden coatrack in a corner behind the door, shaking loose the multiple coats and hats that had been hung upon it, until only the rack remained.

Standing upon the struggling Cherubim's chest, he allowed the divine fires of Heaven to flow through his hands and into the wooden shaft that he held. The wood glowed suddenly with an unearthly light, suddenly so much more than it had been.

He raised the new weapon high, preparing to bring it down like a spear. Zophiel, though badly injured, still had much fight remaining in him, flailing his muscular wings and tossing Remy up against the opposing wall.

Zophiel rolled onto his side, using the gigantic blade to help him rise.

Remy leapt into the air as Zophiel lunged, swinging the burning blade. The sword buried itself deep within the plaster wall. Zophiel tugged upon his weapon to free it as Remy dropped down upon him.

Riding the Cherubim's back, Remy wedged the shaft of the glowing coatrack beneath Zophiel's chin. He yanked backward with all his strength, causing the monstrous angel to stagger backward, leaving the burning sword stuck within the wall.

Zophiel flailed, slamming his enormous bulk against the hallway walls, desperate to remove the troublesome Seraphim pest.

Remy held on as tightly as he could, pulling up on the burning coatrack beneath the Cherubim's throat with all his might until the muscles in his arms were screaming. His own hands now burning with Heavenly fire, Zophiel attempted to reach behind him, to grab enough of Remy to tear him from his perch. Avoiding the Cherubim's wanting fingers, Remy continued to hold on.

At last the great angel dropped to the floor, but Remy did not let up, continuing to pull upon the heavy wooden rod.

From the corner of his eye he saw movement, and Remy turned his head to see Jon over by the stairway wall, where the Cherubim's sword was still buried. The man was pulling up on the hilt of the giant blade, attempting to free it.

"Leave it," Remy yelled to the man.

Zophiel saw Jon and what he was doing and became roused by the sight. A low growl from the angel's constricted throat vibrated the burning shaft still clutched beneath the Cherubim's chin as Zophiel pushed himself to his feet.

Jon pulled upon the blade, the wall surrounding the weapon beginning to smolder and burn.

With a newfound strength Zophiel reached up with his clawed metal fingers and began to tear at the shaft wedged under his chin, ripping away chunks of wood, as well as his own flesh.

Zophiel lurched across the brief expanse of floor toward the man who sought to claim his weapon. Jon saw the angel coming, increasing his attempts, but still the sword remained trapped in the wall.

Yanking back with all that remained of his strength, Remy heard the fateful snap of the makeshift weapon falling away from the Cherubim onto the floor.

Heavenly fire no longer burning at his throat, Zophiel grabbed for his sword, just as Jon managed the incredible feat of pulling it free.

The sword of the Cherubim dropped heavily to the hallway as Jon attempted to lift it. The strain of this action apparent, the Son of Adam brandished the Heavenly weapon with a surprising display of strength.

"Come on," Jon said, fighting to keep the blade up.

He thrust the burning sword at Zophiel, the angel easily moving aside to avoid any harm. Lashing out, he struck the Son of Adam, knocking him ruthlessly to the stairs, the flaming weapon falling from his grasp.

As the Cherubim reached to reclaim the blade, Remy reacted.

The Seraphim was crying out for blood, and Remy saw no reason to deny it its fill. Holding two jagged ends of the broken coatrack that still smoldered with the divine fires of the Heavenly Father, Remy leapt, pushing off with his wings, propelling himself at his foe with great speed.

Sensing the imminent danger, Zophiel spun to meet his attack, but the Seraphim was faster. With a bloodthirsty roar, Remy thrust the two jagged ends of the poles into the already ravaged throat of the monstrous Cherubim.

The pair flew back, crashing into the wall just before the stairs, narrowly avoiding Jon, who darted partway up to the second floor to avoid being crushed.

The Cherubim struggled, gauntleted hands going to his injured throat, but Remy did not let up, leaning forward with all his strength, hands still gripping the two ends of the twin spears that had pierced his enemy's neck. Zophiel's hands glowed with the fire of the divine, but they began to subside, as did the bestial angel's struggles.

Remy could feel the angel growing slack, the extensive injuries already received coupled with this latest abuse at last taking their toll. The Cherubim went limp, his powerful, armored body becoming still. Sensing that his foe was down, Remy released his grip upon the two pieces of pole and stepped back. Zophiel stood for a moment, swaying from side to side, before lowering gradually to his knees, and then falling face-first to the floor.

Remy stared at his fallen foe, but strangely enough, even as the warrior nature at his core howled in victory, he felt nothing but trepidation.

"Is it dead?" Jon asked, venturing down from safety.

"If not, I'm sure he soon will be," Remy said, his voice sounding tired . . . flat. There were missing pieces to this puzzle, and he hated missing pieces.

The Seraphim was eager to finish what he started. . . . Remy, not so much.

He could hear Zophiel's struggles to live, multiple, wheezing gasps as the angel sentry fought to breathe.

Remy approached his fallen foe, considering the merciful thing. If the Cherubim did not pass from this existence shortly, Remy would assist him on his way. Moving closer, Remy allowed the power of Heaven to fill his hands. Fire hotter than the surface of the sun snaked from his fingertips as he grew nearer.

Jon watched from his perch upon the stairs, crying out as Zophiel again fought off approaching death, reaching out to grab hold of his fallen weapon, dragging the burning blade to him.

Remy drew back, preparing for yet another round of battle, but quickly sensed that maybe this was not the case.

The Cherubim pulled the sword close, using the blade to prop himself up.

The two pieces of wood still protruded from his throat, dark blood oozing down their lengths, sizzling and smoking like grease on a hot stove.

Fire in his hands, Remy was ready for just about anything, watching the angel with a cautious eye. The Seraphim whispered in the back of his mind: *Kill your enemy. Do it now.* . . . But Remy didn't feel that this was necessary, which just made his warrior side all the more frantic.

Zophiel reached up, removing one of the burning spears sticking from his throat, and then the other. Angel blood flowed freely, running down the front of once golden armor in glistening, dark rivulets.

Attack. Attack. Attack. Attack, the Seraphim urged, but Remy stayed his hand.

Swaying as he stood, the Cherubim hefted his mighty sword. It now glowed brighter—hotter—in his grasp, happy to be back in its master's possession.

It had been a very long time since Remy last held a weapon that he had bonded with, a weapon as much a part of him as any appendage. Flashes of the Great War exploded in his mind, and of the blood-caked sword that he had dropped upon the battlefield when the war was done.

When he was done.

"I am at an end," the Cherubim weakly gurgled, holding the burning blade up so that he could look upon it. "I can do no more."

Zophiel whipped the blade forward, tongues of flame leaping down its tarnished length to lick eagerly toward him.

Remy recoiled, but did not attack.

"Take it," Zophiel commanded, releasing the large sword from his grip, letting it land at Remy's feet. The fire that covered the blade dimmed as it lay there. "If the warrior's heart still beats within your breast, you must rouse it, for the Kingdom of Heaven is threatened by things most foul."

Zophiel slowly slid to his knees, the life going out of him as the blood from his injuries continued to flow.

"A cancer grows in the bosom of the Garden," the Cherubim warned, his voice weaker. "A malignancy that cannot be allowed to spread."

On his knees, Zophiel's once fearsome form grew more and more still, as fire as well as blood streamed from his wounds.

"Stop him, Remiel of the host Seraphim," Zophiel begged as his body was slowly consumed by the fire of God leaving his dying body.

"Stop Malachi before it all crumbles to ruin."

The words broke loose from Zophiel's lips in a final whisper, the white-hot flames licking at the flesh of his body, surging to engulf his entire form in an inferno.

Remy watched as the fire burned white, temporarily blinding him with its intensity, before it receded, growing softer, until nothing remained but the burn mark where the Cherubim had knelt upon the wooden floor.

That and the still smoldering sword lying at Remy's feet.

The Garden was in pain.

She had felt the illness growing inside of her for quite some time, felt it writhe as it slowly grew over the ages to maturation.

The sickness was inside . . . beneath her cool, fertile earth, feeding off the life energies of this vibrant Paradise.

Suckling upon the roots of the Tree.

It was new life that grew, dangerous life that yearned to be born.

Eden had tried to thwart their growth, making her skin shake and shift, inciting the more primitive life that lived upon and inside her to feed freely on this malignant invader.

But the illness was created to be strong, even in its earliest stages.

She had attempted to communicate with the multiple life-forms gestating within her bosom, wanting to know their purpose, and she learned that they had been created to survive, to usurp what had come before.

The Garden knew that this was wrong, that the things nestled inside her should not come to be, but she was helpless.

Those who could have protected her were long since banished.

She felt their presence out there in the ether, and she had reached out, singing for them to notice her, but they had been too far away to hear her voice.

To hear her pleas.

Until now.

After drifting for so very, very long, she was near her children again. There were more of them now: more to hear her cries for help.

Weakened by the goings-on inside her, the Garden called out as loudly as she could, hoping they would hear her call.

Hoping they would come as she grew nearer to them, and their world.

That they would come to the aid of their mother.

CHAPTER FIFTEEN

The sword cried out to him.

Remy gazed down to the floor, listening to the blade's pleas. It was calling to him—begging him—to pick it up.

It wanted to tell him what it knew; it wanted him to be its new master.

He felt the Seraphim stir, the song of the blade incredibly powerful. It had been too long since the divine being had held a weapon forged in the fires of Heaven.

Before he could even question the action, Remy bent down, fingers wrapping around the sword's hilt.

It was like taking hold of a live wire. His mind exploded in a searing flash of white, images forming from the fire that spread across the surface of his brain.

He saw the Garden. . . . No, he felt the Garden in every way that was possible. He saw through the eyes of the sword . . . through the eyes of Zophiel.

Something was wrong there. War was on the horizon, the air tinged with the acrid smell of blood, growing stronger as it drifted on the thick currents of air.

But there was something else. Something that had begun to affect the thick vegetation of the Garden paradise, tainting the earth beneath the sentry's feet. The blade was warning him, driving him through the thick underbrush toward what would desecrate this most holy of places.

He emerged from the jungle to stand before the Tree.

The poison was there, and the Garden called out to him.

And then he saw that he was not the only one of God's divine creatures there.

The elder called Malachi was there at the Tree, and in his arms he held something that squirmed with life.

Something that did not belong.

The elder explained that everything was as it should be, though the sentry felt that something was wrong. Something was horribly, horribly wrong. Looking upon the pale thing that undulated in the elder's arms, he felt a sense of revulsion, that what he was observing was not of God's design.

Of God's plan.

He was about to question the foul thing's existence, but he did not have the chance. The elder moved faster than the speed of thought, a flash of burning dagger the last thing Zophiel saw before it plunged through the bone of his face and into his brain.

Turning the ordered world of the Lord God to madness.

There was a fire in Zophiel's mind, a ravenous conflagration that consumed everything that he had ever known, replacing it with a jabbering insanity.

He could not remember what had led him to this, only that he was filled with a bloodlust that could not be quenched.

He must find what was responsible for this . . . and it must burn, and maybe then he would have the answers that eluded him.

Destruction would be his sustenance, feeding the madness that enshrouded him, and hopefully satisfying it so that one day, his sanity would be returned to him.

The images came in a torrential flow, the sentry's ability to process what was happening, and the world around him, now nothing more than a jumble of sights, sounds, and smells.

For a moment Remy—Remiel—remembered who he was and that these were not his experiences, but the experiences of the Cherubim who had been given the sacred task of guarding Eden, but the recollections came furiously and the Seraphim was almost drowned in their relentless intensity.

The fires of madness raced across the surface of his mind, and Zophiel tried desperately to hold on to some recollection of the evil that threatened the Garden.

But it was gone, leaving only the insanity and a berserker rage over what had been stolen from him.

The battle in the Garden with the Seraphim Remiel was fierce. He had wanted to tell the warrior angel that something wasn't right, but he was unable to do so. The thoughts and the words that needed to follow would not come. There was only the anger . . . and the disease of madness that plagued him.

The Cherubim fled the realm of Heaven to the stars, hoping to escape the insanity, but it clung like burning oil, eating away at him and his most holy purpose. Soon, the sentry knew, there would be little left; only the fury and destruction that followed in his wake would define him.

But in the world of God's man, there came a change.

He could hear it far in the back of his mind, something that spoke to memories that had been buried so deep beneath layers of smoldering ash.

He did not understand what it spoke of, but felt the emotion that it roused in him, and knew that if he found this source, this irritating cacophony of visions, sounds, and smells, and destroyed it, that maybe . . . maybe he would remember what it was all about.

There were countless millennia of searching, most of the time the source of what he hunted having grown eerily silent, leaving him with only the jabbering insanity that had come to personify him.

The Cherubim haunted the Earth, searching . . . hunting . . . for the thing that would clear his mind, and free him from the slavery of madness.

He'd even worn the guise of one of God's humans, hoping that perhaps whatever it was that he stalked could be tricked into emerging into the light so that he might see.

And eventually he did in fact see, and slowly, little by little, it was returned to him.

Zophiel recalled the dire threat to Eden, Heaven, and all the Heavenly hosts, as well as the one who was responsible.

Just in time to die.

Remiel felt the death of Zophiel as if it were his own, the fire of Heaven that burned hot and powerful at the center of his being suddenly burning so brightly . . . so furiously . . . and then it was gone, leaving behind a cold, creeping darkness that eventually became . . .

Nothing.

The shock of oblivion was enough for Remy to take his humanity back, to suppress his angelic nature enough to resume control, but it wasn't an easy task.

The Seraphim was enraged by the thought of something that dared to threaten his Lord God, His Kingdom, and the Garden that He loved.

Remy placated the angry creature that lived inside him, promising him he would be set free to deal with the offenders in the only way that the Seraphim knew how.

Through the rite of combat.

The Seraphim knew that this was a battle that would test him, that there was a chance that he would not survive—that he could be vanquished by the Shaitan—but that was something the divine being always knew was a possibility.

And it made him yearn for the taste of violence all the more.

"All those years with the Sons of Adam," Remy said, holding the blade tight, lifting it to eye level. "It wasn't Malachi at all."

"What?" Jon asked, moving closer, but stopping just before the pile of ash that had once been the Cherubim Zophiel.

"It was a Shaitan," Remy explained.

"Shaitan," Jon repeated. "And what exactly is that?"

"Something that shouldn't even exist," Remy said, his eyes drawn to the beauty of the blade that he held. He could feel it bonding with him, and he with it.

The Seraphim was very happy about this, a hum like some sort of prehistoric cat's purr vibrating at his core.

"The Shaitan were an idea—a concept—when the Lord God and Malachi were creating the beings that would serve Him."

"The first angels?" Jon suggested, attempting to understand what Remy was saying.

"No, something far darker," Remy said. "Rumor has it that they were going to be made from the cold darkness that existed before God brought forth His divine light. But the Lord didn't trust the darkness, choosing instead to fashion His messengers from a portion of His own inner glow."

Remy paused, considering what he now knew.

"They were never supposed to exist," he said. "They were never created."

"Well, at least one of them was," Jon reminded him.

"Yeah," Remy said, remembering what he had seen from Zophiel's memory of Eden: that Malachi had left something in the Garden. He saw the rich, fertile soil as if he were there, sensing that something very wrong had been planted there.

Something that was growing . . . maturing.

"At least one . . . for now."

"For now," Jon repeated. "Are you suggesting that there might be more of these things . . . these Shaitan?"

"I believe as Zophiel did," Remy said. "That Eden . . . and eventually Heaven itself, could be in great danger."

Jon looked at him with eyes desperate for answers, the events unfolding traveling far outside what he was capable of comprehending.

The Seraphim knew what had to be done, and this time Remy did not seek to argue, or squelch his bourgeoning emotion.

If the Garden and Heaven itself were threatened, there could be only one response.

"We need to go to Eden and destroy the threat," Remy said, gripping the sword all the tighter.

"Do we have a chance?" Jon asked nervously. "Do you think you can take on Malachi and the Shaitan?"

Remy did not answer his question, letting the silence of the moment say all that was necessary.

Izabelle Swan pulled her bare feet up underneath her and took a long swig from her third beer of the hour, and continued the conversation with her parents.

"How was I to know he was your friend?" Izzy said to her father as she held the photo of the nightclub in one hand, the bottle of beer in the other. "Alls you said was to watch out for an angel that wanted to do Mama harm, and that's exactly what I was doin'."

She took another drink from the bottle, feeling emotions swirl around inside her that she hadn't felt in many, many years.

Izzy barely knew her parents, having been just a little girl when they left, but there was still some sort of connection. She felt them out there in the world somewhere, and wondered if there would ever be a day when . . .

Her anger flared, and she set her beer firmly down on the floor beside her, grabbing the wrinkled paper bag and shoving the photograph back inside.

Those were foolish thoughts. She used to have them when she was a little girl growing up alone. They hadn't seemed quite so foolish then. Izzy had always hoped that they would come back for her, that they'd all be together someday.

Protecting one another against anything, and everything, that might try to harm them.

But a lot of years had gone by, and that hope had become pretty silly, and she had to wonder how she could even think about it with a straight face.

Must've been the beer, she thought, wrinkling the top of the paper bag closed and preparing to hide the photos away again.

She got up from her chair, heading toward her bedroom, when she felt it.

It was like somebody had taken a dull screwdriver to her soul, plunging it in and giving it a good twist. Izzy gasped, the paper bag of photos falling to the wood floor beneath her feet.

She stood perfectly still, waiting for the intense pain to pass, when her mind became filled with visions of green.

Visions of the Garden.

She'd been having dreams lately about this place, but never as vivid as this. Not only could she see it inside her head, but she could smell the heavy dampness, the rich soil.

But also the smell of rot.

And she could feel something growing ... stirring. Something that didn't belong. The perverse sensations stirred her elemental power, and the magick churned inside her.

Outside the wind picked up, and she could hear the rumble of a forming storm.

And Izzy could sense that she was no longer alone.

A snarl played upon her full lips as she let her magick flow, arcing power jumping from the tips of her fingers, eager to be unleashed.

It had been quite some time since she'd used her powers this frequently, and she had to admit it felt really good.

She had no idea what she would find outside her home, but it didn't stop her from striding across the floor, taking hold of the knob, and throwing the door open.

"All right, then," she said, the pain in her chest—the pain of the Garden—making her all the more angry. "Who wants to play?"

She noticed the man called Jon first. He was leaning against the railing of the porch clutching at his chest—feeling Eden's pain as well.

The angel was standing stiffly behind him, a nasty-looking sword that burned with an eerie, supernatural flame in his hand.

And then she noticed the swamp below her home, and the many rowboats and motorboats that bobbed there upon the water. The Sisters had come as well, drawn to this place ... to her. And she knew that they could feel it as well. Feel the Garden ... feel *her* pain.

"No playing," Remy said to her. "Just some serious business."

The magick was begging to be released, but she pulled it back inside her, where it squirmed unhappily.

"What the hell do you two want now?" she asked, fearing the answer. Knowing the answer.

"Your help," Jon said. "Do you feel it? It's almost here . . . just beyond the pale."

"I don't know what you're talking about," Izzy lied, starting to turn back to her home as the angel spoke.

"We have to go to the Garden," he said. "You know it . . . and they know it too." He motioned with his hand to the Sisters who had gathered around her home.

"Fine," she spat. "Go. It don't have nothing to do with me."

"But it does," Remy said. "Your mother will be there, and she could be in great danger."

Izzy had turned her back to him, not wanting him to see how his words affected her.

"She probably doesn't even remember who I am," she said, those silly feelings coming back to haunt her.

"Then maybe it's time to remind her by helping to save Eden, and quite possibly Heaven itself."

She turned back around to face them.

"Knew I should have killed you both when I had the chance."

CHAPTER SIXTEEN

The Garden was arriving.

Through space and time she surged, sensing a world thriving with life just beyond the veil, and pulling herself toward it.

Eden had been lost for so very long, moving from place to place—world to world—searching for what would make her complete again.

It had been so long since she was last whole.

Since she had last held her children.

This place—this world—sang as it approached; kindred sprits, they were, for both had been shaped by the Almighty.

But the closer she came, the more pain the Garden experienced. The illness at her core was growing, becoming more dangerous as the world of God's man drew near.

She did not wish to endanger the world, but Eden had grown weak as she traversed a multitude of realities, and she did not know if she had the strength to move on.

The Garden reached out to the world, searching for a place where she could be, where none who lived upon her would be harmed. The planet Earth welcomed Eden, and guided her to an inhospitable place—an area mostly devoid of life.

A place where she had a chance to be saved.

For the Garden could sense beings of great strength walking upon the Earth, beings of unimaginable power.

Beings that could save . . .
Or destroy her.

The North Pole

Gregson Paul pulled himself tighter into a ball inside his sleeping bag and listened to the freezing winds howl hungrily outside his tent.

As he had done since joining this expedition, he shivered to the point that his bones nearly broke, and wondered about when he had turned into the world's biggest fucking idiot.

He guessed, as he had guessed before, that it was when he first saw Marjorie Halt in her cutoff jeans shorts.

The tent undulated, battered by the relentless current of air. It wanted him to come out; it wanted to show him how fucking idiots were treated when they volunteered for a scientific expedition to the North Pole to provide the most accurate survey of the thickness of the Arctic ice.

There were three others in the expedition, lying alongside him, wrapped in their sleeping bags as well. There was Terrance Long, the expedition's environmental scientist; and project leader Daniel Hiratsu, engineer in charge of the various pieces of high-tech equipment that they were using to survey the polar ice's thickness; and then there was Marjorie, grad student and ecological savior. She wanted to be the one who told the world about how the Arctic ice caps were melting due to global warming, and he had hung upon every word that left her beautiful mouth on that hot—very hot—summer's day at the University of Michigan, as they lounged in the grass out in front of the student center.

By the time she had finished talking he wanted to tell the world about the melting ice caps too, and anything else she might suggest . . . and possibly to see what lay beneath those ridiculously short but awesome cutoffs.

There were no cutoff shorts now—maybe beneath the layers of special thermal clothing that they were wearing, but he wouldn't know. Marjorie had very little interest in him in that way.

She was as cold as the ice they were measuring.

When it was time to rise, they would be on day one hundred and twelve in their mission to reach the Pole. According to Professor Long, they and the ground radar unit that they were using to penetrate and take readings of the ice depth every eight inches would likely reach their destination today, and their mission would pretty much be complete.

Curled up and shivering inside their tent as the below-zero windchill mercilessly assaulted their shelter from outside, Gregson began to dream of another place, a warm place with thick, tropical growth.

A primitive jungle older than recorded history.

Gregson awakened with a yelp, the heady, humid stink of the jungle lingering in his nostrils. He could see that the others still slept, huddled against one another within their cramped confines. Listening to the relentless winds outside, he was about to lie back down, to perhaps escape again to the dream of that wonderful and warm tropical place, when he smelled it.

He sat up in his sleeping bag, a mummy rising from his tomb, and sniffed the frigid air.

Was he going crazy, or did he actually smell that thick, wet jungle? He'd vacationed with his parents in Costa Rica a number of times while growing up, and he remembered the aroma fondly, often thinking of the South American jungles to help him drift off to sleep at night after a long and grueling day of taking readings in below-zero temperatures.

But there was no mistaking it: Gregson could smell the jungle.

He considered waking the others, but, still doubting his sanity, decided against it. Squirming from his sleeping bag, he put on the protective clothing he had shed before going to bed, trying to be as quiet as possible so as not to awaken the other members of the team. And even if they did wake up, they'd probably just think he was going outside to perform the uncomfortable task of relieving oneself in a subzero-degree environment.

As strange as it seemed, the jungle smell was stronger—thicker—the closer he got to the tent's exit. He quickly unzipped the opening, temporarily allowing the howling, razor-sharp winds entrance as he crawled outside into the snow, turning around to seal up the opening behind him.

Standing, Gregson slipped on his protective goggles, looking through the tinted lenses in the eerie twilight of the Pole, searching for the source of the unusual smell.

He didn't have to look for long.

Gregson thought that he had to be dreaming. It wouldn't have been the first time. Exhausted from pulling sledges loaded with equipment across the ice, he often had bizarre and incredibly vivid dreams of being home in Michigan, or even back on campus.

But this was unlike anything he'd experienced before.

The wind had piled a few feet of snow just in front of the tent, and he pushed through the powdery drifts in order to get closer.

He half expected it to vanish: a mirage on the bleak, frozen landscape.

But it didn't; it remained, its details becoming more precise the closer he got.

There was a jungle at the North Pole—not a chance they could have missed it, not even in a blizzard. Gregson was about to turn back and rouse his fellow explorers, but the jungle called to him, the warmth of the place radiating outward and enticing him forward.

The Garden drew him closer.

He pinched his leg through his thermal pants, wanting to be sure this wasn't just the product of a dreaming mind.

Thick, billowing steam rose up from the mass of trees that spanned for miles in either direction. It became warmer the closer he got, and he swore that he heard the sounds of squawking birds.

How was this even possible? His mind wanted to know. It didn't make the least bit of sense, but here it was, right before his eyes.

One second Gregson Paul was walking across ice, and the next his heavy rubber boots were falling on grass. The temperature becoming increasingly hot, he could feel the sweat pouring from his body beneath the layers of his clothes. Before he could even question the act, he found himself stripping away the layers, basking in the heat of this magickal place.

And that was exactly what it had to be, he thought, as he dropped his heavy jacket onto the ground ... onto the thick green grass.

Magick.

He found himself drawn to the place, compelled to enter the jungle, but the man could see no discernible entrance, his passage blocked by thick, thorny vines, massive trees, and tangled underbrush.

Gregson looked for a way in, moving along the jungle's edge until he found it.

It loomed above him, between two enormous stone pillars, intricately forged from what appeared to be iron: two ornate gates.

But the gates were closed.

Barring him entrance to the Garden beyond.

CHAPTER SEVENTEEN

Before Taranushi knew himself to be Shaitan, he knew only that he had been shunned by God.

He dropped from the night sky down to the city rooftop in a swirling maelstrom of howling wind, dust, and dirt. In his multiple arms he still carried the nearly lifeless body of Adam, and the descendant of the first woman who, along with the ancient man, would complete the key, and allow him and his master access to the Garden.

And to his still-gestating kin.

The pale-skinned creature crouched upon the roof of the building, making sure that his charges were still intact; the use of magick often had diverse effects upon the frailer examples of humanity.

Adam was unconscious, but still among the living, and the woman was crying and trembling with fear.

How pathetic, he thought, observing the life-forms that the Creator had deemed worthy, while discarding one such as he.

Taranushi remembered as if it had happened only moments before being presented in his infant state to the Lord God by he who had fashioned him from the stuff of darkness: his master, Malachi.

He could not recall the Lord's face, but remembered the feel of His eyes. He was to be the first of the Creator's servants: the soldiers of His glory as He created the universe and all that existed within it.

But the Holy Creator cared not for what Malachi presented, deeming it unfit to exist, and brushing it aside to move on to the next.

The Messengers.

The angels.

But Malachi saw his potential, and refused to erase him from existence.

The Shaitan gazed up into the evening sky, sensing a presence in the pitch-black that surrounded the blazing stars in the sky. Sometime soon that darkness would be hungry enough to consume the stars.

And the Lord God would know the experience of being discarded.

Deemed unfit to exist.

The human woman looked at him with disbelief in her old eyes.

"If only your tiny mind could comprehend the mightiness of the gift that He has bestowed upon you," Taranushi said with a snarl, resenting the woman for everything that she was.

He shrugged off the rage he felt welling in his being, and flowed across the rooftop to the door that would allow access to the building below. Another muscular limb erupted from his torso, grabbing hold of the doorknob and pulling it with all his might. The knob disintegrated in his grip, and he found himself creating other limbs to tear the barrier from its hinges.

Standing in the now open doorway, the Shaitan sniffed the air, seeking the scent of what had brought him here.

"There it is," he growled, his bottom half having become like liquid as he flowed down the stairs, his captives under a powerful arm each, to the levels below.

The building was quiet except for the rustling of vermin and the rumble of the structure's heat source. No one currently resided in the building, but the scent of previous tenants caused his nose to wrinkle in disgust.

Fallen angels—they were the worst-smelling of their kind.

The Shaitan reached the apartment building's lobby, his

muscular neck extending outward, nose twitching as he continued his search.

"It is below," Taranushi said with a sly grin, moving toward another door. He reached out, sensing that there had been defenses placed there. His fingertips tingled the closer his hand got, powerful angelic magicks infused within the wood to prevent unauthorized entrance.

The creature sneered at the pathetic attempt, throwing himself full force against the barrier and reducing the door to splinters. Angel magick was nothing against the power that had created him.

The disgusting smell of a fallen wafted up from the room below, but there was also another scent beneath it, a smell that made the black sigils upon his pale flesh writhe like maggots.

Taranushi descended to the basement apartment, eyes scanning the darkness for what he had been sent to find.

Though it was weak, and beginning to fade, the stink was unmistakable.

He placed the frail form of Adam down upon a nearby piece of furniture, while uncoiling his tentacle-like limb from around the old woman's waist.

"Stay where you've been put," he warned her, snarling as he spoke to show off his pointed teeth. He realized that it had been quite some time since he'd fed at the biodome, and found the human before him quite tempting, but he wasn't about to jeopardize his entire species to satisfy his hunger pangs.

The old woman's gaze suddenly hardened, and he thought he might need to teach her through pain, but she instead moved herself across the floor to the prone form of Adam lying naked upon the furniture.

"If you're not meaning to kill him you might want to be a little gentler," she scolded. She reached into a pocket of the clothes she wore and produced a cloth. Licking the fabric, she proceeded to clean some small wounds upon the first man's skeletal body.

"Everything is going to be all right," she cooed to the cadaverous figure. "You just hold on and see."

Adam remained silent, unmoving, as if dead.

Taranushi was tempted to tell them what their fate would be, but he had already wasted enough time, interacting for centuries with the fragile life-forms that had stolen God's affections.

Turning toward the lingering aroma, he rushed toward it, eager for his mission to finally be over. After all this time, the pieces had at last fallen into place, and the beginning of the end was about to commence.

At the far end of the basement room the first of the Shaitan stopped before a closed door. He pulled it open to reveal what appeared to be a storage closet. Inside there was an old metal bucket and a mop, and some boxes stained and mildewed from water damage.

Gazing inside, Taranushi felt his smile grow wide with excitement, for he did not see an empty closet; he saw so much more.

He saw through the drifting malodor what had once been there not so very long ago.

Not a closet, but a passage to Hell.

A passage that would soon exist again.

Hell

The entire cave was shaking, the shrieks and moans of a Hell being gradually murdered echoing down the stone passage to where they were.

"It won't be long now," Malachi said wistfully, gazing off in that direction. "Changing . . ."

Francis dropped his bare feet down from the stone table to the floor, feeling the violent vibrations increasing in intensity. The entire place—the entire mountain—was just a few minutes away from being shaken to rubble.

The Hellion had risen from where it had patiently lain the entire time he was being tortured—the elder angel rummaging through his brain as if looking for a favorite winter hat. The foul beast paced nervously, glancing toward the sounds of its world being torn asunder.

Francis didn't know what he was going to do. To say

he was weak was an understatement. If asked, Francis would have had a difficult time admitting that he was even alive, but if he wasn't going to attempt something, who was?

Malachi wasn't right in the *cabeza*—a trait that he'd noticed seemed to be quite common in many of the Lord's more powerful creations of late—and he certainly wasn't up to anything good. Francis missed being able to pick up the Batphone to give Remy a call. Struggling to stand, he wondered whether Eliza had reached out to the angel, the memory that he had left her one of Remy's cards, just in case, giving him a warm feeling in his tummy.

Or that just could have been his insides melting to slag.

Maybe Remy would be arriving any minute now, he thought, as the floor of the cave hummed beneath his feet. Flying down the cave corridor, guns blazing—no, Remy would most likely be carrying a sword—sword blazing, coming to save the day.

"You're smiling," Malachi said to him, raising his voice to be heard over the commotion outside.

Francis leaned back against the stone table, still too weak to stand on his own two feet.

"Was I?" he commented. "Must be a touch of gas."

"I thought that perhaps you had resigned yourself to the approaching change . . . a moment of clarity before . . ."

Francis could sense it coming.

"Before what?" he asked, tensing to do something, but what, he did not know.

"Before your usefulness was brought to a close."

Malachi struck with the speed of a cobra. That fucking scalpel was out again, and whenever that bad boy made an appearance, nothing good followed.

At first Francis thought that nothing had happened, that whatever Malachi was going to do was somehow avoided as the elder stepped back away from him.

But then he followed the elder's eyes, and felt the growing tightness in the flesh of his stomach.

"You fucking didn't," Francis slurred, not wanting to look down at himself, but really having little choice. He leaned farther back against the table and slowly tilted his chin down to see the extent of the damage.

"You have always been a prominent fixture in the visions gifted to me by the fruit of the Tree," Malachi said.

Francis looked down at his chest, seeing the fine line that started just below his sternum and went down to his groin. Blood had started to seep from the edges, making the line—the cut—that much more noticeable.

"And little by little I figured out why."

His legs began to give out, and he caught himself on the stone table's edge, the sudden movement causing the incision in his belly to tear apart, exposing his inner workings to the outside world.

"In using you as their agent, the Thrones provided me with the perfect all-purpose tool for my needs: strong, cunning, ruthless, penitent, and quite resourceful."

Francis's hands went to his belly, and he pressed them against the diagonal cut, desperate to keep his insides from sliding out onto the floor.

"And they gave you certain gifts . . . certain useful gifts to make you a better executor of God's will."

Malachi retrieved what looked to be a bowl from a collection of crap cluttering a formation of rock jutting from the cave wall used as a shelf.

"One of those gifts is in your blood."

Someone had pulled the cave floor out from beneath him, and Francis found himself dropping down to his knees. The impact was jarring and he felt what was inside him—what he wanted to keep inside him—press against his hands. He was successful in preventing his inner workings from leaving his body.

But there was nothing he could do about the blood.

Malachi placed the bowl beneath him, capturing the scarlet spill as it rained down from his belly.

"The Thrones gave you the gift of passage . . . the ability to open doorways from here to there."

Malachi's eyes looked around the cave, dust and bits of rocky debris raining down as the Morningstar continued his renovation project outside.

"From here . . . to there."

The elder bent down to Francis's level, looking at him eye-to-eye.

"The gift is in your blood," Malachi said as he retrieved the bowl, its contents splashing out over the rim.

The cave shook as if having a fit, huge cracks suddenly appearing in the floor as well as the wall. Unable to stay upright, Francis fell onto his side, his hand momentarily leaving his stomach—the results unpleasant. Despite its anxiety, the Hellion was there to sniff at the bloody innards that had temporarily spilled. The beast growled at him, snapping at his fingers as he attempted to retrieve them and shove them back where they belonged.

Malachi stood there, silently watching as Francis struggled with the beast over a section of his intestine.

"I'm done with you, Fraciel," the elder announced. "My visions of you end with the collection of your blood, and my escape from . . ."

He looked around the cave again, larger pieces of rock and dust raining down from the ceiling.

". . . this place. Strangely enough, I've grown rather fond of it during the time I've waited for your arrival."

Francis had managed to take back the rubbery piece of his guts, shoving it deep inside his abdominal cavity, while giving everything that he had to remaining conscious.

A large section of rock dropped from the ceiling to land atop the Hellion's skull-like head. The beast yelped, retreating back toward a patch of shadows along the wall.

The place was coming apart at the seams; it wouldn't be long now.

Malachi turned his back to him, approaching an area of wall with the bowl of his blood.

Francis willed himself to get up; despite all the pain, and his current *opened* condition, he forced himself up onto his knees.

Standing at the wall, Malachi casually glanced over his shoulder, smiling as he dipped his fingers in the bowl of fresh blood and began to paint upon the wall.

"I'd like to reiterate how important you've been to this entire process," he said, painting the angelic sigils—the beginnings of a spell—upon the cave wall. "It could not have been done without you."

The sounds coming from outside were pretty scary, and Francis could only imagine what was happening.

Exactly what's going to be happening inside not too long from now, he thought, swaying as the cave shook, and the large cracks branched off to smaller cracks that begat even more cracks than that.

A powerful wind rushed through the chamber, traveling down the passage and carrying with it the stink of brimstone and transformation.

Malachi continued to smear the angel blood upon the wall, dropping the still partially filled bowl to the cave floor when finished.

"But now it's time that I said good-bye."

The blood sigils had begun to glow with a thrumming black energy—the shapes growing steadily larger, colliding with others and eventually merging to become a single piece of expanding darkness.

Francis could do nothing but watch . . . hold in his insides and watch.

A black portal grew steadily larger upon the wall, an annoying hum of expended magick cutting through the ruckus of the crumbling cave. He thought about maybe using his intestine as a lasso, preventing the elder from escaping, but had doubts about his aim.

Malachi chanced another glance over his shoulder before ducking into the passage to be swallowed up by the bottomless darkness that had manifested there.

So much for that, Francis thought as the cave convulsed fitfully, the walls crumbling, the floor shifting violently beneath him, knocking him back to his side.

For a moment he imagined his situation couldn't get any worse, but then he noticed the rope of bloody intestine—*his* rope of bloody intestine—cooling upon the rubble-covered floor.

That isn't good.

And the crazed Hellion emerging from its hiding place, drawn again by the smell of his exposed insides.

It was totally fucking awesome that life—what little he had left of it—could still manage to surprise him.

The Hellion lunged, opening its cavernous mouth to take a bite from his intestine.

Is it my large or small intestine? the former Guardian angel wondered, before deciding that it truly didn't matter.

He looked into the beast's horrible maw, at all its teeth and its fat, sluglike tongue, and hoped that the monster got the nastiest case of food poisoning from him.

Francis watched as the Hellion's snout dipped down; the front razor-sharp-looking teeth were about to close upon the slimy, dirt-covered piece of flesh when the floor beneath the creature suddenly disappeared, and the beast that was about to nibble upon him was gone.

It was like something out of a classic Warner Bros. cartoon, and Francis actually managed to let loose with a barklike laugh that just about ended his life.

Consciousness leaking away, he watched through dimming eyes as the remaining sections of floor around him continued to fall away, the ground beneath him eventually disappearing as the walls of the cave collapsed, exposing it to the outside world.

To the hell outside.

Francis was falling, the sudden sensation of weightlessness triggering a treasured memory of the last time he'd flown.

Before *his* fall from grace.

The mountains of Hell were crumbling all around him, clouds of dirt and debris being sucked up into the swirling maelstrom that his broken body had now become part of.

And to think he actually believed he was going to die under the teeth and claws of a Hellion. It just went to show how one could never be sure about anything.

Except that he was finally going to die.

Buffeted and deafened by winds, Francis found himself accepting his fate, letting go as his body drifted upon the currents of air choked with the remains of Hell's former landscape.

He found that he could no longer breathe, and gave in to the darkness, calling it to him with open arms and minimal regrets, wishing only that he could have seen her again—the beautiful Eliza Swan whose memory had been stolen from him till now.

And sorry that he hadn't earned the Lord's forgiveness, even though he'd tried so very hard. He would have also liked to have seen Remy again, but since the son of a bitch never came to his rescue, he could go screw himself.

The sound within the vortex went from cacophonous to silent.

And then Francis sensed that he was no longer alone.

He struggled to open his eyes, and in the eye of the storm a familiar figure floated.

Lucifer was as beautiful as he remembered, and Francis was surprised to see the Morningstar gliding toward him on wings blacker than the darkest nights.

There was a smile upon the Morningstar's beatific face, and Francis believed that Lucifer actually remembered who he was.

And that he was happy to see him.

CHAPTER EIGHTEEN

Eliza stroked the face of the man who appeared dead, sensing through the tips of her fingers that there was still some life left inside him.

He was holding on for something, and she seemed to know that.

The far corner of the room lit up as if in the midst of a lightning storm, and she looked up to find the monster who had taken her standing in front of an open closet door. The flashes of blue light were coming from inside it.

Memories that had been denied her for so very long suddenly rushed in to fill their places.

This was what Pearly had wanted to save her from—why Pearly had left her, and taken her memories. And now she understood how much he really did care for her.

The light from the closet grew even brighter, more violent, as crackling bolts of electricity shot from the doorway, their intensity driving the monster back.

Eliza thought briefly about running, but then looked at the man lying on the couch. The man called Adam. How could she leave him there, alone with the monster? And she most certainly couldn't manage to take him with her. So she resigned herself to staying.

"Don't you worry," she told him again. "I won't leave you."

She knew exactly who he was, and could feel the pain of the life he'd led.

Her own family carried a similar guilt, descendants from Adam's bride—Eve. But the Daughters of Eve had chosen instead to accept the first mother's sin and her punishment, and channel their guilt into efforts to do good upon the world. Eliza's mother, and grandmother, and great-grandmother before her had always believed that God accepted this, and gave them the special gift of longevity so they could continue their work for as long as possible. Even Eliza believed this as she left the protection of her family to spread happiness through her music.

But there were forces that wanted to silence her songs, and others that wanted her—*needed* her—for something that still remained a mystery.

The lightning was abruptly replaced by complete darkness, as if the storm had passed, and the closet was filled with liquid night.

Eliza watched as the monster crouched at the threshold, peering into the solid shadow, cautiously moving closer, then plunging its many arms into the undulating wall of black. Her captor screamed, tossing back his head in agony, but it did not stop its search.

"I have you!" the creature finally bellowed, and Eliza saw the muscles tense on the monster's pale back as it yanked something from the thick pool of shadow, something covered in layers of ice and frost.

Eliza was fascinated by the frozen shape lying on the floor of the apartment, and although she couldn't ever remember feeling so frightened, she found herself cautiously moving toward it.

"I thought I told you to stay put," the monster snarled, extending one of its frostbitten arms toward her. A surge of invisible force erupted from its fingers, hurling her backward, where she hit the couch and rolled to the floor, her old glasses knocked from her face.

Stunned, she lay there, watching as the monster knelt beside the shape. The ice was beginning to melt in an expanding puddle on the hardwood floor.

"Master," the monster spoke softly. "I have you." It was

running its hands over the object, and where it touched, the ice fell away in clumps to reveal a man.

He was dressed in filthy, bloodstained robes, and as he opened his eyes, his gaze fell upon the monster. A smile formed upon his bearded face at the sight.

"Taranushi," he whispered.

"Yes, my master."

Suddenly there was a blinding flash, and when her eyes cleared Eliza was shocked to see the robed man standing directly before her, that strange smile still on his face.

"Hello, Eliza," he said, his voice as smooth as velvet.

All of a sudden she remembered this man. He had come to Pearly's aid when that thing pretending to be an angel had attacked the club.

"I . . . I know you," she said from where she lay upon the floor.

And for a moment, she almost believed that things were going to be all right. But the bearded man reached down and yanked her up from the floor by the front of her apron.

"So sorry, but the time for pleasantries is at an end."

She struggled in his grasp, as he pulled something that glowed as if it were red-hot from within his disgusting robes.

"You have something I need," he said, his velvety voice now more of a growl, and jabbed that burning something into the middle of her forehead.

To think she had almost believed that things were going to be all right.

Her mama and daddy always said she was a damn fool.

Remy knew this place.

He was standing naked atop one of the many spires surging up from the Kingdom of Heaven, staring out over the resplendent City of Light.

He had buried the memory of how beautiful it was— before the war—but the Seraphim had found it.

Saved it.

Cherished it.

This was where he wished to return.

This was what he had been denied.

Something passed overhead, momentarily covering Remy in a blanket of cold shadow. He turned his gaze skyward, at the awesome form gliding above him on wings of gold.

"I think we need to talk," he called out, and the figure banked to the right, then dropped from the sky, hurtling straight for Remy.

Remy dropped to the base of the spire, dangerously close to the edge. Carefully he pulled himself away, eyes locked on the towers below, wondering about his fate should he fall from such a great height in this strange, dreamlike state.

From behind him, the Seraphim laughed, a joyless sound, bitter and angry.

Remy rose to his feet and turned to address his angelic nature. "All right, you're pissed; I get it," he said.

The Seraphim studied him with cold, emotionless eyes. The angel was wearing his armor of war, shined to a glistening brilliance, looking as though it were forged from the sun itself.

Remy remembered that armor, before its radiance was dulled by the blood of his brothers.

"You shouldn't be here," the Seraphim growled menacingly.

"You're probably right," Remy replied. "So you can probably guess how bad the situation is."

The angel tilted his head to one side, a smile cutting across his perfect features.

"You fear the Shaitan," he stated.

"We should all fear the Shaitan," Remy retorted. "Born from the darkness that was everything before His light chased it away. They were too monstrous . . . too dangerous to even be considered."

"There is only one," the Seraphim spoke.

"For now."

"Kill it," the Seraphim said with a smile.

"You know that isn't possible," Remy said, making the angel smile all the wider. His teeth were incredibly white, and appeared sharp.

Did I really look like that once? he wondered, transfixed by the sight of his angelic persona, absent of any humanity.

"Weak and pathetic," the Seraphim stated.

"Yeah," Remy agreed. "You're probably right . . . but I'm not sure how even you'd do against the Shaitan."

"Why are you here?" he asked.

Remy considered his answer a moment, then decided to be as honest as he could. "I'm afraid."

The Seraphim laughed. "Of course you are."

"I'm afraid of what Malachi has up his sleeve. I'm afraid that once the Shaitan are born, we won't be able to put them back in the bottle . . . and everybody . . . *everybody* . . . will be forced to pay the price."

"What makes this threat so different from all the others?" the Seraphim asked with genuine curiosity. His wings slowly unfurled, stretched out, and then folded back. "Why don't you just force me . . . bend me to your will as you always have. Give me a taste of freedom, and then lock me away, deep in the darkness until you need me again."

"This is different," Remy said. "We have to be together on this . . . need to be. . . ."

Remy hated to have to admit this, especially to his angelic nature, but it was true. Humanity would not be an asset in dealing with the Shaitan. He remembered what it had done to Zophiel, and it frightened him more than anything.

"We have to be more like we once were."

The Seraphim's eyes widened. "How we once were?"

Remy nodded. "It has to be if we are to survive this."

"And what of your precious humanity?"

"It'll still be here, but . . ."

"Pushed down in the darkness," the Seraphim growled, enjoying the words.

"Until—"

"Do you even remember what you were?" the Seraphim interrupted.

He moved fast, dropping directly in front of Remy with a single thrust of his powerful wings. The Seraphim stood before him, studying him, but Remy did not flinch. The angel tore the metal gauntlet from one hand, exposing pale, alabaster flesh and long, delicate fingers.

"I remember," Remy said, not quite sure what the Seraphim was about to do.

"Do you?" the Seraphim hissed, as he placed his cold fingertips upon Remy's brow.

And then Remy did remember. But this time, he saw the reality of it all, the true memory no longer dulled by the passage of millennia, no longer softened by the fabrication of his humanity.

He saw.

He saw that he was an instrument of God, an extension of the Creator's love and rage. He was an extension of the Almighty, as were his brethren. And all was right in the mechanism of the universe . . . until the birth of humanity.

When they were placed within the Garden, things went horribly awry.

The war came not long after that, and his full potential became tapped. No longer was he just a messenger of God; he was transformed by battle into a thing of violence, a thing that channeled the wrath of the Almighty.

And he reveled in it, smiting all who would raise their weapons against his—*their*—Creator.

How dare they do this? How dare they question His most holy word?

Those he had known as brothers fell beneath his hungry sword, and as each died, a little bit of him died with them.

Stained with the blood of his family, he found that he could no longer be there—no longer bathe in the light of his Lord God.

For the light had dimmed.

Bitter and confused, he left Heaven, hoping to make sense of it—to find some meaning—upon the world that God had fashioned for His favorite, yet disobedient, creations.

It was there that he lost himself, where the separation of what he was and what he would become began.

Yet he still carried all that anger, buried away, festering. Seething.

Infected and pustulated, covered with a thin bandage of humanity.

He saw.

The Seraphim stepped back, studying him as he pulled the gauntlet back onto his hand.

Remy was shaken; the powerfully raw emotion of what his angelic nature had experienced—was still experiencing—was stunning.

"What do you want me to say?" he gasped, as the Seraphim walked away. "That I can give you answers to your questions? That I can somehow make it like it used to be? I can't do that ... it will never be the same."

Remy paused, feeling the rage as he once had. "There are no answers; it's just how it is. Everything had lost its meaning until I started to watch them."

"To become like them," the Seraphim said with a sneer.

"Yeah," Remy agreed. "And was that so bad?"

"It is not what you are."

"No, but it's what I've become."

The Seraphim stared with an intensity that was nearly palpable. But Remy stared back, refusing to back down.

And suddenly the angel spread his wings, a sword of fire—Zophiel's flaming sword—appearing in his hand. The armor that adorned it was suddenly dirty, stained maroon with the blood of his memory.

"Look upon me," the angel commanded, his voice booming like thunder. "Look at what I've become."

The Seraphim was a fearsome sight indeed.

"Right now, this is what I need you to be," Remy said, walking across the top of the spire toward the Seraphim, and offering his hand.

"You," the Seraphim snarled, staring at Remy's hand as if it were covered in filth. "What Eden ... the Earth ... and the Creator need you to be ... What *I* need to be."

And with those words the Seraphim turned swiftly, unfurled its wings, and leapt from the spire, gliding down to disappear amid the elaborate structures of the holy City of Light twinkling below.

*   *   *

"Are we ready?"

Remy blinked repeatedly, first seeing the multiple boats and those who manned them in the water below where he stood, before turning his gaze to Jon and Izzy, who stared wide-eyed at him.

"Are you all right?" Jon asked. "You got kind of quiet."

"I'm fine," Remy said, remembering—*experiencing*—the rage of the Seraphim. "We should get going."

They were standing close together on the porch outside of Izzy's house, having decided that they were going to Eden.

"We was waitin' for you," Izzy said. "You was goin' to tell me how to get to the Garden when you went all strong-silent-type on us."

"Sorry," Remy apologized. "I was just thinking."

"Well, how about you think me an explanation as to how we're going to find that place."

"We need some blood," Jon said before Remy could reply.

Izzy looked at him as if he had three heads. "I'll give you blood," she said, making a fist that crackled with repressed supernatural energy.

"He needs it to track the location," Jon explained, throwing up his hands in surrender. "If you can sense where Eden is, then he can track it through the magick in your blood."

She looked at Remy.

"I'm afraid he's telling the truth."

"How much blood?" Izzy asked.

"Enough that I can catch a strong scent," Remy explained.

Izzy shook her head in disgust, reached into the pocket of her jacket—she'd put it on because she could sense that Eden was resting someplace cold—and removed a pen-knife.

She unsnapped the small blade and let it hover over the index finger of her left hand. "This all right?"

"Should be fine," Remy answered with a nod.

She dug the blade into the center of the finger's pad, the

blood welling up on either side of the blade. "Shit," she hissed. "Now what?"

"I need to smell it."

She raised her finger toward Remy's nose. He closed his eyes and inhaled, taking the scent of her magickally tainted blood into his nose.

Images exploded in his mind, pictures so vivid it was as if he were already there.

"Got it?" Izzy asked.

He opened his eyes and nodded, then spread his wings wide.

"Come closer," he told them. They shuffled toward him, and his wings began to close around them as if in a hug.

"This isn't gonna hurt, is it?" Izzy asked.

"When was the last time that you ate?" Jon asked, as their reality began to shift.

And they were gone.

Gregson Paul had been raised a good Catholic boy.

Church every Sunday for most of his life, followed by an hour of Sunday school, where he'd learned the wonders of the Holy Bible.

He'd always thought of the stories inside the Good Book as that—just stories, parables that sought to teach the reader something about how to live life as a good Christian.

He never thought of any of it as true: Noah's ark, Lot, Sodom and Gomorrah, Moses and his commandments.

But here—at the North Pole—right before his eyes, one of those stories had come to life.

"It's Eden," he said to Marjorie Halt as he gazed through the metal of the gate at the thick greenery beyond.

"You're fucking crazy," she said, hands on an impressive hip as she studied the gated jungle that had appeared amid the ice and snow.

"Then explain it," he said. "Look at us."

They were in their T-shirts and underwear, the heat from the mysterious jungle overwhelmingly tropical.

"There has to be an answer," she said, pacing back and forth in front of the gate.

Daniel Hiratsu knelt silently in the grass, his scientific instruments scattered uselessly about him. All he could do was stare. Terrance Long stayed back on the ice and snow, clothed in his heavy gear. He was attempting to communicate with anyone who would listen, but was met with a wall of interference. It appeared that Eden would not let him.

Gregson knew that it was Eden before them, as crazy as that sounded. There wasn't a doubt in his mind. It was as if the jungle were broadcasting something directly into his mind, telling him that this was true.

"I want to go in," Marjorie said as she wiped trickles of sweat from her brow. She was standing before the gate, a look of determination on her pretty face.

An uncomfortable feeling suddenly twisted in Gregson's gut.

"I don't think that's a good idea," he said.

"Why?" she asked. "Why isn't it?"

"Because we're not allowed," he said, having no idea where his answer had come from but knowing it to be true.

"Yeah, right," Marjorie said. She turned, rushing the gate and grabbing hold of its metal bars.

She didn't even have a chance to scream.

The lightning arced from the sky, striking the top of her pretty head, disintegrating her in a flash of brilliance that caused small, colorful blobs to dance before Gregson's rapidly blinking eyes.

All he could do was stare at where the girl whose remarkable ass had brought him to the North Pole had been standing, now nothing more than a smoldering mark upon the ground before the gate.

After a moment, the sound of sobbing distracted him and he turned to see Hiratsu rocking back and forth, his face stained with tears. Long was standing nearby, having ventured onto the grass, the hissing walkie-talkie he'd been using resting by his boot, where he had dropped it.

"I told her," Gregson said, his voice cracking. He could feel his sanity slip just a little bit more. "I told her not to do it."

"We should go," Long said, his voice cold and emotion-less. "We should get out of here before ..."

Before we're all struck down by lightning ... by the wrath of God? Gregson wondered.

He slowly turned from the Garden on wobbly legs and caught sight of figures in the distance near their tent. He hadn't noticed their approach; they just suddenly seemed to be there.

"Who ... ?" Gregson began.

The others turned to follow his gaze; then almost as one they began to move toward the strangers.

But the closer they got, the more wrong they appeared.

The lead figure was dressed in long, tattered robes, like some sort of twisted monk. The other appeared naked, his flesh as white as the snow they trod across, but covered in strange, angular black markings. An even odder observation was that he appeared to be carrying two people beneath his arms, an older black woman and ...

A mummified body.

Alarms went off in Gregson's brain and he felt the grip of madness embrace him that much closer; first the Garden of Eden, and now this.

Gregson called out to warn Terrance, well in the lead, but he was too late. Terrance had stopped before the robed figure. Gregson could just about make out the scientist's excited voice as he spoke to them.

The pale-skinned man—if he was a man at all—seemed to lose his shape, dropping the two figures that he carried and lunging at Terrance Long.

What happened next was indescribable.

The monster—there was no doubt in Gregson's mind as to what he was now—pounced upon the scientist and, in a display of preternatural strength, began to rip the man to pieces, eating the body parts as if starving, as the leader of their expedition's blood stained the snow.

Hiratsu screamed and started to run, but the white-fleshed monster simply reached out with an arm that grew incredibly long to coil around the Asian-American's ankle and draw him toward the beast.

Gregson couldn't move, watching as Hiratsu struggled to halt his progress, digging his fingers first into the grass, and then into the ice, but to no effect.

Finished with Long, the white-skinned thing pounced upon Hiratsu, its protean form flowing over the man as his screams intensified.

Gregson finally looked away as Hiratsu's pathetic cries died away, to be replaced by the sounds of something hungrily eating.

He did not hear the approach of the robed man, but found him standing before him.

Gregson knew, could feel, that he was in the presence of someone—some*thing*—unearthly. He was going to speak, but could think of nothing to say.

The robed figure turned his attention toward the gate and the lush, steamy jungle behind it. "Your kind had its chance," he said, his voice low and melodious. "But you tossed it all away."

He looked back at Gregson, his eyes cold and mesmerizing in their intensity. "I could never understand His fascination," he said. "I could have given Him something so much more . . . worthy."

Gregson had no idea what the robed man was talking about, but continued to listen.

"And now it's come to this."

He stepped forward and leaned close to Gregson's face. "Do you have even the slightest idea what I'm talking about, monkey?" he asked.

"No," Gregson croaked, and began to cry.

The man's intensity softened, and he put his arms around Gregson's shoulders, drawing him into an embrace.

"It's all right," he whispered. "It's not your fault; it's as if He wanted you to fail. Engineered it to be so."

Gregson was sobbing now, his face buried in the collar of the filthy fabric of the man's robes. It smelled strongly of blood, and of the air just before a storm.

"But I believe I can do better," the robed figure said, suddenly pushing Gregson away. "I must do better if reality is to survive the coming cataclysm."

Gregson's brain was on fire, trying desperately to hold on to what little sanity he had left. "Who . . . who are you?" he managed to ask.

The robed man seemed genuinely pleased by the question, and his posture straightened as he spoke.

"I am Lord God," he pronounced.

But that just made Gregson Paul laugh as the final strands of his hold on reality snapped, and he began a free fall into madness. First the Garden of Eden, now God.

Gregson didn't think he'd ever heard anything funnier, but the robed man—God—didn't appear to be the least bit amused.

Gregson tried to control himself, but the laughter of madness would not be contained. Stumbling back in a fit of giggling, he bumped against something, turning around to look up into the horrible, blood-covered face of the monster that had consumed his friends.

And Gregson kept laughing.

Even as the thing of nightmare reached for him, pulled him up into its many arms.

And into its mouth.

Malachi brought a hand close to the gate, feeling the energy radiating from the black metal, an energy that could destroy even him.

The gate had been closed by an edict from God. It could be opened again by neither the divine nor man.

Not unless one possessed the key.

The Lord God had given them the ability to see the error of their disobedient acts, and to someday return to the Garden from which they were banished. But there had to be penance; they would have to be truly sorry.

Then, and only then, would they be allowed to pass through these sealed gates.

The elder turned to look at the two pieces of the divine key that he had endured so much to obtain. The old woman had draped her body across the naked form of Adam, protecting him from the elements, her own fragile body shivering in the cold.

Again he questioned the Creator's fascination with imperfection, wondering if he would understand once he himself assumed the role of Lord of Lords.

His eyes shifted as he watched his own creation finish its meal, blood glistening upon its face and muscular body. It saw that its master was watching, and came to attention, eager to please.

"Bring them to the gate," Malachi commanded.

And the Shaitan obeyed.

Just as it should have.

Eliza tried to protect Adam from the harshness of the elements. It was in her blood, and at first she did not understand.

But now, in this cold, frozen place, with the warmth of the Garden before her—calling to her—Eliza Swan understood.

They had always said she was special, that there was something inside her that made her different from all the other Daughters. This was the reason they were so upset when she left them.

And yet, she had never realized how special she really was.

So special, in fact, that there would be folks in Heaven who would try to kill her.

The monster was before them again, pulling them up from the snow with its snaky arms, and hauling them closer.

Closer to the Garden.

She remembered now that she used to have dreams as a child: vivid dreams of this very place. And she used to tell her grandma, and her mother, and all the other Daughters, and they would look at her in that knowing way and smile.

The monster tossed them roughly onto the warm, green grass before the heavy metal gate.

"Keep treatin' us like that and you'll kill us," Eliza said, her body aching in so many places she was surprised she could still move.

"Not yet," Malachi said, staring hard through the thick metal bars at the Garden beyond.

Eliza felt the pull of the place, like a piece of metal being drawn to a magnet. She couldn't fight it if she wanted to. Adam lay silently beside her, but now his eyes were open.

Malachi was watching her, his monster—all covered in blood—standing obediently beside him. She was reminded of the big man Leo, and his dog, Cleo, at the Pelican Club, only she had liked them.

"Do it," Malachi said, eyes still locked on the lush green beyond the gate.

Eliza lay on the ground, pretending she hadn't heard him, picking blades of grass from Adam's pale, naked flesh.

"Did you hear me, monkey?" Malachi asked, his voice deceptively calm and pretty.

"I heard you," she replied. "But I haven't a clue as to what you're going on about." Even though deep in her heart, she did.

He looked at her then, his cold, icy stare so intense she could practically feel his eyes inside her. "You lie."

"Guess you know me best," she said, realizing that she was staring at the metal obstructions that barred their entry. Something stirred inside her, fighting to get out. It was the Garden pulling her, calling to her from the other side.

"Far better than you know yourself," Malachi purred. He knelt down beside her, that horrible knife of fire appearing in his hand.

She gasped, remembering the feeling as he'd used it on her, cutting loose the pieces of her forgotten life. Cutting loose the location of Eden.

Malachi brought the blade down toward Adam. "He has so little life left. I would hate to see it wasted ... out here ... so close to home."

Eliza shielded the man with her own body, the instinct to protect him strong. Almost as strong as the instinct that pulled at her from beyond the gates.

"You leave him alone," she cried. "The poor man's been through enough."

"And now it's time for him to rest," Malachi said with a nod.

"Yes," Eliza agreed.

"Then do as you're told. Open the gates."

Holding Adam in her arms, Eliza felt suddenly whole, complete. The feeling in her chest had grown to bursting, and she wondered if her old heart was about to give out.

"Open the gates," Malachi said again, his attack dog looming behind him.

She looked down at the ancient man in her arms and saw that he was looking at her. Malachi had been so right: he didn't have much life left, and it was only a matter of time before it would all run out.

She saw the corners of his mouth twitch first, and she was surprised by the movement on his sunken features; then she realized he was trying to open his mouth.

"What is it?" she asked, pulling him closer. "What are you trying to . . . ?"

But she knew the answer, the feeling in her own chest bubbling up, threatening to explode from her.

They were both feeling it. Together.

Adam's ancient mouth slowly opened, releasing a soft, whispery sound.

And Eliza could not help herself. She found herself doing something she hadn't done in so very long—not done since Pearly Gates had used his magick to take away her memories.

She was doing what she loved to do.

What she had been born to do.

Eliza Swan let it out, the sound of her voice joining with the weak sound from Adam to form the most beautiful of songs.

Eliza and Adam were singing a song of absolution.

And the gates swung wide to welcome them home.

CHAPTER NINETEEN

Remy did not feel the bite of the severe cold, only the heat of Zophiel's sword, and the pull of Eden upon it.

He opened his wings to the sight before him: a jungle, enshrouded in a roiling tropical fog, growing up from the bleak surroundings of ice and snow.

The blade flashed with an angry fire, and he felt it pull him toward the gates, which were yawning open.

Remy remembered the last time he and the Garden were together—it had been his duty to close those gates, severing its connection to Heaven.

The Garden called to him now, and Remy answered, trudging across the frozen landscape, burning sword clutched firmly in his hand. The Seraphim was with him; Remy could feel him inside, burning in his muscles, joined with his being, no longer struggling for supremacy.

For now.

The angel nature must have understood; he must have realized that for them to survive there must be unity.

At least, that was what Remy hoped.

"A little help here," said a voice, barely audible over the polar winds.

At first it startled him; he had almost forgotten he hadn't come here alone. He turned to see Jon supporting Izzy, who was bent over and vomiting onto the snow.

Remy returned to his friends, a sudden, burning spark of

annoyance that he needed to do this confirming that the Seraphim was indeed with him in more than spirit.

"Feels like you turned me inside out," Izzy slurred, wiping her mouth with the back of her hand.

"If it means anything, the more you do it, the less awful it feels," Jon offered.

They were shivering with the cold, and Remy held out his burning blade, letting the heat of the sword warm them slightly.

"We might want to get moving," he said, his attention drifting back to the open gates. "Before the cold finishes you two off."

He started to walk, and they followed, eager to stay close to the warmth of the blade.

"Do you think they're here?" Jon asked through chattering teeth.

Remy noticed patches of blood on the snow, and what appeared to be a crumpled tent off in the distance. The scent of violence, though fading in the wind, still wafted heavily on the frigid air.

"They're here," he said, stopping at the gates. "The last time I saw this place I locked the gates behind me."

"Looks like they found a key," Izzy said, carefully stepping from the ice onto the thick green grass.

"That's exactly what they did," Remy answered, staring into the Garden. The Seraphim was ready for anything. . . . Remy was ready for anything.

"So, what's the plan?" Jon asked. The man had already begun to sweat profusely in the stifling heat radiating from the jungle.

Remy considered the question.

"We go in and we kill the bad guys," he answered, and then started through the opening, into the Garden of Eden.

"That's it?" Izzy asked, following Jon, who followed behind Remy. "Sure am glad you guys worked this out so carefully," she griped. "For a while there I'd almost convinced myself this whole business was suicide."

*   *   *

Her face was numb.

Linda led Marlowe into the lobby of her apartment building, letting the door slam closed on the cold behind them.

"There," she said to the dog, relieved to be out of the icy January cold. "Happy now?"

Marlowe's thick black tail wagged as he looked at her with his deep brown eyes. She had never owned a dog before, but the last few days with Marlowe had been special.

"C'mon," she said, holding on to his leash and leading him toward the stairs. "Let's get back to the apartment and get you an apple. . . . You like apples, right?"

Marlowe barked, as if telling her yes, and galloped up the stairs, pulling her eagerly behind him.

Once inside the warm apartment, Linda kicked off her boots and settled on the couch, feet curled under her. She sipped a cup of chamomile tea, watching the black Lab happily eating his apple, and thought of his master.

Remy had been gone for more than three days, longer than he had expected, and had called only once, leaving a message apologizing for the inconvenience, and telling her that the job was proving more complicated than he'd thought.

Marlowe finished the apple, getting up from the floor and approaching the couch.

"Hey, there," she said, smiling as his tail wagged.

He rested his chin on the sofa cushion beside her, gazing up at her with soulful eyes.

"You miss him, don't you?" she asked. "You miss Remy."

The dog let out a low moan, tail twitching ever so slightly.

And Linda had to admit that she missed him too. In all her years she'd never met a man like him, and she'd known quite a few.

There was something about this Remy Chandler.

"Want to come . . . ," she began, but never got a chance to finish as Marlowe leapt up onto the sofa, plopping heavily beside her, his butt pressed firmly against her hip.

"There you go," she said with a laugh, leaning on him, hugging and scratching behind his ears. "How's that?"

Marlowe sighed, closing his eyes to begin another nap.

She continued to think about Marlowe's master, and what it was that attracted her so. She had noticed it the first time they'd met, out in front of the brownstone on Newbury. She couldn't quite put her finger on it, but he seemed to give off a strange kind of vibe, as if he had the weight of the world on his shoulders.

A weight that she would be perfectly willing to share, if he'd let her.

"Oh, my God," she muttered aloud, horrified that she had thought of such a thing.

Marlowe lifted his head wearily and looked at her, wanting to be sure that she was all right.

"Can you believe it?" she asked the black dog, reaching out to pet his square head. She loved the feel of his fur, his velvety soft ears. "I've got a crush on your master, and we've only been on two dates. Can you say '*mucho* desperate'?"

She bent down and gave him a loud smooch on the top of his head as she got up from the couch. "Promise me you won't tell him?"

Marlowe's tail thumped on the cushion.

"It'll be our little secret, okay?"

He barked softly as if to say, *Your secret's safe with me*, and Linda laughed.

She loved it when Marlowe answered her.

It was almost as if he understood exactly what she was saying.

Steven Mulvehill was in a half-awake, half-asleep limbo in the emergency room of Brockton Hospital, waiting for the doctor to either discharge him or admit him.

Machines beeped and chimed on the outskirts of his consciousness, along with the chattering of voices and the tormented moans of the injured.

He was hurting, but the physical pain was nothing compared to the agony inside his head.

Mulvehill had gotten a glimpse behind the curtain—a peek inside Pandora's box, so to speak—and knew that no matter how hard he tried, life would never be the same again.

Drifting down deeper into sleep, he saw his friend waiting for him, ready to tell him that everything would be just fine. And wanting to believe, Mulvehill let his guard drop.

Remy tore the flesh from his own face, revealing something pale and tattooed, with teeth like needles. Something horrible, and hungry to eat the world.

Mulvehill screamed, thrashing upon the hospital bed. The machines beeped loudly, and he guessed a nurse would soon be in to check on him.

Good, he thought as his heart raced painfully in his chest. And after she had checked him out and hooked him back up, he would ask her to turn on some more lights.

It was too damn dark in the room.

Marlowe waited outside the bathroom door as Linda showered.

He could have stayed on the sofa, but decided to accompany the female instead, preferring not to be alone.

He lay on his side on the rug in the hallway, closing his eyes, and in a matter of minutes he was dreaming.

He traveled to the place where his master was, a place of many trees and grass, surrounded by ice and snow.

A place filled with danger. Even in his dream, Marlowe could smell it, heavy in the air, drifting up from the ground, and from the leaves on the trees.

He began to bark, warning his master of the impending danger, but Remy did not hear, so Marlowe barked some more.

And would continue to bark until Remy heard him.

CHAPTER TWENTY

For Jon, it was like stepping into a fairy tale.

Like climbing the beanstalk and finding the old woman who lived in a shoe, and all her kids were being babysat by Cinderella.

It was that weird.

He'd been raised to believe in this place, that someday he and all his cousins would be allowed to return to Paradise.

To Eden.

Now, standing just beyond the gate, he tried to take it all in. It was an odd place, a foreign place. Jon had been to many a jungle in his lifetime as the Sons moved from place to place, but he'd never seen a jungle like this.

"Something's wrong here," Izzy said.

Jon noticed the trees, their branches twisted and malformed, the vegetation covered in dark, malignant spots. A smell hung heavy in the humid air; it was the smell of sickness, of rot.

Izzy bent down to the ground, and Jon watched as she extended her long fingers and stuck them into the moist earth.

The woman gasped.

"Oh . . . ," she said, eyes growing wide, her body rigid.

Thin, snaking vines began to emerge from the ground, entwining around her fingers and moving up her hands, wrapping around her wrists.

Her breath was coming in quick gasps, her eyes blinking rapidly as they glazed over.

"Oh, my God. Oh, my dear God . . ."

Jon reached for her, but Remy grabbed his wrist, stopping him.

"Wait," he ordered.

"The Garden," Izzy said between troubled breaths. "The Garden . . . the Garden is in my head. . . . Oh, God . . . she's sick. . . . Something . . . something is growing inside of her. . . . Something is going to kill her if . . . if she can't fight it."

A strange moaning sound filled the air. Jon looked around for the source, but realized it was coming from all around them. The tree branches were moving, creaking in protest as they bent in their direction. Even the grass beneath their feet had begun to squirm.

"This isn't good," Izzy screamed, trying to pull her hands from the ground, but the vines held her fast. "She's crazy from the pain . . . from the sickness."

Tree limbs lashed out with whiplike speed.

Remy grabbed Jon, driving them both to the ground as a branch swiped at them, passing dangerously close to their heads.

"She . . . she's trying to fight back," Izzy said, now sitting upon the ground, still connected to the Garden. "She doesn't know that we're here to help."

Thorny vines dropped from some of the higher trees, wrapping themselves around Remy like tentacles, and pulling him up into the air.

Jon watched in horror as the squirming tendrils yanked Remy higher into the thick foliage, the angel practically disappearing into the growth.

"She's trying to save herself," Izzy yelled.

Jon scrambled to his feet, standing beneath the struggling form of Remy Chandler, who was now completely enshrouded in sharp, spiny vines. He looked toward Izzy; she had the power to help but was held in the grip of the Garden. She had started to struggle, her body becoming covered in thin, slithering roots.

Jon moved to help her, but the ground beneath him turned to watery mud. He sank instantly to his waist, clawing at the ground for purchase, but wherever he touched, the ground turned to insubstantial muck.

Pulling him deeper, until he felt the cold touch of wet earth beneath his chin.

Ready to swallow him whole.

Taranushi dispatched the tigerlike beast with cold, deadly efficiency, wrapping his pliable body around the great cat and snapping its bones one at a time, slowly crippling it, before he began to consume its still-warm flesh.

The great cat had sprung at them from the thick underbrush as they fought their way through the living jungle, another example of how much the Garden had changed.

These changes disturbed Malachi, a seed of worry germinating in his mind. Something was amiss.

Thick, serpentine roots erupted around them, attempting to snatch Adam and Eliza from where they lay upon the ground. Malachi brandished his scalpel, lunging at the vegetation, cutting the tentacle-like growths in half before they could do any harm.

"It is obvious that the Garden does not want us here," the angel said, brushing the signs of conflict from the fabric of his robes. "It too must sense the end of the old, and the inevitable approach of a new beginning."

Malachi paused, waiting for Eden to respond, as Taranushi finished his snack and rejoined the group.

"Though a wonderful thing, birth can always be so ... traumatic," Malachi continued.

The jungle again began to tremble, shifting and moving as it readied to resume its attack on them.

"Tear it down," Malachi said with a wave of his hand. "We do not have time for this."

Taranushi did as he was ordered, his liquid form flowing toward the thickening wall of vegetation, bolts of magickal power erupting from his hands, reducing the jungle before them to drifting particles in the air, and cutting a swath of destruction into the very heart of Eden.

The old woman moaned, her face pale and flushed, damp with sweat and tears.

Malachi studied the humans; he hoped they would stay alive long enough to help him fulfill his plans.

"Bring them," he commanded the Shaitan as he turned and strode down the blackened path.

The jungle surrounding him grew steadily darker, the growths more perverse and mutated. He was getting closer—closer to the seeds he'd planted so very long ago, the seeds that would now bear the fruit of his supremacy.

Malachi stopped before a wall of vines adorned with ebony flowers. The flowers hissed menacingly, blowing puffs of some noxious, organic poison into his face. Annoyed, he slashed at the growths with his glowing scalpel, burning and cutting the thick vegetation, the stink of poison in his angelic lungs reinvigorating his determination to see Heaven reduced to smoldering ruins.

And from the ashes, a new beginning would emerge.

He had no idea how long he went on, his anger blinding him to time's passage, stopping only when he was summoned by his servant.

"Master," Taranushi called tentatively.

The elder whirled, blade clutched tightly in his hand and murder in his eyes.

"We are here," the Shaitan said, pointing behind him.

And Malachi turned to see what he had endured so much, for so very long, to reach.

"The Tree," he exclaimed, clambering over the remains of Eden's last defense.

With a cloud of buzzing insects swarming around his head, Malachi finally stood before the Tree.

And was horrified by what he saw.

The Tree was withered, its branches sagging with the shriveled remains of fruit once filled with the knowledge of God.

Something's wrong, Malachi thought, and then his eyes fell to the ground surrounding the base of the great Tree.

The grass was brown—dead—and the ground roiled as something stirred beneath it.

Something that he had placed there.

Something ready to be born.

For a moment, Izabelle Swan ceased to exist, and there was only the Garden.

Izzy and Eden were one. Izzy felt the Garden's yearning, her desire to be complete again, to have her children returned to her.

But she also felt her sickness.

Something had been planted within her, something that fed upon her. It was beyond hungry . . . voracious, and it wanted the knowledge.

God's knowledge.

And it would not be sated until it had consumed it all.

And as it grew, it fed upon the tree, suckling upon its roots, using the enlightenment of God as its source of nourishment.

The evil grew within the soft, dark womb of her earth. She tried to kill them, to abort this dangerous life inside her, but it was too strong, and the longer it was inside her, the weaker she became.

She did not how much longer she had, but Eden would fight until there was nothing left of her but dust.

Izzy threw back her head and sucked in a mouthful of air and annoying insects, gasping for breath as the thoughts of the Garden receded in her mind.

"We want to help you," she cried out, her hands still buried deep within the soil. "Please let us help you."

The Garden shivered, a noticeable tremor passing through the lush vegetation as the woman's words reached the sentient jungle surroundings.

She heard the sound of coughing, and turned to see the muddy form of Jon, climbing out of a deep pool of muck, roots snaking across the ground allowing him to pull himself free.

"Thank you," she said, feeling suddenly joyous, but that joy was short-lived as there came an explosion from somewhere above them, and something dropped to the Garden floor, still burning.

"Sweet Jesus," Izzy said as she watched the angel slowly stand, his body burning as if doused with gasoline.

"Remy," Jon called out as he stood, dripping thick mud.

But Izzy wasn't quite sure it was Remy he was calling to.

The angel stood there, flaming sword in hand, a sneer of contempt upon his burning face.

"Jon, you might not want to get too close," she warned.

The Son of Adam stopped short as the angel's gaze fell upon him.

"Remy?" the man asked again.

The angel's fire seemed to burn brighter, and for a moment Izzy feared for the man's life, but the angel's expression suddenly softened, and the fire around his body extinguished.

"Yeah," Remy said.

"She didn't want to hurt us," Izzy explained, as she pulled her hands free of the twining roots and joined her friends. "Eden's sick. . . . Something very bad is growing inside her, something evil. . . ."

Remy looked at her, and for a moment she sensed that he might have been replaced again by something far colder, and more angelic.

"Then I suggest we help her," he said, holding out his burning sword. "And cut this cancer from her womb."

CHAPTER TWENTY-ONE

The sword burned in Remy's hand.

The heat of the weapon radiated internally, amplifying the rage of the Seraphim, drawing it out like an infection from a wound.

Remy held on to his control, but didn't know if he had the strength to continue. Wrapped within the constricting embrace of the thorny vines, he had let his defenses down, allowing the Seraphim to emerge without restraint.

There had been something horribly liberating about the experience, and yet terrifying. To think of the Seraphim—to think of this being of divine power filled with rage—unleashed upon this holy place . . . it scared his human side.

But their options were few, for he knew that he didn't have the power to face the Shaitan without the unbridled fury of the Seraphim.

He could feel the scions of Adam and Eve staring at him. They were looking to him for guidance, unaware of the struggle going on inside him. It was taking everything he could muster to hold on to the leash. . . .

"What now?" Jon wanted to know, nervously looking about him. The jungle was moving, writhing as if in pain.

"We find the nest of the Shaitan, and kill them before they can be born," Remy answered as the Seraphim howled for blood, testing his resolve at every turn.

"Then we'd better find them fast," Izzy said. She was leaning against a nearby tree, her complexion wan—sickly.

"I'm not feeling so good since hooking up to the Garden," she explained. "Think I might be sharing how Eden is feeling . . . and it isn't good. I don't know how much time we have left."

The flaming sword began to vibrate in Remy's hand, and as if the blade had a life of its own, its tip suddenly pointed toward the earth.

Jon jumped back as Remy struggled with the unwieldy weapon.

"What's happening?" he asked, afraid.

"I don't know," Remy answered, fighting the blade. The pull was incredible, his muscles straining to keep the sword from stabbing the ground.

"Let it do what it wants," Izzy hollered. "It has a connection to this place. . . . I think it might be trying to help."

Remy did, allowing the burning blade to drop, stabbing into the soil of Eden with a sibilant hiss. Images from the Garden began traveling through the sword and into his mind.

And what he saw filled him with horror.

The Tree of Knowledge, withered and dying, the ground beneath it churning with unholy life—as Malachi and the Shaitan looked on.

It was more than he could stand, and the Seraphim raged, charging forward to wrest away control.

Let me out, the divine power demanded.

And Remy knew he had no choice.

He let the Seraphim come.

The angel Remiel considered the humans before him.

And, finding them of no importance to the coming conflict, he stretched his golden wings and leapt into the sky.

There was evil to be vanquished.

Blood to be spilled.

Battles to be won.

All in the name of Heaven, and the Lord God.

The Tree was nearly dead.

"Master, what is wrong?" Taranushi asked with concern.

It's been drained, Malachi thought, as he placed a hand against the dark, dry bark. *The fetal Shaitan have feasted upon the knowledge of the Almighty.*

They should never have been capable of such a task. They were never supposed to do something such as this.

They were not designed to do something like this.

All that knowledge, the elder thought, eyes turned to the soil around the base of the Tree. The ground bubbled as the Shaitan stirred.

And he began to wonder if perhaps he'd made a mistake.

He looked up as the fearsome form of Taranushi approached. Malachi recalled the ferocity of this first Shaitan, the violent acts he had mercilessly performed throughout the ages in Malachi's name.

The knowledge of God contained within such a vessel . . . perhaps it wasn't the best of his ideas.

He revisited his vision of a future plagued by a war that would bring about the end of all things. He saw the Shaitan in this vision, believing at one time that they were fighting under *his* command, but now . . .

"What is wrong?" Taransuhi asked again.

"Nothing," Malachi lied. He looked to the writhing ground again and felt nothing but disgust.

"They're not ready," he stated flatly, turning his gaze back to his servant. "It is not yet time for them."

Taranushi's expression was one of confusion. "I do not understand. I can feel my brothers and sisters . . . desperate . . . wanting . . . ready to be born . . . unleashed into the world."

Eden trembled angrily beneath them, and Malachi lost his footing, stumbling to one side. Taranushi caught his arm and their eyes locked.

"Finish what you have started with me," the Shaitan pleaded. "I no longer wish to be alone."

Malachi could hear the desperation in his creation's voice, and considered what it would be like to be the only one of your kind. God had created him first, mere seconds before Lucifer, and he remembered that feeling.

The intimacy between creator and creation. It was something that could never be forgotten. Fleeting, but so powerful.

If only the Lord had stopped there, what a reality they could have shaped.

"Sometimes alone is best," Malachi said, pulling his arm away, already considering alternatives to his future. A future that did not include the Shaitan. "There's a cave nearby that I used for my work," he began. "We'll go there before we leave Eden and—"

"No," Taranushi roared.

The symbols on his pale skin began to flow, like the warning of a snake's hiss just before the strike.

Malachi reared back, startled—but not surprised by the creature's insolence.

"You will do as I say," he ordered, exerting his will over his creation.

The markings upon the Shaitan's skin slowed, and the creature backed down beneath his gaze.

"Remember that there are even worse fates than being alone," Malachi warned, a sudden niggling thought entering his mind as he looked upon the powerful beast. *Am I strong enough to defeat the Shaitan?*

And as if the beast could sense his sudden inkling of weakness, Taranushi's body became like smoke as he emitted the most bloodcurdling scream.

"I have waited long enough!" the Shaitan proclaimed, swirling around the Tree of Knowledge, flowing past to reconstitute before the two humans.

"You will do as I command," Malachi ordered.

But it was too late; the Shaitan was beyond all that.

"I hear them," the creature said, breathing rapidly. "They are calling out to me ... questioning why they are still beneath the cool, damp earth of this place, while there are kingdoms and worlds to conquer.

"Gods to usurp."

Malachi knew he had to do something. Things were spinning rapidly out of control. Carefully, he approached his creation.

"Taranushi, please," he pleaded in his calmest tone. "Trust me. Your species *will* be born; they are just not yet ready."

"You lie!" the monster bellowed. "I can feel that they are ready."

"A tragic miscalculation on my part," Malachi said, closer now. He palmed his dagger from within the folds of his robes. "They need more time."

He was closer now, and Taranushi seemed to be listening.

"If we were to complete the process now, they would be deficient. Imperfect."

Malachi was close enough to strike. At least he'd been smart enough to build in a weakness for the Shaitan. He would strike at the monster's heart; even though it wasn't often in the same place as the beast shifted its shape, the elder could sense—could hear—where it was at that moment.

"And we wouldn't want that."

Malachi lunged, his burning blade plunging into the solid flesh of his creation's chest, and into where its monstrous heart beat.

The elder's eyes met Taranushi's, and he expected to see the light of life failing, but the Shaitan only snarled.

"What you seek is no longer there," Taranushi growled.

Malachi attempted to pull back, but it was too late. The Shaitan's flesh bulged outward to engulf his hand, trapping him.

"Perhaps it is a cycle," Taranushi said, his form shifting to resemble Malachi.

"You betray your Creator, and I betray mine," the monster spoke with Malachi's voice, a sinister smile appearing on his bearded face.

The Shaitan struck, dark energies flowing through his form and into the elder. Malachi screamed out in pain as the force of the energies ripped him from Taranushi's clutches and sent him flying to land at the base of the Tree of Knowledge.

He lay for a moment, stunned, feeling the Shaitan in the ground below him moving toward the surface.

"You dare," Malachi said with great indignation, as he slowly climbed to his feet. He summoned the remnants of his divinity, and even though he had been stripped of most of his angelic power when sentenced to Tartarus, he was an elder, and the power that still remained was awesome.

Heavenly energies flowed from his body; Malachi was ready.

Taranushi crouched at the edge of the jungle, the black markings upon his pale form flowing again, forming larger and bolder shapes, in his attempt to distract his opponent.

The Shaitan moved, but not in the way the elder expected.

Malachi had counted on a full-on attack, the servant versus the master, but the monster moved quickly to the left, toward the humans cowering on the ground.

"If you will not bring them forth, I will," the Shaitan proclaimed, snatching up the cadaverous form of Adam and heading for the Tree. The old woman screamed, leaping to her feet, trying to drag the man from Taranushi's muscular tentacle, but the monster was too fast.

Malachi tried to block his way to the Tree, but Taranushi was fury incarnate, moving with incredible speed, dodging the elder's pathetic attempts to strike him down. Multiple limbs, flowing with their own arcane energies, lashed out, and the elder was tossed aside, tumbling from the base of the Tree to lie upon the trembling ground.

Taranushi stood beneath the Tree, Adam's limp and naked form before him.

"A sacrifice," the Shaitan cried to the Garden. "Let the blood of the first feed the hunger of a new beginning."

And as Eliza Swan screamed, Malachi watched, helpless, as Taranushi brought Adam toward his mouth of razor-sharp teeth, biting into the old soul's withered throat and letting his ancient blood ooze from the gaping wound onto the soil.

What have I done? The question reverberated through Malachi's mind as he watched the horror unfold.

Adam's blood rained down upon Eden's flesh, the disease beneath her surface becoming more active as it fed upon the ancient life stuff. The ground began to tumble and roll as if in the grip of convulsions. And from the cold, dark womb of dirt, a new life started to emerge.

Taranushi let the limp and bleeding body of Adam fall to the ground, as pale, childlike hands shot up from the soil, like some perverse fungus. They attached themselves to the ancient one's body, sinking tiny claws into the withered flesh and tearing pieces away.

The old woman wailed for the first of men, her sad tears running down her face to water the soil of Eden.

And from her tears the most beautiful of flowers began to grow.

Malachi was paralyzed by the sight, one part fascinated, the other filled with terror over what was to come. *It's too late*, he realized, knowing that he did not have the strength to face off against Taranushi and the emerging brood. Slowly he rose to his feet, careful not to arouse the Shaitan's attentions, and started for the cover of the thick jungle foliage. He would find his cave, and there he would begin to compose his escape.

Images of the Shaitan forces invading the Kingdom of Heaven oozed into his mind, followed by the presentation of total darkness, and he had to consider the fact that perhaps there would be no tomorrow.

The thought came upon him like a shroud draped over the face of the dead.

He was just about to turn away from the horrors unfolding at the base of the Tree, when a sound from above made him stop.

He had heard this sound before when last he'd stood in the Garden.

It was the sound of God's terrible fury taken shape.

The war cry of the Seraphim.

Remiel dropped from the sky, burning blade in hand, a scream of furious indignation on his lips.

How dare this thing taint the Lord's Garden with its presence, the Seraphim thought as it swooped down upon the Shaitan.

The blade arced as he dropped, seeking out the muscular flesh between the beast's head and shoulders. Remiel watched the fiery sword, anticipating the sensation of its razor edge biting into thick muscle.

But it was as if the blade passed through water.

The Shaitan's body shifted, flowing away from the descending soldier of Heaven, to reconstitute directly across from him.

The monster smiled, attacking with the speed of thought.

Multiple sets of limbs rose, fingers like worms writhing in the air as bolts of snapping blue energy leapt from their tips. Remiel spread his wings, lifting off from the ground and blocking most of the supernatural energies with his sword, but one of them got through. The dark magick pierced his shoulder, an electrical fire igniting in his veins, causing his wings to grow numb.

He fell through the withered limbs of the Tree of Knowledge, landing on the body of Adam, the stink of the first human's blood flowing up into his flared nostrils. He could feel the sickness of the Garden, feel the evil bubbling up just below its surface, and was almost taken to the brink because of it.

The Seraphim began to rise as tiny, white hands with claws like hooks reached up from the ground, grabbing at his armored form. Remiel watched in horror as the claws pierced the Heaven-forged armor with little effort, holding him in place as more and more of the birthing Shaitan attempted to feed upon him. He furiously beat his wings, pulling away from some of their clutches, and was able to kneel upon the churning soil, raising the flaming sword that once belonged to the sentry of Eden, and stabbing it down into the ground.

There came a muffled explosion, followed by unnatural, high-pitched screams from beneath the dirt. Remiel could feel their pain, hear the psychic screams of the injured and the dying, as the hold they had upon him loosened, and he was able to free himself.

He withdrew his blade from the earth, which was hot and sizzling with the life juices of the unborn Shaitan. Eager to see them all dead, the Seraphim readied the sword to strike again at the base of the Tree, when the newest attack came.

The adult Shaitan exploded at him, running upon all fours like a bull and ramming its bony head into Remiel's midsection, pinning him to the side of the Tree.

Remiel recovered quickly, bringing the pommel of the sword down on top of the Shaitan. Its head seemed to break apart, flowing up the Seraphim's arm. The damnable creature's entire body went to liquid, oozing over Remiel's armored form, covering him in its malleable flesh.

The angel could feel what it was doing, seeking out the weaknesses in his protective covering. He could feel the thing squirming through the openings, writhing against his divine flesh beneath the armor. The sensation was sickening.

Remiel thrashed, dropping to the ground, beating his wings, but the flesh of the Shaitan had spread onto them as well, preventing him from taking flight. He tried to use the sword, poking and jabbing at the thick second skin that had engulfed his body, but the Shaitan endured the stabs of the flaming blade, squeezing him even tighter, while forcing the armor from his body.

Pain like he had never experienced before flowed through him. The angel attempted to cry out, but his mouth was filled with the oozing, liquid flesh of his shapeless attacker. His own flesh was burning as the Shaitan released its destructive, dark energies.

The Seraphim fought fitfully as his body was completely engulfed in the constricting mass of the forbidden lifeform. From all around, he heard a rumbling chuckle, as the Shaitan continued its relentless assault. The creature knew it was winning.

The monster was whispering now, telling him to give up the fight, that there was no dishonor in this defeat, for it was all inevitable.

He could feel the Shaitan inside him now, forcing itself down his throat. Remiel called upon the fire that was his gift from God, and his body started to radiate a heat as hot as the fires of creation, but it wasn't enough.

The fire could not burn bright enough to repel the darkness that now held him in its constricting embrace.

Stealing away his light.

Feeding upon his life.

Jon was holding Izzy up by the waist, helping her move across the twisted landscape as they tried to follow Remy.

"I can't believe he left us," Jon said, stumbling as the ground pushed up suddenly beneath their feet, sending them both falling to the ground.

"He's doing what he needs to do," Izzy said, breathing heavily. She looked even sicker now; her mahogany skin had taken on a grayish pallor. She didn't even try to get up.

"But I thought we were part of that picture," Jon said, trying to help her to rise.

"We are," she said, pushing his hands away.

"You have to get up," Jon told her. He was looking around. "I can't imagine it's much farther. . . . How big can this place be?"

"Very big," Izzy said. "Much bigger than you could ever imagine, and she needs our help."

"Which is exactly what we're going to give her," Jon said, bending down to wrap his hands around her waist and lift her to her feet.

"No," Izzy said firmly, her dark eyes looking deeply into his. "She needs us."

"Well, we can't stay here." Jon was really annoyed now. "Remy is over there somewhere and he—"

"She needs our help," Izzy repeated firmly. "My help . . . and your help."

He didn't know what she was getting at as she sat upon the ground, one of her hands again buried beneath the soil.

"I don't . . . ," he started to say.

"Think about who we are." She grabbed his pants leg, attempting to pull him down with her. "Whose blood courses through our veins."

The moist ground dampened the knees of his slacks as he knelt with her.

"She's going to die. . . . Eden will die if we don't try . . . if we don't lend her some of our strength.

"I can't do it alone," Izzy continued weakly. "Will you help me?"

Jon didn't know what to say at first, even though it was obvious. This was what it must've been all about, the true reason he had been born into the Sons.

His purpose.

"Will you help her?" Izzy whispered pleadingly.

Tentatively he extended his hand above the soil, curious as to whether or not it would hurt, and then brought it down.

Knowing Nathan would have been proud of him as he plunged his fingers into the dampness of the earth.

"Why are you hiding?"

Remy Chandler opened his eyes at the sound of the familiar voice.

"Madeline?" he called into the sea of gloom surrounding him.

"Yeah," she answered casually, her approach bringing a warm yellow glow to the nebulous surroundings. "Who else would it be?"

He pushed himself up into a sitting position. The aura around her was warm, and it felt good upon his naked skin as she drew closer.

"Are you going to answer my question?" she asked.

"I'm not hiding," he said indignantly. "Why would I be hiding?"

"That's what I want to know."

Remy said nothing as he stared at the woman he loved, the woman who had given him so much.

"Do you know what's happening out there?" she asked, hooking a finger toward the sea of black behind her.

He looked past her, squinting into the shadows.

"Not going well, is it?"

Madeline's mouth opened in disbelief. "I can't believe you," she said.

"What?" Remy asked. "What can't you believe?"

"You," she said incredulously. "I can't believe you. He's dying out there, you know."

Remy was still staring into the darkness behind her when he looked away.

"There's nothing I can do," he said, looking at his bare feet.

"Really?" She placed her hands on her shapely hips. God, she was beautiful. Just one look was enough to get his heart racing.

"The Seraphim is out there fighting for Eden . . . for Heaven, for Pete's sake, and there's nothing that you can do? What's wrong with this picture?" she asked him.

"This is where I'm supposed to be," he said. "There's no room for humanity out there." Remy shook his head.

"There's not going to be room for much of anything once the Shaitan are born," Madeline said. "I'm not going to ask you if you know how dangerous those creatures are, because of course you do—I'm nothing but a manifestation of your subconscious—and if I know, you certainly do too."

"I'm here because I need to be," Remy said. "I'm his weakness. . . . The matter of the Shaitan should be faced with a cold, divine efficiency."

Madeline laughed, a delicate hand going up to her mouth to stifle the sound of her merriment.

"Sorry about that," she said. "It's just that that was really funny."

Remy almost smiled, loving the sound of her laugh, even if it was at his own expense.

"Are you that big of a dummy?" Madeline asked.

Remy was a bit taken aback by the question.

"Excuse me?" he asked.

"I asked if you were stupid."

"No, I don't think that—"

"The Seraphim has gone into battle incomplete," Madeline stated.

"You're wrong; the Seraphim is out there . . . complete, all fiery rage and righteous indignation," Remy explained.

"Then what are you?" she wanted to know.

"I'm what isn't needed right now," he said. "Which is why I'm here."

"Which is why you're wrong," Madeline corrected. "You're his humanity ... not some useless thing that was picked up at a yard sale a few years back. Whether he likes it or not, the Seraphim has evolved ... his human aspect is just as important as his angelic one."

Remy didn't know how to respond to that one.

"He's missing something," Madeline explained. "Like going into battle without his armor ... without his sword."

The darkness began to swirl behind her, growing lighter as forms began taking shape—as images of a world appeared.

New York at night ... Chicago ... Japan ... Australia ... the Boston skyline.

Remy felt his mood lighten at the sight of his adopted home.

"This isn't what he's fighting for," Madeline pointed out.

The backdrop quickly changed, melding to scenes of the past. Remy saw when their relationship was young—he and Madeline walking on a beach at Cape Cod, their love uncontrollable in its growth. It would grow so big ... so powerful.

"This isn't what he's fighting for."

The disheveled image of Steven Mulvehill appeared, and for some reason the sight of the man ... his friend ... it hurt, made him want to reach out and ...

Marlowe running at the Boston Common, his black fur shiny in the afternoon sun as he chased a tennis ball thrown by ...

Linda Somerset dressed in a heavy winter jacket and jeans, clapping her hands for Marlowe to return the ball to her. Remy smiled. She would probably have a long wait. Marlowe was a ball hog, preferring to tease, running around with the prize clutched proudly in his mouth before ...

"This isn't what he's fighting for."

The following scene made him gasp, not real but torn from the imagination.

The Earth was in ruin, infernos burning that permanently blackened the sky. The Shaitan swarmed upon the world like locusts, dismantling everything that He—the Lord God—was responsible for.

"Up there, in the Garden," Madeline said, pointing off in the distance behind them. "He fights for his Creator, and the Kingdom of Light. . . ."

Remy saw the Garden and the battle going on within it. The Seraphim was covered in the flesh of the Shaitan, being crushed . . . suffocated. . . .

"And there's so much more to fight for, Remy," Madeline said. "Don't you think?"

So much more, he thought as the images of the world, of people, places, and things, fired past in staccato blasts.

Madeline came to him, putting her arms around him and drawing him close.

"Glad you agree with me," she said with her most seductive smile as she brought her lips to his. And they kissed.

And it was like he had been awakened from a very long slumber, like the sun rising powerfully in the sky to chase the darkness away.

So much more.

CHAPTER TWENTY-TWO

Remiel had failed the Creator.

He could feel the corrosive, supernatural energies flowing from the Shaitan digesting what remained of his armor, and starting to work upon his flesh.

And there was nothing he could do.

The angel considered crying out to his Lord God, but he was too ashamed. If this was to be his fate, he would accept it. He had met a foe more powerful than he.

This realization seemed to fuel the angel's anger, and he struggled fitfully in the Shaitan's grip, but the darkness at the center of the creature's being was like nothing he had ever experienced before.

It was so cold, and it was drawing the light from him.

Soon there was only shadow, and Remiel was flying in the endless night, not toward the sky, but down . . . down to where the light would never reach.

Down to where he'd cease to be, swallowed up by the endless night.

At first he believed it a trick of his failing system, flashes of light heralding his approaching death, but then he realized that something was with him.

There were shapes in the flashes, and he came to know that they were of his human persona and its deceased wife.

Come to gloat? the angel of Heaven wondered, as he drifted closer.

The woman was smiling, and he didn't know why. For

soon they would be no more ... their life forces consumed by a horror with the potential to level the Kingdom of Heaven. He wanted to ask her why she smiled, but he was too weak, already wavering on the precipice of oblivion.

And then she reached out, taking his wrist and bringing his hand toward the other, toward the hand of the human self that had dominated his form.

"I doubt I can make the two of you kiss and make up," the woman said, as she joined their hands. "So a handshake will have to do."

Malachi was loath to admit it, but at the moment, he was quite in awe of his creation.

Despite the angel's divine power, Taranushi had managed to immobilize the Seraphim, completely envelop its body, and was now in the process of consuming him.

This was a design to fear, and maybe the Almighty had been right in His decision not to create the Shaitan.

But that was neither here nor there. If Malachi wanted to save reality, he had to move quickly, before the rest of the Shaitan were born. He started back into the jungle's thickness when he heard the sound of crying. Glancing across the clearing, he saw the old woman, Eliza Swan, kneeling just before the Tree as Adam's corpse continued to be fed upon by the emerging Shaitan. She was weeping, mourning his death, but at least he had gotten his wish: to die in the Garden.

Malachi was going to leave, but thought better of it. The woman, this descendant of Eve, might prove useful in escaping the Garden. Quickly, he made his way around the withered Tree, emerging from the jungle at the woman's back.

"Do not mourn for him, human," Malachi said. "For he has achieved his heart's desire, to return to the Garden from which he was banished."

She turned her head to him, her face awash with tears.

"You killed him," she spat. "This poor old soul, and you killed him like a dog."

"You are incorrect, woman," Malachi said as he grabbed

her arm and hauled her to her feet, pulling her back toward the jungle. "*I* did no such thing."

He chanced a quick look back at the Tree of Knowledge, and what unfolded beneath it. Taranushi was still covering the Seraphim, moaning aloud. At first Malachi thought them moans of pleasure as the spawn of darkness fed upon the angel's light.

But then the moans turned distinctly to screams of agony.

Taranushi had only imagined how wonderful an angel of Heaven—a Seraphim—would taste.

He had thought about it for centuries, and longer, as he searched the world for the keys to Eden. Now the power of Heaven's warrior host flowed into him as his body continued to spread across that of the Seraphim, expanding and contracting, using powerful muscles to crush his victim, and allow the delectable juices to flow.

To think that there was an entire legion of these beings to feast upon was enough to drive him mad with pleasure.

Taranushi groaned in satisfaction as the angel struggled within him. He wanted to tell the Heavenly being to cease its efforts, that it was only prolonging the inevitable, but the truth was, he enjoyed the feeling, the power that he had over this arrogant messenger of God.

The sensation of supremacy.

The Seraphim's movements grew weaker, and Taranushi felt his own digestive fluids increase in flow. The beast was tempted to release the angel, so he could rip the flesh from its bones and stuff the bloody pieces of Heavenly meat into his mouth as the Seraphim slowly passed from life, but this form of consumption would more than suffice.

The first twinge startled the Shaitan, but that moment quickly turned to excitement as he realized that the Seraphim still had some fight in him.

More life to feed his insatiable appetite.

The Shaitan constricted his muscles all the tighter, giving his prey little space to move.

"Fight, pretty angel," he cooed, stretching his head

above the undulating mass of black, marked flesh that was his body. "It will just make your meat all the sweeter."

The monster began to laugh, but his amusement turned to concern as he realized that the Seraphim's movements were growing stronger.

Concentrating with all his might, the Shaitan tightened his body's pliant muscles, just as a clenched fist savagely punched through the mass of its body, and into the air.

"Yeeeeeeeeeearrrgh!" Taranushi cried out.

His flesh flowed over the arm and drew the limb back down into his body. But another fist forced its way through, followed by the flexing of a mighty wing.

The Shaitan was in trouble, and he doubled his efforts to put his prey down, but to little avail. It was as if the Seraphim had been given a second opportunity at life.

An intervention on behalf of the divine, he almost considered, before pushing the disturbing thought away.

And that was when he began to feel the heat. The angel had attempted the same trick before, radiating the fire of its divinity, but the darkness inside Taranushi had been enough to suffocate that flame.

Now, however, hands burning white with fire hotter than the heart of a star tore through Taranushi's flesh, the meat of the Shaitan's body sizzling as his juices were cooked from within.

The Seraphim tore himself out from the prison of flesh, body glowing white-hot, and tossed his head back in a savage scream that informed the universe he still lived.

Taranushi recoiled, flowing away from the intense heat of the angel's form. He was hurt, his body damaged in ways that it had never been before. Gazing down at the wounds, he considered escape, giving himself time to heal before resuming the struggle.

But the ground beneath his feet pulsed with life.

The life of his kind, and he knew there wasn't much time before they were born, and unleashed from the Garden unto the world.

There was no choice.

The angel stood naked before him, the fluids from his

captivity smoldering upon his superheated flesh. Slowly he flapped his wings, shaking off the burning residue.

Taranushi let the rage come, ignoring his pain to once more challenge the soldier of Heaven.

"Time to die, messenger," the spawn of darkness said as he lunged for his prey.

For the fate of his kind.

There was a balance within the Seraphim now.

Before there had always been a sense of struggle, of holding back.

But now that was gone.

He had been about to die when the change had come upon him, but two opposing forces joined together to form one.

Dispelling the darkness with light.

Dispelling the darkness with holy fire.

Seraphim and Shaitan came together at the base of the Tree of Knowledge, two bodies colliding with such force and strength that the Garden trembled with the intensity of it.

They both knew that this was the moment their fates would be decided.

They smashed into the base of the Tree, tearing away huge pieces of bark, revealing the pale, oozing flesh beneath.

The Shaitan was up to his old tricks at once, his body like water, attempting to engulf his foe. But this time the Seraphim was ready. He refused to allow the malleable beast to take hold. Instead, he made his hands burn with the heat of the righteous.

The Shaitan drew back, roaring his displeasure. He shifted part of his mass into a muscular tentacle and lashed out with all his might, swatting the angel away, the intensity of the blow picking him up from the ground and launching him through the air.

Sensing an opportunity, the Shaitan slithered across the ground in pursuit of his prey.

Remiel climbed slowly to his feet, attempting to stave

off the encroaching unconsciousness. He could hear the
monster approaching, its breathing excited and eager,
probably imagining that victory was at hand.

The Seraphim decided to let it continue to think that
way, for he had found his own opportunity.

Unwittingly, the Shaitan had knocked him within inches
of his weapon. He had lost Zophiel's sword when the struggle had first intensified, but now he looked upon it, protruding from the ground, covered in winding vines and
thick leaves that were constantly burning, only to regrow
twice as large, and twice as thick, only to burn all over
again. To the normal eye it appeared as a small tree, but to
the Seraphim ... to Remiel, it was so much more.

The blade of Eden's sentry was crying out to him,
screaming into his mind to take it up and destroy the foes
of the Garden and Heaven.

Almost, he thought, the sounds of the eager Shaitan
nearly upon him.

Closer.

Closer ...

The damnable thing was almost there; he could smell
the evil sweating from its pores, hear the sound of its flesh
as it abandoned its shape, becoming molten, preparing to
envelop him.

Remiel reached for the sword, tugging the burning
blade from a scabbard of thick vines and leaves, and spun
to meet his attacker with a cry of fury. Their eyes met as
Zophiel's blade hissed through the humid air on its designated course.

The Shaitan attempted to bend its body around the
sword, but the blade forged in the fires of Heaven would
have none of that. It was starving for the blood of its enemy.

Gouts of black, foul-smelling blood spurted into the air
as the blade cut through the twisted thing's rubbery skin.
The Shaitan cried out in pain, and dropped to the ground,
slithering back from its foe.

Remiel spread his wings wide and flew after the monster, relentlessly hacking at its thick, trunklike body, each
blow cutting spurting gashes in the thing's ever-shifting

flesh. The Shaitan managed to reach the Tree of Knowledge, winding itself around the trunk like a serpent, and up toward the expanse of withered branches. Huge, leathery wings began to take shape from its body, beating the air, as it attempted escape.

Remiel shot up into the air, intercepting the beast as it exploded through the diseased, fruit-covered branches. He slashed one of the monster's new wings, crippling it. It began to fall, and the Seraphim joined it, holding on, pushing the monstrosity down through the Tree's branches to the hard ground below.

Remiel landed atop the thrashing Shaitan, raising his fiery sword and plunging it into the monster, pinning it to the ground. Screams filled the air ... the Shaitan's, as well as those of its fetal brethren still gestating and waiting in the soil beneath.

The Shaitan's movements grew frantic as it attempted to right itself. Its blood flowed into the ground, exciting the young beastlings that waited below and enticing them toward the surface.

The earth began to seethe and Remiel quickly stepped back. The Shaitan struggled to be free of the sword, but it held fast, pinning the monster to the churning earth.

And then it began to scream.

The baby Shaitan were emerging, pale skinned and hungry, crawling up from the darkness into the murky light of the Garden. They shrieked angrily at the light, the sudden illumination hurting their sensitive eyes, but it did not stop them from their purpose.

To feed.

The blood of their brother had created a feeding frenzy—the blood of their brother rich with the taste of Seraphim.

It was a horrific sight to behold, and the unfortunate Shaitan survived much longer than Remiel would have imagined possible.

He was not sure how long it was before his foe was completely consumed, but the Seraphim realized that, little by little, the babies were starting to notice his presence. Those that had fed sniffed the air, zeroing in on his scent, and began to claw their way toward him across the overturned earth, dragging malformed limbs in their wake.

Hungry for their next meal.

And Remiel did not know if he had the strength left to defeat them.

The old black woman struggled in his grasp as Malachi peered through the thick jungle foliage at the battle raging before him.

This Seraphim, he thought, watching as the angel Remiel finally dispatched the Shaitan. *There is something different about him now, something that wasn't part of his original design. Something new is present.*

Something deadly.

The Shaitan's death screams spurred him to action. He began to drag the woman away, but she fought him.

"I know that one," Eliza Swan cried. "That's my Remy," she said, voice trembling with emotion. "That's my Remy Chandler."

Malachi savagely pulled her away. All he needed was for her to draw the attention of the Seraphim—especially *that* Seraphim.

The ground still moved beneath each footfall, trees swayed, and plants reached weakly to snag them as they passed. The Garden was dying, but she still tried to stop those she believed had harmed her. He wondered how long she had before all the life left her.

A wall of thick vegetation blocked the opening to his cave, but the scalpel of light was more than sufficient to gain him entrance. The vines squeaked in death, and wilted away as the blade cut through their tubular bodies to expose the gaping cave mouth.

Eliza planted her feet, not wanting to enter, but the elder had little time for the human monkey's games. He dragged her with ease, the grip upon her wrist so powerful that he could feel the frail old bones grinding together as he pulled her along.

The chamber was just as he'd left it, and he headed to-

ward his workstation, tossing Eliza aside. The old woman
fell to the ground, stunned.

Malachi ignored her, his mind abuzz. He found a deep
bowl made from the bottom portion of a gourd, and
plucked it from the table. Turning, he focused on a section
of wall and recalled the forbidden piece of angel magick he
would recite, and the sigils he would have to draw, in order
to make his escape.

Now all he required was the blood to draw with.

Malachi turned toward Eliza and brought forth the
ever-so-versatile blade of light. "One last chore before . . . ,"
he began, only to stop short when he saw that they were no
longer alone in the cave.

A figure knelt beside the woman, tenderly touching her
face as she lay stunned upon the floor of the cave. At first
he did not recognize him, clothed as he was in a dark three-
piece suit, but as he rose there was no mistaking the former
Guardian angel.

"Fraciel," Malachi said excitedly. "How nice it is to see
you again."

"Yeah," Francis said, adjusting the sleeves of his jacket
so the white of his shirt showed just below the cuffs. "And
it's Francis now.

"Bet you didn't see this coming."

Francis could practically hear the gears turning inside the
old angel's skull as he slowly approached.

"This day is just full of surprises," Malachi said, dark
eyes shining in the weak light of the cave. "Surprises and
revelations," he added.

The elder stopped halfway to Francis, who continued to
stare in stony silence.

"The surprise, of course, being that you're still alive,"
Malachi said with a chuckle. "And the revelation that we
are somehow linked, you and I."

Francis was mildly interested to see where this would go.

"Ever since I first partook of the fruit from the Tree,"
the ancient angel explained, "you have been part of the future that I foresaw. . . ."

Malachi paused.

"I had thought your part at an end with my escape from Hell, but now . . . seeing you here, I realize that our lives—our futures—are far more intricately entwined than that."

"You gutted me like a fish," Francis said, still feeling the excruciating pain.

"I did," Malachi agreed. "And yet here you are. Don't you see, Francis? We're supposed to be together."

Malachi was inching closer, and Francis let him come.

"The survival of this reality—of all realities—is our responsibility," the elder stressed. "We are the future."

"*I have a job for you*," Francis heard Lucifer Morningstar say, as he balanced on the precipice of death. "*If you are so inclined.*"

There must have been something in his eyes, something that told Malachi he wasn't about to buy into his bullshit. And that was when the ancient being made his move. The scalpel was out, slicing through the moist, stagnant air of the cave, as Malachi darted forward to try to kill him again.

But Francis had been expecting as much, willing the golden pistol from where it waited in the ether, to his hand, pitilessly firing a single, Hell-forged bullet into the center of Malachi's forehead.

The elder's head snapped violently backward, the glowing scalpel flying from his open fingers, an amusing look of surprise frozen upon his ancient features.

"Always wondered what would happen if I fucked with the future," Francis said, watching his victim fall backward to the floor.

He walked over to where Malachi lay, surprised to see that he was still alive, even with a bullet of Hell metal lodged inside his skull.

"*I have a job for you*," he heard the Morningstar speak again.

The golden peacemaker was still in his hand, and he held it above the angel's chest, firing another round into Malachi's black heart.

The angel twitched as the bullet entered his body, and then went still.

"If you are so inclined."

Francis closed his eyes, recalling the offer, and the answer he gave, as he was yanked back from the edge of death.

There was a scuffling sound somewhere behind him, and he spun around, finger twitching on the trigger of the deadly pistol.

But it was only Eliza Swan.

Eliza Swan. Even thinking her name brought a smile to his lips.

Willing the gun away, he went to the woman.

She was leaning up against the cave wall, and it was then that Francis noticed how incredibly old she had become. He tried to do the math, and gave up. She was of Eve's bloodline, and would live much longer than the average human woman, but even by those standards, she was pretty damn old.

Francis approached the woman, whose love he had remembered only a short time ago, and knelt down beside her.

"How are you, girl?" he asked, emotions that he would never admit to bubbling to the surface.

Eliza lifted her head to look into his eyes. "Pearly," she whispered. "I never forgot you."

She lifted a hand to stroke his face, and he leaned into it, reveling in the affection, but suddenly taken aback by the scent of blood.

"Eliza?" he questioned, taking her hand and staring at it. Her fingers were stained red. "Are you hurt?"

"You told me to leave the writing where it was," she said, her eyes locked on his. "That if I didn't, I would put myself in danger ..."

Francis began to panic; the smell of blood was stronger.

"Why is it that I never listened?" she asked him. "Why did I always ignore the people I loved? My parents ... you ... I guess I was always bad news, wasn't I?"

"You were never bad news. ..."

She began to cough, and that was when he saw it.

Malachi's scalpel protruding from her belly.

He gasped and reached to pull it free, but she caught his wrist, demanding that he look at her.

"I did this," she told him. "If I had listened . . . if I had listened, none of this would have happened. Figured I'd best put an end to it . . . before I messed up anything else."

He was about to tell her that she would be fine, that he would find a way to fix her, but he didn't want to lie, not to her.

Her hold on his wrist grew weaker, and her hand eventually fell into her lap.

Francis reached for the blade, pulling it from her. He stared at it, listening to its faint hum and occasional crackle, before slipping it into the pocket of his jacket.

Claiming the weapon as his own.

Eliza's eyes had begun to close, and he knew that she didn't have much longer. There was so much he wanted to say, to tell her before she left, but all he could do was watch.

"I have a job for you."

And remember what he had done to be here.

"If you are so inclined."

Eden was still dying, but she wasn't as sick as she had been before.

Izzy could feel the connection with the Garden now, the thrum of her life through her own body.

And Jon's.

He had been the key to saving her, the two of them somehow providing the place with what she needed to fight . . . the strength to fight and possibly survive what was happening to her.

The ground still trembled violently beneath their feet as they pushed their way through the thick jungle, an effort on the part of Eden to fight back against her foes.

Izzy could feel where she needed to go, holding on to Jon's hand, leading him to their destination. He believed that they were going to Remy, to assist the angel in his fight against the Shaitan, but she knew otherwise.

There was someplace else she was supposed to be right now.

She brought them to a stop before the gaping mouth of the cave.

"What are we doing?" Jon asked. "This isn't where . . ."

"Yes," the woman said. "Yes, it is."

And as the words left her mouth she and Jon watched as the man in the suit emerged from the darkness of the cave, the body of an elderly woman held in his arms.

Izzy knew at once who the old woman was, and that she was dead, for the Garden was telling her this.

"That . . . that's your mother," Jon spoke aloud, seemingly knowing the information as well.

A pistol had appeared in the man's hand, aimed at them both.

"You don't have any need for that," Izzy told him.

The man continued to stare. It had been a very long time since she'd seen either of them, but she knew this man before Eden had begun to tell her who he was.

"Don't you remember me, Dad?"

His expression barely changed, but in his dark eyes she could see that he knew her . . . that he remembered.

"Izabella," he said.

The gun was somehow gone; she hadn't seen where, or how he'd put it away while still holding the woman, but it wasn't pointed at them anymore.

Her father looked at the dead woman in his arms with a gaze so intense that she could feel the energy passing between them.

"She blamed herself for what's happening," her father said, lowering himself to his knees. "Said that it was all her fault. Purposely hurt herself so that she couldn't be used anymore."

Izzy knelt in the moving grass beside her mother and father.

"Why'd you have to go and do that?" Izzy said quietly, reaching out to cup the dead woman's cold cheek in her hand. "Wish I could have spent some time with you before—"

A violent tremor passed through the earth, and a jab of pain like an ice pick to the skull caused her to double over.

Eden was in trouble again. Eden was in pain.

"We really don't have the time for this," Jon said. He was holding the side of his head, a slight trickle of blood leaking from his nose.

Her father was now staring at the man, as if noticing him for the first time.

"Who's he?" he asked. "Boyfriend?"

Izzy smiled at the idea—after so many years of hate, the Sons and Daughters coming together again . . . here.

"No," she told her father. "But you don't have to worry about that."

She stroked her mother's hair.

"You need to get her out of here," Izzy told him. "You need to bring her home. . . ." She looked at him squarely through the lenses of his dark-framed glasses.

"Her real home."

Her father nodded, understanding what she was asking of him.

"We have some business to take care of here first," Izzy said.

He stood, gently holding the body of the woman in his arms.

"It was nice to see you again, Dad," Izzy said.

"Nice to see you too," her father told her.

And in his eyes she could read that it was true—he was glad to see her.

Remiel held the young Shaitan at bay with the Cherubim's sword.

The fire burned brightly as he held it out before him, the light from the blade preventing them from advancing.

But for how long?

The small monsters, no bigger than newborns, hissed and snapped at the light thrown from the blade, squinting and covering their eyes with nastily clawed hands.

The angel considered his options: He could flee the Garden, leaving the situation as bad as he'd found it, or he could attack, wading in among the pale-skinned creatures and attempting to slay them all before they reached their full, deadly maturity.

He didn't particularly care for either choice, but running away was not an option.

The Shaitan were getting braver by the second, charging at him, teeth snapping. As one did this, the others followed suit. They were learning from one another, and it wouldn't be long now before they came at him in full force.

His body was still weary, injuries slowly healing, but still healing nonetheless. He wasn't even close to peak battle form, but all that would need to be set aside if he were to fight in hope of slaying them all.

One of the younglings charged with a horrible shriek, and Remiel sliced the head from its body. They had not yet learned of their shape-shifting abilities, but he guessed that it was only a matter of time before they did.

Their dead brother provided him with a little more time, the others pouncing upon the corpse and eating it before the body could even grow cold.

They were soon back, their full attention on him in seconds.

There seemed to be more of them now, even more newborns crawling up from the dirt.

The Shaitan were clumped together, a mass of snarling, snapping teeth and claws, hungry for the flesh of the Heavenly.

"Come at me, then," he said, steeling himself for the approaching battle. And his thoughts quickly reviewed all the things that would be lost to him if he should fall, all the friendships, all the loves, and even the dislikes that would be greatly missed.

He hoped those things would give him the strength to do what was required of him this moment, the strength to be victorious.

The strength to survive.

The Shaitan flowed like a wave, and Remiel was ready, the slaughter of his foes the only thing that mattered.

He waited for them, but the earth itself reacted before he could.

Jagged teeth of rock and dirt pushed up suddenly from

the ground, creating a wall and preventing the Shaitan from reaching him.

Remiel was confused, but remained ready for what might possibly follow.

The abominations screamed their displeasure, pushing against the blockade, and began to climb over. Roots like tentacles reached up from the ground, snagging them around their malformed limbs, dragging them back behind the wall.

A cacophony of bird cries filled the air, and he gazed up to see a cloud of strange, sparrowlike birds descending from the trees to peck at the Shaitan.

The wall of rocks and dirt continued to grow in thickness and in height, and began to push them, herding the newborn Shaitan back toward the Tree of Knowledge.

"You need to get out of here," came the familiar voice of a young man.

Remiel turned to see Jon and Izzy emerging from the jungle. The two were holding hands, and he didn't really understand until he noticed the jungle around him, and what was happening at their feet.

Where there had once been sick and wilted vegetation, it was now green and healthy, growing up from wherever they passed or stepped.

They were connected to Eden now, and this connection was providing the Garden with what she needed to fight back, and to survive.

"What happened to your armor?" Jon asked.

"Lost in the belly of the beast," Remiel answered. "Good to see you, Jon . . . Izzy."

"Good to see you too, Remy," Jon said. "But you've got to do what we said and get out of here as fast as you can."

"I can't," he said, looking back to the Tree, and to the Shaitan that were trying to escape the Garden's attempts at confining them. "Something needs to be done about them before . . ."

"Don't you worry about that," Izzy told him. "That's why we're here."

The Garden then shook with such force that he almost toppled.

"You've got to go now, Remy," Jon said.

Remiel noticed that both their noses were bleeding, and their ears as well.

"We're helping her fight, but I'm not sure how much longer we can keep this up," Izzy said.

Strange, catlike animals were padding from the jungle and going to the Tree, attacking the Shaitan on the other side of the rock wall.

"You need to go and do what you did before for her," Izzy said, her face squinted up with exertion. "You need to cut her loose by closing the gates again."

Remiel understood what they were asking of him.

"What about you two?" he wanted to know. "I think I could fly both of you through the jungle and—"

"We're staying," Jon said. "Somebody has to make sure that these things aren't allowed to escape."

"And with our help, Eden should be strong enough to keep them prisoner here for a good long time," Izzy added, wiping a fresh trickle of blood from her nose with a sniffle.

Remiel stared, in awe of their sacrifice.

"We're sure about this," Jon said, Izzy nodding beside him. "Please . . . get out of here and close the gates."

He was about to leave when he heard the unmistakable sound of magickal energies being unleashed. They all looked toward the Tree as jagged fragments of rock and hunks of tree root exploded into the air. The Shaitan were learning about their abilities, unleashing them against the forces that attempted to keep them at bay.

Remiel lifted his sword and was heading in that direction, when Jon grabbed his arm in a powerful grip.

"Go," the man commanded. "We have it under control, but we don't know for how long."

He hated to leave them like this, but the thought of the Shaitan getting out of the Garden was even more troubling.

Moving toward the jungle, he passed the sad, mangled body of Adam, and as if in response to his troubled thoughts, he watched as the ground began to draw the corpse down into its embrace, swallowing him up, returning his body from whence it came.

The sounds of heated battle erupted behind him, but he did not turn. He had a mission to perform, and there would be nothing to deter him from it.

Remiel spread his wings, leaping into flight, maneuvering through the low-hanging limbs and vines, flying toward his destination. Eden looked healthier, greener, thicker, and he believed that maybe the great Garden would survive the horrors she had been forced to endure.

And in doing so, keep the monstrous race known as the Shaitan from swarming out into the world of man. He could see the gateway up ahead, and pushed himself to fly faster. As he dropped to the ground just before the opening, so as to not overshoot his goal, excruciating pain exploded in his back as something raked its claws down his bare flesh.

Remiel fell to the ground, rolling over and lashing out with his sword.

A young Shaitan crouched there, licking his blood from its hooked claws, a malicious smile growing upon its monstrous face as it enjoyed its snack. He had to wonder if any more of the beasts had escaped Jon and Izzy, and gradually climbed to his feet. The wounds in his back throbbed in pain so sharp it was as if he were being stabbed over and over again.

He didn't know whether it was his eyes playing tricks, his senses dulled by the incredible pain, but he could have sworn that the Shaitan was growing—maturing—before his eyes.

Finished with the blood on its claws, it obviously desired more, coming at him with a ferocious hiss. The flaming sword lashed out, but the beast was quick, ducking beneath the swing and darting forward to rake its claws along his side.

Remiel cried out.

It was all proving to be too much, his body shutting down a little at a time, not leaving him enough to work with.

The Shaitan seemed to sense this, moving in to attack again, tatters of Remiel's flesh still dangling from its claws.

There was no mistaking the sound of gunfire.

The shot hit the beast in the chest, dead center, and tossed it backward into the jungle.

Remiel turned to see Francis, smoldering pistol in hand, standing in the gateway. Was that one of the Pitiless—weapons imbued with the power of Lucifer Morningstar? he asked himself briefly, before the sound of screaming drew his attention back to the jungle in front of him. Even with a bullet hole in its chest, the Shaitan was coming again. Remiel readied himself, sword in hand to fight.

But snaking tendrils of green shot out, vines wrapping themselves around the Shaitan's thrashing limbs. The creature continued to squeal, struggling as it was dragged backward into the jungle.

A face that he recognized as Izzy's took form in the bark of a tree nearby.

"Get out of here," the face of wood commanded. "Close the gates behind you."

Remiel passed through the gate to the world outside.

Francis was standing there, the body of Eliza Swan lying at his feet.

Remiel felt sadness come at the sight, but quickly pushed it aside to deal with the problem at hand.

"We have to close it," he said to his friend.

Francis nodded, saying nothing as he went to one of the heavy metal gates, and Remiel went to the other.

There were noises coming from within the Garden, something that told him that more than one of the Shaitan had escaped his friends. They needed to do this, and to do this quickly.

"Ready?" Remiel asked him. "On the count of three."

The sounds were louder now, multiple things fighting their way through the thick jungle growth.

"One," Remiel said, taking the cold metal in his hands.

He looked across at his friend, feeling a strange combination of joy—to see him still alive—and revulsion.

He was concerned what that meant, and wondered

whether it had anything to do with the weapon he'd seen in Francis's hand.

"Two."

"Three," Francis grunted, pushing on his side, as Remiel joined him.

It was as if they did not wish to be closed again, but the gates eventually gave way, hinges crying out unhappily as they came together with a nearly deafening clatter.

The two stepped back, away from the locked gates as the Garden of Eden was again detached from a particular reality, gradually slipping in and out of focus as it resumed its journey behind the veil.

Cast adrift, and out into the sea of realities once more.

Jon thought he was going to die.

The power of Eden rushed through him like a raging river, threatening to pull him from the safety of shore out into deeper and far more dangerous waters.

"Got to hold 'em," Izzy said, squeezing his hand all the tighter.

He didn't answer, choosing instead to focus on the job at hand.

The Shaitan were trying to escape, newly acquired magickal energies shooting out at the Garden that tried to imprison them. A few had managed to escape the clutches of the jungle, but only a few. The majority still remained in their possession . . . the Garden of Eden's possession.

Thanks to Jon and Izzy, Eden was stronger now, filled with a strength that she had not had for countless millennia.

The Garden told them how happy she was.

How happy she was to have her children back.

The gunmetal gray sky of the North Pole above their heads suddenly went to a weird kaleidoscope of colors before going completely to black . . . burning lights like stars igniting one by one, shedding their light down upon them, lending them some of their fiery strength.

"Remy did it," Izzy said. "These nasty sons a' bitches ain't getting away from us."

And Jon had to agree. He felt suddenly stronger, capable of getting the job done, now that the threat of the Shaitan's escape out into the world had been averted.

"Let's put them down," he told Izzy . . . he told Eden.

And they obliged him, their combined strength pouring into the Garden. A wall of earth like a tidal wave rose up from the ground above the struggling Shaitan. The roots from the reinvigorated Tree of Knowledge had created a kind of jail, keeping them in one place, as the other aspects of the holy jungle worked at keeping the monsters from escaping.

The wave of dirt plunged down, burying the squirming beasts, as the Garden drew them deeper into herself.

"She's going to create a place for them," Izzy said, the sides of her head and neck stained crimson with blood. "A prison that she holds close to her heart."

"And she'll hold them there for as long as she is able," Jon joined in, feeling Eden's message to them. "For as long as she is strong."

They stood there for a good long time, waiting for the Shaitan to reemerge, for the battle to continue, but they did not come.

For now, Eden was capable of holding them.

The Garden soon calmed: The ground beneath their feet ceased to tremble; the plants, trees, and animals returned to their natural states. It was a Garden of peace again.

A Garden of peace with a malignancy at its core.

Jon was so exhausted that he dropped to the ground, releasing the viselike grip that he had on Izzy's hand. His head swam, and he dropped it between his legs, taking deep breaths, trying to keep from passing out. There was an annoying whine in his ear, and he reached up, plucking out the damaged hearing aid and dropping the squealing device on the ground. It was then that he realized that he didn't need it anymore, that his hearing had completely returned to that ear.

The damage had been healed. As he had helped heal the Garden, the Garden had healed him.

"Where do you think we are?" Izzy asked him.

He looked up to see that she was staring at the strange sky above them. It was like no night sky that he had ever seen before. The stars all seemed so incredibly close.

"I haven't any idea," he said. "But as long as we're away from Earth, it's all good."

She sat down on the ground beside him.

"Never would have seen this coming," she said with a chuckle.

"You're right there," Jon answered. He picked a stick up from the ground and started to play with it. Healthy green buds began to grow upon the stick, blossoming into tiny pink flowers.

"Look at that," Izzy said. "Looks like you've got a green thumb now."

He let go of the branch and watched as it took root before his eyes. It had grown nearly twice its size before one of them spoke again.

"So, what now?" he asked, wondering if Izzy had any idea of their purpose. He glanced over to her, waiting for the answer.

Izzy shrugged. "We're the gardeners now," she said. "I guess we tend the Garden."

"Makes sense," he agreed.

"And when we're not tending the Garden, who knows," she added.

He looked and saw that she was staring at him, eyebrows going up and down lasciviously.

"You're not so bad-looking . . . a little bit skinny for my taste, but . . ."

Jon couldn't stop himself; after everything they'd gone through, this was just the last straw . . . the perfect release, and he laughed so hard that he fell over onto his side.

"What's so damn funny?" Izzy asked, obviously annoyed.

"I'm sorry," he apologized, trying to control his laughter. "I'm not laughing at you; I'm laughing at the situation."

"The situation?" she asked.

"It's not that I'm not flattered, but . . ."

She looked at him for a moment, and then it dawned on her.

"You're . . . ," she started, but didn't finish.

He nodded, trying to keep from laughing again.

"You've got to be fucking kidding me," she cried.

Jon couldn't hold it back, laughing hysterically, his laughter so contagious that Izzy soon started as well.

It had been a long time since laughter had been heard in Eden.

And the Garden liked the sound.

CHAPTER TWENTY-THREE

The Garden of Eden was gone.

The spot where she had rested was still warm, but cooling rapidly.

Remiel stood motionless in the wind and snow with his friend Francis.

Both were uncommonly quiet.

"She was an amazing woman," Remiel said, staring at the body of the woman Francis held in his arms. A large flake of snow landed upon her cheek, where it rested without melting.

"I didn't know about the two of you ...," he began, but then wasn't certain how to continue.

"Neither did I," Francis answered, looking at his lover's still, cold face. "Not until a little while ago."

"What happened, Francis?" Remiel asked. "I thought you were dead."

Francis did not look at him, continuing to look at Eliza's face, as if searching for a sign of life. More snowflakes had collected there.

"Should be," he said at last. "But I'm not."

Remiel waited for Francis to say more, but he remained silent.

"Is that it? Is that all you're going to tell me?"

"For now," Francis replied.

The grass at their feet was dying as the intensifying snowfall gradually covered it.

"I need to bring her home," Francis said finally, looking up at his friend.

Something's missing from those eyes, Remiel thought. But he couldn't quite figure out what it was.

"There's something different about you," Francis commented, as if reading the angel's thoughts.

Remiel looked down at his naked, angelic form. His wings slowly flapped, stirring the powdery snow at his bare feet. "Yeah, there've been some recent changes."

"Looks good on you," Francis said, with a barely perceptible nod. "Might want to get some pants, though."

Remiel laughed. No matter what, it was good to have his friend back, alive.

Wasn't it?

"Do you want me to take you somewhere?" Remiel asked him.

Francis shook his head. There came a strange crackling sound and the air behind him began to swirl like a whirlpool, sucking in all existence and leaving behind a spiral opening.

"I'm good," he said, moving toward the portal.

Since when can he do that? Remiel wondered, but keeping his question for another time. If there was another time.

"Be seeing you?" he asked instead.

Francis didn't answer right away as he ducked his head into the portal.

"Yeah, I'll be around," he finally offered, giving Remiel a quick look over his shoulder as he disappeared into the passage, taking Eliza Swan home.

It was then that Remiel realized what was missing in his friend's eyes.

Hope.

And for a moment, the Seraphim felt the awful bite of the northern wind, before wrapping himself in the embrace of his warm, feathered wings, leaving the cold and barren place behind.

Remy Chandler sat with his car running on the street in Brookline.

Yes, Remy was back, but this time the guise of the Sera-phim warrior had been put aside gently. There was no struggle, as there used to be, only the painless replacement of the angelic with the human. And although the angelic nature floated just below the surface, Remy was all right with that. It was where it needed to be: side by side with his humanity.

He was a Seraphim, but he was also a man.

Returning to his apartment this last time had felt strangely wrong—not only because it was empty, but be-cause he wasn't the same as when he'd left.

Shedding his warrior guise had been easy. He'd showered, dressed his wounds, and made himself presentable. He'd then driven right over to Linda Somerset's apartment, not even bothering to call first.

But here he sat.

"Aren't you going in?" a sweet voice asked from the passenger seat.

Remy looked over and saw Madeline sitting there, as beautiful as she always was.

"Don't rush me," he said, and smiled.

She smiled back, but then grew serious. "What's wrong, Remy?"

"I have to get used to this again," he explained. "It feels like I've been gone from this sort of ... normalcy for so long."

"You need to get used to being human again? Is that what you're saying?"

"I guess that's it," he said, looking through the wind-shield at Linda's third-floor windows. There was a light on, casting a warm glow through a white curtain. It was inviting ... comforting, and Remy focused on that.

"You weren't gone so long, y'know," Madeline com-mented.

"I know," he said. "But it felt like forever ... and the changes."

"Sometimes changes are good."

"Yeah, they are," he said, and truly believed it.

"Go on," Madeline encouraged. "The baby needs to see his father."

Remy looked at his wife, terribly missing the reality of her.

"I think I might've screwed things up pretty good with Linda," he said.

It was Madeline's turn to look through the windshield.

"Well, you'll never know if you don't go up there."

"As profound as always," Remy said as he turned off the engine. He looked toward his wife to say thank you.

But she was already gone.

Remy was halfway up the third flight of stairs when he heard the sound of a door unlocking ... followed by the familiar jingling of a chain collar. And then he was met at the top of the stairs by the most excited black Labrador retriever he'd ever seen.

"Hey, buddy." Remy laughed, squatting down so his face could be thoroughly licked.

"*Hi,*" Marlowe barked between kisses. "*Hi. Hi. Hi.*"

"Did you miss me?" Remy asked, rubbing his velvety soft ears and kissing his cold, wet snout. "I certainly missed you."

"*Missed you,*" Marlowe said, panting excitedly. "*Missed you much.*"

And suddenly Remy found himself that much more in tune with his humanity, the events of the last week already receding into memory.

He rose to his feet, dog dancing happily around him, and walked down the hallway toward Linda's apartment.

She appeared in the doorway then, leaning against the jamb, arms crossed.

"Hey," he said with a sheepish smile.

"I thought he was going to tear my door down to get out," Linda said. "I knew it had to be you to get that kind of a reaction."

"He must've smelled me coming up the stairs," Remy said, keeping a respectful distance.

"Must have."

Marlowe jumped on Linda, knocking her back against the doorframe. He barked excitedly before returning to Remy.

"I know, I know, Remy's home," she said with a laugh. "We thought he'd left you forever."

Ouch! Remy felt that one.

"Yeah, about that," he said as he affectionately thumped the dog's side.

"Yeah?" she asked.

He stepped closer, drawn to her annoyance.

"Things just got out of hand with the case, and I'm sorry," he told her.

"Marlowe was worried," she said.

He looked down into his dog's deep brown eyes. "I'm sorry for worrying you, Marlowe," he said.

"*Okay*," the dog barked in response.

"He's forgiven me," Remy said, moving closer to her.

"I was worried," she said. Her eyes grew slightly wider as the words left her mouth, as if they surprised her.

"I'm sorry, Linda," he said in all earnestness, hoping that she could see how bad he felt.

She was quiet for a moment. "I'm not sure I believe you," she said at last, a hint of a smile playing at the corners of her mouth.

"You're not?" Remy asked, pretending to be serious. "Marlowe, Linda doesn't believe I'm sorry," he said to his dog.

Marlowe whined, ears going flat.

"I know. It's a terrible situation. But what can I do?"

Marlowe tilted his head to one side, crying again, then letting out a pathetic bark.

"Kiss her?" Remy said.

He looked from the dog to her.

"He said I should kiss you."

"*Did not*," Marlowe barked.

"What'd he say, then?" Linda asked.

"He was stressing just how much I should be kissing you."

"Do you always do what your dog tells you to do?"

"He's never steered me wrong before," Remy replied, staring deeply into the warmth of her eyes.

"Hmm, you should probably do as he says, then," Linda suggested.

"Do you think it'll work?" Remy asked. "That whole proving-I'm-sorry thing?"

"Never can tell till you try," Linda said.

Remy moved closer, drawn to her heat, drawn to her beautiful humanity. It was all here now, everything he'd been missing since his return from Eden.

The spark to reignite what it was all about.

He leaned his face close to hers, their lips on the verge of touching, then finally coming together, soft at first, gradually becoming harder, more forceful.

Eager.

Remy broke the connection first. "Do you believe me now?" he asked.

Linda looked surprised, her cheeks flushed red. "Not quite." She reached up and pulled him closer.

Marlowe was barking now, telling them to stop, to pay attention to him.

"What's your problem?" Remy stopped kissing Linda to ask the dog.

"He thinks we should move this inside before we get complaints from the neighbors," Linda answered instead, taking Remy's hand, tugging him toward the open door.

"Did you say that?" Remy asked Marlowe.

"*No*," he barked, tail wagging furiously.

"Just wanted to be sure."

Remy allowed himself to be led inside Linda's apartment, Marlowe following obediently behind.

They kissed again just inside the doorway, lost in the heat of passion.

Lost in the passion of their humanity.

ABOUT THE AUTHOR

Thomas E. Sniegoski is the author of the groundbreaking quartet of teen fantasy novels titled *The Fallen*, which were transformed into an ABC Family miniseries, drawing stellar ratings for the cable network. With Christopher Golden, he is the coauthor of the dark fantasy series *The Menagerie* as well as the young readers' fantasy series *OutCast*. Golden and Sniegoski also cocreated two comic book series, *Talent* and *The Sisterhood*, and they wrote the graphic novel *BPRD: Hollow Earth*, a spinoff from the fan-favorite comic book series *Hellboy*.

Sniegoski's other novels include *Force Majeure*, *Hellboy: The God Machine*, and several projects involving the popular television franchises *Buffy the Vampire Slayer* and *Angel*, including both *Buffy* video games.

As a comic book writer, he was responsible for *Stupid, Stupid Rat Tails*, a prequel miniseries to the international hit *Bone*. Sniegoski collaborated with *Bone* creator Jeff Smith on the prequel, making him the only writer Smith has ever asked to work on those characters. He has also written tales featuring such characters as Batman, Daredevil, Wolverine, The Goon, and The Punisher.

His children's book series, *Billy Hooten: Owlboy*, is published by Random House.

Sniegoski was born and raised in Massachusets, where he still lives with his wife, LeeAnne, and their Labrador retriever, Mulder.

It had been quite some time since Remy had last listened.

That was why he was here, standing before the high front gates of the New Hampshire Correctional Facility, staring at the harsh angles of the prison beyond.

He had come because he had listened again.

Thunder crashed, lightning pulsed across the nighttime sky, and rain fell in straight sheets to the earth. Remy was soaked to the skin, but he didn't give it a thought, his mind occupied with the reason for his being in this inhospitable place on this most inclement of evenings.

He had come in answer to a prayer.

A prayer that he, a former emissary of Heaven, had overheard as someone had pleaded for God's attention. And although Remy had struggled to block out those prayers in his quest to be human, tonight he had heard, and was compelled to act.

Invisible to the video cameras that watched the comings and goings from the prison, Remy spread his powerful wings to their full span, and with a single mighty thrust, he lifted himself up and over the fence to the open yard beyond.

The world was changing. He could smell it in the air, taste it on the tip of his tongue, feel it, like a faint electric current on the surface of his skin. Remy knew it had to do with how close the earth had come to the Apocalypse a year or two back, a catastrophe that he had had a major role in averting. Ever since then, life had been growing stranger, deadlier, with every passing day—as if being that close to the end had set the world on a different path.

Stirred things up like silt from the bottom of a lake.

Remy had changed as well, for the love of his life had died, and without her strength, he'd found himself fighting to hold on to the humanity that he'd worked so hard to fabricate. His human nature had begun to tatter, his angelic essence trying to assert itself as he drifted further away from the mundane existence he had created as a private investigator—and husband.

But as the world that he loved—and fought for—continued to transform, Remy had to face the fact that the warlike nature of the Seraphim was needed. If he was going to continue to protect this changing world and all he loved from the rapidly escalating supernatural threats, the two warring natures at the core of his being would have to unite.

Finally, with the help of the memory of his beloved Madeline, Remy had embraced a side of his nature that he had been attempting to stifle for thousands of years. Remy Chandler was transformed.

Whole.

The human and the angelic were one. He was a creature of both Earth and Heaven, and tonight he had chanced a listen to the prayers of humanity. It was a mother's plea that had touched him tonight, compelling both the human and the Seraphim to action.

Remy walked across the puddle-covered blacktop of the prison yard and stopped beside a guard who stood outside the main entrance smoking a cigarette beneath an overhang. Patiently, he waited in the steady fall downpour as the man finished his smoke, then followed him into the brightly lit building, the heavy metal door slamming closed behind them.

Remy had been relaxing on the roof of his Beacon Hill brownstone, sipping a glass of scotch as his canine friend, Marlowe, snored loudly at his feet. The rain hadn't started, but the dampness permeated the air, and he'd known that it was only a matter of time before it did.

He had seen the glow of the lights at Fenway Park, and

absently wondered if the Sox would be able to get their game in before the deluge. He had allowed the effects of the alcohol to wash over him. His psychic connection to the world's inhabitants danced in the corners of his perception. Normally he would have blotted it out, not wanting to eavesdrop on the pleas of the needy and devout, but something about this particular night had encouraged him to open himself up to the cacophony of prayers.

It had been like being in a sea of sound—a multitude of voices in every worldly dialect, all speaking at the same time.

Remy had been tempted to pull back from the deafening roar, but he forced himself to concentrate, whittling down the sounds from many to a select few, until he was focusing on only one, the strongest and most plaintive of them all.

The prayers of Catherine Perlas.

Remy was deep inside the prison now. The noxious smell of violence and desperation hung stagnant in the air, despite the nearly overwhelming stink of industrial cleaner. He'd left his escort to wander on his own and was passing the prison infirmary when his acute hearing picked up the sound of heavy breathing—someone fast asleep.

He stepped inside a darkened office to find an older man sleeping at his desk, file folders spread out before him as if sudden sleep had claimed him in the midst of work. Silently, Remy approached the man.

"Robert Denning," he said softly in the voice of an angel.

The man twitched with a grunt and slowly raised his head, leaving a small puddle of drool on one of the folders. He looked around the room bleary-eyed, and still mostly asleep, searching for the source of the voice.

"Where can I find him?" Remy whispered into the man's other ear.

The man could barely keep his eyes open. His head bobbed up and down, as sleep tried to pull him into its embrace once more.

"Where is Robert Denning?" Remy repeated.

"Maximum Security," the man mumbled. "Special Housing, unit six."

His eyes closed again, and this time they did not reopen. His breathing grew deeper as he laid his head back down upon his pillow of folders. He was snoring as Remy looked around the office searching for some kind of floor plan. On the back of the door he found an emergency map of the facility and quickly located the Maximum Security wing.

Catherine Perlas had lost her daughter and twin grandchildren to murder, and she prayed with all she had that God would punish their killer.

The story had been all over the local news. Charlotte Marsh, a thirty-three-year-old single mother, and her six-year-old daughters had been found, brutally murdered, in their home in Camden, New Hampshire. They had been together, maimed so as not to be able to escape, and Charlotte had been the last to die.

Who could do such a thing, and why? asked everyone who heard the tale of horror. The answer was far from satisfying, and more disturbing than most could bear.

Robert Denning was a twenty-year-old college dropout, and according to the testimony at his trial, he had always been curious about how it would feel to take a life. After one particularly taxing day, when he'd fought with his girlfriend, Robert had felt the overwhelming desire to satisfy that murderous curiosity.

He'd seen Charlotte and her daughters, Amanda and Emily, at a local supermarket and followed them home. He had parked his car and waited, unnoticed, until the house grew dark. Then he'd entered through an unlocked door in the garage. Details were sketchy, but they said he'd taken his time with them.

Remy found his way into Maximum Security, transporting himself through the locked doors by wrapping his wings about his body and picturing the other side.

It was as if the prisoners asleep behind the doors of their cells could sense his divine presence, many of them crying out pathetically as he strolled past. Most simply returned to a restless sleep when he paid them no mind—the prowling Seraphim on the hunt for a specific prey.

Denning had tried to escape human justice by declaring that he was insane at the time of the murders; but the jury hadn't bought it, agreeing with the prosecutor, who had portrayed the man as a cold, calculating killer.

Remy stopped before a white metal door with a large black number six stenciled above the single Plexiglas window. He stood for a moment, staring at the door, imagining what was on the other side. A part of him—*his human side*—yearned to sense some unspeakable evil emanating from the cell, something beyond the norm that would explain why Robert Denning had done what he had.

A form of demonic possession, or some such manifestation of evil.

A way to make some strange kind of sense from the senseless.

But Remy felt nothing out of the ordinary, and that just made it all the more maddening.

The angel stepped closer to the cell, peering into the small, darkened space, seeing a shape huddled beneath a blanket on the bed.

He opened his wings and wrapped them about himself once again, and then he was there on the other side of the door, beside the bed, watching the figure in the embrace of a seemingly peaceful sleep. Remy wondered briefly about Catherine Perlas; he wondered if it was possible for the poor woman to sleep peacefully again or if she would be forever haunted by the memories of her murdered family.

His emotions had never been more acute than they had been since embracing his angelic side once more. Even the most mundane feelings affected him with startling acuity. Never had he experienced love so strongly or, as in this particular instant—

Hate.

"Robert Denning," Remy said into the darkness, his voice resonating with divine presence. "Awaken."

Denning stirred upon the bed, the angel's command pulling him up into the waking world.

"What? Who's there?" the young man asked sleepily, pushing himself up on his elbows, squinting into the shadows.

Remy chose to remain visible this time and had not hidden his wings. The brilliant white of their feathers cast an unearthly radiance about the cramped cell.

And Robert Denning saw what had come into his room. He sat up with a sucking gasp, throwing himself back against the wall, clutching his blanket tightly beneath his chin.

His eyes were wide and filled with fear, and Remy wondered if the young man was thinking of Charlotte, Amanda, and Emily then . . . thinking of how afraid they had been in his own presence that night he had yearned for, and sampled the act of, murder.

Remy hoped that he was.

"What the fuck?" Denning screamed.

"Keep your voice down," Remy commanded, not wanting the murderer's cries to summon any of the prison staff.

Denning opened his mouth to cry out again, but Remy was across the small room with the speed of thought, snatching the prisoner up by the front of his jumpsuit. "You will not cry out again," Remy ordered, his face mere inches from that of the young man.

He had taken on the full guise of the Seraphim warrior; his body was adorned in golden armor, stained with the blood of recent battles, of which there had been many.

Denning's mouth moved like that of a dying fish desperate to feel the flow of water over its gills again.

Remy looked into his eyes . . . *really* looked into his eyes. They were welling up with tears, but there was little else there—no signs of some otherworldly evil that might have taken up residence in a frail human shell.

All Remy saw was a terrified human being.

"I . . . ," Denning was trying to speak, but having difficulty forcing the words from his gaping mouth. "I . . . I'm . . ."

"What?" Remy snarled. "What do you have to say for yourself?"

"I'm . . . sorry," Denning managed, and then fell limp in Remy's grasp, sobbing uncontrollably.

"You're sorry?" Remy asked incredulously, barely able to control the anger in his voice. "You took the life of a mother and her two children in cold blood, and you're sorry?"

Remy could feel the divine fire building up inside him, traveling through his body as he remembered the prayers of a mother who had lost so much. It took a mighty effort not to allow the hungry flame to emerge, to consume the flesh of the lowly human he held—to award him an excruciatingly painful death.

It would be the closet thing to Hell that Remy could manage.

The fire . . . the fire of Heaven would start with the soul first, burning it away before moving on to the physical . . . the flesh and blood, organs and bones. It would happen quickly, but a pain like that would seem to last forever.

And it couldn't happen to a nicer guy.

The flames moved down Remy's arm toward his hand, and he struggled to hold it back, trying to convince himself that this wasn't what he wanted to do.

But it *was* what he wanted . . . what the Seraphim wanted.

He heard Catherine's plaintive prayers again, echoing inside his skull, begging the Almighty to punish the man who had taken her loved ones.

And wasn't that what the angel Remiel had been created to do? To carry out God's will? To be His divine messenger?

Denning was looking up at him, tears streaming down a face flushed with emotion as he jabbered on.

"I never believed in you . . . I never knew . . . so sorry for what I did . . . sorry that I didn't believe . . . so, so sorry . . ."

Remy could feel the fire at his fingertips now, straining to be released.

Hungry to feed upon the flesh of the sinner. To return this one to the dust from whence he had come.

Suddenly his fingers began to glow, and Remy knew he could no longer hold it back.

With a growl, he roughly tossed the young man back onto the bed. Then Remy threw his wings about himself like a cloak of feathers and was transported high above the prison into the storm-swept sky, where he released the fire of Heaven into the night, his own furious screams drowned out by the roar of thunder.

His rage temporarily spent, Remy returned to the prison cell to find Denning kneeling, his face pressed to the floor, his body trembling uncontrollably and stinking of urine, as he prayed for forgiveness to a God who was not listening.

Denning slowly raised his head, and Remy felt a certain satisfaction when he spotted five circular burns on the man's face, where he'd gripped him with a hand engorged with Heavenly fire. And in the young murderer's eyes was terror—a terror that had taken him beyond the brink.

It had been a struggle not to kill him, but Remy had come to the realization that it wasn't his place. Human justice had prevailed here, and now, for as long as he lived, Robert Denning would never know another moment without fear.

Fear of living, and what awaited him beyond.

For now that would have to be enough.

The air warped and rippled just above the road outside the New Hampshire Correctional Facility. There were a brief flash of white and the sound of wings beating the air as the fabric of time and space was rent, appearing to disgorge Remy Chandler.

The Seraphim stumbled as he came forth, folding away his appendages of flight as he caught his balance and began to walk.

Remy knew that he'd done the right thing in leaving the young murderer alone with his fear, but a part of him still wasn't satisfied, and if he'd stayed any longer, Denning would have been dead.

That was what he'd always been wary of, why he'd pushed the angelic essence of the Seraphim deeper and deeper inside himself, locking it away. It had always been wild, always reacting on instinct only.

It was what Remy feared.

What if he continued to think more like an angel? What if the more rational, human side of his dual nature hadn't won this time?

The urge was still there, like an itch at the center of his spine taunting him to scratch.

A vibrating sensation from the pocket of his jacket suddenly, thankfully, distracted him from his troubling thoughts, and Remy pulled out his phone, seeing that Linda was calling.

He guessed that he would call her his girlfriend, but something still didn't feel quite right about that. It was odd talking with another woman after having been with Madeline for so long, even odder to know that he was beginning to develop feelings for Linda. He still felt guilty at times, that he was somehow cheating on his dead wife. His issue, of course, and something else that he would have to deal with.

"Hey," he answered.

"Hey, yourself," Linda replied. "What's going on?"

"Nothing much," Remy lied, as he continued to walk down the center of the deserted road. The rain had temporarily ceased, but the air was still saturated, causing a writhing mist to snake up from the ground as the evening temperature gradually cooled. "Just wrapping up some stuff for work. What's going on with you?"

"I got out of class early," she said. "I'm planning a date with some lounging clothes, a bottle of Merlot, and *The Real Housewives of New Jersey*."

"Sure one bottle will be enough for all of you?" Remy joked. "I hear those housewives can really put it away."

She laughed, and he was reminded again of how much he liked the sound, and her.

"I miss you," she said.

Remy stopped walking, experiencing that moment of electricity that proved he wasn't the only one starting to have those kinds of feelings.

"I miss you, too."

"So what are you doing now?" Linda asked again.

He was about to suggest that he join her and the housewives, when he remembered that he still had something left to do.

"I was planning on stopping by Steven Mulvehill's," he said.

"Has he returned any of your calls?" she asked, concern in her voice.

Linda was aware that a rift had formed between the two friends, but hadn't been made privy to the specifics. The homicide detective had become involved in one of Remy's recent cases and had received a full dose of the kind of world that Remy often walked in.

A kind of world that Steven would have preferred never to see.

"No, he hasn't," Remy admitted. "But I'm thinking of dropping by his place anyway, to try and straighten this business out face-to-face."

"Good luck with that," she wished him.

"Thanks. I think he just needed some time to himself. Things should be fine once we've had a chance to talk. No worries."

"Do you want to stop by after?" she asked.

"I'd love to, but Marlowe's been alone for most of the day, and—"

"Bring him with you," she interrupted.

Remy felt himself smiling at the suggestion. It had been a few days since the dog had seen Linda, and Remy knew he'd jump at the chance to go for a ride in the car, especially if it meant seeing his new friend. It would definitely make up for having been left alone for most of the day.

"Let me see how late it is once Steven and I get finished."

"No pressure," Linda said. "Just thought it would be nice to see you."

"And Marlowe?"

"And Marlowe," she laughed. "I've been missing him, too."

"I'll give you a call when I leave Steven's, okay?"

"I'll be here."

"Talk to you later."

"Bye."

Remy put his phone back in his pocket and looked around, surprised to see how far he'd wandered while chatting. The prison was off in the distance now, practically hidden by the thickening fog.

Far enough away that he was able to resist the temptation to go back.

"Th..is a compelling character as he constantly struggles to hold on to the shred of humanity he forged for himself by suppressing the Seraphim.... Sniegoski adds a creative new spin to the good-versus-evil scenario while bringing in some biblical characters that are decidedly different than what you read about in Sunday school."
—Monsters and Critics

The best yet ... an exciting fantasy PI story with such compelling characters and a plot that will keep you guessing until the very end."
—Night Owl Romance

"This exciting urban fantasy is fast-paced and filled with action from the moment Remy sees the last drawing and never slows down as the hero realizes all hell is about to break out over a child. Remy is super as he struggles to contain his power though he would not mind burning a few worthless souls yet will move heaven, hell, and earth to protect an innocent little girl. Delilah is a terrific villainess who will do anything to further her power; except for Remy, she makes the rest of the cast including her former husband look emaciated. Fans will relish this fine tale and seek the hero's backstory."
—The Best Reviews

A fast-paced detective-noir fantasy, both refreshingly gritty and imaginative, a dark realism mixed with intriguing fantastical elements ... an exciting noir-flavored world with a grittiness that feels like chomping on sandpaper, a beautifully crafted world that I'd definitely like to revisit.... *Where Angels Fear to Tread* is a solid fantasy noir with nice characterization and an intriguing pseudorealistic urban fantasy feel."
—Blood of the Muse

Dancing on the Head of a Pin

[Sniegoski] nicely blends action, mystery, and fantasy into a well-paced story ... a very emotional read with the hero's grief overshadowing his every move. An intense battle is fought, new secondary characters are introduced, and readers should gain a more solid picture of the hero's past."
—Darque Reviews

continued ...